THE FRAME

BY
JAMES M. MURPHY

To Mrs. Mitchell
Regards

James M. Murphy

AmErica House
Baltimore

First printing

ISBN: 1-59129-205-0
PUBLISHED BY AMERICA HOUSE BOOK PUBLISHERS
www.publishamerica.com
Baltimore

Printed in the United States of America

For Joan M. O'Reilly

The air that I breathe

CHAPTER ONE

Along with my check, the Fed-Ex package contained a large white envelope with instructions hand-printed on the outside: WATCH VIDEOS BEFORE VIEWING PHOTOS. Inside were two videotapes and two envelopes of still pictures. Clay Oeland's lawyer, Toni Conboy, hadn't sent the emergency room report, medical examiner's report, interrogation transcripts, depositions, and the usual contracts and confidentiality agreements. The omissions suggested that she was either lazy or new.

But the $200 check looked authentic, and overnighting three pounds of material to my apartment in Arlington, Virginia hadn't come cheap, so I poured a glass of orange juice, put the tape labeled Video #1 in the VCR, sat on the futon, and pushed Play on the remote.

On my television, in black and white, a camera mounted near the ceiling monitored a hospital emergency room. Rows of sparsely populated, molded plastic chairs ended at a pass through window where a nurse was writing on a clipboard. Near the camera, a young woman in a plastic chair was nervously flipping the pages of a magazine. Nearby, a man in working clothes was watching a television that was out of sight to the camera's left, its audio garbled. Near the back, an older woman was asleep, her head bent nearly to her chest. The video date stamp indicated January 25, 2001, over three months ago.

At the rear of the room, the swinging doors were rammed open, and a heavyset, gray-haired man rushed in. Probably in his middle fifties, he was wearing a suit jacket but no shirt. He hurried to the pass-through desk, almost yelling, "There's a girl in my car who's been shot. Please hurry." In seconds, three people rushed a gurney through the swinging doors, the man running to keep up. "The Gold Lexus right over..." His voice faded as the doors shut.

There was a motionless body on the gurney when the doors reopened.

5

They rushed off camera so rapidly that I had to back the tape and push Pause on the remote. The woman on the gurney had long, straight, dark hair matted underneath her head, framing a round face covered with an oxygen mask. She could have been asleep, oblivious to the nurse wrapping a blood pressure cuff around her arm and the doctor holding a towel on her belly. Like the man who brought her in, she was shirtless, wearing a blood covered bra and skirt.

The man reappeared through the doors when I restarted the tape. A nurse asked if he was injured. He shook his head and then he was ignored. The scene stagnated so I fast-forwarded the tape. At the fast speed, the man was wringing his hands, the scene suggested Macbeth complete to the blood on his hands. When two uniformed cops appeared, I pushed Play to return the tape to normal speed.

"You brought in the girl who was shot?" the shorter cop asked. The man's voice sounded hoarse when he said, "Yes." The cop positioned his pen over a notebook. "Your name?"

"Clay Oeland. She said her name is Sally Krestas."

When Clay Oeland looked to his right, I could see four long scratches on the left side of his face. I froze the picture. The scratches were recent, one was still seeping. After I pushed Play, the cop pointed to Clay's face and asked, "Did she do that?"

"Yes, but..."

"Did you shoot Ms. Krestas?" The cop was reaching for his handcuffs.

"No." He hesitated as the cop fingered the handcuffs. "We were parked off Monterey Road, near Morgan Hill. A man came out of the orchard. He had a gun. He made both of us get out of the car. Then he..."

The cop interrupted. "Take us there." The tape lost signal for a moment, and then a different camera was looking through the windshield of a car speeding down a dark and deserted four-lane divided road. "What were you doing out here?" the cop asked.

Clay Oeland's long answer was partly unintelligible, lost in the car's noise. What I heard was that Sally Krestas had hidden on the floorboard of the car and directed him to some location where they wouldn't be seen. She told him she had papers in her purse that she wanted him to sign. The papers had to do with the reward for identifying the person who had stolen a shipment of ball bearings from Clay Oeland's company, Microfix.

"What time did this happen?"

"We got there before five, it was still light." Clay Oeland's voice was very clear, he had evidently leaned forward. His hand came into the picture, his index finger pointing. "The next road on your left. Where the power lines are?"

A paved but rutted road appeared, a strip of black fading into the darkness. Trees lined both sides of the road, their shapes menacing in the headlights.

"Stop us before we get to where your car was parked," the cop said. "We'll want to rope that off to preserve evidence."

The paving ended and a dirt road bent to the right and ended at a wire fence. "There," Clay Oeland said, "at the fence."

The car turned around and stopped. Four police cars could be seen, uniformed police spilling from the cars and swarming out of sight, shotguns at the ready. Minutes later, the officers drifted into view, gesturing and pointing. The tape ended after a tour of the crime scene, essentially two wheel ruts.

I slid Video #2 into the machine. The tape, in color, began at the same location at 10:22 a.m., January 26, 2001, according to the time stamp. The hand-held camera focused on three people standing next to a police car. Clay Oeland, dressed in a gray business suit, stood to the right of a casually dressed, large man with closely cropped black hair. On his left, a petite brunette in a dark blue police uniform looked tiny.

The large man explained to the camera, "San Jose Police Department investigation of the circumstances of the murder by person or persons unknown of Sally Krestas. Present are Clay Oeland; Police Officer Duncan Chivers operating the camera, and..." he pointed to the diminutive woman, "Police Officer Ann Wilentz. I am Sergeant Javier Olivera."

It took two replays of the tape before I understood his name: Javier, pronounced HAH-vee-are. Sergeant Javier Olivera was wearing rimless glasses on a hook nose. A bushy black mustache adorned a very Mexican face. Brown corduroy pants and a tan pullover shirt hugged a large and athletic frame.

With Clay Oeland directing, they stepped through his version of the events of the prior evening. After Clay parked the car, a man with a gun had appeared at the driver's window. He ordered Clay out, walked him around to the passenger side of the car, ordered him to take off his shirt, and then made him lean on the hood. Sally Krestas was out of the car, leaning against the passenger door, when the man suddenly ripped her blouse and slapped her until her face was a bloody mess. He then held her by the arms and shook her violently. According to Clay, Sally made no move to protest or protect herself during the assault. When the gunman stopped slapping her, he nodded toward Clay. Sally Krestas then assaulted Clay with her fingernails, stopping when he pushed her away.

Sergeant Javier Olivera questioned Clay about Sally Krestas' blouse at each step of the reenactment. Javier obviously knew something about the blouse beyond what he'd told Clay. When had she taken it off? Clay didn't think she was wearing it when she scratched him, yet she couldn't have been holding it. Was it on the ground? How did it get back into the car?

To each question, Clay emphasized that he was looking at the gun, it mesmerized him, he said, so he wasn't aware of what Sally Krestas was doing.

When Clay was allowed to continue, he described how the gunman then ordered him back into the car, and told him to keep both hands on the steering wheel. Clay got into the car to show how the gunman shoved him forward into the steering wheel, and then leaned in and shot Sally Krestas twice. The gunman then dropped the gun on the seat, and disappeared into the orchard.

On the tape, Clay's voice trembled. "She was thrashing; the spasms were very violent. I saw blood gushing from her hands where she was holding on to her stomach."

Clay put his right hand on the seat. "The gun was here. I picked it up. The slide was open so I knew the gun was empty, but I ejected the clip anyway. It was empty."

"How did you know how to eject the clip?" Javier asked.

"The eject button is obvious."

"Is that the only reason?" Javier asked, writing something in his notebook.

Clay seemed confused. Javier interrupted whatever he was going to say. "It's your gun, isn't it?" Clay's mouth refused to work. "Did you think that the gun had never been registered to you?"

Clay's face drained to an ashen pallor. He seemed to wilt when he said, "I won't say anything more until I talk to a lawyer."

Javier pulled Clay out of the car and handcuffed him, saying, "That's a good idea, you're gonna need one." Javier took a white card out of his shirt pocket and began reading the Miranda warnings.

The next video, taken through a one-way mirror, showed four men gathered around a small, rectangular, metal table in a narrow, windowless room. The time stamp indicated January 30, 2001, five days after the shooting. Javier introduced a balding, chubby guy as a stenographer. Clay sat beside a small man wearing a very expensive suit. Jim Shaw stated his name for the record and said he represented Clay Oeland.

Javier hurried through the preliminaries for date, time and case. Jim Shaw interrupted. "My client has been framed in a clever plot to make this shooting look as if he murdered Ms. Krestas. Since it is in our interest to help you find the person who actually did the shooting, we will cooperate to the extent that we do not jeopardize our defense strategy. A question that I instruct Mr. Oeland not to answer does not imply the avoidance of self-incrimination. Some questions will not be answered to preserve the viability of our defense strategy. Is that clear?"

Javier waved his hand in a sarcastic gesture. For a few minutes, he listened as Clay argued that the incident was intended to wreck the merger between his company and a Los Angeles company. Javier didn't care about Clay's theory. When he finally addressed Clay, it was to ask, "Did you ever call Ms. Krestas' apartment?"

Clay nodded. "I made three calls to a number she gave me. I assumed it was her home."

"What were the calls about?"

"She left a message on my answering machine on January 20, Saturday before last. When I returned her call, she said she knew who had stolen the ball bearings from our receiving area."

"Did you know her previously?" Javier tried too hard to make the question sound like idle curiosity.

"No, I didn't." Clay had caught the inference, he waited for Javier's bombshell. Javier shrugged so Clay continued, "Needless to say, I was very interested. The stolen shipment cost $80,000. She wanted a $10,000 reward and I agreed. She said she'd call me when it was safe to get together."

"How long did this call take?" Javier sounded bored.

"Not long, five to ten minutes."

Javier hesitated as if unsure of his next question. "And that was the first time she contacted you?"

"Yes."

"What were the other calls you made to her about?"

"I called her on January 24 in answer to a call she left on my answering machine. She wanted to get together the next day. I told her I could meet her at four-thirty. She wanted me to pick her up at the Santa Theresa and Baily bus stop."

"And the third call?" Javier asked quietly while he wrote on a pad.

"I got home at three on the 25th, so I called to see if she wanted to make it earlier. She told me she couldn't, so we left it for four-thirty."

Time stopped in the tiny room while Javier wrote on his pad. He consulted a calendar, and made another note. Then he waved the pad at Clay when he asked, "So she made two calls to your house: the first on January 20; the second on the 24th. Is that right?"

"To his knowledge," Jim Shaw interjected.

"As far as I know," Clay confirmed.

"And you made three calls as you've stated, beginning with the one on January 20. You're positive about that date?"

"Yes."

Javier ripped a sheet of paper from his notebook and slid it across the table. "How about the 23 minute call on January 5, at 8:22 in the evening, to her number from your office. How about the 34 minute call on January 8, at 9:37 a.m., to her number from your office. How about the call from your office at noon on January 12, that ran for an hour and five minutes. Or the 18 minute call on January 19, at 1:23 in the afternoon, from your office."

Clay looked stunned. He pointed to the paper for Jim Shaw, then reached in a pocket, retrieved a small book and opened it. "I was at work during all those times," he said finally. He ran his hand across his face, pulling it away when he touched the scratches, as if they were hot. He said, "I can't explain those. I didn't make them."

Javier abruptly changed the subject. "Do you remember the swabs we took of your hands the night of the murder?" Clay nodded. "You told me during the reenactment at the scene that you picked up the gun. You're right-handed, so you grabbed the gun with that hand?" Clay nodded; his face indicating he knew some other rock was about to fall. Javier continued, "That would explain why you have GSR, ah, gunshot residue, on the palm of your right hand."

"I ejected the clip into my left hand and, after I put it back, I closed the slide with my left hand."

"So we'd expect to find GSR on the palms of both hands." Javier waited for Clay to nod before he continued, "What we can't figure is why the back of both your hands had the most GSR, if you didn't fire the gun."

Clay looked stricken. Javier's voice was quiet as he asked, "Got any idea how that happened?"

Jim Shaw turned to Clay and said, "I think we ought to end this now. Mr. Olivera is not interested in pursuing any other suspects."

"I wouldn't be either," Clay said quietly. "This is all unbelievable."

"Yeah, it is," Javier agreed. He stood up, slammed the metal chair against the table, and walked out of the room.

I had to agree, talk about braiding the rope.

While the tape rewound, I looked through the stills. There were pictures of Sally Krestas taken in the morgue, the first a close-up of her battered face. Grotesque swelling had pulled a cut apart on her upper lip. Her left eye was bloody. Greenish welts marred her forehead, cheeks, and her upper arms.

In a photo of her blood-covered bra, the strap between the cups was notched. The bullet that hit her in the chest took that chunk out of the bra strap first, a perfect half-circle in an elastic strap. I couldn't imagine the force and speed that it took to cut elastic that precisely.

The photo of Sally Krestas' chest showed that powder burns had blackened the skin that wasn't covered by her bra. The bullet hole made the same notch in the bra's white shadow on her skin.

The wound to her belly was another matter, the shock of an expanding bullet had opened the entire abdominal cavity from her rib cage to her pelvis, a mass of gore that didn't resemble anything human.

The next three pictures were Clay Oeland, naked from the waist up. Fingernail wounds marked both sides of his chest and the underside of his arms. The final pictures were of the crime scene and the interior of Clay Oeland's car.

It was an unplanned murder. Clay Oeland's story was ludicrous. It was the third request in as many weeks from obviously guilty men, requests sent by lawyers wanting me to develop an alternate scenario, something to hang a jury with reasonable doubt.

The story had kept me interested, I had forgotten my appointment. I looked like shit; unshaven, uncombed, worn pants and a T-shirt from Puerto Vallarta advertising Corona beer, but I didn't have time to change. I ran out to the carport, drove like a madman through the traffic in Arlington, and got to her office building in nine minutes.

As I parked my car behind the glass and steel tower, it occurred to me that I had become one of those rich fucks who go whining to a shrink when life hands them a lemon. Why didn't I follow the plan I had prescribed for them: Go to a resort in the Caribbean and chase skirts until the problem disappears.

Despite that sage advice, I ran up the stairs to the third floor office of Dr. Slocuse, entering just five minutes late. She opened the door to her inner office and invited me in.

Dr. Mildred Slocuse is the shrink of choice for the District of Columbia's cops. When a District cop I hang with told me about her, he didn't use a nickname, which was weird, cops give everyone nicknames. When I met her, the absence of a nickname seemed very strange. To put it unkindly, the lady dripped possibilities. No one would ever call her handsome; she was built like a tree stump, and, in the dim light of her inner office, she had a mustache.

Minutes into our first session, I understood why. She took the concept of intelligence into a realm I had never glimpsed. She had dissected my rationalizations, emotions, and confused reactions; digging through the debris until she found the core problem. Then she made me look at it by asking, "When you arrived at this illogical solution, why was it so attractive?"

This was to be our third session. She gestured me to the couch that faced a fireplace where gas flames danced over cast iron logs. As usual, she sat off to the side in a low rattan chair, facing the opposite wall so that we both had to turn our heads to look at each other. It was easier to watch the fire, and her words seemed to appear in my mind.

"How was your week?"

"Boring. Chasing deadbeat dads mostly."

"Look up any domestic violence perps?"

"Some."

She is silent then, I can feel her eyes. I stare at the fire, trying to find some other conversation to divert her. Knowing it is a lie, I say, "If they have warrants, I could find them for the police."

She knows it is a lie, she even knows that I know that, so she says nothing, obviously waiting for the truth. The truth comes embedded in rage, I want to scream it at her, punch holes in her office walls, break something. Just as quickly as it comes, the rage subsides, leaving me drained.

She asks, "Gary, why did you come to me?"

"Because of that situation."

"Don't use euphemisms; don't equivocate, be specific."

Her request feels like psychological bullshit. I hadn't repressed anything, I had relived the incident every night for two months before I could go to sleep. The eerie feeling that I'd stepped out of my body and watched myself catch up to John Whiley while cocking the gun, intending to place it against the back of his skull and fire it. Ahead, a woman turns the corner and walks toward us, saving his life, and perhaps condemning his wife to death.

"Gary?" she prods.

"What's the point?"

She waits, knowing that I know the answer, forcing me to confront each

·

illogical thing that I do. I am a logical person, I like that I am a logical person, yet I want to kill strangers because of this thing inside me. I need to get rid of it before I do kill.

I feel tension evaporate as I say, "I stalked an abuser with a gun, looking for an opportunity to kill him."

"You knew that you'd have to kill 500 abusers to have even odds of saving one woman's life, yet you prepared to kill him. Are you any closer to knowing why?"

"I don't think I decided that I wanted to kill him. I only remember thinking that I could kill him and get away with it."

"If your mind is capable of substituting a decision about opportunity for one of intent, you should be on medication."

I feared her truth. "I'm 34. If I medicate my problems away at this age, when will I ever learn coping skills?"

"This isn't a problem, you are arranging a murder. Without prevention, there will be no coping."

I didn't see that coming, and it staggered me. The rage flashed and I countered without thinking. "Fuck the pills, do your job. If you can't give me coping skills, refer me to someone who can."

Her voice was unhurried and calm when she said, "Do you really believe another recitation would be helpful? You know all the appropriate coping skills."

"Change locations, immerse myself in work, fall in love, plan for the future, that kind of thing?"

"Those are your coping skills."

The rage subsided into pain. There was no magic. I had to get through each day without thinking about the past.

Resigned, I said, "I've been offered a complex case that should keep me mentally occupied for some time. If I'm still hung up when that's over, I'll try the pills."

"Does this job have anything to do with violence against a woman?"

"No."

I'd changed my mind about taking the job by the time I got back to the apartment. I could lie to the shrink but there wasn't any point in lying to myself: I hated Clay Oeland for killing that girl.

I called Oeland's lawyer, Toni Conboy, in California. She kept me on hold for several minutes. When she picked up her extension, her perfunctory apology for the long wait irritated me. I told her bluntly that I didn't want the case.

"Clay Oeland figured that." She paused for my comment before she launched what sounded like a rehearsed pitch. "He wants you to go beyond your first impression. He will pay you $20,000 for 40 hours of investigation."

"I don't think so. People who kill ought to go to jail."

"I believe he's been framed, just as he said." She paused, perhaps expecting an argument, before she added, "You've seen what they have. I have a snowball's chance in hell of getting him off. Mr. Oeland is much too smart not to cut his losses and cop a plea if he did this thing."

I wondered how long she'd been practicing criminal law. Guilty people are always optimistic. "He does seem very convincing," I inserted a timely pause before I concluded, "but I've learned not to rely on impressions."

"What if it did happen the way he said?" She waited, obviously giving me time to take that leap. "What is going to be hurt if you take his $20,000? Come out and look around for a week."

Thinking there might be some mitigating evidence in the materials she hadn't sent, I asked, "Do you have any facts that support his story?"

"If I did, I wouldn't need you, would I?"

The lady had an attitude problem. I was thinking about hanging up when she said, "That was a bitchy thing to say; I apologize." After a brief pause, she asked, "I don't know what you want, Mr. Charboneau."

"I made my reputation helping innocent people. There's no point in working for the defense if the person is guilty. I need to believe that Clay Oeland is innocent."

She might have sighed. "The evidence shows that the gun was fired behind his back, just as he said. The police think he fired at her that way, holding his left hand behind his back. That doesn't make sense, he's right handed."

If that was her only reason, we were through talking. "I agree with the police. He had GSR on both hands, not too likely if he only handled an empty gun. If Sally Krestas saw the gun in his right hand, she probably grabbed his right arm. If she braced herself against the passenger door with her feet, she would have had enough leverage to hold that arm against the steering wheel. Jammed into the wheel, he couldn't move, so he transferred the gun to his left hand, put it behind his back, and shot her. He could hardly miss."

I paused before I concluded, "As I said, I work to clear innocent people. I think Clay Oeland shot her."

"I know he didn't shoot her." Toni Conboy sounded almost desperate. "I can't prove it, but I know it."

The passion in her voice intrigued me. "Tell me why you think that."

Again, she made some noise that sounded like a sigh before she said, "I've watched the man at work. His typical day is chaotic. People are continually in his office with all sorts of emergencies. The guy never raises his voice, never gets upset, never micro-manages. He encourages, he suggests, he puts people together and nudges solutions out of them, and he usually does it with humor. He seems gender blind, he treats men and women with courtesy."

Some noise intruded. She said, "Excuse me." The phone was muted, then she came back on. "Anyway, the point I'm trying to make is that Clay Oeland is not a volatile man. Everyone who knows him is willing to testify that he has no temper. The police think he shot her because she scratched him, but he boxed in college. It isn't likely that he would have a murderous reaction to a physical assault." She sighed again. "It's not proof, I know that, but I also know he didn't do it."

The passionate tone in her voice was unusual for a lawyer. She did believe him. The tape had shown him to be a very calm man, Javier had pushed and taunted him throughout both interviews, yet he had never looked or sounded so much as piqued.

If it had happened as he described it, the cleverness of the frame would make the national news. My lagging career could sure use the publicity. I hadn't had a good case in over a year. And it would keep my mind off killing abusers.

Without Deborah, my one-bedroom apartment felt empty. I had stored all the touches she had added, so the furnishings had reverted toward nonexistent. The apartment wasn't neat either, the TV trays flanking the futon were buried under books and magazines. A relief map of the world on the wall above the futon was the only decoration. The wall-length, built-in bookcase crammed with paperbacks provided the only color in an otherwise unbroken sameness of beige and brown. I could walk out and let the place burn without feeling any regret at all. Maybe I needed to get away from the memories.

"Did you hang up?" Ms. Conboy asked.

"There's one thing you should know. I really hate men who abuse women. If I find evidence that he has a history of assaulting women, I'll give it to the prosecutor and help him use it."

"She doesn't need it. She has more than enough to cream me now."

"Reimburse me for first class?"

She wasn't that impressed. "Get real, Mr. Charboneau, take coach and have a lousy meal like the rest of the world."

"All right," I said, sighing loudly into the mouthpiece. "When do you want me?"

"As soon as you can get here."

CHAPTER TWO

From the air, San Jose formed the apex of the "V" shaped megalopolis anchored by Oakland and San Francisco. San Jose's airport occupied the triangle formed by a massive rail yard and two freeways. As we slid below the surrounding hills, the wing on my side aimed at a dirt, mile-long race track. The airplane pivoted as flaps whined into position and then the landing gear shuddered into the air stream.

Satisfied with the new direction, the pilot applied more power. Tall buildings formed a corridor for the airplane. A freeway flashed underneath, close enough to see that a woman driver was smoking. The airport appeared and we fell toward the concrete runway. Terminal buildings flashed by and still the wheels hadn't touched.

After the concrete yanked the airplane out of the sky, the pilot was in a hurry. Large panels rose from the wings to spoil the lift. After the thrust reversers deployed, the Niagara noise hurled momentum away, but we were still moving very fast when the engines faded into a whine. The pilot was on the brakes in spurts. Every time he lifted, the plane seemed to gain speed. Despite that impression, we made the right turn at the boundary of the airport. I saw tire smoke curl around another jet just touching down on the runway. No wonder our pilot was in a hurry.

After the long wait to get off the airplane, walking the length of the crowded airport, and then waiting forever for my suitcase, the car rental process was going to be a breeze, I was the only customer. Unfortunately, the eager young man must have been trained by a religious cult.

I rent white Dodge Neons because they are invisible, people don't see a tail because there's always a small white car behind them. Since I own one, I have everything I need to install all my electronic gear. As the fresh faced young man pointed out at length, I could upgrade to a midsize for the money

I had paid to reserve the color. Maybe he saw that I was getting pissed, I don't know, but he abruptly dropped the spiel and started filling out the paperwork.

Once I had the car keys in my hand, I compounded my error by asking him for directions to Toni Conboy's address. I snatched the map out of his hand when he began retracing the route for the fifth time.

It took less time to find the street than to listen to his directions, it was only two miles from the airport. Older homes with large front yards lined the street. Huge elm trees rippled the sidewalks, streets, and shaded lawns. All the houses looked freshly painted, and the shrubbery was manicured; an upscale neighborhood.

Toni Conboy's office was in a Disneyland Victorian done in shades of blue with white filigree. The carved oak door had an etched-glass inset. Like a brave little heroine raising a puny spire in protest, the Victorian was a counterpoint to the square, cinder-block, three story building on the corner.

Inside the foyer, three secretaries were wedged into a small cubicle festooned with phones, fax machines, files, and computers.

"Can I help you, Sir?"

The lady who greeted me reminded me of my ex-wife, Sandy. That wasn't her fault so I gave her my best smile when I said, "Gary Charboneau. Toni Conboy is expecting me."

She thought I was lying. Her voice dripped suspicion as she repeated, "Gary Charboneau?" When I nodded, she keyed an intercom and repeated my name, still sounding skeptical.

Toni Conboy was big. She wasn't overweight, just not a typical Playboy candidate: thick waist, small breasts and a long torso. Close to forty, I estimated, but it was hard to tell. "Gary Charboneau?" she asked, obviously surprised. The receptionist was standing, the phone in her hand, ready to call nine-one-one.

The eerie tension made me laugh. "What'd I miss?" I asked. "Were you expecting a linebacker?"

Toni Conboy's face softened as she grasped my hand. "We watched you on 60 Minutes. Have you had plastic surgery?"

I almost told her to get real, I certainly wouldn't have chosen bland looks, even if they are an advantage for an investigator. At 34, I can pass for ten years' difference in either direction. People either mistake me for someone else, or they don't remember meeting me. The interviewer on 60 Minutes was short, so people had the impression that I was a big guy. At six feet even,

I'm tall enough to see over most people, yet short enough so that I don't stand out in a crowd. My weight fluctuates around 180, a medium build that attracts no attention. My brown hair is short, my hazel eyes take on the color of my shirt, everything about me is forgettable.

I gave both women a quick description of George, the make-up man used by 60 Minutes. I wanted my face disguised; George wanted a challenge. "He began the make-up session by asking what sex I'd like to be."

I mentioned that I'd done a couple of local shows without any disguise. I tapped my unshaven upper lip. "So I grow this while I'm working, just in case someone has a picture."

Once I passed inspection, Toni Conboy invited me into her office and motioned me to an overstuffed leather chair. Her short, straight, black hair accentuated her long face and large nose. She had applied too much color to her cheekbone ridge. Her eye shadow was heavy and dark, lending a cadaver look. She would be good looking getting out of bed in the morning, but then I always vote for the "before" pictures in makeover articles.

I asked, "Where did you get the 60 Minutes tape?"

As she sat down, she said, "I save all sorts of things I think I might need. I have tapes of a few investigators." Her unrelenting stare made me uncomfortable. She escaped the obvious question when she asked, "How was coach?"

"The meal was very good." I took a package of peanuts out of my pocket. "I brought you these, just in case you're suffering withdrawal pangs."

She accepted them. "Thanks, they're my favorite." She had seemed aloof on the phone. In person, her warm voice and smile felt sensual.

The office was expensively cluttered. The desk looked as if it were carved out of an oak tree. I couldn't find a change in the grain where the wood was joined. Matching the wood that precisely must have been expensive. "Beautiful desk, Ms. Conboy."

"Toni. May I call you Gary?"

"Please."

She looked as if she wanted to say something and didn't quite know how to start. I jumped into the pause to say, "I'll want to talk with Clay Oeland as soon as possible."

She picked up the phone. "I'll make an appointment for you to meet him at Microfix."

I shook my head. "At his house, tonight, with his wife and kids."

My success as an investigator is the result of illegal eavesdropping. I use cheap, throwaway bugs that are good for a couple of days before they become whatever they look like, small blocks of wood or plastic phone connectors, that kind of thing. I wanted to hear the truth Clay Oeland told his wife after I left.

He agreed to meet at eight that evening. When Toni hung up, she wrote his address on a note pad, and, at my request, the address for Microfix. When she handed me the paper, she said, "There's something else you should know."

She looked guilty as hell. I waited for the shoe to drop.

She smiled morosely. "I've been out of law school ten years, mostly writing briefs for other lawyers. When this broke, every lawyer in town put in a bid with Clay. Deep pockets are very attractive. When he fired his first lawyer, I decided to make a bid to represent him." In spite of her best efforts, she grinned. "I told him that I could deliver you."

That made me laugh. "Why did he believe you?"

"I told him we had a thing once." She stared at me, probably trying to read a reaction.

"Was I any good?"

She waved her hand in a so-so gesture. "Anyway, in case he asks, I didn't want you to be surprised." She watched me when she asked, "Does this make any difference to you?"

"Only if you dumped me."

She grinned. "We just grew apart. Although I have to say, you were a lot cuter on 60 Minutes."

"Well, that's show biz." I managed to sound cranky.

"You aren't upset with me, are you?"

I shook my head. "I'll be tolerant since we're lovers."

"Were."

"Yeah." I grinned. "In case he asks, shouldn't I know something about you?"

"Like moles? Whether I make noise when I come?" She was going for a laugh but there was some undercurrent I couldn't identify.

"I was thinking more along the lines of how old you are, where you're from, where you went to school, are you married, that kind of thing."

She blushed. "Of course you were, I knew that."

"Do I make you nervous?" I asked, grinning unkindly.

A wry expression wrinkled her mouth. "Lying makes me nervous." She saw the remark coming. "I know, I'll never be any kind of a lawyer with a defect like that." She laughed, then picked up a pencil and studied it. "To answer the questions, I'm 34. Both parents were addicts who managed to OD within a year of each other, I was too young to remember either of them. I was raised by my grandparents. I went to the University of Santa Clara Law School."

She turned sideways to the desk, looking out the window at a bougainvillea-covered fence. She talked to the window. "I was married at twenty-four. It only lasted six months. His name is Pete. He lives in the city and we're still friends." She watched me when she said, "You and I met at a class I took during the summer at Georgetown two years ago." When I made no comment, she shrugged. "You need more?"

"Do you have any moles, and do you make noise when you come?"

She wrinkled her nose disdainfully. "Moving on, is there anything else you need?"

"The drawing of the shooter sucks, it looks like the 'Bushy Haired Stranger' stereotype." I used my fingers to put quotation marks around the "Bushy Haired Stranger." A BHS is an automatic flag to law enforcement. The one who sees the Bushy Haired Stranger commit a crime is usually guilty of it. "Is Oeland familiar with the legend?"

Toni winced. "Yes. Like everything else in this case, his description wasn't adequate." That was an understatement, all Oeland had recalled was a white guy with a mustache. She continued, "He doesn't like the drawing either, he just can't tell the artist what's wrong with it. He spent hours looking through the mug books."

Maybe there was no guy to find. If his wife knew that, one well-placed bug could have me on my way back to the District tomorrow with his $20,000. He'd pay to keep me away if his truth was what I expected.

I told Toni, "That's all I have." I half rose to hand her my card. "That's my cellular number, leave me a voice mail if I don't answer."

She rummaged in her middle desk drawer. "I'll write up a contract for you. How do you charge expenses?" When we finished the list of expenses, she tucked the paper into a manila folder, put that in a drawer, then she leaned back in her chair and toyed with a hand-grenade paperweight. "Out of curiosity, what did your expenses average for your last few cases?" She pulled the pin.

Pointing at the grenade, I asked, "Is this your idea of a subtle negotiating tactic?" She laughed; replaced the pin, and put the grenade down without commenting. I wondered if she would throw the grenade when I said, "One cost 200 K, one was 10 K, 20 K must be close to usual."

"Two hundred thousand? Wow. The McBride case?"

"The DA had a good case against McBride, and almost none against the killer, so guess which one he chose to prosecute? I knew, he knew, everyone in San Diego knew who committed the murder, but it took a year and two hung juries before the DA quit trying to convict an innocent man." I should have been grateful to the prick, he had made my reputation, but thinking about him seared my emotions.

Toni pushed a form across the desk toward me. "Is this acceptable for billing? It asks you to itemize your time down to the nearest tenth of an hour."

I shook my head and pushed the form away. "I'll find the killer for $20,000 plus expenses. If it takes me eight hours or eight weeks, it'll cost the same $20,000. Will that be acceptable to Mr. Oeland?"

She nodded. "He'll jump at it."

Despite having been up for eleven hours, it was only noon in California. I went shopping for area maps and a deli, used a phone book to find a motel with a kitchen near Microfix, then drove there and got a room on the second floor facing the parking lot. In the room, I put the food away, unpacked, put the stuff I needed with me in the car, then I returned to the lobby and bought a newspaper. Back in the room, I took out a pint of potato salad and settled in with the newspaper.

Halfway through the potato salad, an article caught my attention. It seemed Aaron Grady of Maid Drive had been arrested for breaking his wife's jaw. His bail had been set at $10,000. I called the jail and found out that Aaron Grady hadn't made bail. Lucky for him. Using the cellular to access the internet, I logged on to the reverse directory site that I subscribe to, and found Aaron Grady's address.

I wanted to know more about Aaron Grady. I drove to his address, cruising slowly by his single story yellow house. The yard was well kept, as was the outside of the house. Several feminine touches: flowers in baskets, a spring wreath on the front door, and fuchsias in hanging baskets, told me something about Aaron's wife, and revived memories that hurt. I was short of breath, my face felt flushed, and I was sick to my stomach, as if I feared Deborah was inside.

I parked the car two blocks away on a busy street. From the make-up bag I keep with me, I glued the fake bump on my nose, and added the oversize mustache and goatee combination. I glued the scar to my right cheek; an ugly, two inch long purple scar with stitch lines. I used foundation to blend both the scar and the lump on my nose. Then I walked back into the subdivision.

At the house next door to the Grady's, an older woman warily opened the door. I flashed the ID that has PROBATION in large letters across the face. That didn't open the door any wider.

I asked, "How well do you know your neighbors, Aaron Grady and his wife?"

"I don't know them at all. You should ask the lady who lives on the other side; she and the wife talk all the time."

"Do you hear any fights next door?"

"Just her screaming in pain. We call the police when we hear that." She seemed disgusted as she closed the door.

The lady who lived on the other side of the Grady's was a young mom with two toddlers. Jennifer invited me in, and I watched her corral her son who carried a smelly load in his diaper. She wrestled him to the floor and changed the diaper while telling me about Karen Grady.

This was Karen's fourth trip to the emergency room. Unlike her other injuries that had been treated on an out-patient basis, this time they kept her in the hospital to wire the broken jaw. I supposed they were also keeping her under observation for a possible brain injury.

Jennifer was through trying to persuade Karen Grady to leave her husband. According to Jennifer, she had told Karen about all the options, and now it was just too painful to continue.

I knew why Karen couldn't run, and why Jennifer couldn't help. Deborah had told me about finding herself alone after all her friends disappeared. Her husband, Roger, seemed to be the only human who cared that she existed. He also seemed to know what she was thinking, so after the first time he put her in the hospital, she didn't dare even think anything that might upset him.

The courts were useless, they only delayed the moment of reckoning, and waiting for punishment was so much worse than enduring it. As she had told me, the beatings were such a release from tension that she preferred them to the waiting.

I thanked Jennifer and left. As I walked by, I thought I saw Deborah move by the window inside the Grady's house.

CHAPTER THREE

I thought I'd parked in front of a single story ranch house that evening. I was wrong. The marble tiled entryway faced a golf course through cathedral-shaped windows. The house and windows extended down three stories. The tall, too thin woman in her forties who had answered the door let the view work its magic before she asked, "Mr. Charboneau?"

She introduced herself as Pat Oeland, Clay's wife. She seemed nervous and self-assured, perhaps an uptight lady who disliked dealing with riffraff like private investigators. She walked toward the rear of the house, showing me the way. Her black slacks and black pullover sweater matched her black hair. Other than a gold wedding band, she wore no jewelry.

The third floor loft surrounding the entryway included a kitchen and a dining room. The kitchen was new. The drop-in designer sink featured a $500 faucet. The refrigerator had the door in the door and a hot and cold water dispenser. I commented about the raised burners on the European stove.

"There's a stove up here?" She pantomimed surprise then did a "How about that" expression before she said, "Live and learn." Her laugh sounded brittle.

"Do you have a cook?" I asked.

"Why?" she asked as if I had the answer. "I eat salads; Clay works so much that he's never here for meals. My son, Rob, prefers junk food."

As we walked down the wide curving oak stairway, the cathedral-shaped windows took my breath away. I'd never have enough courage to put windows like that on a golf course. I would have opted for paned windows. One ball, one pane, a few bucks at most. Some people risk everything to create the proper impression. An errant incoming would take out $10,000 worth of glass.

The stairs dropped to a second floor loft that connected to another stairway leading to the ground floor. Just the stairs had cost well over $100,000. The house would go for two, maybe three million. The taxes alone would break a wage earner.

I had considered that paying me $20,000 might mean that Clay was innocent. Judging by the house, $20,000 might be his pocket change.

Clay was waiting in the ground floor living room. He seemed both thinner and older than the man in the videos. He carried some extra weight but not that much. Although age had not treated his face kindly, women would like his rugged looks. The fingernail scratches on his face had faded to pink lines.

He examined me with a salesman's frankness as we shook hands. He asked about drinks. As usual, my request for tap water created some confusion. He went behind a small bar, handed me a glass of water, then began mixing two different drinks.

Four bar stools, four unmatched upholstered chairs, and a small couch that matched one of the chairs provided seating arranged to admire the view of the golf course. Other than a cabinet, a bookcase, and a coffee table, the furnishings were decorator items. A small tree hid one corner of the room, an oriental screen hid another.

Pat Oeland hovered near the bar, watching Clay mix their drinks. I had the impression that she didn't want to look at me, so she looked at him. Abused wives are afraid to look at other men.

As Clay worked on the drinks, he said, "Tell me about yourself."

I gave him the highlights. An electrical engineer by schooling, I took FBI training to do surveillance work for the DEA. I helped a computer contractor's employee make a fraud case against his employer. We split the $3.2 million reward when Justice convicted the guy's boss of receiving $32 million in kickbacks. For some reason, DEA management didn't want me around after that, so I set up shop as an investigator.

I told him about the McBride case. I didn't tell him that my success in that case, and several others, was due to a liberal sprinkling of illegal eavesdropping devices. I also didn't tell him that the reporter who profiled me in two stories in the Post was a girlfriend. Those articles got me invitations to two talk shows, which led to the 60 Minutes story.

Clay asked some pointed questions. As Toni had said, he was not stupid.

I could hear rap music. "Are your children home?"

"Rob," Clay said. "Andrea's married; she lives in Portland."

"How old is Rob?"

"Twenty-two. He's a college student."

"Would he sit in on this?"

As Pat moved toward the coffee table, she said, "If you can get him to talk, you'll be doing better than we have." She picked up a cordless phone and pressed the intercom button. After some delay, she said, "Rob, the investigator would like you to join us."

A few seconds later, Rob came down the stairs, taking three steps at a time. He was easily 6-4 and probably weighed 160 or so, just a rail. His baby face looked out of place on someone that tall. A shock of unruly brown hair seemed to tug at his forehead so that he looked permanently surprised. As he shook my hand, he said, "I don't think I can help you."

"The killer had your father's gun," I told him. "That means someone connected with the killer was in this house. You may know something that could help."

He shrugged and collapsed on the couch next to his mother. Sitting slouched, he was a head taller than Pat. They shared eyes but little else.

I wanted to walk Clay through the police tape. As I handed it to him, Clay nodded toward Pat and Rob. "There's nothing in there they need to see."

Pat said, "We do need to see it, we aren't disinterested parties here."

Clay seemed surprised, but he took the tape. A big screen television rose majestically from the top of what I'd assumed was a cabinet. He loaded the tape in a VCR hidden behind a door near the bottom of the cabinet. I took the remote from Clay and asked him to sit next to his wife on the couch. Potential objections flashed across his face before he sat down without comment. He and Pat carefully avoided touching one another.

I sat in a chair facing them. I'd seen the tape, now I wanted to see their reactions. Sloppy killings happen when someone loses control. I had just taken control away from Clay, I had the remote. I would use the tape to push him into little corners. I wanted to be looking at him, some people get angry very quietly.

I paused the tape just as Sally Krestas was wheeled into the emergency room. Since she had been shot in the heart, I wanted to ask Clay if he knew she was dead when he got her to the hospital. Before I could ask, Pat Oeland grabbed for her mouth, her face ashen. She struggled to her feet and then rushed from the room. In a bathroom just down a short hallway, we heard her get sick.

"Weak stomach," Clay explained. Rob looked amazed. The frozen picture showed Sally with some blood on her bra and skirt, but the towel on her belly hid the large wound. Considering the slow motion bloodshed normally shown on television, this was suitable for very young children. A weak stomach was an understatement.

When I asked if he had known Sally was dead, Clay told me that he thought she might be. It was some weeks before he learned that she had been DOA.

There was nothing else I wanted to ask about on that tape, so I rewound it. As Clay loaded the second tape, Pat came back into the room and quipped, "That's what I get for eating my own cooking."

When she was seated between Clay and Rob again, I pushed Play on the remote. On the videotape, Sergeant Javier Olivera asked Clay to reconstruct Sally's beating, blow by blow. Clay didn't remember much except that the man had put the gun in his waistband to free his hands, and that Sally hadn't raised her hands to stop the assault.

Javier had held up a hand to silence Clay. "So this young girl was casually leaning back against the door while the guy almost ripped her blouse off, then he beat her so badly that it would have required several stitches to close the wounds on her lips and eyelid, and she didn't once groan, or cry out in any way?" Clay looked helpless. Javier put his hands on his hips, his face very close to Clay's. "Did her eyes tear up? Somebody splits my eyelid open, I will have tears in my eyes. You will have tears in your eyes if it happens to you. So let me ask you again, how did she react while she was being beaten?"

"He had the gun stuck in his belt," Clay said. "I was thinking about making a grab for it; I wasn't watching her."

"Were you listening? Did you hear the buttons pop off her blouse?" While Javier's verbal assault continued, I watched the three of them on the couch. Clay had his eyes shut, Pat seemed frightened, her face pale, her eyes wide, while Rob winced as Javier's sharp voice lanced the room. "Did you hear the sound of his hand hitting her?"

"Yes, I..."

"So you would have heard her cry out if she had. I tell you what, Mr. Oeland, Sally took some incredible punishment. Every one of those blows must have hurt her brain, I couldn't have taken it without making some kind of noise."

Javier suddenly puffed his cheeks, raised his hands in a surrender gesture, and asked, "Did she have her blouse on while he was beating her?"

For the next several minutes, I watched the Oelands as Javier used Sally's blouse to poke holes in Clay's faulty memory. Although ripped, the blouse was intact, yet she wasn't wearing it when she was shot. Javier wanted to know when she took it off. Clay thought she didn't have it on while she was being beaten, yet he didn't remember her taking it off. He didn't know where it was when she attacked him with her fingernails either.

Pat Oeland suddenly erupted. "Why did he do that? What was the goddamn point?"

I stopped the tape and waited, hoping her anger would open some door in Clay's facade. Instead, Clay put his hand on Pat's shoulder and said, "Truth is in the details. He was looking for truth."

Rob suddenly unfolded his lanky frame and stood. "If you'll excuse me, I have studying to do."

"Perhaps we can talk later?" I asked.

He shrugged. "Whatever." He took the stairs three at a time. Pat and Clay watched him, concern on both their faces.

I asked Clay, "You've had three months to think about it. Did you remember what happened to the blouse?"

Clay looked annoyed. "At the time, I remembered that the blood from her face splattered her bra, so I assumed the blouse was gone, but it must have just been open, hanging from her shoulders. Forensics found that she had the blouse on while she was being beaten, and she was wearing it after she scratched me. They found my blood in four long smears near the bottom, as if she'd wiped her nails there. She evidently took the blouse off as she was getting back into the car because she was sitting on it when she was shot. If that's when she took it off, my back was turned, that's why I didn't remember."

"You said on the tape that you couldn't stop looking at the gun. Why didn't you recognize your own gun?"

Clay nodded as if he agreed with something I'd said. "Exactly the point that Sergeant Olivera made. But when I had time to think about it, there was no reason for me to recognize my gun. I was looking down the barrel of a .45 and all I could think about was dying. I knew it was an old Army .45, but why should I think it was mine?"

Clay winced. "Until he told me it was my gun, I thought the killer wanted to murder Sally Krestas and pin it on someone else. As soon as the police found out who needed her dead, I'd pick him out of a line-up and the whole nightmare would be over. That's why I look so goddamn stupid on the tape when he told me. I was going to say it wasn't, I didn't think mine had wooden grips, but then I could tell by the look on his face that he knew the gun belonged to me. I realized then that I was the victim of a truly elaborate frame, that someone who had been in my house had set me up." Despair

29

wrinkled his face when he added, "By the time I realized the extent of the setup, I looked guilty as hell."

I looked at my notebook. "I don't have any information about the gun. When do you think it was taken?"

Pat Oeland volunteered, "As Clay told the police, I ran across it when I cleaned out the closet some years ago. It could have been taken any time since then."

I took advantage of the opening. "Can I see where you kept the gun?"

I lagged behind them while we walked up the stairs to their bedroom on the second landing. I removed the plastic coating from the tape on the bug I wanted to plant, then palmed it. Like most married couples with children, they probably did their serious talking in the bedroom.

In their bedroom, two dressers, two night stands and a closet flanked a king-size bed. If someone knew Clay had a gun, there weren't that many places to look. "Everyone keeps their guns in the bedroom," I told them as Pat opened the heavy mirrored closet door. "If someone was looking on the off chance you might have a gun, it probably took less than ten minutes to find it."

Pat pointed to the shelf above the hanging clothes. "It was in a shoe box there."

As I looked into the closet, I pushed the tape side of the bug against the back of the door next to the overlapping metal edge. On the heavy mirrored door, the small wooden rectangle could pass for a shipping block. After the battery expired in two days, that's all it would be.

Turning to face them, I asked, "Do you have any idea who might have taken the gun?"

Pat moved, a slight shifting of balance. I looked at her expectantly, but in my peripheral vision, I saw Clay flash her a warning glance. "Do you suspect someone?" I asked her. She shook her head and turned to leave.

As we walked back to the living room, I guessed Clay's glance must have been about some marital sore point, perhaps the gun had been a source of friction. I mentally sorted through a list of questions that might probe sore spots. If I put enough thorns in their obviously strained relationship, the conversation after I left would be heated.

In the living room, Clay and Pat sat on opposite ends of the couch. I sat in the chair to Clay's right so I could watch both. I focused on Pat Oeland and said, "A wife's lover might not want her grieving for a dead husband; a convicted killer would be so much neater. Any chance that's what happened?"

She shrugged when she looked at me. "Sorry, no one comes to mind."

"Clay ever hit you?"

She seemed surprised by the question, then she joked, "I'm the physically abusive person in this relationship."

Pointing at Clay, I asked her, "Do you know whether he was having an affair?"

That question worked its wonders yet another time. She answered in a flat voice. "He does have his flings." They looked at each other over that chasm. "It's a different smell each time," she said quietly, still looking at Clay, "so I'm guessing they're casual."

"And when was the last one?" I asked.

"A few weeks before the incident." Her face was a montage I couldn't decipher.

Clay said, "I'm sorry, Pat, I had no idea you knew." He reached across the gulf separating them and made contact by holding her hand. She seemed frozen, as if she couldn't believe what he'd just admitted.

"Do you want to change your story now?" I asked Clay.

Still looking at his wife, he said, "They were hookers. I... They were hookers. I'm sorry, Pat."

"I hope you were careful," she said quietly. Her face showed some change. Whatever it was, I couldn't read it.

"Of course." He looked at her for another moment before he looked at me. Wearily, he said, "No, there's nothing to change, I wasn't involved with Sally Krestas in any other way. It happened exactly as I told the police."

Satisfied with the rift I'd created, I took out my notebook and opened it to the notes I'd made when I viewed the tape. "When you were talking with Sergeant Olivera, you seemed sure that the frame was put together to wreck your firm's merger with another company. Why do you think that?"

"My company, Microfix, makes positioning tables, tables that move in precise increments. They're used to position circuit boards for drilling, parts that require machining, they're even used for engraving trophies and etching glass. ANA, Advanced Numerical Applications, a company in Los Angeles, makes the automatic controls used on 85 percent of our tables. Customers had to buy our table, then negotiate with ANA for the controls. The merger of Microfix and ANA would give the customer one-stop shopping, the combined company would be able to market a turnkey unit.

"The merger was announced on November 1 of last year, and it would have been complete on March 30. When I was arrested for Ms. Krestas' murder, the financing fell through because ANA would absorb all of Microfix's liabilities in the merger. Even if I'm exonerated, there will be millions in possible awards to Ms. Krestas' family that Microfix will have to pay, because the shooting occurred while I was on company business."

I asked, "But why did you tell Javier that undermining that merger is the only motive that makes sense?"

He opened his hands. "Take any other motive you can think of: someone wants my money, my wife, my job, or someone wanted to kill Ms. Krestas and blame it on me. With any of those, killing me would have been a better solution. On the other hand, killing me wouldn't have stopped the merger, the liabilities would have been covered by insurance."

If ruining the merger was the reason for the shooting, then finding the brains behind the frame was going to be easy. "If that's true, then you know who set up the frame."

Clay looked the obvious question at me. I held up my index finger. "Judging by the phone calls you didn't make, the person who set this up is someone you work with." I raised two fingers. "Since he or she had to steal your gun, that person has been inside your house." Three fingers were up. "He or she was going to lose something valuable as a result of the merger." As I raised the fourth finger, I said, "This is probably the most important point. That person has to know you well enough to fabricate a story that would get you out to the boondocks with a woman you had never met." I let him absorb all that before I asked, "Who is it?"

He didn't hesitate. "It would have to be one of six managers at Microfix who were going to lose their jobs. The severance compensation was very generous, all of them seemed happy with it, but they are the only people who were going to be affected. No one else would have seen any change."

"How many of them could have been in your bedroom since they were informed about the merger?"

"All of them," Clay said. "We had a Christmas party. We put coats in there, so they all could have been in the bedroom during the party."

When Clay leaned on one hand, he touched Pat's hand accidentally. He apologized, and Pat put her hands in her lap.

"I'd like pictures and the W-4 forms for those managers. Is one of them the purchasing manager?"

Clay looked concerned. "Gene Addison? Yes, he's one of the six. Why?"

"Purchasing is the department where large amounts of money can be stolen and it's also the entry point for drugs. Sally Krestas wasn't killed over anything minor."

"Gene does live well, but we have very good controls in purchasing. He's also a minister."

"Religion is an excellent cover for crooks. But besides stealing money or running drugs, is there any other reason someone might want to wreck the merger?"

"I had our marketing people look into the obvious reasons. No one shorted Microfix stock, and our competition wasn't that impressed, so those avenues are dead ends."

While I noted that in my book, Clay picked up the remote. "We don't need to see any more of Sergeant Olivera making me look guilty, do we?" We didn't, so he rewound it, handed me the tape, and then pushed a button that submerged the projection TV into the cabinet.

Clay watched the TV descend as he said, "Knowing all six managers as well as I do, I just can't believe any of them are running drugs. And we don't single-source any parts, so stealing money would require the collusion of two or more companies as well as buyers and engineers. That's hard to imagine."

"You have a factory in Mexico. Parts shipments from Mexico are known conduits for drugs."

He nodded. "When we joined the Maquiladora program, we worked with the Border Patrol to devise a method of getting our trucks through the border with no delays. We run with minimum inventory, delays cause havoc with our production line. At the suggestion of the INS, we employed a retired Border Patrolman who seals the trailers. According to the INS, if he says there aren't any drugs on those trucks, there aren't."

"That's all I have for now," I said as I stood up. "I'll want to look at your phone at Microfix tomorrow. Is that a problem?"

"No, anytime is fine."

Clay walked toward me, but instead of shaking hands, he grabbed my arm. "Sylvia Vance, the prosecutor, has no reason to seek any other suspect. If I'm going to be cleared, the mastermind behind this frame has to be found. Can you do it, or should I call someone else? The money I've promised is yours, whatever your answer."

Clay dropped his hand as I said, "I don't know of anyone who could do a better job. If you're right about the merger being the reason, I can find the guy inside your factory who set you up." 'Even if it was you,' I added silently.

Clay looked relieved. Pat shook my hand as we exchanged the required polite comments. I shook Clay's hand as I said, "I would like to talk with Rob."

He pointed up the stairs. "The second door on your left. It's on the second landing farther down the hallway from our room. Follow the beat, you can't miss it."

I walked upstairs and located the rap beat at Rob's door. The music died when I knocked. Rob opened the door. The clutter in his room seemed arranged. Magazines, books and sports equipment were grouped by subject. He was either a flea market aficionado or he had a wide range of interests. As I entered, I nodded at the scuba gear in the center of the room. "You do much diving?"

"No," he said quietly, "just taking it up. My first ocean dive is scheduled for Saturday."

I wandered the room, deliberately invading his space. Snow skis were propped against the wall. The handles of several tennis racquets stuck out of a black bag. A large poster of a water skier in a sharp turn dominated the wall over a double bed. No doubt the family had a boat somewhere.

Rob had remained near the closed door as I nosed around. He didn't look anxious, he seemed upset. I watched his eyes when I asked, "Did you take your dad's gun?"

"You believe his story?" he asked, watching me.

"You don't?"

"It looks so bad." He seemed near tears. He sat down on his bed, looking at the floor between his feet.

"Did you take your dad's gun?"

"No."

"Does your father ever hit your mother?"

He shook his head, turning to look at me. "One thing you should know about Dad. He has no temper. None. When I was 15, I got in his face. He didn't even raise his voice, he just told me to go to my room." Rob looked at the floor for a moment and then said, "He used to box, he wouldn't shoot anyone over some scratches."

I asked, "Sally Krestas went to San Jose State, is that where you go?" He nodded. "Have any classes with her?"

"No. From what the student paper published, she was taking freshman G.E. courses."

"How about her roommate, Alicia Stowe? Any classes with her?"

"No, the paper said she was a part-time student."

I nodded and turned to leave. With my hand on the doorknob, I asked, "Does blood always make your mom sick?"

"I didn't think anything made her sick."

As I opened his door, he unfolded his lanky frame as if it hurt, then walked with me to the third floor landing. As he leaned by me to open the door, he said, "I hope you can help Dad." His eyes were brimming.

"I'll find the killer," I told him as I shook his hand.

I hurried to the car, drove around the corner, and then parked next to a large shrub. A receiver in a small tape recorder was tuned to the bug's frequency. When I turned up the volume on the tape machine, two people were in the master bedroom; a toilet flushed and a drawer moved at the same time. The closet door was moved, setting up a low rumble in the bug.

After several minutes of random noises, Clay said, "You don't have to sleep in Andrea's room. I'm the one who should be sorry, Pat."

"Sorry for what? Driving me over the edge?" She sounded sad.

Clay's voice was very loud, he must have been standing near the closet door. "You always used the term 'affairs.' I chose to interpret that narrowly, probably so I could feel comfortable lying to you. I wasn't having an affair, I was only buying sex."

"Oh, Christ," Pat was almost screaming, "did you believe I went off my rocker because I heard a female voice on the phone? Didn't that give you a clue? Didn't you care about why I did that? Did I have to say that I knew you were fucking around?"

Clay's voice faded as he walked away from the bug. "I didn't want to confirm what you suspected, I thought it would only hurt you more."

"As if the lying didn't." After a short silence, she said, "I am confused. Why would you pay for sex and risk infection when you could have me any time?"

Clay sounded tired. "Pat, I know what you need me to say. I can't help you. You know everything I knew about Sally Krestas. It happened just as I told the police. If she was a prostitute, I didn't know it. I'm sorry, I wish it could be different for your sake."

Pat said, "I'm not talking about her. Why did you pay prostitutes for sex?"

"I paid for oral sex."

The conversation came to an abrupt halt. Finally Pat made a noise that might have been a sigh. "All that because I give lousy head." Her sharp laugh sounded bitter. "There's an epitaph for you: 'A good wife except she couldn't do a decent blow job.'" A slamming door ended the conversation.

I waited, hoping to hear more. The exchange about Sally Krestas was very confusing, why did Clay apologize for the truth?

I rewound the tape and listened from the beginning. I stopped it after Clay told her, "Pat, I know what you need me to say. I can't help you. You know everything I knew about Sally Krestas. It happened just as I told the police. If she was a prostitute, I didn't know it. I'm sorry, I wish it could be different for your sake."

It made no sense, what should be different for her sake? She hadn't been at the scene because Clay assured her his story was accurate, hardly necessary if she had been there. Yet she obviously felt guilty about Sally's death, but why?

That was the trouble with bugs, no one ever explained anything.

CHAPTER FOUR

The next morning, Toni left a terse message on voice mail while I was in the shower. "Gary, meet me at nine for breakfast at Ezee's." Perhaps a test: can the investigator find a restaurant. Whatever the reason, I didn't like her taking up my time.

The rush hour was at full tilt when I left the motel. The logical route to Ezee's wasn't moving. I pulled into the tiny parking lot at ten after, the five miles had taken me a half-hour.

Ezee's was a 40s style coffee shop near Santa Clara University. Toni was waiting in the enclosed porch attached to the front of the restaurant. Inside, paunchy men in working clothes, elbows planted on the Formica of the U shaped counter, sat on round vinyl seats perched on chrome pedestals. Three walls had booths with new upholstery; the blue vinyl was unmarred. Experienced waitresses, their eyes searching, padded by on soft shoes, juggling impossible armloads of plates, coffee pots and cups. Even with the door shut, the food smelled delicious.

While we were waiting, Toni and I wedged into a niche between a potted tree and a cigarette machine. Her chocolate brown make-up matched the color of her suit.

"How did it go?" she asked.

"I didn't learn much. His wife did, though."

We lapsed into silence as we were beckoned into the restaurant by a hostess who took us to a booth near the back. As soon as we were seated, our waitress was there with two coffee pots. She poured mine and then poured Toni's decaf from the pot with an orange rim. Toni gave her a brief smile, waited until the woman left and then asked me, "What did Pat learn?"

"Clay frequents hookers."

Pain flickered on her face. "That won't be any help," she said. She built a mound of sugar on a spoon before she dumped it into her coffee.

I tried the coffee; it was fresh, strong and hot. As I put the cup down, I asked, "What do you know about his wife?"

Biting her bottom lip, Toni considered the question. I wondered if the "bite your lip" was an unconscious warning to herself. "She makes a good cup of tea," she said, submerging a second teaspoon full of sugar in the coffee.

"And?"

Her face shrugged. "I don't know what I'd do if my husband was facing murder charges, but she acts as if it's none of her concern. Does all the right things; says the right words, but her tennis game is the only interesting thing going on in her life."

The waitress stopped, a pencil poised above her pad. Toni ordered a spinach omelet. After I ordered, Toni waited until the waitress walked away, then asked, "Why did you ask about Pat?"

"She tossed her cookies when she saw the tape of Sally Krestas being wheeled into the ER."

"Really? That made the Ice Lady sick?" Toni stirred the sugar for a moment. "If I remember right, the wounds weren't visible."

I nodded. "Strictly 'G' rating." I sipped my coffee, then put the cup back into the saucer before I dropped the bomb. "Her reaction makes me wonder if she shot Sally."

Toni looked astonished. "That sure doesn't fit. The footprints where the car was parked show Sally's sneakers and four or five sets of men's shoes, three of which were matched to Clay and the cops, but no woman's shoe prints." Toni tried the coffee, then drank half of it like water. When she put the cup down, she added, "It doesn't make any sense."

I proposed a masochistic sex tryst that was interrupted by the vindictive wife carrying a gun. Toni thought that scenario was ridiculous so I told her about a civil case in New Jersey; both participants had sued the other after they were released from the hospital, no hard feelings about the beatings, they just wanted to recover their costs.

I said, "If she did shoot Sally, Clay needed a story to cover for her."

If I wasn't mistaken, Toni's look said she had another idea about Pat. I went with my gut. "What don't you want to tell me?"

"She's having an affair." Toni looked embarrassed when she noticed the waitress standing at the table with our order. The waitress didn't care, she put the plates down, asked if we needed anything else, then left. As I put jam on my toast, Toni added, "With the tennis pro at the Camden Racquet Club, Charles Newton. He's a buddy of the pro at my condos' tennis courts, who told someone, who told someone, who told me."

I wrote "Charles Newton—Camden Racquet Club" in my notebook before I turned my attention to mashing my eggs, hashbrowns and bacon into a stew.

Toni finished her coffee, then talked to the cup. "I asked Cliff, the pro at my place, if Charles is the type who could kill for love. He says the only ambition Charles has is to get his zipper into the hall of fame."

I nodded and continued eating. The eggs were over easy, the hashbrowns were hot, and the bacon was crisp. Those three things almost never happen together; I was very impressed.

She was toying with the omelet when she asked, "Does Clay's using prostitutes mean something to you?"

"It doesn't make me feel any better about his innocence. I worry about a married man who uses hookers."

"I use a vibrator," she said amiably. "What's that have to do with anything?"

I managed to keep a serious expression when I said, "Hookers and blackmail are peanut butter and jelly. Sally thought she was blackmailing him."

"She was a college student," Toni reminded me.

I shrugged. "Those two occupations are not mutually exclusive." The waitress stopped and refilled Toni's cup. While Toni poured sugar on a spoon, I asked, "Why don't we know more about Sally. There was nothing about her in the materials."

Toni nodded. "And that's how much we know. Everybody I talked to in her home town hadn't seen her since she left town years ago. Talking to her father was an exercise in futility. Her mother was worse, she might be certifiable. We couldn't find anyone who knew how Sally earned her money. It was like she dropped in from outer space."

Toni gingerly tried the coffee. She grimaced and poured more sugar while she said, "You read about Sally's roommate, Alicia Stowe, in the materials?" I nodded. "So you know that she told the police they hardly knew each other, despite being roommates. The police weren't too surprised when she disappeared shortly after the murder; they're positive that she was a hooker, so they think she left to avoid problems. They don't suspect foul play."

I finished the stew on my plate, then went looking for survivors with my toast. While I swabbed the plate, Toni asked, "So let's say Sally was a hooker and Clay has been known to wade in that pool. What difference does that make to you?"

"Suppose Clay has problems relating to women. You've heard of the Madonna and the whore syndrome?"

Toni nodded, her attempt at a serious expression ruined by the smile tugging at the corner of her mouth. "Certainly. I'm a Madonna myself. That means you don't get much."

"Can we be serious here?" I complained, failing to contain a smile.

Suddenly she was a little girl whose patience was being tested, shoulders slouched, eyes looking toward the ceiling, perhaps sad but unmistakably bored.

The pathos cracked me up. "It must have taken years to perfect that expression."

She shook her head, smiling. "Had it down pat since I can remember. Grandpa tended to be wordy and that expression could shut him off like a faucet." She smiled again. "Sorry, I'll be serious. Go ahead with what you were saying." She made an exaggerated serious face and then adopted a "please continue" expression.

"If a man believes that any woman who arouses him is a whore, and therefore scum, he could be the kind of man who would shoot a hooker if she pissed him off."

Toni grimaced. "Why are you coming up with these theories? You're supposed to believe his story and develop the proof I need."

Like most lawyers, this lady regarded truth as relative, so I didn't bother responding. I watched four cops as they came into the restaurant. Their eyes never stopped moving. Amazing people, cops. The public beats on them; their bosses treat them with disdain, and most cops consider themselves garbage collectors, yet most love the job. Thank God someone does.

Without warning, Toni asked, "Are you married?"

"I was once, for two years." She waited for more, so I added, "It failed due to boredom."

"Whose? Yours or hers?"

"Hers. She wanted to be married to someone who was fun."

Toni understood. "No one else catch your eye?"

"Yeah, a year ago, I fell in love with a woman who had been tortured by her husband for six years." I didn't want to tell her the rest, so I said, "I learned that some wounds don't heal."

After a moment, Toni said, "I have the same problem, it's tough starting over when the last one was so good. Pete was wonderful, everyone else I've dated is tied for last."

I wondered why she divorced him. Wisdom prevailed and I didn't ask. I finished my coffee before I said, "I'm going out to Microfix to look at Oeland's phone. He says it would have been impossible for anyone else to make those calls to Sally Krestas from his phone. That means a tap. If it's still there, it'll be a great lead."

As we left the restaurant, I told her about shipping my high-tech hardware to her office. "Glad to be of service," she said as if she meant it. "I hope we're not talking the size of a piano?"

"No, but I see your concern. An extra newspaper would totally clog your reception area. I'll get it out of there as soon as it arrives."

In the parking lot, she got into a Jaguar. She wasn't doing badly for someone who only wrote briefs.

During the five mile drive to Microfix, I called Clay, hoping to bypass the usual security delays. The cellular lost the signal when I dialed his number. I had to wait until the freeway topped a rise before the phone acquired another cell. When Clay picked up his extension, I asked him if this was a good time to visit.

"I'm off to a meeting. My secretary should be able to help you. I'll leave the W-4 copies with her."

"Thanks." My dark side suddenly moved my mouth. "Do you know Charles Newton?"

"There's a tennis pro by that name at our Racquet club. Why?"

"The name just came up. Is he a good friend?"

"No, I've never met him. I know him by sight but that's about it."

Someone in a hurry was attached to my rear bumper. While I changed lanes, I asked, "Would Mrs. Oeland know him?"

"I don't...oh yeah, that's right, she took lessons from him some time ago. Sure, she would know him."

"Would you ask her if he's done anything that would cause her to wonder about him?"

"Sure, I'll ask."

After we disconnected, I laughed; that question would smoke her out. Lovers had done weird things before; framing a husband would only be a variation on a very old theme.

I felt smug about that until I realized that if Charles Newton was the killer, he was capable of killing me. I had no protection, I'd shipped my gun UPS. I cursed my dark side for not thinking things through.

Microfix was a tilt-up single-story building with large mirrored windows reflecting the lush landscaping. Rolling mounds of lawn and shrubbery gave the impression that the building was sinking. The surrounding business park had several similar buildings, all with facades inspired by California mission architecture.

The lobby was in the rear, facing a large parking lot fenced with hedges. I found a space in a far corner, and then walked toward the lobby. Most of the cars weren't new; a predominately blue collar work force, I guessed.

Inside the lobby, my name impressed the security guard. He handed me a badge with VISITOR printed on it, and directed me down a hallway to Clay Oeland's office.

Clay Oeland's secretary, Michelle Corbett, regaled me with the corporate smile. The slim, conservatively dressed lady, perhaps in her late twenties, seemed distant until I introduced myself, then she was very friendly. "Mr. Oeland is in a meeting in the building. Do you want me to interrupt him?"

"No, I want to look at his phone." She watched from the door of Clay Oeland's office while I worked. For a CEO, his office was very functional. A massive wooden desk surrounded by eight metal chairs took up most of the space. Four metal filing cabinets used the corners of the office. A white credenza and bookshelves kept Clay's black upholstered chair close to his desk. The only wall decoration was a large red button, an emergency circuit breaker evidently.

I unhooked the bottom of his phone and connected the bug detector, a small unit about the size of a pocket calculator. Its red light indicated a transmitter. I asked Michelle, "Does Clay have a portable?"

She nodded and pointed at a cordless base unit on top of a steel filing cabinet. I pulled its electrical plug and the detector light went green. No bug.

Judging by the antenna, the portable was old. It turned out to be ancient, it had no security code and it operated on a single frequency. Anyone with a modified CB, common among the marginal members of society, could use his phone from the parking lot.

"He's got it with him now?" I asked.

"Perhaps." Michelle waved her arm vaguely toward the factory. "It's out there somewhere. He took it out to the floor this morning. If things are normal, he'll forget where he left it. I look for it before I go home; it has a beeper or I'd never find it."

So much for the phone calls. "Tell him to spring for a new phone, one that scrambles the conversations."

She smiled indulgently, silently informing me that he liked his trusty phone; he didn't want a new one.

Nodding to let her know I understood, I asked, "Did he leave some papers for me?"

She handed me a manila envelope. I sat in one of the chairs in Clay's office and looked at the W-4's. Gene Addison, the purchasing manager, and Raul Valazquez, the shipping manager, both claimed zero exemptions. That's an indication that they might show unusual sources of cash income on their taxes. Money gets laundered when a taxpayer claims sales of antiques, or rare coins, or anything else that's hard to trace.

Another reason to claim zero is the marriage penalty. I asked Michelle if either Gene or Raul had a wife with a high income.

"Raul's wife is a very successful decorator. She runs a business called 'Old Almaden Decor.' I've read articles about her work, she's that good. Raul said she did $500,000 worth of business last year."

"And Gene's wife?"

"No, I understand that she's not well. Lupus, I think."

"Does he have his check deposited electronically?"

While Michelle looked up his account number, I wrote Gene's address in my notebook, then his account number as she read it to me.

Since Gene Addison was in the meeting with Clay, I asked if I could look around the shipping area where the ball bearings had been stolen. Sally had used that theft as the reason for meeting Clay, so it seemed a logical place to start.

She picked up the phone and pushed three digits. "Mr. Valazquez, an investigator, Gary Charboneau, will be down to talk with you about the missing parts. Are you available?" She nodded and then said, "Fine, I'll send him down now." She replaced the phone in its cradle and looked at me with an odd expression. "He said 'no' but I said 'yes.' He may be a bit difficult but do persist, he's terrified that he'll make a mistake and say the wrong thing."

She pointed down a corridor to her left and said, "Just keep walking toward that end of the building. When you reach the shipping department, you'll see Raul Valazquez's office."

When I thanked her, I glanced at the day-timer notebook on her desk. Michelle's neat and tiny handwriting filled half the open page. I pointed at it and asked, "May I?" She gestured a "go ahead." Clay's day had begun at six in the morning with a meeting. Each person who had been invited had a notation after their name recording whether they had attended the meeting. I asked Michelle, "Does your log show Clay's schedule when the calls to Ms. Krestas were made?"

"Yes, his attorney, Ms. Conboy, has copies of all the relevant dates."

"Can anyone confirm that he wasn't on the phone then?"

"He didn't make any of the calls. Someone remembered being in the meetings during the time each was made. Ms. Conboy has those names," she said. "As you can see, he's always in a meeting. Most of the calls were on Fridays, and he can't find the time to eat lunch on Fridays."

He could prove that he didn't make those calls; I could show how easily anyone else could have made them, so the DA's evidence was going to bite her in the ass. Obviously, Toni and Clay were guarding that ambush, waiting and hoping the DA would introduce the information during the trial. Once the trap sprung, the jurors would have to accept the calls as proof of a conspiracy to frame Clay.

I thanked Michelle and walked toward Raul Valazquez's office. The long corridor formed a break between stacks of parts on my left and rooms on the right side. Steel benches filled the assembly rooms. Workers in yellow smocks sat on high seats at the benches, assembling mechanical units with power tools. Dropping from the ceiling, helical cords supplied power for the tools. The small rooms confined the noise; the factory seemed very quiet.

Raul Valazquez, impeccably dressed in a dark blue, pinstriped, vested suit, studied a paper on his desk. Good looking, probably a Mexican-Indian, he carried just enough weight to round out his features. He gave me a curt, "Just a minute," when I knocked on the metal frame of his office door. After that comment, all I saw was his hair. For all I could tell, he corrected the grammar on a paper, then took another paper off a stack and attacked that.

While I waited, I made a notation in my notebook. "Raul Valazquez, asshole."

He was still correcting the papers when I pocketed my notebook, so I turned and walked into the shipping area. That brought him running to my side as if he'd been shot out of the office. "You can't go out there without an escort."

"I thought I might be rushing you, standing there like that."

That caught him halfway between the hay stacks and he started in two directions. "No. Well...I am busy. What is it you want? I've already told the police what I know."

"What's the market for ball bearings?"

"They're like cash. We paid $40,000 for each of the two pallets. The thief probably fenced them for half that."

"How did it happen?" I stopped walking and looked at him, trying to read his face.

He looked pained if anything. "Someone took them at lunch time. All my people were celebrating a promotion at the local pizza parlor, so I stayed to watch the warehouse. I heard a lift-truck moving around, but I assumed it was legit so I never looked." He shook his head before he added, "I was surprised that Clay didn't fire me. I would have."

"Are the ball bearings identified in any way?"

"They're stamped with a lot number." He suddenly stuck his tongue between his front teeth and whistled. A tall woman with shoulder-length, black hair looked over at us. Raul waved her over. She placed a tool she was using on top of a box and came toward us. "Gina can answer any other questions you have."

I stopped him before he could get away. "You were going to be let go when the merger went through?"

His eyes narrowed—I'd hit something. "'Let go' isn't the way I saw it. That annuity was going to give me $5,000 a month for the rest of my life." The tall beauty, in her late twenties, walked up. Taking no notice of her presence, Raul concluded, "I'd have given my left nut to see it completed." He turned to the woman and said, "This is Mr. Charboneau. He's investigating the stolen ball bearings. Will you show him around?" Raul walked off without introducing her.

I extended my hand. "Gary Charboneau."

Her grip was warm and soft, the dark eyes turned my brain to mush. "Gina Rawlins." She was wearing jeans and a starched white shirt with the collar turned up in back. Silver hoop earrings matched a silver chain around her neck. She nodded in the direction Raul had gone. "What did he want to see completed?"

"The merger."

She nodded as if I'd said something incomprehensible and looked at me expectantly. Her chest rising and falling in my peripheral vision ruined my thought process. Trying to act like an adult, I asked, "Can you show me where the pallets of ball bearings were when they were last seen?"

She nodded politely and motioned toward the corner of the warehouse. Walking beside her, I realized that she was nearly six feet tall. Trying to make conversation, I said, "Your boss is an asshole."

She grinned and tried to repress a soft chuckle as she said, "We see each other."

"As I said, your boyfriend is a nice guy."

She blushed. "I'm sorry, I just thought it was funny. You being a detective, you know. I'm sorry."

"I should be apologizing and I do, I'm sorry."

She looked horrified that I'd embarrassed myself. "Oh, no, really, that's all right, he can be abrasive at times." She stopped and pointed at two pallets holding what seemed to be large metal castings. "The ball bearings were about where those are. The pallets weighed 1430 pounds each. There was no path to any other part of the warehouse so they must have been put into a truck that was parked in this loading bay."

The pallets were next to a large roll up door. When I asked, she pressed a switch on the wall. The door moved upward slowly, accompanied by an incredible din akin to a violent thunderstorm. "Jesus, how could Raul have missed that racket?"

Her expressive face showed chagrin for Raul. "That's what he wants to know. He heard the lift truck but he didn't hear the door go up."

"When was the theft discovered?"

"About three that afternoon. A work order said to move them into manufacturing and the lift-truck operator asked me where they were." She raised her eyebrows. "We looked all over. It was embarrassing."

"Are there any rumors about who might have stolen the ball bearings?"

Her face clouded. "They're like cash, honest people would steal them. Someone saw an opportunity and took it."

"Since they're identified with a lot number, would the thieves have to sell them overseas?"

Gina looked at me as if I'd just arrived in the real world. I understood I'd asked a really stupid question. Who would look at the lot number of a ball bearing once it was installed in a machine?

We wandered through the drop area, Gina giving me a cram course on the flow of parts. She charmed me. Warm, self-deprecating, laughing easily, she was the girl next door. She used facial expressions to convey paragraphs.

I asked, "Are there any rumors about who might have wanted to wreck the merger?"

Her face reflected deep sorrow. "Everyone here thinks Mr. Oeland killed the girl."

"But not you?"

"No, not me." She knew I wanted more, so she stopped, putting a hand on my arm so that I would wait. She frowned with the effort. "It's something I don't want to believe. Mr. Oeland is really nice." She looked frustrated. "'Nice' is not the right word. He's thoughtful. He likes people. He feels things. You know what I mean?" Satisfied that I understood, she made her point. "So if a man like that could beat and murder a defenseless girl, then no one is safe. So I can't believe he did it."

When we reached the door, I opened it with my left hand and held out my right to shake her hand. "Gina, thanks for your time."

She held my hand without shaking it, forcing me to turn toward her. "Would you like to come over tonight?" she asked seriously. "Being famous must be very interesting. I'd like to hear about it."

My brain was slobbering, I couldn't think of anything intelligent to say.

She upped the ante. "I'll cook you dinner." Her deep brown eyes held mine in a lock.

"Would Raul object?"

"He's married. We only see each other on Tuesdays and Thursdays." She felt that was sufficient explanation.

My mouth said, "That's very generous of you. I'd love to, but my time isn't my own just now."

She smiled pleasantly. "If you find time, I'm in the book: Gina Rawlins." She turned to go back to work while I mentally kicked my butt for not taking her offer.

I was outside and walking toward my car before my mind returned to the real world. I regretted warning Pat Oeland that I knew about her lover; I could feel cross-hairs on my forehead. If Charles Newton was a killer, I wanted to find him before he found me.

CHAPTER FIVE

Charles was the tennis pro at the Camden Racquet Club in the Almaden Valley, an upscale bedroom community south of San Jose. The trip was fast, the tennis club was easy to find, located on the slope of the coastal range and visible from the expressway leading into the valley.

Up close, the block of screened tennis courts besieging a two-story wooden clubhouse looked very posh. The entry was through a single-level, rustic building that guarded a small parking lot. I parked the Neon among large SUVs, BMWs, and Mercedes, and walked into the cool hallway that separated a tennis apparel shop from the reception counter. A tall, big-boned, blonde in her forties stood at the counter. A handsome woman with a smile that could wreck cars, she looked at me expectantly.

"Could you help me?" I asked.

"God, I hope so," she said seriously. She joined my laughter before she said, "Sorry. What can I do for you?"

"I'm looking for Charles Newton."

She pointed at a tennis court just outside the window behind her desk. Charles Newton was demonstrating the backhand to a cute redhead who was having trouble keeping her eye on the tennis ball. Charles was tall, tanned, and handsome in his spotless whites. He moved with easy grace, using his racquet as if it were an extension of his arm. He was very young to be Pat Oeland's lover, in his late twenties, I guessed.

"The lesson should be over in ten minutes," the receptionist said.

"Gary Charboneau," I said, holding out my hand.

She shook it, holding on too long. "Britt Goetz. Are you interested in joining the club?"

"No, I'm here on business." I pointed at her window. "Are there any rumors about which lady Charles might be seeing currently?"

Britt leaned on the counter, a smile playing with her mouth. "Currently? As in today?"

I laughed, then asked, "Would his current lady be Pat Oeland?"

Britt raised her eyebrows. "That's not nice, Pat's a married woman." She looked at me as if trying to read something. "Are you a cop?" Her look said that she loved cops.

"No, I'm investigating the shooting that involved Mr. Oeland."

"A private eye," Britt said admiringly. "Don't you have to wine and dine me to get me to spill my secrets."

"Could I?"

She tried to look indignant. "Of course not, I don't know you." She laughed. She liked to laugh and it did wonders for her face. "To answer your question, I won't answer your question, you'll have to ask Charlie."

Out the window, Charlie leaped to snare a bad shot. He looked very fit.

"Is he likely to get angry when I ask?"

She looked surprised. "Charlie? He's a lover, not a fighter." She leaned close and almost whispered, "I don't know if he and Pat are getting together, but if they are, you'll probably need her picture to jog his memory." Britt wasn't one of Charlie's admirers.

When I asked, she pointed to the upper deck of the clubhouse. "There's a soft drink machine up there. You should be able to find a quiet corner."

I met Charles as he came off the court. I stuck out my hand, introduced myself, and asked if I could talk with him. "Buy you something to drink?" I asked, pointing toward the clubhouse.

He said that he had a Gatorade in the refrigerator in the clubhouse.

I sidestepped his questions until we were seated, then I said, "The company I work for sent me to investigate the shooting that involves Mr. Oeland."

Charlie's tan faded to a sickly yellow. "Oh shit, I knew it. God damn it, I knew it." He leaned forward and put a death grip on his Gatorade. "Does her old man know?"

"That you're boinking his wife? I don't think so."

"But you have to tell him." Charlie thought it was my duty.

"I'm trying to find out who killed Sally Krestas."

"Who?"

"The girl Clay Oeland is accused of killing."

"Yeah, shit, that's right, he blows some girl away for scratching him, can you imagine what he'll do to me for banging his old lady?" He downed half the bottle of Gatorade as if it were liquor. When he could, he said, "God damn, I knew it was a bad idea to get mixed up with her. God damn." He finished the quart in another long pull. As he set the empty bottle on the table, he said, "He's gonna kill me, isn't he?"

"When did you and Mrs. Oeland start the relationship?"

"She invited herself to my place a couple of weeks after her old man got arrested." He shrugged his helplessness. "It happens a lot. I listen to their troubles, take 'em to bed, everybody feels better. No harm, no foul, usually."

"What has Mrs. Oeland told you about the killing."

He looked lost. "She talks non-stop, and it gets to be kind of a blur." He wiped his face with a towel that had been wrapped around his tennis racquet. Squinting with the effort to remember, he said, "She's angry at her son because he smokes grass. She says her daughter won't talk to her." He looked at the ceiling before he continued, "The lawyers are costing a fortune." He examined the table, looking up to say, "Oh, yeah, all of her friends have gotten too busy to see her. And the major complaint they all have, her old man's never around." He scratched his neck. "Unless I missed it, she hasn't mentioned the killing."

Obviously Charlie was not in love with Pat Oeland. His fear of Clay Oeland seemed real, he looked frightened when he asked, "When are you going to tell her old man?"

Convinced that Charles Newton had nothing to do with the shooting, I said, "I'm not going to tell him."

"That is cool, man. I won't see her again, I promise you."

For a reason I didn't understand, that pissed me off. "Don't do it for me, I don't give a rip, she's not my wife."

I left Charlie wondering what he had said that punched my buttons. Britt was busy with another customer; she waved and smiled as I walked by.

Back in the car, I rearranged the list of suspects. Pat Oeland didn't have a lover who would kill for her; she didn't shoot Sally herself; and her access to a scumbag who would shoot Sally for pay had to be nil. I hated to cross her off the list; there was something there, but I had to move on.

Eliminating Pat as a suspect had moved Gene Addison to first place. He didn't have an obvious reason for claiming zero exemptions on his W-4. He lived in Portola Valley, a long freeway ride north. I wanted to see his house and cars; people with off-the-books cash buy expensive toys.

I took I-85 and sailed right along until it merged with I-280. Evidently the rush hour started at 2:30. Silicon Valley commuters risked expensive sheet metal to gain twenty feet. When it was my turn to merge, I pretended not to see the Porsche already in the lane, letting the Dodge proclaim that I didn't care if something got bent. Ignoring the angry horn blowing, I entered the traffic flow; made my way to a middle lane, and idled along until the clot broke up.

Portola Valley was a riverbed twisting through hills dotted with very large houses on sizable lots. Pine and eucalyptus trees added privacy. Gene's house-of-many-gables was very impressive and nearly invisible in a stand of tall trees. On the driveway outside the three-car garage, a BMW and a British Range Rover sparkled in the sunshine, Gene's salary for a year if they belonged to him. I guessed the house would go for better than a million dollars. Unless he had won the lottery, he had some other source of income.

Gene's check was electronically deposited to Portola Valley Thrift. I took my ID out, removed the PROBATION overlay and fitted the ID with a clear plastic overlay that included a United States Treasury seal with SECRET SERVICE printed underneath.

After a few wrong turns, I found the Thrift. At the manager's desk, the SECRET SERVICE worked its usual magic. Bankers know of the Secret Service role in counterfeiting, but they are unsure of what else the service does. When I gave her Gene Addison's account number, an older lady presented me with Gene's financial records that went back ten years. There were two huge deposits, one for $300,000 in February of 1999, another for $200,000 in September of 2000. That wasn't anything I could use, no one launders money by reporting it to the IRS. Just for the form, I asked to see the checks. They were from Portola Valley Thrift itself. Like most of Silicon Valley, Gene's house had soared in value, and Gene had refinanced twice. He was living well on borrowed money.

Back in my car, I tried regrouping and I came up blank. Looking for something that I could focus on, I drove to a gas station and found a pay phone. I called the jail; Aaron Grady still hadn't made bail. He didn't know how lucky he was to be broke.

I checked my voice mail; Pat Oeland had left a message. I called her at home; she asked if we could talk. We made a date to meet at a park near her house about eleven the next morning. I remembered the look she gave Clay in the bedroom that night when I asked if they suspected anyone of taking the gun. I wanted to ask about that look.

CHAPTER SIX

At ten the next morning, I drove to the park where Pat wanted to meet. From her description, I'd pictured a playground with grass. Instead, it was landscaping and walking paths that followed a stream. Other than a woman walking her Cocker Spaniel, the park was empty.

At eleven, Pat pulled into the parking spot nearest the small children's play area she'd selected as our meeting spot. Black jeans and a red cardigan sweater hugged her skeletal frame. She walked slowly to a redwood bench at the rear of the park as if muscles hurt. I watched for a few minutes; she seemed depressed.

She saw me walking toward her, and she looked away. I sat beside her on the bench facing the park. The stream paralleling the walking path created a peaceful murmur. She blew her nose. Still not looking at me, she said, "I thought you might find out."

"When did you start this affair?"

"A couple of weeks after the shooting. It was my idea."

"Why start an affair that could damage Clay's defense?" Her shoulders slumped. "It was very bad timing."

"My world was collapsing," she said in a choked voice, wiping her hands on the tissue as if they were damp. "My friends don't talk to me, Rob acts like I don't exist, and my daughter makes excuses when I call." She suddenly sat back, as if she needed to relax her body. "Clay's at the company all the time, I know he does that to keep from thinking about the future. I understand what he's going through but the reality is he's abandoned me just when I need him most. I'm facing the same uncertainties as he is, and it's ripping me apart." She turned to look at me. "Charlie listens and he makes time for me when even my children won't. Fidelity is small price to pay for some human contact."

We watched as an overweight woman in sweats jogged by, the baby steps not producing any speed. As the woman slowly shuffled up the hill, Pat said, "You have to understand Charlie. He's been with every lonely woman in that club at one time or another. I told him my troubles; he invited me to his place." She had twisted the tissue into a string, now she wrapped it around her finger. "It's what he does."

"What questions does he ask about the case? How interested is he?"

"He doesn't ask about the case, he asks about me. How am I doing? What did I do this morning?" She suddenly looked at me. "You can't think he's part of this."

I stood up. "I don't, but I had to check."

She nodded, and I turned to leave, giving her the impression that I was through, hoping she would relax her guard. I turned back to face her when I asked, "Did you shoot Sally?"

She seemed to withdraw into some shell—I could have sworn she got smaller. Then she looked up at me, defiance tightening her face. "Is that how you work, accuse everyone and see who admits it?"

"Did you shoot Sally Krestas?"

She looked at her hands when she said, "No, but Clay thinks that it was my fault." She looked up, watching my face when she said, "He wanted to get rid of the gun when Rob was small. I persuaded him to keep it."

That was pure bullshit considering what Clay had said to her. I could repeat it in my sleep. "Pat, I know what you need me to say. I can't help you. You know everything I knew about Sally Krestas. It happened just as I told the police. If she was a prostitute, I didn't know it. I'm sorry, I wish it could be different for your sake."

Clay wasn't blaming her. Even if he had blown up about her wanting to keep the gun, that wasn't what he was talking about. He was trying to absolve her of something to do with Sally Krestas. He'd said, "You know everything I knew about Sally Krestas." Why would that matter if all she felt was guilt about the gun?

Unless she felt guilt for something she didn't want to tell me. Had she been hammering on him for the affairs? Maybe Sally had been in love and was threatening to tell Pat. Maybe Sally was blackmailing him, asking for money for her silence. Either way, Pat threatening divorce could have been a motive for murder. Maybe Clay had blamed Pat because her threats had forced him to shoot Sally.

"Did you back Clay into a corner when you suspected he might be having affairs?"

Her laugh sounded bitter. "Oh, sure, I really made him worry. He tripped me up on a technicality. I asked about his affairs, not his whores."

I walked away, disgusted, I hate being lied to.

That afternoon, I put over 200 miles on the rental car visiting houses. With the exception of Gene Addison, all the managers who would have been retired in the merger lived in tract houses. They all had expensive toys like cars, RV's, and boats, but nothing their salaries couldn't handle.

When I returned to the motel just after four, I called the jail. Aaron was still safely locked away, the California penal code evidently tough on abusers.

I called the San Jose Police Department and asked to speak with Sergeant Javier Olivera. Fame worked its magic yet again; Sergeant Olivera agreed to meet with me. He suggested a restaurant near the police station at eight the next morning. I was hoping he had some loose ends that might suggest a lead, because I had squat.

CHAPTER SEVEN

Sergeant Javier Olivera's choice of a coffee shop was a converted restaurant without windows, the only natural light came from glass doors. The dark interior was fine when the clientele expected dinner by candle light; for a coffee shop, it sucked.

Sergeant Olivera entered at nine, squeezing by me in the entryway. The guy was 6-4 or better, and probably 250 lean pounds. His size hadn't been obvious on the tape. When I stopped him by introducing myself, he glared at me through small rimless glasses as if I'd insulted him. "You don't look like the guy I saw on 60 Minutes."

I told him about the fake nose and chin. He accepted the explanation by extending his hand, saying, "Javier. It's Gary, isn't it?" My hand felt lost in his. The small round glasses perched under bushy eyebrows gave his eyes a piercing quality, as if he were looking at my character rather than my face.

Noting his brown slacks and a brown tweed sports jacket, I said, "You guys dress much better than the detectives in the District."

"Nah," he said seriously, "this isn't the usual. Kid popped his ex, I'm going to the funeral just in case he shows." The bushy mustache hid most of his facial expression, and what I could see suggested contempt. Despite that, he seemed friendly and deferential.

A waitress waved her hand to indicate that we could sit anywhere. Javier picked a booth with a view of the doors. The waitress brought two coffee cups, the menus and a glass coffee pot. After she poured the coffee and left, I asked, "Is California tough on domestic violence?"

"We are if the woman will testify, which most of them won't. Like this woman they're burying today; we kept her ex-husband for 72 hours after he beat her up, but that's all we could do. She was afraid she would make him mad if she testified."

I sipped the scalding coffee; it was so hot I didn't get any idea of the flavor. The menu listed my usual breakfast.

Javier shoved his menu to the side without looking at it. "You're aware of the limits to what I can say?"

"If I ask anything that's out of line, just tell me. Unless the prosecutor is hiding something from the defense, I've seen all of your relevant work. I was hoping to get your impressions of the case."

He nodded curtly while pouring cream into his coffee. Leaning in close, he softly asked, "Just so I know what's going on," he shifted abruptly in the seat, moving the booth, or the floor, or perhaps the entire restaurant, "are you fucking a dog here?"

I addressed the serious question. "I'm investigating the crime that Mr. Oeland says happened. He's paying me. If he did it, he's wasting his money."

His nod seemed impatient, and he suspected bullshit. While he stirred his coffee, I tried for a better explanation. "I don't worry about things I can't know. I look for facts."

"I liked what you said about the two cops on 60 Minutes. You could have dumped on them for screwing up the original investigation."

"But they didn't," I countered quickly. "The DA didn't want them investigating leads that didn't support the case against McBride. They led me to the shooter by my nose. They were as tickled as I was when the prosecutor gave up on McBride. We celebrated together when the jury gave the guy first with special circumstances."

He sipped his coffee, put it down, and said, "Well, for the sake of my career, I wish I had evidence that could help you. You see the tape?"

I nodded. "I have to assume that he's telling the truth. Ms. Krestas believed she and the bushy haired man were setting Oeland up for blackmail. The BHS had his own agenda. Oeland thinks it was to wreck the merger between Microfix and ANA. That's where I'll start."

The waitress returned. We ordered before Javier asked, "So what do you want to know?"

"Did you get the names of any of Sally's classmates?"

He nodded. "We interviewed in all her classes. No one in any of the classes had ever spoken to her." Javier picked up on my facial expression. He nodded and said, "It bugged me, too. I finally asked one kid why no one talked with her. According to him, she dressed worse than a slut, either her ass or her tits were showing. The kids had her for a flake."

I asked, "Sally's roommate? Alicia Stowe. She could nail the case for you. She didn't know anything?"

"According to Alicia, all they shared was the house. Alicia said that she didn't like Sally." Javier tried the coffee, and frowned. He didn't hold the cup by the handle; I guessed his finger wouldn't fit. "She never saw Oeland at the house; never heard his name. She said that Sally didn't have any visitors." He wrinkled his forehead as if something hurt.

Javier answered my next question before I could ask. "She was cool when I showed up at her place. She answered all the questions but never once asked about Sally. That felt fuckin' weird: a cop shows up and asks questions about a missing roommate and Alicia doesn't ask if she's okay. Finally, I just came right out and told her Sally was dead. She came unglued; started throwing things in a bag, insisted that I wait until she could leave with me. Oeland hadn't been arrested, and she said she was afraid he might think she knew something and try to kill her too.

"She was so frightened, I let her stay at my place." He grinned at my obvious surprise. "It wasn't the best move I've ever made. I knew she wasn't telling the whole truth, so I thought if I made her feel comfortable, she might start talking. Didn't work; she was gone the next morning."

"Have you looked for her?"

"Sylvia Vance, the DA prosecuting, doesn't want her testimony." He responded to my puzzled look by adding, "She likes the case she has."

He sipped his coffee, watching me over the rim of the cup. When he put the cup down, he said, "My hunch is that Oeland visited Sally regularly. There are two witnesses who say they saw Oeland's car parked near Sally's apartment on two separate occasions."

I tried hard to maintain but the news stunned me. The phone calls could be explained as part of the frame, but how would he explain his car being in the neighborhood? "Why doesn't Oeland's lawyer know about those witnesses?"

He looked disgusted. "Because Sylvia Vance thinks she's clever. She's not going to decide to use them until just before the trial." While he talked, he took a notebook out of his shirt pocket. "This thing has been a political football. The DA doesn't want to piss off the high rollers, he wants to be mayor, so he was too busy to handle the case. The press made it high profile with a 'rich CEO caps poor college kid' slant, so the DA assigned an aggressive feminist. Sylvia wants to nail him so bad, she's cutting corners." He tore off a page and slid it across the table. "Whoever told you about the witnesses also gave you their names and addresses."

I nodded my thanks. "How did they know it was his car?"

"His personalized plate is MICROFIX; both wondered about the meaning." When he looked toward the person coming through the door, the glare on his glasses blanked his eyes. For that second, he reminded me of death.

I asked, "Did Sally need money badly enough to try blackmail?"

"Maybe. She was a typical college kid, broke all the time. She was behind on almost everything except the rent. I talked to her dad, he sent her what he could. She also had some sort of grant as well as a student loan." He sounded angry when he added, "I'm pretty sure she was hooking, but it wasn't a successful career."

The waitress brought my daily ration of cholesterol and the bear claw Javier had ordered. While I mashed my eggs, potatoes and bacon into a brownish stew that I call the Heart Association Orgasm, Javier said, "I have a theory about why Oeland shot her." He took a bite of the bear claw, then waved the fork to make his point. "I discovered that Oeland is a regular customer of some of our finer ladies. When I looked for kinks, I turned up missing girls."

A cop shouldn't be surprised by that. "Which is what you'd expect to find. Prostitutes are very transient."

He set his glasses with the knuckle of his index finger. "They might have moved, but if two of his regulars are missing, maybe he was doing number three when Sally got him with her nails."

He continued after a bite of the bear claw. "That is wild-ass speculation, but there is one tantalizing piece of evidence we found in his car." He let that ferment while I mentally went through the inventory of the items you'd find in a car. It hit me about the same instant he said, "There was a shovel in the trunk."

"That isn't too unusual."

"In snow country, maybe," he countered. "Why would you need one here?" He waited and then added, "We're digging up the orchard in case he planted the missing girls in the same spot. If we find them, you can go home."

I wrote down the names of the missing women before I said, "Why wouldn't he have buried Sally if that's what he intended?"

"Right," Javier said sardonically. "Blood all over his upholstery and scratches all over his body. He is a smart man. He knows that if she's reported missing—don't forget about Alicia—the phone calls to her place from his office will point at him. The scratches and a freshly upholstered car are going to be tough to miss. What he really needed was a story that would account for all those things."

Recalling my conversation with Pat Oeland, I said, "Pat Oeland thought he was having affairs, and he denied it. I wonder if she could have been retaliating in some way."

"Getting her own lover to shoot her husband's latest?"

When I shrugged, reluctant to nail my employer just yet, Javier shook his head, then had to set his glasses. "I've watched Oeland's phone records since the murder. The only thing I've found is Mrs. Oeland calling a number listed to a Charles Newton. He's the tennis pro at a Racquet club in Almaden Valley. I checked the guy; he has no sheet. Also, the phone listings prior to the murder don't show any calls to him. If they are lovers, it started after the murder."

Javier sat back abruptly; the booth slapped me in the back. He took a sip of coffee before he continued, "We know that Sally wasn't beaten by a woman, so I don't see any possibility of Mrs. Oeland being directly involved. A welt on Sally's face gave the M.E. the width of the guy's hand. He also found a pinch mark on the underside of her arm that gave him the length from the tip of his thumb to the tip of his middle finger. The guy who shook her and hit her had a big hand, about the size of Oeland's."

He brought the cup almost to his mouth, then lowered it without drinking. "The M.E. determined that Sally was shot within minutes of getting the split lip, so she was probably shot at the scene. That means we had a man beating her just before she was shot."

"Did Oeland's hands show any bruises or cuts?"

"We didn't expect to find any. As Oeland said, she was hit with an open hand."

We were silent while the waitress refilled our coffee cups. As I put jelly on a slice of toast, Javier said, "I must be slipping, I almost missed your point, didn't I?"

I raised my eyebrows in a question. Javier grinned when he said, "Pat Oeland is on his back about screwing around; Sally is on his back because she thinks it's true love and is threatening to tell his wife, so he shoots her when the rock meets the hard place." He toyed with his bear claw before he added, "If that's the way it went, it's still murder two. I could give a fuck why he did it."

Javier pointed his fork. "There is proof that Oeland's original story is a lie. There were bullets left in the clip after Sally was shot. The clip should have shown residue on the top, but it was clean, as if someone had pushed bullets out. When we opened the clip up, the GSR distribution inside suggested that the clip was almost full when the two shots were fired. It isn't conclusive for the number of bullets, but we're positive that the clip wasn't empty when the second shot was fired. The only prints on the clip were Oeland's." He dug the fork into the bear claw. "If he wanted us to believe the guy dropped an empty gun in the car, he had to get rid of those remaining bullets."

He raised his eyebrows, then had to re-seat his glasses. "Another thing I'm sure of is that he knew it was his gun. What he didn't know was that the seller had registered it using the information from his check."

While Javier ate some of the bear claw, I asked, "Oeland never tried to register the gun?"

"No, and after that many years, why would the original owner remember who he'd sold it to? After I told Oeland that it was his gun, it took him a few days to come up with the excuse that he suddenly realized he'd been framed, and that's why he asked for a lawyer." Javier chewed while contempt crossed his face. "Give me a fucking break, an idiot would have seen a frame without the gun, and Oeland is no idiot." Javier wiped his mustache with a napkin before he added, "When I asked him how he knew how to eject the clip, why didn't he say he had the same type of gun? That's what an innocent man would have said."

He took another bite and chewed while he poured cream into the steaming cup. "Ever since this thing got dumped in my lap, I've been up and down like a fucking yo-yo. When he said that no one else could have made those calls to Sally, that bothered me. Why didn't he have an explanation? He had to know we'd find them. The guy is too smart to make dumb-ass mistakes."

Yes, he was. Oeland would go to trial and let Sylvia hang herself proving he acted alone. As soon as she'd made that the linchpin of her case, he'd ambush her with the phone calls he could prove he didn't make, and the portable phone that anyone could have used to make the calls.

Javier continued, "Then he hires Jim Shaw, the best criminal lawyer in town, a sure sign that he's going to cop a plea. I've nailed the right man, so I'm a pig in shit."

Javier sipped his coffee, put the cup down, and blotted coffee from his mustache. "Then Oeland fires Jim Shaw, supposedly because Jim is working Sylvia for a plea. That just kills me, the guy is lunch if he doesn't do some serious bargaining. Then he hires Toni Conboy: who the hell is she? When I find out she has never been to court, it bothers me, a lot. He has to hire a novice lawyer because no one else wants to lose this big of a case? If he's risking his ass with a novice, maybe he is innocent."

Javier toyed with his cup on the saucer. "Then I hear on the grapevine that Toni Conboy was hired because she has connections somewhere. And sure as hell, here comes Gary Charboneau, the famous investigator."

Javier leaned his elbows on the table, slanting it. His eyes were locked on mine, looking for truth. "Now I wonder if Oeland is smart enough to know that a famous investigator might generate enough publicity to draw some damaged soul out of the swamp, a citizen who will admit selling Oeland's gun to the Bushy Haired Stranger, or any other two items that may get Oeland off on reasonable doubt?"

Javier's speculation was on the mark. If there was a sudden burst of publicity, the confessors would be out in force, trying to be the person sitting beside the famous investigator on television. It had happened to me before, more than a few people were willing to risk jail for fifteen minutes of fame.

Javier finished the bear claw and wiped his mustache with a napkin. His face flushed as he sat back, looking at me with a malevolent smile. His voice was quiet and clipped when he asked, "Is Oeland that smart?"

He didn't expect me to answer; he looked at his watch, mentioned the funeral he had to attend, and handed me the bill. His laugh was unforced and relaxed. As he got up, he shook my hand. "Let me know if you turn up anything interesting."

"You, too," I said.

He laughed at that and waved. As he walked toward the glass doors, he darkened the restaurant.

CHAPTER EIGHT

I drove to Sally Krestas' apartment building, a dilapidated Victorian with eight cars shoehorned into the narrow driveway. Evidently mass transit didn't exist, cars stashed haphazardly on streets, sidewalks, and lawns flooded the neighborhood. After ten minutes of looking, I wedged the rental into a just abandoned parking spot four blocks from her apartment, and walked back.

The screen door to Sally's building leaned against the scarred wooden door. I moved it gingerly, afraid the single remaining hinge would give up. Inside, a narrow corridor with a worn hardwood floor provided access to several plywood doors, most with padlocks.

A boy who looked to be about twelve, wearing baggy, gaudy shorts and a T-shirt, came out of a room sliding a large book bag with his oversized running shoes. He padlocked the flimsy door while he struggled to keep the book bag from falling over. He ignored me; a stranger standing in the narrow hallway wasn't unusual.

"Excuse me."

When he made eye contact, I saw a mixture of fear and curiosity. He gave my clothes a quick once-over. I probably looked too well dressed to be hitting on him for money. "Can I help you?" he asked in a surprisingly deep voice.

"Did you know Sally Krestas, the girl who was murdered?"

"A girl was murdered here?" he whispered.

"A girl who lived in one of these apartments was murdered in Morgan Hill three months ago."

He looked relieved. "I didn't hear about it. Mac—top of the stairs in 2A—would know. He's the manager."

There weren't any numbers on the rooms except for 2A. It was the only room with a painted door, "2A" lettered free-hand in the center.

Mac was a tall black man in his late fifties. Reed thin with wild hair and a narrow face, he reminded me of Chuck Berry.

"What can I do for you?" he asked in a soft voice.

"Did you know Sally Krestas?"

He looked interested. "Are you from the police?"

"No, I do investigative work for the insurance company that handles the affairs of Microfix." I let that hang there for a moment but he waited for me. "I need to talk with anyone who might have known Sally or her roommate."

He flashed a smile and said, "That would be me. Do you want to come in?"

It wasn't a rhetorical question, he wanted to know the answer. "Would you mind?" I asked.

"No," he said expansively, holding the door open.

"Gary Charboneau," I said, holding out my hand.

"Will Greene."

"A kid downstairs called you Mac," I said, shaking his hand.

He chuckled. "It's a nickname. I carry a pig-sticker so they call me 'Mac the Knife.'" He raised his left pant leg, revealing a steel throwing knife in a Velcro holster. "Never had to use it; hope I don't; I don't know shit about fighting with a knife. The rumor keeps the peace."

His room was small. A bed, table and dresser holding a hot plate were the only furnishings. A refrigerator and sink crowded an alcove that might have been a closet at one time. The room was neat, clean and shabby, perhaps worn colorless by repeated scrubbings. It smelled of soap and Pine Sol.

When he closed the outside door, I saw another alcove. Clothes hung from a length of water pipe that crossed the ceiling. Mac motioned me toward one of the two vinyl kitchen chairs flanking a small table. The chipped Formica on the table gleamed. "Would you like some tea?" he asked. "Don't have any coffee, can't drink it anymore." When I declined, he nodded and sat down carefully, a bad back I guessed.

"How well did you know Sally?" I asked.

Mac watched my eyes while he talked. "She came over a lot. She was a real nice girl. Quiet. Studied most of the time. She was serious about getting an education." He paused and then concluded, "She didn't socialize much."

"You've seen the drawing of her killer?"

He rolled his eyes.

I ignored the meaning. "Did you ever see anyone with her who looked like the drawing?"

He shook his head. "I guess in your job you have to believe what's-his-name didn't shoot her, but I don't."

"Clay Oeland."

He nodded. "To answer your question, there are people in the hall constantly, I try not to see them." Mac shifted carefully in the chair. He winced in pain but his voice betrayed nothing when he said, "The cops asked if I'd seen Clay Oeland here. I hadn't, but that doesn't mean he didn't visit her."

"How did Sally earn her money?"

He shrugged. "She was always broke; I used to fix her dinner when she hadn't eaten. She and Alicia always managed to scrape up the rent." I waited for more. "Sally might have turned tricks to do that, but I don't know, I never asked." Mac did not attach any shame to that occupation, but he evidently felt it necessary to explain. "It wouldn't have been any big thing for her. She had love and sex all screwed up, thanks to her father." Mac looked sad when he said, "She was sure carrying a lot of hurt."

Covering up incest was a reason for murder. I filed that away.

"What about her roommate, Alicia? Did she work the streets?" I asked. He nodded.

"Why did she live here?" I regretted the innuendo as soon as it was out of my mouth. I tried to undo the damage. "She should have been able to afford an expensive place." Mac smiled as if the answer should be obvious. "Drugs?" I asked.

Mac looked almost angry. "Alicia was screwed up, big time. According to Sally, Alicia did speedballs when she was flush." He winced again and carefully resettled himself in the chair. "Some of the people Alicia partied with terrified Sally; she'd wait here while Alicia did her business."

"Sally do drugs?"

"I don't know." Mac wasn't going to elaborate.

There wasn't much more. Even though he'd already dismissed the idea, I asked Mac to look at the drawing of the Bushy Haired Stranger. This time he laughed before he handed it back, saying, "At least he didn't make the guy black."

After I left Mac's, I knocked on a few doors. No one had known Alicia or Sally. Most had no idea who lived in the building now.

I walked back to the car, and then called Javier. When he came on the line, I thanked him for the help and then asked, "Did anyone tell you that Sally accused her father of incest?"

"Talk to Mac?" When I said I had, he continued, "Yeah, we followed up on that. Her father lives in a small town named Linda Vista in the San Joaquin Valley. I called the Sheriff there to see if her father needed her dead. Talk about your alibis, the guy was playing poker with the Sheriff that evening, their regular Thursday night game."

He excused himself to answer someone's question. When he returned to the phone, he said, "Her father is dirt poor. 'Couldn't afford to hire a babysitter,' is the way the Sheriff put it. If it went down the way Oeland said it did, someone took a lot of time and trouble to develop the best frame I've ever heard of. It would have cost more than her father could afford."

Broiling in the hot sun, I rolled the driver's window down while I asked, "Did she have a pimp?"

"I'm sure she didn't. She worked sporadically, no pimp would put up with that."

Javier waited a beat, and then asked, "You like tamales? Mom's fixing a batch for dinner tonight."

"I love tamales. What can I bring?"

"A couple of Corona six-packs would be good."

He gave me the directions to his mom's place, finishing by warning, "Suck it up, the relatives will be there, tamales are a big deal."

I called Toni's secretary to see if UPS had delivered my high-tech stuff. Toni wanted to talk with me. She picked up the phone and explained, "I'll take it home with me. You can come over for dinner; I'm not great but I'm very good."

If she intended the double meaning, I was happy I had Javier's offer. "I'm sorry, I've already accepted another invitation for dinner tonight."

After a moment of silence she said, "Of course, I should have asked." She disconnected abruptly. For a lawyer, she had very thin skin.

I wanted to talk to the people who had seen Oeland's car. I got the witnesses' addresses from Javier's note and located them on the map. Both lived within a block of each other; two blocks beyond Sally's apartment. Not sure I could find a closer parking space, I got out, locked the car, and began the trek.

On the walk, I got the impression that there were three distinct groups fighting for the crummy housing. The flood of college kids lugging books far outnumbered the indigent residents, damaged souls engaged in angry conversations with imaginary enemies. One freshly painted house with a well-tended yard had a group of neat and clean scumbags pruning shrubs and sweeping, evidently a halfway house.

Norm Ryan lived in a newer, two-story stucco apartment building that showed signs of serious wear. Short and fat, well into his sixties, Norm had a flushed, round face and a bulbous, vein-lined nose. He invited me in before I had a chance to explain what I wanted. Inside, sunlight peeking though a torn window shade was the sole illumination in the room; Norm liked his space gloomy.

Norm's suspenders were too tight. His pants, riding up over his huge belly, tended to bunch his shirt, creating crevices where crumbs had congregated. As he moved through the shaft of sunlight, particles fell off his clothes in a continuous stream.

A police dispatcher's voice reverberated in the room. "Apple 4, are you 10-7?" The scanner lapsed back into silence while the dispatcher waited for an answer.

Norm's apartment was a larger variation of Mac's room. The scanner was on a wood dresser next to a hot plate. A closet-sized indentation contained a refrigerator and sink. To the side of the kitchen, a door opened on a tiny bathroom.

Norm collapsed into a recliner that must have doubled as a bed, creating an explosion of dust that hung in the shaft of sunlight. In profile, his jutting jaw lent a combative air. When Apple 4 didn't answer, I asked about Oeland's car.

"You want to know when I seen the car? Told them cops I didn't 'member when exactly, sometime early January, maybe late December. Silly bastard parks car like that in this neighborhood, you notice is all. Big gold fucker with one of them personal plates on it, said 'Microfix.' Wondered if..." He paused when the scanner broke squelch.

"X-RAY 3, are you clear for traffic?"

"X-RAY 3, 10-4."

"X-RAY 3, see the RP at 1043 Magee.

"Ten-four."

Norm continued, "Wondered if it was stolen. It was gone the next day. Saw it again: two, three times."

"Why did you remember the plate?"

He broke into a fit of coughing. As the coughing moved into a different pattern, I realized that was his laugh. "Like to figger 'em out. Microfix could mean guy has a tiny pecker." He wheezed into another bout of coughing or laughing that ended abruptly. "Maybe his girl gave him the plate and he don't get it." That really broke him up, I was afraid he'd die but he finally calmed into an irregular wheeze.

"Nighttime? Daylight?"

He gave me a contemptuous look. "Shit, you don't wander around here at night. Fucking crazy if you do, some wacko will cut your nuts off."

"Morning? Afternoon?"

"Don't remember." He sounded defensive, perhaps bothered that his memory wasn't good.

"Do you think you saw the car back the next day, or a week later? Do you have any feel for that?"

The scanner boomed, "Eleven-oh-two, Control."

"Eleven-oh-two, 11-84 at Morrison and McInery."

"Eleven-oh-two, 10-4."

Norm waved his hand, dismissing my question. "Shit, I don't remember what I did this morning. Can't remember when I saw the car, just saw the fucker."

The second witness lived just around the corner. Jessie Minathab, a single mother in her mid-twenties, looked tired. The children shrieking in the apartment explained the look. Overweight with a very bad complexion, Jessie wore a purple crepe headband that barely restrained her greasy blonde hair. Dingy gray stretch pants accentuated the lumps on her massive thighs. Doe-eyes belied the harsh sounding "Yeah?"

"Gary Charboneau. I'm with the insurance company that represents Microfix. I wonder if we can talk about your seeing a car that belongs to a Mr. Oeland."

She stood aside and reluctantly invited me in. Three small girls stood in the wreckage, each a slightly taller replica of the younger copy, all with short, dark brown hair, and large brown eyes, smudged dolls in ragged clothes, unbelievably beautiful children. Kneeling, I introduced myself to Meghan, Margaret and Melissa. They all solemnly shook my hand. Melissa, the oldest at perhaps seven asked, "Are you from AFDC?"

"No, I work for an insurance company."

"What's insurance?"

Jessie gently shooed her away before I could answer. "Mr. Carbo and I have to talk. You go play, quietly."

When I left a few minutes later, I'd heard the same story that Norm had told. Jessie saw the car in January or December, although she couldn't remember if it had been in the morning or afternoon. She too, had wondered about the meaning of the personalized plate. She did know that she'd seen the car at least two times.

On the walk back to the car, a scenario began to emerge. Suppose, as Javier suspected, Sally was not the first to die, that Oeland liked to kill hookers. He might have taken the women to that location to beat and kill them. Perhaps Sally fought better than the others, she stopped him momentarily with her nails, and then fled to the car. Somehow he got into the car, perhaps he apologized for his behavior. Once inside, he pulled the gun out from underneath the seat. Bracing herself against the door, Sally pinned him against the steering wheel. Unable to use his right hand, Oeland moved the gun to his left hand, and shot her with the gun held behind his back.

As with Sally, Oeland had assaulted the girls outside the car, probably killing them there. Now he had scratches on his face and blood on his upholstery. As Javier said, he needed a story that would account for all that evidence.

Oeland might have prepared an alibi in case something went wrong. Before each fatal tryst, he could have phoned his next victim from his office, leaving his phone connected to the woman's phone machine while he chaired a meeting. With proof he hadn't called the woman during those times, and an expert who could demonstrate how anyone could have called the woman on his ancient portable phone, he could convince a jury that he was the victim of a conspiracy.

As Javier had asked, "Was Oeland that smart?"

By the time I reached the car, I was kicking my butt for getting carried away with the theory. I didn't know Oeland was a serial killer, all Javier had were prostitutes he couldn't find, almost a normal condition for working girls.

For my own peace of mind, I needed to find a hooker who had serviced Oeland and was still alive. If one lady could tell me Oeland was a normal client, then I could get on with the task of proving his innocence.

At a pay phone, I found out Aaron Grady was no longer in jail. According to the woman in charge of releases, the charges had been dropped. If his wife wouldn't testify after he broke her jaw, he was worthy of my time.

I called his house, there was no answer. Tomorrow then.

When Javier introduced me to Rita Olivera that evening, I assumed she was his wife, I guessed her to be around forty. She was small and thin with classic Native American features. The hook nose and sharp bone structure of her unlined face didn't fit today's definition of beauty but she was beautiful. A restless good humor tugged at her mouth and eyes. Perhaps shy when she was younger, her mannerisms hinted at a lingering reserve. When she realized that I thought she was Javier's wife, the reserve evaporated. She hugged me and asked Javier if she could keep me.

As she stepped out of the hug, she looked at me critically. "You looked healthier on TV. You could stand some meat on those bones."

"Tamales should work," I said. Tamales were to be the center of attention as well as the meal. We all sat around a large circular dining room table while Rita set the table. The smells from the steaming pot of tamales filled the room.

The relatives Javier had promised were a sister, Stacy, and her husband, Rick. They were a matched set: short, dark, chunky, and very young. Their year-old daughter, Veronica, was a miniature version of her parents. Veronica instantly adopted me. She wanted me to pick her up when I sat down. Once on my lap, she stuck her thumb in her mouth and watched me from the crook of my arm, evidently content to stay there. Stacy gave me several outs but I didn't want to give up Veronica. Holding a small child provides a spiritual lift, I don't get many opportunities so I clung to this one.

Rick wanted to talk about 60 Minutes. I told him about the weird feeling as Morley asked me the same questions I'd just answered, for the reverses, the camera angle looking over my shoulder. They had edited out most of the praise I'd made sure to include for the cops. To make it up to them, I'd written to the cop's supervisor in San Diego, so they'd know I'd tried to put the credit where it was due.

The tamales were the best I'd ever tasted, and Rita had made too many to count. Javier, Rick and I did our best to hurt ourselves. The women exercised fantastic control and stopped after a couple.

Ignoring her protests after the meal, I helped Rita clear the dishes. I needed to move around anyway, my stomach needed help dislodging the food, so I told her, "You need to relax, I know how hard it is to make tamales."

That shamed Rick and Javier into helping. While we washed the dishes, Stacy and Rita joked about our technique, perhaps uncomfortable with the role reversal.

When it was time to leave, Javier walked me out to the car. As we stood on the darkened driveway, I asked, "I hate to ask a favor after this treat, but I need to find hookers who might have known Sally or the women you're looking for."

Back-lit by the porch light on his house, I couldn't see his face, but his voice was sharp when he asked, "Why?"

"Your theory is driving me crazy, I have to find some girl who knows Oeland professionally. I know you've looked, but I can afford to pay for information."

He leaned against the front fender and folded his arms. "You're right, no one will talk to us. Give it a shot." He put a hand on my shoulder. "Do it quietly, okay? Every working girl we collar will be giving Oeland up if they know what we suspect."

"I understand."

He stood away from the car, towering over me with the slant of the driveway. "Tomorrow's Friday, the hookers will be thick around south Second and Keyes. Look for a guy named Glen Hubbard, he knows all the girls. He's a guy my size, long hair in a pony tail, Van Dyke beard. He has his right wrist in a cast at the moment. Don't fuck with him, Gary, he got the broken wrist fracturing a guy's skull."

CHAPTER NINE

I got to Toni's office just a little after nine the next morning. My lucky day, she was in court. I picked up the UPS box and drove back to the motel.

In my room, I unpacked the gear I might need. I tested the batteries in the tracking units; the directional microphone and the electronic lock-pick. The eavesdropping bugs hadn't moved from the anti-static foam during shipment.

A wooden box protected the large 9 millimeter handgun. Originally a target pistol, it was similar in shape to a German Luger. I had modified it to take back-to-back 16 round clips inside an enlarged grip. I ran 16 rounds through the gun, working the slide manually. They chambered smoothly. The aiming laser didn't work, its battery needed charging.

The gun's fright factor is very high. With the aiming laser, it looks like something made to stop tanks. Carrying the mother is a pain, the special holster has straps that cross my back and both shoulders, and the gun is suspended upside down with the barrel nuzzling my left armpit. A Velcro strap over the grip holds it. One yank on the Velcro and the gun falls into my hand, some of the time.

I put on my grubbies and set to work turning the rental car into my office. I installed the UHF transceiver and the printer in the trunk using double sided mounting tape. I put the laptop in the front footwell and connected the cables for the transceiver controls and the printer. I ran the cables under the rear seat and into the trunk through the opening behind the fold down seat backs. Under the dash, I found a hot wire and spliced into it for power.

I installed the tape recorder in the glove compartment, and connected that to the serial port in the laptop. Using a superglue that would dissolve with acetate, I installed a through-the-glass antenna to the windshield for the cellphone inside the laptop, and another to the rear window, and then attached that cable to the UHF transceiver in the trunk.

The laptop diagnostics ran fine until I tried them with the engine running, then the computer spewed error messages, evidently unhappy with the noise on the 12 volt power source I'd used. It took me an hour to find a power wire it did like, and it stopped bitching.

I tail people the easy way, I put transmitters on their cars that tell me where they are. These "trackers" have weak transmitters, so I rent access codes to a powerful "repeater" transmitter to extend their range. I found a business radio service in the phone book, and with credit card magic, I got the codes. I entered the codes in all four trackers, put one on the porch railing outside my apartment, and went for a drive. I was well out of range when the tracker checked in, the repeater working as advertised.

When I returned to the motel, I stashed the briefcase with the other electronic gear in the trunk of the car. Then I took a long, hot shower. The week of non-stop work had sapped my energy, I slept for an hour. When I awoke, I put on a business suit and went to hunt up Glen Hubbard, the pimp who Javier had said knew all the working girls.

As I drove the short distance to south Second and Keyes, Javier's warning about Glen Hubbard echoed in my mind. I treat scumbags with respect anyway, but my adrenaline kept pumping. I found him at two that afternoon on my fourth pass by the corner. Hubbard was leaning on the front wall of a Laundromat.

I would have treated Hubbard with respect in any case. The guy was huge and he wore his hard-time on his skin. A tattoo of a chain with large links circled his thick neck and a blue lace filigree covered both massive arms. The cast on his right wrist seemed too large, as if he intended to use it as a weapon. As I walked toward him, he watched me approach with an easy contempt; he had me for a cop.

"Mr. Hubbard?" I asked politely.

"Can I help you?" His voice was as flat as his expression. The man had all the empathy of a tiger looking at a gazelle. Even his cowboy boots were weapons, the toes covered by chrome steel caps sharpened to a knife edge.

"My name is Gary Charboneau." I didn't offer my hand, respecting the cast. "I'm an insurance investigator for Microfix. I need to find a recently deceased woman's coworkers."

His face slid toward boredom. He looked away. His unadorned white pullover shirt was a second skin over a body sliding into middle age and a beer belly. His gray-streaked hair worn in a pony tail and his brown Van Dyke beard were both precisely trimmed. One of his ladies had lavished a great deal of attention on her man.

Hubbard's apparent disinterest was a gambler's move; he wanted to play this hand. Otherwise he would have suggested that I get lost. Without waiting for eye contact, I said, "You may have read about the case. The CEO of Microfix is accused of shooting a Sally Krestas. The police think that she may have been a prostitute. I would like to talk with anyone who knew her."

His eyes challenged mine when he decided to answer. "Any expertise I might have would be revealed at some risk."

"Of course." I took out the hundred dollar bill I had in my right-hand jacket pocket and handed it to him.

He took it with the fingers sticking out of the cast and deftly rolled it into a small cylinder. He watched as a tall woman wearing an outrageous blonde wig and no panties under a very short skirt displayed her all as she leaned into a car. "Word is that Sally was working as a punching-bag. I can put you in touch with others who work that specialty."

That stopped me. I waited, hoping he would volunteer an explanation. He thought he had. "Is that what you want?" he asked, glaring at me.

"I apologize. I'm not familiar with that term."

He winced as if it physically hurt to educate a citizen. "Punching-bag. Some girls allow the customer to beat them. The specialty pays well if they can take it."

I had never heard of such a thing. "These women are masochists?"

"Don't none of them like it." His glare was withering. "The punching-bags allow some slapping around, some blood, but no fists. The fee is very high, takes time to recover."

"Do you know if Sally Krestas provided that service to Clay Oeland?"

His eyes shifted toward the woman just climbing into the Chevy. The guy driving looked to be about 70.

When Hubbard continued to watch the car drive away, I guessed that he wanted a different question. "Two women Oeland did see no longer work in San Jose. Charlotte Alcar and Victoria Wilson. Do you know if they worked the same specialty?"

"I heard that they did."

The answer came too quickly, it didn't ring true.

"Perhaps someone could put me in touch with them?"

He looked at me with that flat expression again, perhaps deciding if killing me would be worth the bother. A rational society would put this animal in a cage and forget him.

With exaggerated patience, he said, "There is a more direct route to the information you need." I waited, it was his ball. "That information would reveal knowledge that could have risk for me." I took the hundred out of my left hand jacket pocket and handed it to him. He began rolling that bill around the first. "I hear there is another girl that works the specialty. She told someone that your man put her in the hospital twice, but he paid her very well so she didn't swear out a complaint." He held up the small cylinder so that I could see how tiny it was. "If you had her name, I'm sure you could save yourself a lot of time."

I gave him two hundreds.

"Brenda Cooper. 1919 Krandell," he said.

I thanked him and turned to leave. He stopped me by putting the cast on his right arm against my chest. "These girls are admired for their courage. If some harm comes to Brenda, I will make sure that either you or Mr. Oeland pays for that."

My guess was that he wouldn't lift a finger to keep his mother from being beaten, but I played it straight for him. "If she reveals that Mr. Oeland is an abuser, then the DA will be given that information. It is in everyone's interest that Mr. Oeland be put away if he is dangerous."

If he gave a rip, I couldn't tell. He turned away and I left his turf, resisting the urge to wipe off my shirt where he'd touched me.

In the car, I looked up the route to Brenda Cooper's address. Since it was five minutes away, I decided to check it out. It was before three, maybe she would still be in.

I drove to her street. Brenda Cooper's house was a 50s style, white stucco bungalow with a red tile roof. Large shrubs hid two paned windows from the busy street. I parked around the corner and walked to her front door. I couldn't hear the doorbell, I was opening the screen door to knock when the inside door opened. The lady with cropped blonde hair had the same flat expression as Hubbard. Wearing tight denim cutoffs and a sleeveless white blouse, she languidly looked me over, insolently pausing to stare at my crotch.

I resisted the urge to ask if I passed. "Is Brenda Cooper here?"

"Does she know you?" The buttons on her blouse, stressed by an oversize bust line, seemed potentially lethal.

"No, but I was hoping I could talk with her."

The door opened wider, pulling the blonde girl with it. The brunette pulling on the door had a child's face. Her mouth verged on laughter without smiling. "Oh my God, he looks good enough to eat. Let him in." She pushed the screen door open and grabbed my arm.

"I'm Brenda," she confirmed. She was modestly dressed in a blue, knee-length, tailored dress that buttoned to the neck. A single strand of pearls matched pearl stud earrings. Short, tending toward stocky, her large bust line accented narrow hips. She pointed at the blonde woman. "This is Jane."

"Gary Charboneau."

That piqued Jane's interest. "You're French?"

"As in French fries."

I looked around while Jane pondered that riddle. Their conservatively furnished living room had a sofa and two chairs done in a matching dark blue fabric, and the color was continued in the drapes and valances. Dark mahogany tables contrasted with light gray carpeting, all very tasteful and upscale, yet comfortable looking.

I wouldn't feel comfortable with Jane. Her clientele had to like their women in stiletto heels and holding whips.

Still looking at me, Jane told Brenda, "He's a cop."

If anything, Brenda seemed happy about that. "Really? Why would a cop come to my house?" Her voice was high pitched yet soft, with a hint of the South in her past.

I shrugged. "Since I'm not a cop, I don't know. I work for an insurance company."

Brenda shook her head and said to Jane. "That makes a real estate agent and an insurance salesman you've called a cop. Give it up." Brenda still hadn't smiled but she had a comic's timing with a deadpan delivery.

Jane flopped on the couch, looking disgusted. "We don't want any. Don't slam the door on your way out."

"I don't sell insurance. I'm an investigator."

Jane pointed triumphantly at Brenda. "I was close, he's probably an ex-cop." She looked at me. "Fired for brutality? Am I right?"

Brenda ignored that. "Have we made some claim, or are you here on personal business?"

"I need to know if either of you knew Sally Krestas?"

"We knew Alicia better," Brenda said amiably. "Why don't you ask if I know the guy who killed Sally Krestas." I feigned surprise and she added, "He beat me up twice."

"Who?" I asked.

"Clay Oeland." Brenda toyed with the pearls. "He called himself George something or other, but I recognized him by his picture in the paper."

"Clay Oeland beat you up? Are there police records?"

"I don't think so." Brenda couldn't believe I was that stupid.

I said, "Tell me about it. He beat you up twice?"

"Want to see pictures?" She didn't wait for an answer. She disappeared into a hallway and returned clutching two handfuls of instant pictures. "This was the first time." She handed me a picture. In it, she was nude, her body bruised from shoulders to mid-thighs.

I had a hard time breathing. "Oeland?"

"Cool, huh?" Brenda seemed pleased. "He paid big bucks for that."

"When did he do this?"

"February of last year."

Jane walked over and stood between us. She sorted through the pictures, then handed me a close-up of Brenda's badly bruised stomach. "She had internal injuries. That was the first time."

"And you let him come back?" Who could believe that?

Jane said, "Some guys go crazy the first time. They've never hurt a woman before and they weird-out, like a feeding frenzy." She pointed at the picture. "Usually not that bad."

Another picture showed Brenda's back, the bruises looked deep and ugly. Standing beside me, looking at the picture, Jane continued, "Sometimes they cry afterwards, just like Oeland did, like it shocks them to know they're capable of it. After that, they keep it together, hit her with open hands and stay away from her breasts. Oeland promised us that he had learned his lesson."

Brenda added her own perspective. "I thought I could keep him in check, not let him get worked up." She handed me another group of pictures. "It's a good thing Jane was here, she saved my life." The woman in the first photo was a gross caricature of Brenda, a balloon painted to look like her. Looking from the picture to Brenda, I could see the lines on her face where the cuts had been.

"Jesus," I said involuntarily as I looked at the second picture. The tooth marks on her breast were deep and livid. "Two days in the hospital," Brenda said, tapping the picture. "The fucking asshole. He really paid for that. Cocksucker knew he was in trouble if I talked." She nodded at Jane's warning look. "I know, I know."

"I'm not a cop and I'm not from the IRS," I said softly, grabbing Brenda's hand for some reason I didn't understand, unless it was an apology for being a man. "I'm trying to find out what happened to Sally Krestas. She was beaten and shot. I'm trying to find out if Oeland is capable of that?"

Brenda almost grinned. "Duh!"

I was sick when I left their house. I wanted to nail Oeland for murder one and let him rot in some cell for the rest of his life. I was so furious, I didn't notice a lady walking toward me until she darted into the street crammed with commuter traffic. She screamed as a car slid to a stop inches away from her. I had been muttering to myself, I must have looked deranged. I felt deranged.

Really wanting to hurt someone, I drove to a nearby strip mall and found a pay phone. I called Aaron Grady's number. When a man answered, I asked for Mrs. Grady.

"Who is calling?" The voice was polite.

"California Special Victims unit. We will be checking on her condition periodically."

There was a long pause before he said, "I'm sorry, she's not here."

"If we aren't able to contact her, we will be sending a unit by to verify that she is not in the residence. The unit has a standing search warrant for your address."

"She's staying with her mother. The number there is 555-5171."

"Will you be home in half an hour?"

"Why?"

"We will be sending a unit by to verify that your wife is not at your location. Will you be there?"

"Yes."

I disconnected abruptly, got back in the car, and took the make-up kit out of the glove compartment. After I glued on the mustache and goatee, I glued the fake bump on my nose and the scar on my right cheek. When I was through applying the foundation to blend the bump and the scar, I drove toward south San Jose.

In a few minutes, I parked the car on the busy street two blocks from Aaron's house. I put on the holster, inserted the gun and secured it with the minimum amount of Velcro, and then put on a windbreaker that would hide the gun. Since it was just after five, the sun was behind the hills skirting the subdivision. The evening was cooling rapidly, so the jacket wouldn't look out of place.

After a fast walk, I rang Aaron's doorbell. There was no answer even though I used up the rage bruising my knuckles on his door.

CHAPTER TEN

The next morning, I was sitting on the steps to Toni's Victorian office building when her green Jaguar turned into the driveway. Toni looked at me sourly as she rolled by, obviously not happy to see me there. I waited, expecting her to go in the back way and have one of the secretaries summon me. Instead, she walked up the driveway and sat beside me on the top step. Her dark blue suit was going to show the dirt.

"Why are you here?" she asked. Screw the chitchat.

"The police think that two hookers that Oeland saw regularly are missing. There was a shovel in the trunk of his car. They're digging up the orchard to see if the two missing girls are there."

Toni snickered. "If Sylvia is hunting for witches, she should look in a mirror."

"They also have two witnesses who saw his car twice near her apartment in January or late December."

"Really?"

"They remembered it because of his personalized plate."

"Ah, boy, when it rains." Toni briefly shut her eyes, then we both watched black birds strafing a crow that was sitting on a light pole. As the little birds found the range, the squawking crow made a run for it, the attackers adding their own cacophony as they renewed their concerted attacks. When the noise faded, Toni asked, "Did you talk to Javier?"

"Yes, you bought him breakfast."

"Did he ask Alicia if she'd seen Clay with Sally?"

"She said she hadn't, but she was scared to death that Oeland, or someone, needed to kill her. Javier is sure that was why she ran."

"She's going to show up at the trial. How the hell do I prepare for her?"

"Ask Clay what she knows. It's his ass if she blindsides you."

"So you and Javier working together now?"

"He's trying to make a case. I want to find the truth."

"And what case are you trying to make with your truth?"

I ignored the snide remark, watching a jetliner as it approached the airport, its noise a waterfall sound until the airplane sank out of sight. In the ensuing silence, I said, "I talked to a hooker yesterday. She has pictures of the beatings both she and her roommate swear Oeland did."

"Beatings? As in plural?"

I nodded. "Brenda Cooper says Oeland put her in the hospital twice: in February of last year, and on January 7th of this year. Her roommate, Jane, was a witness to both beatings."

Toni put her elbows on her knees, her head slumped. She muttered, "Shit."

I put my hand on her back. "The good news is that being beaten up is what Brenda Cooper does for a living."

Toni's face registered shock. "You're kidding?" She noted my expression; put her hand over her mouth and then removed it to ask, "Why?"

"The pay is good," I said quietly.

She threw her arms up and almost yelled, "Of course, why didn't I think of that. Let guys beat me up for money. Sure, that would work." She dropped her head and whispered, "Unbelievable." The silence dragged until she asked, "I see what you mean about her occupation being good news, who would ever believe her."

"The bad news is that she was admitted to a hospital both times, so there have to be police reports. I know she didn't name Clay, but if she described him accurately..." I let that simmer before I added, "The sticky decision you have to make is; do I ask the police to see the records. If they don't know about her, they will, once I ask."

"Uh huh," she said, perhaps lost in thought. "But if you found her, the police probably will too." Toni rested her chin on her knees, looking down at the steps. "I'll let Clay make the decision, he's the one in the hot seat."

"And if he doesn't want me to ask?"

"I have to know, don't I?" She pointed at me. "Ask the police to look at the hospital records. Whatever the truth, I have to know what's in those admission reports." She hugged her knees, watching a light plane in a steep left turn as it aimed for the near runway. She said, "I think the hooker is lying. There is just no way that man is abusive to women, she's got to be lying."

"They've been known to do that."

Toni watched the quiet street for a few moments. With a slight southerly wind, the morning was pleasantly cool. Wisps of low clouds were brilliant white strands of angel hair against a deep blue sky. "Smell the garlic?" she asked.

I nodded. "Where are the fields?"

"Thirty miles south." She pointed east.

"Potent stuff, no wonder it wards off vampires."

She rubbed at her blue eye shadow. "When I took this case, Clay told me that it happened exactly as he told the police. He said if we can't prove that, then he'll do the time rather than accept a plea." She looked at me as if I might object before she said, "I can understand that, can't you? If it happened as he said, pleading guilty would have to eat you alive."

I got up and walked down the stairs, then turned at the bottom to look at her. "I'll check the hospital reports with Javier and call you."

"Do you think the witnesses to his car are credible?"

Brenda might be lying; the witnesses to his car might be lying, but I had a hard time believing that they were all lying. If he had visited Sally, if he liked to beat up hookers, there had to be a point where the evidence would become overwhelming. "I want to confront him with what I have. Face to face. With you there. His story isn't credible if just one of the four is telling the truth. I want him to see the weight of it all."

She looked worried. "I'll see when he's available."

After breakfast, I tried to call Javier. His weekend fell on Saturday and Sunday this week. I'd have to wait until Monday to ask him to look up Brenda Cooper's hospital admission records.

With no leads, and wanting to kick the shit out of Clay, I thought about Aaron Grady. From a pay phone, I called his number. No answer. In my notebook, I found the number for Mrs. Grady's mother. When a woman answered, I asked to speak to Mrs. Grady.

"She can't talk, she has her jaw wired. Can I help you?"

"I'm looking for her husband, I thought you might be able to tell me how I might find him."

"I don't know and I don't want to know." The click in my ear sounded final.

Tired and cranky at ten in the morning, I tried to think of something useful that I could do. Nothing came to mind, but shooting holes in things sounded therapeutic. I let my fingers do the walking and found a shooting range south of San Jose.

Getting there was half the fun. Within spitting range of highway 101, you couldn't get there from here, and it was seven miles before I could turn around and try again. Going north on 101 was no better, still no way off the freeway. I hate it when that happens. I'm so good at finding my way around, I have no patience for getting lost. Assumption was the mother of the foul up, a road that I assumed ended at a small pond went under the freeway.

The range was expensively rustic, each shooting station a tidy window with bench and gun rest. The 50 foot pistol range dug into a hillside had an open spot. I rented ear protectors and bought five paper targets.

The sound of the 9mm slugs going flat drew a crowd. They flutter for an instant, the noise a feeling instead of a sound. I didn't notice the group gathering until I'd fired six rounds. At fifty feet, the bullets only managed a group of eight inches, appallingly bad but quite acceptable accuracy. I felt a hand on my shoulder. I put the handgun down on the bench before I turned around. The range safety officer, a small black lady in her thirties, asked, "Is that ammunition legal?" The men standing in a semi-circle behind her seemed very interested in the answer.

I ejected the clip and slid a bullet out. Using pliers, I extracted the slug from its cartridge. I explained to the group that I wanted a non-lethal bullet that could stop a man without killing him. I also wanted a bullet that would fall out of the air before it had a chance to fell some innocent bystander.

I unfolded the slug while I explained the work I'd done. My first attempt was the obvious solution, a flat aluminum blank folded into a barrel shape. When the open end came out of the gun at high velocity, the aluminum would unfold, I thought, forming a flat surface the size of a quarter. The best laid plans of engineers and mice are approximately equal, the bullet did everything but unfold. It tumbled; it spun, it even went sideways.

After months of failure, I tried inserting the open end of the slug into the cartridge, more from frustration than logic. Sure enough, that worked, sort of. The slug never quite unfolded all the way, remaining lethal out to fifty feet or so. The groves in the barrel were designed to spin bullets for stability, not to unfold them, so I had a new barrel machined with tighter turns. That worked to perfection. More spin, more unfolding. The slug was lethal up to 15 feet but after that, it rapidly assumed the dimensions of a quarter. Since the metal was never exactly flat until it hit something, the slight cone shape and spin prevented the slug from tumbling.

One of the men, probably a cop, brought up the obvious failing. "That makes glass bulletproof." Cops can't shoot the bad guys in the back while they're running. The bad guys know that. So a common gun battle happens after a bad guy has found suitable cover. The cop's answer is to carry a cannon that will penetrate concrete.

So I explained the back-to-back clip arrangement. One side contains 16 non-lethal bullets, the other side has 16 regular steel jacket bullets. All I had to do was eject the clip and turn it over to go from one to the other.

All seven men and the lady were cops. They disagreed with me about the wisdom of the arrangement. They liked the laser, though, all of them tried it. The lady shot a group of five that a quarter could cover.

When I left the range two hours later, I felt good, my mood much improved. On my voice mail, Toni said Clay would be in her office at eight this evening. Good, if he cracked, I'd be on my way home tomorrow.

When I got to Toni's office that evening, she and Clay were watching the emergency room video. I watched with them until I remembered the first time I watched it. I paused the tape and asked Clay, "On fast-forward, you seem to be Macbeth wringing your hands. Were you aware of that?"

He removed his glasses and put them in the jacket pocket of his suit coat. "I worried about AIDS. I'd feel guilty worrying about her blood on my hands when she might be dead, then I'd rub at it again. Petty, just petty."

"When did they swab for the GSR?"

"As soon as they were through taking my statement that night."

"Wringing your hands might explain how the residue got where it did." He looked pleased so I decided to hit him with what I had, trying to catch him while he was vulnerable and tired. "Why was your car parked near Ms. Krestas' apartment in the weeks before the shooting?"

"It wasn't."

"The DA has two witnesses that say it was. Any chance that Rob parked it there? It's near San Jose State."

"He doesn't use the car." Clay sat straighter in the chair, looking at me with a strange expression on his face. Toni inspected some piece of paper on her desk.

"According to the police, Charlotte Alcar and Victoria Wilson are missing. Do you know them?"

"No."

"They went by the names of Charlie and Vicky."

Clay didn't hesitate. "Yes, I knew them. They're both nice people."

"They're missing," I said.

"They aren't missing. They roomed together. Charlie told me that the police were getting curious. They expected to work some other town for a couple of years."

"Do you know where they went?"

"I didn't want to know."

"There was a shovel in the trunk of your car. Can you tell me why it was there?"

"Ah." His expression of pain made me feel rather good. "They think I killed them." It wasn't a question.

"That's a theory they're working on," I said amiably. "Why did you have a shovel in the trunk of your car?"

"I didn't know there was a shovel in the trunk. I'll ask Rob. He might have put it in there so we could clear the driveway in Tahoe." Judging by the expression on his face, he wasn't happy with the questions.

Feeling that I was close to pissing him off, I pushed. "Do you know Brenda Cooper?"

"No." Anger sharpened his voice. He looked at Toni who was still examining the paper.

"Ever hear the term 'Punching Bag' used for a hooker?"

It was deathly quiet in the room. Clay watched my face as he answered. "No, but something tells me I'm about to find out."

I locked on his eyes. "You deny that you beat up a hooker named Brenda Cooper twice; once in February of last year and again in January of this year, bad enough to put her in the hospital both times."

"Yes, I deny that." His eyes held mine as he spoke.

"She may testify against you. She has pictures and hospital reports that prove she was beaten."

Clay seemed to sag. He leaned forward and put his face in his hands, his elbows braced against his legs. I felt the rush, he was going to crack.

Toni interrupted the silence. "You can still work a deal. Sylvia might settle for..."

Clay's furious expression stopped her. In a quiet voice he said, "I want you both to listen carefully, I'm only going to say this one more time." He stopped to sigh, as if weary of the subject. "The incident happened exactly as I've said. You both know all the truth that I know. I didn't know Ms. Krestas; I never visited her apartment. I have never struck any woman. I don't know any hookers other than the two you know about."

THE FRAME

His eyes held mine. "Is all that clear?"

I shrugged my indifference, reluctant to believe him. His face flushed, he said quietly, "Consider this question, Mr. Charboneau. If someone used my phone to create evidence of a relationship between Ms. Krestas and me; coached her on their plan to create the physical evidence of an assault; and then pulled that off without making any mistakes, wouldn't they be smart enough to find witnesses and prostitutes to lie about my past?"

He yanked at his tie as if it suddenly bothered him. "Did you investigate the motives of the people who led you to these witnesses?" He wanted an answer but I had none, nor did I have an answer to his follow-up. "Who are they and what do they have to gain if I'm convicted?"

He unbuttoned the top button on his shirt. "You assumed those people are telling the truth. Let me make a suggestion. Quit trying to do the DA's work, she has the entire police force at her disposal. Find out why those people are making these accusations. Work for me, not the DA."

His eyes held mine when he asked, "Is there anything else you want me to clarify?"

I shook my head.

He stood up and leaned on his fists on Toni's desk so he could be close to her. "One more time. I'm not guilty. If we can't prove it, I'll do the time." He nodded at me. "If Mr. Charboneau is convinced I'm guilty, hire someone with an open mind." He walked out, shutting the door quietly. The guy had great control.

Toni opened her center desk drawer and took out a checkbook. "I think he'd be more comfortable with another investigator," she said quietly. "What do we owe you?"

"Our deal is for $20,000. You'll pay me that if I leave now, or if I stick around and nail the killer. It's your choice." She began to fill out the check, so I reached over and closed her checkbook. "I'll find out if they're lying. If either the hooker or the witnesses are telling the truth, then you can write it; he'll owe me the money for trying to sucker me."

She put the checkbook in the drawer. "He just told you, they aren't telling the truth," she said vehemently.

"I'll find out."

CHAPTER ELEVEN

Breaking Norm's story would be tough; Brenda's would be impossible. Jessie Minathab had kids to protect, so I picked on her. The flaps of her tattered bathrobe barely met over her belly when she opened the door at 7:30 the next morning. "I'm sorry," I said, trying to look worried, "but I need to talk with you."

"The house is a mess, can't you come back later?" She wanted to shut the door.

I lowered my voice to a whisper. "For your kids' sake, I don't want you to go to jail."

Jessie paled. She opened the door and motioned toward the living area. Judging by the debris, she had spent the evening with a bottle of rum. The kids were putting a doll's dress on the bottle, perhaps reducing the demon to something they could deal with. Cereal littered the floor, the result of small, unsteady hands pouring their own breakfast.

Jessie's shocked expression remained but she asked if I wanted coffee. I nodded and followed her into the kitchen. Speaking very quietly so the kids couldn't hear, I said, "I don't want coffee. Did you know there was another witness who said he saw the car?"

She looked relieved. "I didn't know that."

I nodded. "Nasty old guy with the morals of a serial killer. He called the DA and offered to tell her the name of the person who bribed you."

She seemed to stiffen, clutching at the tattered robe as if it might provide some protection. "I don't know what you mean."

I put both hands up. "I don't want to know if you lied, I'm only here because I don't want those kids to get hurt."

She focused carefully on my face. Positive she would listen, I said, "He offered to finger you, and the guy who paid you, for money. The DA will call you to take your deposition under oath. If you say you saw the car," I hit my hands together, "she's got you for perjury. If you tell the truth," my hands hit perfectly, the noise made her jump, "she's got you for making a false report. Either way, you could go to jail."

I let her stew on the horns of that dilemma for a few seconds. "The DA is waiting for approval to pay him. You have to get to the DA first, and offer to give the guy up for free. She'll give you immunity in exchange for the name of the guy who paid you."

I could see an embryonic protest forming. I raised my hand. "Look, as I said, this has nothing to do with me. I just hate to see those kids get sent to foster homes." To sidetrack any discussion, I asked, "Can I use your phone?"

Back in the living room, she pointed at an end table. A phone balanced on a stack of magazines. She pushed the girls out of the room and then excused herself to get dressed.

As I dialed, I unplugged the phone. While I talked to the vapors, I inserted a UHF transmitter into the phone plug and then reconnected the phone using the transmitter's receptacle. If all had gone well, the UHF radio in the trunk of the rental would pick up her phone conversations.

Jessie emerged dressed, but looking as if she had been assaulted by a hair dryer. As I walked toward the door, I said, "Just don't let the DA know I told you, okay?"

I rushed back to the car but the receiver had already intercepted a call. A phone machine had answered, "You've reached 555-4662. Leave a phone number and I'll get back to you." Jessie had left a breathless message that she needed a call.

The phone directory CD in the laptop found the phone at a Chevron service station in Los Altos. A service station? For a few seconds, I thought perhaps Jessie had her car in for repair. Something bugged me and I replayed the message before I realized that no retail business would answer a call by repeating the phone number. I put the map CD into the laptop. Its software found Los Altos, a small community northwest of San Jose, only twenty minutes away on a Sunday.

I had to wait near Jessie's apartment if I wanted to hear the call back; the bug's range was less than a quarter mile. I tried to get comfortable for what I hoped would be a short wait.

After an hour, I considered leaving the car in range of the bug, and taking a taxi to the motel. Another hour later, I had to pee. I walked to the corner. I couldn't see anything that looked as if it had a public restroom.

Two hours after my kidneys had shut down in disgust, Jessie received a call. "Hello." Did she sound worried or was that my imagination?

"Jessie? Earl. What's up?"

Jessie's clipped voice raised an octave. "Do you have another witness who saw the car? An old man?"

"Why?"

"Because an insurance investigator was here. That old man is going to tell the District Attorney that you paid us. I could lose my kids."

"Ah, Jesus," I moaned out loud. Oeland had called it.

Earl smelled the phone tap. "Now Jessie, I asked you if you'd ever seen the car and you said you had. If you were telling the truth, you have nothing to worry about. If you were lying, then just tell the police that you were mistaken. They can't do anything to you."

"Filing a false police report is a crime, that's what he told me."

"They have to prove you knew it was false."

"You bastard," Jessie shrieked. "They'll know it was false if that old man tells them you paid us." My recorder popped when she slammed the handset down.

Whoever this Earl was, he was risking prison to help convict Clay Oeland. If he was part of the frame, he had just made a major mistake. I started the car, eager to find the asshole, right after I found a place to pee.

The Chevron station in Los Altos reflected the upscale community. It had the same Art Deco motif as the shopping center that surrounded its corner. I watched from the parking lot for an hour. Three mechanics worked on a flood of cars. In the office, a lady took money for the self-serve pumps. The only other employee was a Vietnamese boy who waited on walk-in customers.

I wandered into the office. I dialed Earl's number on my cellular phone. The station's phone didn't ring. "Are you the manager?" I asked the boy, who looked about 12.

He laughed. "For the next 15 minutes, until the owner gets back." He had no accent.

"Another phone number is registered to this address. Where's the phone?"

"Another phone?" Then his face changed. "Ah, yeah, I remember." He walked into the garage and opened the door to a storage room the size of a small closet. Floor-to-ceiling metal shelves held car parts, except for the top shelf, unusable because of the height. I could just see the front edge of a white answering machine.

"Some guy needed a business address for a phone. The owner rents him the space."

"What's the guy's name? Do you know?"

He shook his head. "The owner will be back in 15 minutes. He can tell you."

"What's he look like?" I asked, pointing at the machine.

"The guy who rents the space?" The kid paused, thinking about it. "I've never seen him. From what I understand, he retrieves the messages over the phone. I don't think he ever comes in."

The station's owner was a tough-looking Vietnamese named Bang Vu, and his English was mostly unintelligible. Short and solid, he was warily curious about why I needed to know who owned the phone machine. "He may have suborned perjury," I explained. "We need to find him."

"What did he do?"

"Suborned, ah, he paid someone to lie to the police."

Bang Vu opened a desk drawer and gave me a copy of a lease agreement between himself and an Earl Mitchell of Mitchell Investigations. The address was a post office box at San Jose Main. I've spent many hours waiting for someone to walk out of a Post Office carrying the red envelope I had mailed to them. Since I had his phone number, I wouldn't have to do that with Earl Mitchell, I'd get him to come to me.

I thanked Bang Vu, and returned to my car. As I drove the 280 freeway toward San Jose, I called Brenda Cooper, the woman who accused Oeland of beating her. Her roommate, Jane, answered. "This is Earl," I said, imitating his nasal sound.

"Earl who?"

"Earl Mitchell. Can I talk to Brenda?"

The phone was quiet for nearly a minute. When she came back, Jane said, "She doesn't know any Earl Mitchell," and disconnected.

Glen Hubbard was Brenda's pimp, that much was certain. If Brenda had lied about Oeland beating her, Glen Hubbard and Earl Mitchell might be working together. If they were part of the original frame, their reasons for having people file false police reports escaped me. Why take that risk when the case against Oeland was so strong?

I glanced in my rearview mirror. Poking along at 75 during my reverie, I had jammed up the fast lane. I moved over and a train of cars blew past like I'd pulled a cork.

Back in San Jose, I tried to find a parking spot near Norm's apartment.

After a few minutes of cruising the neighborhood, I saw a man sitting in a black Ford Taurus. When I pulled up beside the car, the guy shook his head and waved me on. I spied a space on the opposite side of the street. I swung an illegal U-turn across all four lanes, driving up on the curb to get into the spot before a speeding truck could flatten my car. All that effort to park, and I was still two blocks away from Norm's apartment.

As I approached his apartment, I hoped Earl had already warned Norm. The crotchety old fart wouldn't bother to lie. And he didn't. As soon as he opened the door, he launched into a tirade. "Asshole, you told that woman a lie; said I was going to the DA."

Earl had paid them both. I grinned my best grin. "And now she's going to turn both you and Earl into the DA. Earl tell you that part?"

"Said you were lying, 's what he said."

I grinned until it hurt. "What made you think $5,000 was worth going to jail for?" I was way too high, I could see that by the way his eyes squinted. Giving him a contemptuous look, I said, "Earl was paying you less than the woman?"

"Fuck you," he snarled and slammed the door.

Back in the car, I called Oeland's home. His wife, Pat, said that he was at Microfix. I thought I heard disgust when she answered an unasked question. "Yes, even on Sunday."

Clay sounded glad to hear from me, as if yesterday was forgotten. I said, "You were right, both witnesses to your car have been suborned by a man named Earl Mitchell." I gave him time to digest the new information. "Does the name mean anything to you?"

"No." Clay sounded intense, maybe excited. "Do you know who he is?"

"I don't know anything about him yet." It was getting hot in the car. Acute embarrassment perhaps. I rolled the window down.

He got in a small dig when he asked, "Any chance he's also paid the prostitute I'm supposed to have beaten."

"She doesn't seem to know him. A guy named Glen Hubbard directed me to her. I'll find out if he and Earl Mitchell are working together. Hubbard's a known pimp, he'll have a police record. If he knows the man who killed Sally, the police will break the case wide open."

While Oeland was considering that, I watched a woman with six small children holding hands as they crossed four lanes at a busy, uncontrolled intersection. A little guy at the end of the string was frightened by the noise, he looked ready to break and run. The woman said something to the tiny girl holding his hand, and she pulled him back into line. The woman had awesome courage, I nearly had a nervous breakdown just watching.

Three trucks blasting by blanked Clay's response. I had to ask him to repeat it. Speaking slowly, he asked, "Could this Glen Hubbard be the same guy who assaulted Sally Krestas?"

"He doesn't fit the description, he's too big, about the same size as Javier Olivera. He's also covered with tattoos, lace work on both arms and a chain around his neck."

"No," Clay said, "he was big but he was wearing a short sleeved shirt; I would have noticed tattoos."

I stepped into the ensuing silence. "I do owe you an apology, Mr. Oeland. I didn't check their stories and I should have. I am sorry."

"When I got over being mad, I realized that you were checking those stories with me. I certainly appreciate how fast you've worked. We've at least got some names now, and that gives me hope." He paused before he said, "I guess I was wrong about the motive for the frame; stopping the merger must not have been the reason."

I felt the hairs on my arms stand up. "What makes you say that?"

"These people want to make sure I'm convicted. A hung jury or, better yet, an acquittal, would prevent the merger. The merger is off until the liabilities are known. The liabilities won't be fixed until the civil trial, and that won't begin until the criminal trial is over. If someone wanted to prevent the merger, they would try to delay my conviction, not rush it."

Broiling in the sun, I got out of the car and leaned against the side. "The only people who have a claim against you are Sally Krestas' parents, is that right?"

"They'll get offered millions as soon as I'm convicted."

The oldest of motives, money. "I'll go lean on Sally's parents tomorrow. Sally told people that her father sexually abused her. Maybe he found two reasons to want her dead."

CHAPTER TWELVE

Monday dawned with a wind out of the south. With the change in wind direction, airplanes were using the motel's roof for a runway extension. The commuters were surly too, the six-lane boulevard in front of the motel reminded me of the back straight at Talladega. I ate breakfast at a nearby coffee shop and watched all the near misses.

Javier returned my call on the cellular as the waitress was pouring my third cup of coffee. "Let me guess," he said, "you need me to break a rule?"

"No way," I said, trying to sound offended, "I saw a guy carrying a concealed weapon and I wanted to report it."

"Really?" His voice reeked sarcasm.

"Of course you might have to check to see if the guy has a permit. We could meet for breakfast tomorrow and discuss whether this person might be a danger to society."

Javier laughed. "I can't do breakfast but what's the name, address and stats?"

"Earl Mitchell and that's all I have."

"White? Black? Tall? Thin?"

"Nothing."

"You saw the gun and you didn't notice whether he was white or black?" Javier's voice was hanging on the edge of a laugh.

"Something like that." I told Javier, "His business phone is 555-4662. His address is Post Office box number 83415 at San Jose Main."

"Earl's Eavesdropping Service?" he guessed.

"Close. Mitchell Investigations."

Outside, a truck locked all the wheels trying to avoid flattening some numb-nuts who had stopped in the curb lane.

"The phone number is a machine in a service station in Los Altos."

Tire smoke drifted by the restaurant windows as Javier said, "Nice address; must be angling for big-buck clientele." He paused before he asked, "Got something?"

"I think Earl suborned your witnesses to the car."

"Do tell. That could be very interesting. I'll call you when I get something."

Before he could disconnect, I said, "I want to do you a favor."

He laughed. "This I gotta hear."

I told him about Brenda Cooper and her injuries, adding, "If she was hospitalized with those injuries, there has to be two police reports."

"If there is, I can't tell you what's in them."

"Perish the thought. If she described Oeland, you've got a big nail to use on him."

Javier laughed again. "Since you're doing me a favor, I'll check the hospital reports."

"Thanks. Just out of curiosity, was it Glen Hubbard who told you that the two hookers Oeland frequented were missing?"

"You didn't hear that from me."

"Do you see a trend here?" I asked. "Did he also know Sally?"

"That would be interesting, wouldn't it. I'll check on that."

Just so he'd know, I told him I'd be going to Linda Vista in the San Joaquin Valley to visit Sally Krestas' parents. "I know you said it didn't seem likely that her father could set up the frame, but her parents are the only people who could profit from Oeland's conviction."

"Worth a look. Keep me up to date."

I left the waitress a good tip, feeling pumped about the way things were working out. In the car, the laptop showed Linda Vista was 140 miles away, not a short trip. Which was fine, I like to drive; being absorbed in a purely sensory task is relaxing to me. Going against the commuter traffic, I drove south out of San Jose past miles of gridlocked cars.

The road into the San Joaquin Valley from Gilroy snaked over steep hills, then plunged into ravines. Spectacular speeds on the abrupt descents were the norm, even for the big trucks. California doesn't allow the police to use radar on freeways, so the Kamikaze had one eye on the rearview as they blasted by me. Great entertainment.

Interstate 5 heading south toward Los Angeles was bland, boring, and fast. It was nearing noon when I reached the overpass for Highway 56 and drove down a long grade into Linda Vista.

Old wooden buildings edging the highway in Linda Vista perched high above the street, as if major floods were a staple of the time. Newer cinder-block stores scattered among the remnants of the past seemed to be sinking into the sand-colored dust of the San Joaquin Valley. Next to the cluttered lot of the farm equipment retailer, a furniture store proclaimed a sale with a sun faded banner. The town had no defined edges, the drifting dirt created its own boundaries.

A tiny green sign pointed the way to the City Hall, two long blocks off the highway. I passed three different fast-food chains on the way to City Hall; evidently the deserted streets came alive at times.

I found the sheriff's office in the basement of the ancient building that housed City Hall. The deputy sheriff offered his hand. "Saw you on 60 Minutes, you don't look anything like that person." In his forties, he still had a farm boy's face that crinkled with delight at my explanation. Other than a chubby Mexican lady sitting in front of three radios, he seemed to be alone. I followed him into his tiny office. He walked with a decided list. "What can I do for you?" He pointed to the steel chair in front of the desk.

"Did you know Sally Krestas well?"

"Sure did. Terrible thing." He frowned. "I suppose you're working with the company president's defense?"

"He's paying me. Do you know if Sally kept in touch with anyone here?"

"San Jose PD asked me to look into that after the murder. Sally only had one friend, a girl named Kim Berry. Her folks run a restaurant in town. Kim hadn't heard from Sally except for a letter two years ago. Even that didn't say much."

It was hard to believe Sally had left no mark in a town this size. My expression must have communicated the thought because he said, "You have to understand, Sally fit in like a square peg in a round hole. No one wanted to know her. She was one of those clueless kids who aren't able to read other people."

The lady from the outer office knocked on the glass window in the door, then opened it without waiting. "Steve isn't coming in. Do you want to call the Willow office and get someone down?"

He shook his head. "If you get anything, I'll take it." She gave him a quick nod and shut the door.

I eased into the pertinent questions. "She left rather suddenly when she was 16. She had trouble with her parents?"

Something flickered across his face but his voice was flat when he asked, "What did you hear?"

The change of atmosphere made me cautious. "Rumors about molestation, that kind of thing."

He shrugged. "I don't investigate rumors."

"Sally never complained to you?" It was a dumb question that I regretted as soon as it was out of my mouth.

He nodded. "She called the day before she left town. She wanted me to arrest her father because he'd hit her across the face. I went out to talk with Will, but they'd resolved the problem before I got there. She was going to move out, and he was going to help her." He nodded gravely. "Things piled up on Will that year. First his kid divorces him and two months later, his wife does the same thing."

"Do you know where his ex-wife lives now?"

"Yeah, she gave me her address up in Willow so I could send her the divorce papers when they got filed." He flipped through a Rolodex and handed me one of the cards. I copied her address and handed the card back.

When I asked, he gave me the directions to Will's place. His eyes narrowed before he warned, "You don't want to make any rash statements around Will, if you get my drift. He can be excitable."

Will's farm barely qualified for the title. A couple of acres of scraggly alfalfa cornered a battered and peeling manufactured home. A tractor and several farming implements rusted in the overgrown side yard. I had to squeeze by the dusty Ford pickup parked inches from the aluminum staircase to reach the front door.

Outside, the doorbell was loud, I couldn't imagine the sound inside the small home. A young Asian girl answered the door. She had a haunted look, as if she'd experienced too much to care about a stranger at the door. She said something I didn't understand.

"Does Will Krestas live here?" Perhaps I'd misread the address.

Her response was unintelligible. She walked away from the open door. A live version of "Yosemite Sam" replaced her after a few seconds. The too-tight Levi's might have stunted the bottom half of his body, the wide leather belt a garrote around his small waist. An impressive belly balanced on an enormous silver belt-buckle. His torso grew progressively larger up to his shoulders, as if the fat had backed up.

Will Krestas walked onto the porch and closed the door behind him. "Not much room and the wife's cleaning. This'll have to do, Mr.?"

"Gary Charboneau." We shook hands—his felt like I'd grabbed a dirt clod. Whatever the state of the farm, he evidently worked at something using those hands.

"What can I do for you, Mr. Charboneau?"

"I'm investigating your daughter's death."

He leaned back against the railing, and it tilted as if it might fall off. Judging by his complete relaxation, he had no such misgivings. His neck was the same size as his bald head, reminding me of a bullet. The walrus mustache was a copy of Yosemite Sam's; I wondered if he'd deliberately grown it so he'd look like the character.

He sounded cranky. "What's to investigate? They got the bastard that did it."

"They might not have the right man."

"And I shit green apples."

"Can you tell me if your daughter had any enemies? A jealous boyfriend? Anyone else who might have had reason to do her harm?"

The walrus mustache developed a sudden list. "She was a sweet girl, careful with other people's feelings. If anyone had it in for her, she didn't know about it."

"You talked with her fairly often?"

"She didn't have the money, she couldn't afford to phone much but she called when she could."

"Your bank won't show any sizable checks to her."

His eyes narrowed, the bushy brows forming a deep "V." "Don't use a bank, don't have enough money to make it worth while. What's your point?"

I tensed in case the sheriff had understated Will's propensity for violence. "She told friends that you had molested her. Was she blackmailing you?"

He looked off toward a towering column of smoke rising in the south. He waved his hand in an impatient gesture as he said, "It's them fuckin' talk shows. Every woman got to have been beat up or raped to feel like they belong. Men tell war stories; women tell them stories, it's the same thing, it's all bullshit."

"Was she trying to blackmail you?"

He stared at me as if I were the dumbest animal on earth before he said, "Damn, son, look around you. What would she get? My palatial home?"

"People blackmail for revenge." I tried a lie to piss him off. "I understand that her mother would confirm the allegations of abuse."

"She surely would," he said, letting a sigh escape. "Her mother needs help, liable to say anything." He watched the smoke, craning his head backwards to see the top of the column. "Don't know how she makes it on her own, being as crazy as she is."

"Do you know Earl Mitchell?"

His pale eyes locked on mine. "Yep."

I didn't expect that answer, I had a hard time keeping my composure. "How did you meet Earl?"

"He came by the house, just like you. Said Clay Oeland had a sharp lawyer that was going to get him off with not so much as a hand slap. So we agreed I'd give him a third of the settlement, up to a million, if Clay Oeland gets murder or manslaughter."

"Why would you agree to that?" He looked at me as if the question made no sense. "Oeland is sure to be convicted. Why would you agree to split any settlement?"

He returned his attention to the smoke column. "Shit boy, I didn't just fall off the turnip truck, I know how the fuckin' law works. The man has money; he can buy his way out of trouble."

He took a small knife out of his pocket, opened a nail cleaner and began working on his thumbnail. "I didn't buy no pig in a poke, I went to see the prosecutor. Cute little thing but she couldn't sell life jackets on a sinkin' boat. She's just out of school and wet behind the ears."

He wiped the fruits of his endeavor on his pants, then tackled another nail. "Saw Oeland's lawyer, too. The guy pays more for his suits than I paid for this farm. You don't get that rich fuckin' up."

He pointed the nail cleaner at me. "And from what I hear, a woman lawyer will defend Oeland in court, just to make sure none of them jurors thinks he has a problem with women. She's probably a mean bitch. He can afford the best."

He folded the nail cleaner, wedged it into the pocket of the too-tight Levi's, then looked at me. "So I shook with Earl. Don't much give a shit how he does it, but I want Clay Oeland convicted."

"Do you have a written contract with him?"

"Didn't need one. We shook on it and that'll do."

"You tell him to suborn perjury?"

"Told him to help the prosecutor convict the bastard." The railing groaned when he shifted his weight. "Didn't tell him how to do his job."

"He paid people to lie."

"Didn't tell him how to do his job." He scowled to make the point.

I unfolded the drawing of the shooter and handed it to him. "Ever see him?"

"Nope."

"Well, thanks for your time," I said, holding out my hand. He shook it. I turned to descend the steps.

I was edging between the Ford pickup and the stairs when he said, "Mr. Charboneau?" He had half his body inside the door, and I couldn't see his left hand. Fear steeled my legs for flight, but his voice remained even. "If any of them accusations about sexual abuse get made in public, say during Mr. Clay Oeland's trial, then I will get that palatial home." He slammed the door so hard I was surprised that the window didn't break.

Will's ex-wife lived in Willow. I retraced my route for forty miles, turning east off Interstate 5 to descend into a small town that seemed to be under siege by farmland. The battlements were recent subdivisions. They must have been a hard sell, the smell of manure permeated the town. Somewhere to the west, a large stockyard smudged the breeze.

The address belonged to a disintegrating mobile home, an ancient single-wide the color of dead sagebrush. Will's ex-wife answered my knock. She might have been 40 or 70. Life had radically etched her face. Despite her frail appearance, her voice was strong. "Mr. Charboneau?"

"Did Will call to warn you?"

"Oh, more than that. He told me to keep my mouth shut or he'd kill me." The threat didn't seem to have dampened her spirits but she lowered her voice and moved closer when she said, "He's a Godless and evil man." She stepped out on the small porch. I had to back down a step to give her room. Her hair, layered in progressively darker shades of red, looked plastic in the sunlight. She was wearing a shapeless blue dress dotted with massive white roses. "He said you work for an insurance company."

"Yes."

She pointed at the late seventies Ford Thunderbird in the carport. The yellow paint sparkled. The dark brown vinyl top glistened; the tires might never have been on the street. "See the dent?" she asked. I didn't. She shook her finger at the car. "In the center of the door."

I finally saw the dimple, a parking lot ding probably from another car's door. "Oh, yes, I see it. Why?"

She smiled shyly, seeming to shrink into the too-large blue dress. "If I cooperate, will you pay to have it fixed?"

"I don't work for an auto insurance company."

She looked piqued; she folded her arms and stared at the car.

"Was your husband abusing your daughter?" I asked.

The sour mood vanished, she seemed excited as she nodded vigorously. "He did what he wanted, to me and to her, whenever he wanted. I hit him one time when he was going after her and he broke my arm. Evil man, standing there naked in front of her. He told her to watch, that this was what would happen to her if she ever told. He took my arm and broke it across his knee. Wouldn't take me to the doctor until the next day. Evil man."

I couldn't take her seriously, her delivery suggested rote recital of an amusing story she had heard.

"Did you report him to the authorities?"

"A wife can't testify against her husband," she said. Her inflection suggested that I should have known that.

"A wife can't be forced to testify against her husband, but she can if she wants."

She looked stunned. "Is that right? Oh, my dear, he'll have to kill me too. Oh, my dear." She seemed to shrink, the hem of her dress rested on white fuzzy slippers.

A sudden gust of wind intensified the smell of manure. Wanting to wrap it up before I lost my breakfast, I held out the drawing of the killer. "Ever see this man?"

She studied the picture seriously before she said, "He's a Godless and evil man." I thought she was talking about Will until she asked, "He's the one that shot Sally, isn't he?"

"We think so, yes."

She moved to the edge of the porch, forcing me down another step. She had done it on purpose, her perch giving her a pulpit from which she proclaimed, "I saw him talking to Will."

My heart seemed to stop. "When?"

"Three years ago. Went back to get some of my things and there he was. Will had to get rid of Sally, sooner or later. She would have told what he did."

I pointed to the drawing. "Three years ago? Does he live around here?"

"No." She shook her head. "Of course, he was a lot thinner then and he didn't have the mustache, but I know it was him. I saw him talking to Will. They stopped talking when I got close."

"Three years ago?" I asked again. She folded her arms across her chest and nodded. "You think Will might have wanted to kill your daughter that long ago?" I asked.

"He'll probably send that man to shoot me next."

"The Sheriff in Linda Vista wasn't able to identify this man."

"The Sheriff is on Will's side." She bent over and whispered, "The Sheriff is an evil and Godless man. They play poker together."

Testing her reality, I held the picture up. "This man is very short, just a little over five feet."

She nodded solemnly. "It's him. I looked down on him, as short as I am. I could see his soul through his eyes. That's why I know he doesn't have God in his life. If you have God in your life, there's a light that shines through your eyes." She bent over so our eyes were level and asked, "You see the light in my eyes?"

She was right, I saw fire in that darkness.

As I drove out of Willow, I realized I'd chased a dead end. If Earl Mitchell and Glen Hubbard had conspired to convict Oeland, they probably concocted the plan after the murder. Sally's father was hoping to get money. Nothing tied any of them to the murder itself.

I was on the long climb toward the San Luis dam when I realized why Oeland had been framed. It was so simple, I couldn't believe that I hadn't thought of it before. I picked up the cellular and hit the speed dial for Toni's number. Toni was out, but her secretary said she would try to arrange a meeting with Clay Oeland for tomorrow.

CHAPTER THIRTEEN

The next afternoon, I met Clay and Toni at her office. Evidently Toni had been in court most of the day, the layers of make-up had vanished. Clay's gray-blue, three-button suit was rumpled, and his face showed the strain of a tough day.

I was fresh, I'd slept late and then spent a fruitless day watching Jessie Minithab's apartment, hoping Earl would be by to mend things with his witness. While I waited, I listened to the bug on Jessie's phone. She hadn't used the phone until mid-afternoon, and then she and a girlfriend engaged in a not entirely friendly discussion about Jessie's married boyfriend. He was upset because Jessie's girlfriend knew about him. That happened to be true, Jessie had told her everything. What Jessie was trying to find out was who had told her boyfriend.

Tiring of listening to that, I called Aaron Grady's house from a pay phone in a nearby liquor store. By the time delay on his answering machine, I guessed that Aaron hadn't picked up his messages for some time. I called the number for Mrs. Grady's mother, and told the woman who answered that the Santa Clara County District Attorney's Office needed to find Aaron. She was polite but the message was the same; she didn't know or care where he was.

She did give me Aaron's work number. After escaping the clutches of phone mail by using the word "emergency" several times, I talked to Aaron's manager, a sultry sounding woman. Aaron had worked last Friday, but she hadn't seen him since then, and he hadn't called in.

It felt eerie. Aaron had disappeared in the half hour between my calling and when I had knocked on his front door. On the walk back to my car, my fertile imagination concocted a scenario where I'd flipped out, killed the guy, and then repressed the memory. Not too likely, the bruises on my knuckles from pounding on his door were still sore.

I walked back to the car and listened to the bug. Jessie continued to grill her girlfriend about every utterance she had ever made regarding Jessie's boyfriend. They were still talking when I gave up.

Now, seated beside Clay in front of Toni's desk, I summarized my trip to Linda Vista, including my impression that Will was telling the truth about the plan being hatched after the murder.

Clay objected. "Earl Mitchell accomplished a great deal in a short time. He had to find Sally's father and convince him that his services were vital. He had to find out what kind of a car I drove; then find two people who would lie. He had to find a prostitute who had been beaten recently, and would testify that I did it. Unless this Earl set up the frame originally, how could he have managed all that?"

I explained, "Earl might not be connected to the hooker. Javier is looking at a pimp named Glen Hubbard. He knew Charlie and Vicki, and he pimps for the woman who accused you of beating her."

Toni asked, "Do Earl and Glen Hubbard know each other?"

I shrugged. "You'll know as soon as I do. I'm going to be in Earl's hip pocket if Javier can find an address."

Toni's mind was creating smoke and mirrors for a jury. "Because if you do put them together, and Earl actively tried to influence the outcome of the case, and he enlisted the aid of a known felon in attempting to suborn witnesses, and he made a deal with Will Krestas to do that for money, then I will ask the District Attorney to bring charges against Earl Mitchell and Glen Hubbard for those offenses."

Toni smiled as she added, "If Sylvia charges them, I'll bring out the possible involvement of these men in creating the frame."

"Will a judge allow that?" Clay asked.

Toni smiled. "The judge will have no choice, both crimes are connected. The jury will see the possibilities."

Clay said, "Go with that, I don't mind being exonerated for the wrong reasons." He turned to me. "Since you don't think these people set up the frame, what will you do now?"

"I didn't say that they didn't set up the frame, I said that Sally's father was brought into the picture only after the murder." Clay squinted his confusion. I moved my chair so that I was facing him. "Suppose the deal with Sally's father was an attempt by Earl and Glen to salvage what they could after you screwed up their original plan?"

"I did?" Clay's face paled, as if he expected me to accuse him of something.

"We've assumed that someone took your gun to frame you. Suppose someone had your gun as the result of a robbery, and wanted to make some real money with it. Imagine what would have gone through your mind if two things had been different. Suppose you realized that Sally had died immediately, and you recognized your gun?"

Finally Clay said, "I see what you're getting at. It would have been very tempting to dump the body and throw the gun away."

It felt right to me. "That's what a low-life would have done, and what he would have guessed you'd do."

I elaborated for him. "The killer might have waited in the orchard. A couple of days later, you would have had an unpleasant visit from someone who had pictures of you dumping Sally's body. He'd know about your phone records. He'd have witnesses that saw your car near Sally's apartment before the murder. He'd have a prostitute that would swear you beat her. He might have taken your gun to a testing lab and paid for a ballistics report. That report would identify your gun as the source of the bullets in her body."

I concluded, "The guy would show you all that evidence. Then he'd tell you how much it was going to cost you to stay out of prison."

"So when I took Sally to the hospital, the blackmail went out the window."

I sat back in my chair. "But they still had all that evidence, and what they needed was a way to make it pay off. It wouldn't take a great mind to think of her family's potential payoff."

Toni said, "It gives us an angle. I'll want you to look at the mug shots of the known criminal acquaintances of both men. If we can tie the killer to one of them, Sylvia will have to pay attention or we'll rub her face in it during the trial."

Perhaps Clay was beat; he stood up, saying, "I'll be available when you need me." To me, he said, "Keep looking, Mr. Charboneau. The first time we talked, you said whoever set this up knew me well. These men didn't know me at all, so I don't think we've found the people we're looking for." He left the office, looking dejected.

He obviously didn't think much of my new theory, but I liked it. Scumbags can be both clever and stupid, and if my theory was right, they had been both. Perhaps Oeland was fixed on the merger as the motive.

Toni's phone buzzed. She picked it up, then said, "Connect him." To me she said, "This will take a minute." When I asked if I should leave, she shook her head. Judging from her half of the conversation, she was arranging for a hearing in a civil case.

I watched her while she talked. Her hair had relaxed into soft whirls. The hornies were working at my brain; it had been too long. Although I couldn't quite picture her as a lover, I was more than willing to entertain the thought.

When she replaced the receiver, I said, "I'm going to follow Earl, maybe he'll meet with the shooter and get this over with."

Toni teased, "Jeez, Charboneau, you sound as if you believe there is a shooter." She laughed when I reached over her desk and pulled the pin on her grenade, sending the lever ricocheting off the bookcase behind her chair.

As I retrieved the lever and replaced the pin, I asked, "Can I buy you dinner?" Her face clouded so I added, "If you say 'No,' I'll have to turn you down next time."

She looked angry. "Are we playing games?"

"Apparently."

"Then you missed the point." She didn't like asking for sex, and she sure as hell didn't enjoy being turned down when she did ask.

"I didn't miss the point, I wasn't free to accept." I watched her eyes to make certain she heard me. "Javier had invited me over to his mom's for dinner. Even if I didn't need his assistance to do my job, I still wouldn't have broken my word, I don't do that."

"Javier?" she scoffed.

"Javier," I answered seriously. "His mom fixed tamales. They were fantastic."

She colored, ever so slightly, and moved papers around on the desk. When she felt my eyes, she said, "There was no rain check in that offer. Do you still want to do dinner?"

I nodded. "I'd like that."

She knew of a restaurant in Santa Cruz that would ruin me financially. She drove us over the coastal range in her Jaguar, the big cat handling the twisting road with aplomb. She drove smoothly, not fighting the road or the traffic and using her brakes sparingly.

We were early for dinner, so we selected an ocean-side table in the nearly empty restaurant. The sunset streaked wispy clouds in deep blues and reds, the sun itself a hazy red glow through an offshore fog bank. The breakers rippled along the rock jetty that channeled water into a marina. I mentioned the beautiful setting.

She nodded, looking wistful. "I like to come to the ocean. For something so awe inspiring, it's very soothing and peaceful somehow."

I smiled in agreement, watching a windsurfer scooting across the waves.

"Makes you forget that Mother Nature's a bitch."

Toni laughed. "Look on the bright side, is that your motto?" When she stopped snickering, she asked, "Where do you go in D.C. for peace."

"There's a park where the Potomac goes through a series of waterfalls. Same as here: awe inspiring, beautiful and peaceful."

The waitress brought our wine. I had picked up the glass when someone said, "Excuse me." A trim little guy with the correct amount of facial stubble, labels on the outside of his clothes and fashionably short hair was standing beside our table.

I raised my eyebrows to ask what he wanted.

"Are you Gary Charboneau?"

"I'm on vacation," I said, expecting a reporter.

"You are Gary Charboneau." He offered his hand.

I shook it. "Can I do something for you?"

"No." He smiled. "I'm a fan of yours. I just wanted to meet you."

"Thank you. You in the business?"

"No, just a fan." He turned to Toni. "Excuse me for interrupting." He turned and walked out of the restaurant.

"Gave me the creeps," Toni said quietly. "Does that happen to you often?"

"First time ever," I told her with a flippancy I didn't feel. I shared her feeling, something about the man wasn't right.

We ordered dinner before she asked, "Do you like what you do?"

"It's really interesting, yeah."

"Are you ever scared?"

"Sometimes." She waited for elaboration. "People are so unpredictable: like you."

"Fuckin' A," she said, doing a passable Bronx accent. She smiled at her joke. We watched the sunset for an awkward minute before she asked, "Is there someone who might replace the abused lady?"

"Not so far. How about you? Any prospects?"

"After the last one, I gave up on men."

"Forever?" I exaggerated astonishment.

She was serious. "I'm just pissed at the whole dating process, it's degrading and demeaning." She responded to my laugh. "If I agree to a date with another lawyer, it has to be some culturally acceptable event."

I asked the obvious question by arching my eyebrows.

"For an evening date, there's the opera or the symphony or a play in the city. Culturally acceptable dates. After awhile I get nostalgic for a home

JAMES M. MURPHY

evening so I invite a friend over to dinner. It's dinner, drinks and some small talk and then he starts undressing me, like he expects sex because I cooked."

She tugged on the sleeve of her blouse as if trying to cover her watch. "I was raised by my grandfather for the most part. Grandma was too busy with a store she ran. It was lonely I guess, but he tried hard to be a pal. He took me fishing, shooting, flying kites, water-skiing and he made up wonderful stories. He was a marvelous man and I thought all men were going to be that way. Maybe disappointment's the real reason for the anger."

"You haven't forgiven the ex-husband?" I asked.

"He was wonderful. It's the rest of you who piss me off."

When I stopped laughing, she asked, "What about you? You come from a fashionably dysfunctional family?"

"Yeah, my father was a domineering asshole, uninterested in his family. He finally divorced Mom to move in with an airhead." I took a pull at my wine to erase the edge in my voice. When the emotion passed, I continued. "There was poetic justice for him, his new wife drove him into the bottle and he died in his forties.

"Mom is a sweetheart. Kind and gentle, smarter than anyone I've ever known. I suppose that's why I hate men who abuse women. My father used to pick at my mother verbally just because he could; he knew she wouldn't fight back in front of the kids.

"I think as a boy, it's natural to put your father on a pedestal. But the picking showed a real weakness. Even as a kid, I knew my father was picking on someone he envied."

Our salads came. We spent the next few minutes eating in silence, both of us fumbling for a safe subject. We finally settled on sex.

I told Toni, "There was a girl a year or so younger than me. She lived two doors away. One day we decided to see what sex was all about." I inserted a pause before adding, "We got caught by her mother."

Toni grimaced. "Oh, how terrible. How old were you?"

"I don't know. Ten, twelve, something like that."

She shook her head. "What happened? What did her mother say?"

"Not much to me, bunches to my mother. I was grounded for an entire summer."

Toni laughed, genuinely embarrassed for the boy I was so many years ago.

"You have too much empathy," I said. "Something tells me there's a story there."

She grinned and nodded. "But you aren't going to hear it."

"No fair. I showed you mine, you have to show me yours."

She laughed and blushed. "My girlfriend and I were having this discussion one day. We'd never seen a penis except for these sex education line drawings. Those things all showed a flaccid penis." She cut at a lettuce leaf with the side of her fork, talking while she worked. "We'd heard the term 'erection' but what did that look like? We didn't know. If whatever it was happened at the same angle, how did you have sex? My best guess was that it had to be like a bull with a cow. The woman had to be bent over something while the male stood behind her. For all I knew, the man might need help, the bulls did."

I was laughing so hard my sides hurt.

Eating her salad, she waited until I calmed before she continued. "We decided the only way to find out was to enlist some boy to show us. Ted lived on a farm a mile away, so I called him and asked him to come over. It was going to be a long, hot trip for him, so naturally, he wanted to know why. No polite reason came to mind so I told him the truth. 'Justine and I would like to see your penis.' All of a sudden, this female voice breaks in and says, 'Justine, you come home right this instant.'"

"Oh man, party line telephones?"

She nodded seriously. "Yes. Very embarrassing. Turns out Justine's mother wasn't the only one listening. For a year, I had offers from boys I didn't even know."

It was late when we started back. The night was warm, balmy and romantic, and I hoped she would invite me to her bed. She didn't, she dropped me off at my car. I felt relieved, go figure.

On the drive to the motel, I circled around a block to look for a tail. The little man had spooked me, my gut said that Earl Mitchell had found me first. Only eight days along, my mustache wasn't a great disguise, but it should have been good enough in the dim lighting in the restaurant. If Earl had found me, he'd probably staked out Toni's office.

In my rearview mirror, the road was empty as I finished the tour. I turned right, heading away from the motel and drove north for a mile before I circled another block. Still nothing. Feeling foolish, I drove back to the motel.

CHAPTER FOURTEEN

I was up at five after a mostly sleepless night, yanked awake by every strange noise. My body felt abused, as if dinner out had been a party. The bathroom mirror agreed, I looked like shit, my abs had disappeared under a layer of fat. Disgusted, I put on my Corona T-shirt and black sweat pants, fished my wallet and keys out of last night's pants, and went for a run.

Even with the light traffic, the six lane boulevard was a zoo, the early commuters were a surly and aggressive bunch. The prevailing wind blew the exhaust toward the south, so I ran on the north side in relatively clean air. It was two miles to downtown San Jose, a loop through the city would give me 40 uninterrupted minutes to think about the case.

Now that I believed Oeland's story, I wanted to get inside the shooter's head. What had he promised Sally to get her to agree to take a beating? Unless they had some reason to trust each other, she wouldn't have done it for the blackmail money, that would take too long. She didn't have a boyfriend she could trust, Mac would have known about him. That left only drugs or up-front money as payment, and I'd bet on drugs. Which meant that either Glen or Earl's candyman was the go-between.

As I neared the center of the city, I ran across a street knowing I could easily beat an approaching car. I must have awakened the driver; he slammed on the brakes as I stepped onto the far curb. Super reactions.

As I pounded on, I wondered what the killer did after he shot Sally. He must have stayed close to see what Oeland would do. On the supposition that Oeland might decide to dump her body and the gun somewhere else, he would have had to be prepared to tail Oeland. If that was true, his car was parked near the shooting scene. I decided to check that out.

When I had run far enough, I went over one block to run back on a parallel street. Nine days away from my usual morning run had taken a toll; the run back to the motel was agony, I was glad I had remembered my wallet so they'd know where to send the body. It felt like three years before I got back to the motel.

After I caught my breath, I showered and shaved and then went to the coffee shop, opting for cereal, blaming those big breakfasts for the pain. After I ate, I went back to the room and looked at the map. The road where Sally was killed wasn't shown but the power lines were.

As I drove south toward the shooting site, Javier called. He abbreviated the pleasantries and then said, "Mitchell Investigations exists only in the phone books, there's no record of a fictitious name application. Earl Mitchell is not a licensed PI, and won't be, he has a felony conviction for assault ten years back. Other than a recent DUI, he's clean. He lives in a mobile home park, 5101 Village Meadow Drive, space 272." I could hear papers being moved. "I can talk about Brenda Cooper's hospitalizations because they were the basis for a trial. Both times were courtesy of her pimp, according to her testimony, and he's doing five years for assault and a parole violation. She's in trouble if she changes her story."

A driver in an adjacent lane, evidently rattled by the traffic on the four-lane freeway, decided to use my space. While I swerved and braked, I said, "Brenda must have a new man in her life." If Brenda had ratted her pimp into prison, a meaner, nastier man had to be available to ensure her safety. "Would you bet on Glen?"

"That would follow. Since he also told me about Charlie and Vickie being missing, I think Glen may have an ulterior motive for helping us."

"Could be." The errant ditz who had tried to force me off the road now decided to do forty in the fast lane. I changed lanes, and the subject. "I have a theory I'd like to try out on you." I spun the blackmail yarn for him. When I suggested that the killer expected Oeland to dump the body after he recognized his gun, Javier supplied another point. "That would explain why the shooter tried to hit her twice in the heart. He wanted her to die quickly but he couldn't afford to ruin the dental work, in case the body needed to be identified after a few years."

Judging by the cars rushing by, the rental's speedometer was far out of calibration; it indicated 75. Even the ditz passed me, having found his accelerator.

I pushed the phone tight against my ear while I said, "So I'm thinking that Earl and maybe Glen could also be responsible for Sally's killing. When that plan didn't work, they thought up this."

"If Glen was in on the frame..." Javier paused and then said, "Listen to me, talking about a frame. I can't believe in a frame when I know Oeland lied about the gun and the bullets. These two geniuses probably read about the killing in the paper and decided to do their bit for justice and the American system of free enterprise."

I thought that was his final take on the theory, but he added, "Still, I'll get with vice and see if Glen has any friends who resemble the BHS."

"Any chance I could get a copy of Earl and Glen's mug shots? I'd like to show Mac, the landlord at Sally's place, their pictures."

"I'll show them to Mac." He must have felt my surprise because he added, "I'm doing my best to help you. I want to go on TV and make big bucks." He laughed and disconnected.

Guided by the power lines, I found the road leading to the shooting site, but I couldn't decide where the killer parked. Even a scumbag would know better than to park on the highway skirting the orchard. I was driving north as I went by the orchard, and barriers in the center divider forced a two-mile long U-turn. Driving south, I retraced the route slowly, stopping on the shoulder several times.

The shooting site was on the northern edge of a walnut orchard. On the south side of the orchard, a dirt driveway led to a house set back from the highway. I pulled into the driveway and then parked between two trees.

I ignored a mongrel dog that gave me a few half-hearted barks as I walked to the house. A pleasant looking woman with beautiful silver hair approached the screen door warily. I introduced myself and asked, "It's about the shooting that happened on the other side of the orchard." I pointed at my car. "Did you see a car parked where mine is the day of the shooting?"

"Yes. I told the police there was a large, dark green American car parked there that night. I couldn't give them the brand or license plate because I only saw that much of it." She pointed toward the driveway. All that was visible was the last two feet of the car. "I thought it was probably lovers so I ignored it. I didn't hear it leave."

"Did you hear the shots?"

"No. The news was on then. I probably wouldn't have heard anyway, because of the highway noise."

"Well, thank you," I said, turning to leave.

"Are the police through digging in the orchard?"

I guessed. "Yes. Did you have something you wanted to show them?"

"No, I was waiting to clean until they stopped raising all that dust." She wasn't angry, just efficient.

I walked through the orchard, guided to the spot by the straight rows of trees. Not a long walk. I set the timer on my watch and loped back to my car. Forty-seven seconds later, I was pulling out onto the highway. The killer was probably a half mile behind Clay as he drove north.

That evening, I drove by Earl's address. The name on the curbside mailbox confirmed that E. Mitchell lived there. A newer blue Chevrolet with a broadband antenna mounted on the roof was in the carport of an older double-wide mobile home. In a park where most of the mobile homes were new and quite large, Earl's faded green home looked dumpy.

I wanted to hang with Earl for a few days. Installing an automatic tracker on his car wasn't going to be easy; too many eyes could see his carport. And considering his line of work, Earl would have an intrusion alarm on his car. But I didn't have much choice; I needed a tracker on his car so I could follow him without being seen. Aware that blind luck beats planning, I decided to wing it.

I drove back to the motel, selected the tracker I'd use, and tested the batteries. The tracker was a one inch plastic cube with a magnet base and a window on top. Attached to metal on the underside of a car, the window faced the ground, allowing an infrared transducer to measure speed while an electronic gyroscope measured direction. The metal in the car would provide the antenna for the data transmission.

After leaving the motel to drive toward south San Jose, I stopped at a drugstore and bought a can of tennis balls. At a restaurant in the shopping center, I ate a leisurely dinner. I waited in the restaurant's parking lot until 10:30 that night before I drove toward the mobile home park.

I parked on the street, then walked through the ornate archway carrying my briefcase with my jacket draped over my arm—my coming home from work disguise. The narrow streets and the resident's fears had resulted in an electrician's paradise, and the park's lighting resembled the Las Vegas Strip.

Two homes down on the opposite side of the street from Earl's, an older single-wide had a "For Sale" sign in its front window. I stepped into the darkened carport and put on my black jacket. When I opened the can of tennis balls, air whistled into the can, the sound very loud in the quiet park.

I missed the decklid of Earl's car with the first tennis ball, hitting the side with a thump that reverberated in the quiet park. The alarm blew the horn and flashed the lights. Seconds later, the same man who had introduced himself at the restaurant came rushing out holding a Glock automatic. I mentally kicked my butt; Earl had found me first. How much did he know about me?

After a few quick looks around the car and the street, Earl went back inside, leaving the alarm alternately blowing the horn and flashing the lights.

Curious people edged onto their porches, then scurried inside when Earl emerged still holding the gun. He aimed a remote at the squalling car and the alarm quit. He took another tour around the car, checked its doors, then walked into the street and looked both ways. Finally he climbed the stairs and closed the door. I was hoping he wouldn't reset the alarm. A curtain in a dark room above the carport opened a few inches, and the alarm reset with a two-tone beep.

A few minutes later, a blue flickering reflection on the ceiling indicated a TV. I couldn't see his head so I threw the second tennis ball. I would never make the majors, I hit the side of the car again, the thump closely followed by the horn and lights.

Earl's face appeared at the window. He turned the alarm off and rearmed it immediately. He continued to watch from inside. With the TV's glare, he wouldn't see a tennis ball, so I let fly. I hit the bumper dead-on, quietly pissing the alarm off again.

As the sound of the alarm died away, Earl's neighbor switched on a blinding floodlight. An older man with an impressive belly opened the door and waddled to his porch railing. He glared at Earl's car for a few long minutes, silently daring Earl to arm the son-of-a-bitch again. He hocked a gob of spit into the junipers separating their property before he went inside. The floodlight extinguished abruptly.

Earl continued to watch, minor movements of the curtain giving him away. An hour later, he closed the curtain. I waited for another hour before I walked across the street and slid under the rear of his car. I had to reach arm's length to find flat metal so the window in the tracker faced the ground. About the time the magnet sucked onto the metal with a loud thunk, a woman walking a dog came by. If she saw me, she didn't say anything. I waited until I couldn't hear the clinking of the dog's collar, then I slid out from underneath Earl's car and walked out of the park.

Back in my car, I waited for the first report from the tracker. The computer needed that input to establish the starting point on the local map. When the tracker checked in, the UHF radio in my car sent the digitized data to the laptop. I clicked on Earl's street on the map. From that initial input, the computer would calculate his location every five minutes for the next four days, until the battery in the tracker expired.

I drove back to the motel, conscious that Earl probably knew where I lived. Going up the stairs, I held the gun against my leg. Standing behind the door frame, I opened it, sniffing for strange smells. Without entering, I flipped on the light, then quickly checked. Feeling a tad foolish about the paranoia, I went in. I put the gun on the night stand facing the door and propped a chair under the doorknob. I balanced a glass on the edge of the window sill with the curtain bunched behind it, just in case someone got creative with a glass cutter. Then I settled in for the night.

CHAPTER FIFTEEN

According to the tracker, Earl was out by nine the next morning. I intercepted his car on a long boulevard leading toward downtown San Jose. A law-abiding and slow driver, Earl made following easy. Two miles after I picked him up, he parked in a restaurant's parking lot, not far from Glen Hubbard's favorite corner. It wasn't coincidence, Glen joined him inside the restaurant a few minutes later.

I had found a parking spot on a cross street that looked into the front windows of the restaurant. Facing the window, Earl was nearly hidden by Glen's back, a broad expanse of blue denim. I called Javier at the police station and gave him the news. He asked where I was. A few minutes later, he walked up and got into the car, dropping it about three inches on the passenger side. I pointed to the restaurant and handed him the binoculars.

He held the bulbous unit as if it might explode. "What do these do?" he asked.

"Automatic leveling binoculars. The optics move to take the jitter out of the image. They're night-vision when you flip the switch on the side."

Javier removed his glasses and rotated the eyepieces until he was satisfied. Earl was facing the restaurant's window, evidently Javier could lip read what he was saying. "'—traded him just after the season started, the asshole. I'm not going to bet the A's now.'... Earl's laughing at something Glen said. I never would have guessed Glen had a sense of humor."

"A very handy talent, lip reading," I said. "I'll have to pick that up."

"Oh, yeah," Javier said, shaking his head in disgust, "then you'll get in on the really interesting things these geniuses say to one another." He raised the binoculars again and picked up the next conversation. "'Asshole parks his Ferrari in front of her place. I'll show him the pictures and tell him how much. If he comes up with one large, I'll let him make up the story I tell his

121

wife. That'll be fifteen hundred for three hours' work, including the five she's paying me to find out what he's doing.'"

Javier lowered the binoculars. "Earl's ethics need work."

I pointed at the restaurant. "This puts the witnesses and the hookers together."

"It doesn't explain the killing."

"Indirectly," I told him. "If all their information came from the news accounts of the shooting, they moved very fast. Too fast. I think they knew a lot about Sally before she was shot. That could be because they set up the frame."

"Sylvia isn't buying it and I don't either, so we aren't going to be doing any work on the case until something new falls in our lap. Mac didn't recognize Earl or Glen; Oeland didn't recognize any of Glen's associates, so there's nothing to go on."

"You knew there was a car parked on the south side of the orchard at the time of the shooting?"

Javier nodded. "No type, tag, or year, and only a loose connection to the right time." He raised the binoculars and watched Earl for a few seconds. "They're getting ready to go. Earl is going to stake someone out." After a moment, Javier said, "Earl thinks he might end up sleeping in his car."

"In that case, there might be a 603 at his place in the next hour." I used the police code for prowler. "Any chance the cop out there could be busy?"

Javier rolled down the passenger side window; unhooked the two-way radio from his belt and held it out the window while he spoke into his lapel microphone, "Control, Nora Two."

"Nora Two, Control." The voice was soft, sexy and very feminine.

"Nora Two. I'll be 10-8 with Nora Six in fifteen."

"Nora Two, Control. 10-4. Nora Six, copy?"

"Nora Six, 10-4."

Javier grinned as he put the radio back on his belt. "If there is a 603, it'll have to wait until we finish our doughnuts."

When Javier left to see Nora 6, I drove to the motel to get ready. I took the make-up kit from the glove compartment and went into the room. I glued on the mustache and goatee, then glued the fake bump to my nose and the scar on my right cheek. When I was through applying the foundation to blend the bump and the scar, I put on a conservative blue suit. When I'm doing a B & E, I look like a salesman, I wear a suit and tie and carry a briefcase. People hide from salesmen, evidently dreading the anticipated knock.

Before putting on the suit coat, I put on the shoulder holster and practiced my quick draw. The gun fell on the floor twice. When I felt confident about the draw, I tried it with the suit coat on. After six tries, I drew the gun successfully without snagging the coat.

Enjoying the adrenaline high, I drove to the mobile home park. I left my car parked on a street two blocks from the park, and then walked to Earl's place. His mobile home had no obvious alarm box and the window beside the front door wasn't protected. Prepared to walk away if it was alarmed, I stood in front of the door, knocking with my left hand while the tines of the automatic lockpick worked inside the lock. The matchbox sized machine whirred, clinked, and then lit its green light. With the deadbolt open, I inserted the tines in the doorknob lock. In seconds, the door opened. I walked in and quickly shut the door.

Earl was a gadget freak, expensive hardware occupied three long planks balanced on concrete blocks in the shape of a bookcase. On the top shelf, a stereo and television shared the space with large, boxy speakers. On the second shelf, a computer was making phone calls, while the adjacent police scanner was feeding an auto-start tape machine. On the bottom shelf, a very expensive communications receiver was scanning cellular telephone frequencies, recording the calls on tape.

Under the front windows, a long sofa faced the hardware. An upholstered chair that didn't match the couch was next to the window overlooking the carport. Judging by the shabby furnishings, Earl put all his money into communications gear.

I brought a wooden chair from the dining area into the living room and sat next to the phone perched on the end of the second shelf. I disconnected the phone and took off the plastic housing. The tiny bug I'd decided to use required 12 connections, and I had seven soldered when Earl drove into the carport. I had the phone together and my soldering gear in the briefcase before he put his key in the lock.

With the drapes closed, it was dark inside. Earl switched on the light and saw me at the same moment. He started to reach under his jacket and then he saw the gun. "Aw, fuck," he said.

"I'd move real slow if I were you," I said amiably. "You want to take out the gun like it was covered in shit, you understand?" He did, he took it out with two fingers and dropped it on the floor.

I stood up and walked toward him, motioning for him to sit on the couch. I picked up his Glock and put it in my left hand jacket pocket. Then I swapped my gun to my left hand and reached into my right jacket pocket.

Silencers are great persuaders. In every movie, the bad guy screws the silencer onto the gun just before he shoots. So I watched Earl's eyes widen as I took what passed for a silencer out of my pocket and screwed it onto the barrel of the automatic. It only extends the barrel, adding about 20 yards of accurate range to standard slugs, but Earl believed it was a silencer. "Why would you want to shoot me?"

I turned on the laser and aimed the gun at his face, letting the laser dot dance over the bridge of his nose until he achieved butt-white. I lowered the gun just a bit when I asked, "Just curious; why kill the girl? You had enough to blackmail Oeland with her alive."

Earl cleared his throat before he croaked, "I didn't have anything to do with that."

I aimed the gun again, saying, "Wrong answer."

Earl rushed an explanation. "I told her father that Oeland was going to get off because he had a smart lawyer. I told him if he gave me a third of any settlement he got from his civil suit, I'd find witnesses to make sure Oeland was convicted."

"Getting the witnesses to lie was stupid," I said quietly, lowering the gun. "Oeland's in enough of a fix."

"A good lawyer could convince a jury that it could have happened like he said."

"This is boring." I placed the laser's dot back on his nose.

"Jesus H. Christ, you can't shoot me. They'll know it was you."

I tried for a thoughtful look. "Hey, good point, Earl." I took his gun out of my pocket and racked the slide. "I'll make it look like suicide." He looked very frightened. "How about some last words? Like who hired the killer? You or Glen."

"I never met Glen until three days after the shooting. You can check. We met at the jail, we started talking about Oeland getting off...all his money..." He pointed at the Glock. "That's got a light pull, it'll go off if you even think about it."

"That's good, Earl, maybe I'll shoot from the floor, the cops will think you dropped it and shot yourself accidentally." I got down on one knee and held the butt of the gun against the floor. I put my gun upside down on top of his and lined it up using the laser. While I worked, I asked, "How'd you get Oeland's gun?"

"It's not Oeland's, it's mine."

That tore it, I was suddenly very weary. If he had known about Oeland's gun being used on Sally, he would know which gun I was talking about. He hadn't participated in the frame.

Afraid that I might shoot him for wasting my time, I picked up my briefcase and walked out of his place without saying anything else. I threw his expensive Glock in a dumpster near the park's entrance.

In my car, I drove north as fast as I dared. Using the speed dial, I called Toni's office, and made my problem sound like life and death to her secretary. When Toni came on the line, I told her, "I need to borrow the trunk of your car for a couple of days. You don't want to know what for."

"I love mysteries," she snorted. "Do I go to jail if the police find it?"

"No, it's nothing illegal. Would you unlock your trunk so I can drop it and run."

"Yeah." She disconnected, probably pissed. If Earl was thinking, he had already called the police. I couldn't afford to be carrying a gun and burglary tools when they found me.

I called Javier's number and got his voice mail. I intended to ask him to check Earl's story about the two of them sharing a jail cell three days after the murder. I recovered my sanity before I opened my mouth. Earl would charge me with assault, and the voice mail would confirm I had talked with him. Not your brilliant move.

Thanks to clear freeways, I drove behind Toni's office minutes after leaving Earl's. Toni was just opening the trunk of the Jaguar. I pushed the gun and the barrel extension into the briefcase with all my other tools, and got out of the car. Toni watched me put the briefcase in the trunk, then she closed it. I held her arm, pulled on the stem of her watch, and turned the minute hand back a half-hour. I asked, "What time did you and Mr. Charboneau meet on Thursday, May 20."

"I'm not going to lie for you."

I shook my head. "Wrong. You should say: 'According to my watch, we met at 11:35.'"

She half smiled, conveying that she'd help put me in jail if anyone asked. "What did you do?"

"Not a thing. Earl Mitchell might allege all sorts of crimes, but we know he lies."

"He might not be the only one," she said sourly. "You do know the difference between legal and illegal investigations, don't you?" I grinned outrageously, and that made her laugh. "If you aren't in jail, come over for dinner tonight. I'll explain the difference." She turned and walked toward the rear door to the building, turning her head to say, "About six-thirty."

I really hoped I wouldn't be eating jail food that evening. As I drove toward my motel, I cataloged my list of sins: Breaking and Entering, Brandishing, Assault with a Deadly Weapon, Possession of an Illegal Weapon, and Armed Robbery for taking Earl's gun.

Savoring my suddenly precious freedom, I went to the public library and browsed the afternoon away. At six that evening, I walked the half block to the library's parking lot, expecting to be surrounded by cops at any second. I felt like a fugitive as I drove out of the lot. Seconds later, I was speeding toward Los Gatos, a short freeway trip south of San Jose.

Toni's address was inside a gated community. The guard examined the sheet of paper on his clipboard and said, "Don't see that name."

"Charboneau. C-H-A-R-B-O-N-E-A-U."

"Oh, yeah, sorry." He sounded annoyed rather than apologetic. "It's 22C. Go straight ahead, then turn right on Foothill."

Twenty-two C was the middle unit in a building housing three townhouses, another example of the ubiquitous mission architecture overwhelming San Jose. The door had a wrought iron ring for a knocker. Toni answered the door wearing a business suit and a fresh layer of mortician's paint. Every hair was improperly restrained with a layer of lacquer. "Sorry, just got home," she lied. "Dinner will be awhile."

The apartment's decor was decidedly feminine; stuffed teddy bears sat on the couch and alongside the potted plants. The living area was open with a wide pass-through from the kitchen overlooking the balance of the first floor. A large, dark mahogany table that could easily seat six defined the dining area.

She handed me a glass of white wine and indicated the couch. She settled into the chair on the opposite side of the room. A gray cat jumped up on the chair and slunk into Toni's lap as if she might not notice as long as he moved slowly. Finding no resistance, he curled up and shut his eyes. "Buddy," she explained. "He lets me live here as long as I feed him."

I indicated the room. "I like the way you've done this. It feels warm."

"The cats and I like it."

"Cats?"

"Two," she said, grinning. "Priscilla. She's hiding somewhere."

"Isn't that a stereotype?" I asked unkindly. "The cat lady."

She took offense. "It works for me. Cats and a good vibrator, love and sex, all a woman needs."

She didn't need a stove either, judging by the meal she served. The meat in the stew was tasteless and tough, the vegetables had long since given up their crispness while the potatoes hadn't. The salad saved me, all the ingredients were fresh, I filled up on that. If she was critical of her own cooking, she hid it well.

While we ate, I told her about connecting Glen and Earl. She loved it, she was going to get Oeland off on reasonable doubt. Her interest in the truth extended no further than winning; she didn't care if they had set up the frame, her job was to get Oeland off. She beat that subject to death, finally running down when her plate was clean.

As we moved back into the living room after dinner, I accepted a cup of decaf. It made dishwater seem appetizing. Maybe jail food wouldn't seem so bad after this.

The thought of jail spooked me. Thinking that I would prefer to spend the night making love, I tried to introduce the subject of sex. "Ever considered marriage again?"

She shook her head. "As I said, Pete was a wonderful husband, everybody else I've dated has come in a poor second. I don't have to settle for second."

"So what happened?" She didn't like that question, I saw the pain. I didn't have any right to pry but I did. "Sounds like there's a story there." I saw her chin tremble, I was probing an open wound. I put up an open hand to stop the explanation. "I'm sorry, professional nosiness, it's a bad habit."

She lifted her cup as if she might drink some coffee, then put it back on the saucer untouched. "I don't know why the pain persists, it wasn't anything either of us did. I came home early one day to tell Pete that I was pregnant, and found him in bed with a man." It did hurt, her eyes filled. She waved her arm as if dismissing the tears. "It wasn't his fault, he can't help what he is."

"I shouldn't have pried," I apologized.

She shrugged, perhaps not trusting her voice. I didn't know what to say so I kept quiet. Finally she sighed and grinned quickly. "Happens every time I tell someone. It's not like he died or anything." She put her hand over her mouth and the tears came again. She cried softly.

Then I knew—it was the baby she was crying for. I wondered if talking about it would help. My mouth moved before I decided. "What happened to the baby?" I heard myself ask.

She dabbed at the tears with a napkin before she said, "I had an abortion." She saw eyeliner on the napkin, so she worked at her eyes while she said, "I didn't have the guts to raise a child on my own."

Awed by the brutal honesty, and desperately wanting to change the subject, I asked brightly, "So, ever had any tough times in your life?" That made her smile; she was attractive when she smiled.

"Have you?" I didn't understand so she asked, "Had any tough times in your life?"

I didn't want to talk about Deborah. "No tough times at all. Swinging playboy, a girl in every city, a new one in my bed every night, looking to break Wilt's record if I live long enough."

Still wiping eyeliner off, she said, "I bare my soul and you give me bullshit. Are you gay?"

I shook my head. "If you don't mind being, ah, number four thousand, three hundred and thirty-nine, I can prove I am a raging heterosexual."

"That doesn't prove anything," she said quietly.

If anyone would know, she would.

We talked about her husband. He had fought what he was all his life. All of a sudden, he was in bed with another man, powerless to fight the urges he'd been suppressing. "He was horrified," she said, "but he couldn't do anything about it. Anyone who thinks being gay is a choice should have to witness the torture that man went through."

"He should have been honest with you."

"He was," she said vehemently. "Before we married, he told me he had no sex drive. All I heard was that he was a man who would be faithful. I could live without sex but I didn't want to be left alone again." She sipped the coffee, and looked surprised. "Cold," she said, placing it on the coffee table. "Do you want a warm-up?"

When I shook my head, she continued, "He was as honest with me as he was with himself. If he had sexual thoughts about men, he ignored them. He'd heard the term male bonding and he thought that's all it was. Even after, he wanted to keep the marriage going, I don't think he could face thinking of himself as gay."

"Why didn't you keep the marriage going, since he gave you the choice?"

"I'm terrified of AIDS," she said quietly.

That seemed reasonable to me. We veered off into a range of subjects that seemed safe until we bumped into her views on feminism. She saw men as the problem. I argued that when women can agree on the solutions, they will use their majority to solve the problems. "At least a third of the men will vote with you, so all you need are half the women."

The exchange was winding down anyway, but she capped it by saying, "At least you're arguing methods. I get pissed at men who wonder what women want. I tell them we want respect, just like they do."

I looked at my watch, it was nearing eleven. "I should go since we have to work tomorrow." I hesitated, waiting for her to say something. "Unless you want me to stay?"

"No, thanks, cats and the vibrator are all I need."

Retaliating for the snippy put-down, I tried to look relieved. "Don't take offense, I just asked in case you expected something for fixing me dinner."

As I walked down the short hallway to the front door, she stood in the living room and watched. I opened the door, waved at her and said, "Thanks." I shut the door quietly; no way was I going to let her see the anger.

Halfway back to the motel, I remembered that Earl knew where I lived, and I was unarmed. Then I almost laughed. Worry about Earl? Cops were probably waiting to arrest me.

CHAPTER SIXTEEN

I circled the block when I arrived at the motel, looking for cops. Parked cars were wedged tight; waiting cops would have to park in the motel's lot. I drove through the lot, not seeing any little hubcaps. I parked next to the stairs and made a run for my room.

At the door, I used my left hand to key the deadbolt, using the door frame for protection. When it opened, the air rushing out of the room had a double odor of stale cigarettes and sweat. My legs seemed anchored in concrete while my brain screamed in fear. I turned to run while still holding the doorknob. A bullet blew a chunk out of the door; the sonic crack from a second bullet popped my ear, the sound of the gun two closely spaced explosions, a magnum for sure. I yanked the door shut. Using one hand to guide my fall, I vaulted over the railing, landing on the steps halfway down. In two long leaps, I was in the parking lot, scrambling to get behind my car.

I heard the broken wood of the splintered door squeal as I went to my knees behind the car. I saw a dark figure fill the opening; he searched for me, swinging the gun in an arc. The angry sizzle of a bullet passing close to my ear warbled the noise of a small caliber gun somewhere to my left. The figure up on the walkway ducked back into the room. Jesus, two of them. I went flat on the ground just as a bullet hit the bumper, ricocheting with a flutter that popped my ears.

On my belly, I scrambled into the gap between cars. The large man came out of the room and edged along the second floor walkway. I couldn't see his face but the gun was all too clear as he aimed. I rolled on my back and pointed my finger at him. He quickly ducked behind a concrete stanchion, then, firing almost blind, he exploded my car's windshield. The next bullet creased the door above me, the horrific noise physical pain inside my head, feeling like something vital had ripped apart. The car bounced as another bullet found something solid. He took better aim, and the gun barrel pointed at my face when it flashed and asphalt hit my ear. I scooted underneath the car. The car bounced as if someone had jumped on the bumper.

He leaned over the railing to get a better angle. Asphalt and blood spattered the car as a hot spear numbed my side just below my ribs. His next shot exploded the rear tire, lowering the car, trapping my head, and enveloping me in a choking cloud of dust.

Pointing my index finger where I'd last seen him, I frantically yanked my way free, blinking my eyes, trying to clear the dirt. As I knelt beside the car, trying to get up and run, I heard someone shout, "Take him, take him." A bullet hit the windshield pillar next to my head, and the side window exploded as if someone had set off a bomb inside the car. Mostly blind, I ran underneath the stairs.

Protected from the shooter, I hesitated, fearing the second man was waiting in the walkway next to the building. I heard the shooter start down the stairs. I was dead if I waited. Not looking, I began running for the end of the building. Running on the edge of my feet, trying to be silent, dreading and expecting that final bullet, I was almost at the corner of the building when someone yelled, "That way."

Just around the corner of the building, a juniper bush sent me sprawling. I could hear people running on the walkway as I scrambled to my feet. Blocked by the chainlink fence surrounding the property, I rushed into the blackness at the rear of the building, only to find myself trapped in an alley just six feet wide.

I heard the bush take out one of the people chasing me, the sound of a fall unmistakable. A shaft of light from a bathroom window illuminated the concrete block wall at the far end. I'd be a silhouette in a shooting gallery. Halfway along the building, I eased to the asphalt, lying on my back and wedged against the chainlink fence.

Both men ran into the opening at the same time, then retreated to the cover of the building, perhaps worried that I did have a gun. My breathing was ragged and noisy, surely they could hear me. One figure slithered around the corner of the building and flattened against the wall. He was thirty yards away and he was going to kill me.

Between us, another bathroom light came on, spearing the darkness. Then another light near the corner silhouetted a second, smaller man before he scrambled back to the cover of the building. I was opposite a window; if the occupants turned on that light, I was dead.

I squeezed against the bottom of the chainlink fence. It gave and I pushed my way underneath. Two feet away, a six-foot high wooden fence loomed. I eased slowly, awkwardly, to my feet, aware that touching the chainlink fence would give me away. I was very thankful I'd worn dark clothes. I kept my face turned away from the men, but my hands seemed very bright against the dark wood on top of the fence.

Slowly, ever so slowly, I pulled myself toward the top, not daring to turn my white face toward the men carefully walking toward me. My arms were trembling, the fence shook as I eased my body up, and boards in another section of the fence rattled. Other noises intruded—a dog was barking, a woman was yelling. I could feel the magnum aiming at my back from inches away; I needed to scream.

Finally, I could lean the upper half of my body over the top of the fence, and I half-somersaulted into the backyard of a house. Each board in the fence slapped its neighbor, a thunderous ripple of noise that traveled away and then back toward me.

As I got to my feet, a floodlight skewered me in its light. A German shepherd, barking and snarling, challenged me. I put the back of my hand out for the dog to sniff, and it stopped barking long enough to do that.

I heard my pursuers scaling the chainlink fence. I ran to the side fence, then struggled to lift myself to the top on arms that felt numb. When the newly enraged dog yanked my shoe off, I fell into a shrub in the adjacent yard. The dog slammed the fence, rattling the boards, pissed and barking loud enough to wake the world.

Between the barks, I heard both men jump from the metal fence, slamming against the wood fence as they landed. One of the men said, "Go that way." The back fence rattled as someone climbed it.

Exhausted and weak, I had to will my body to get up. On my feet; I took one step, stumbled over a raised edging and fell down again. The edging was foot-long scalloped brick. I pulled one out of the dirt; then I hid in the corner where the side and rear fences met.

My hand was wet and slippery. In the light from a gap in the fence, my entire right side was shiny. I shifted the brick to my other hand and probed the burning spot, a finger size hole. I tried to remember what vital organs were there.

Very close, the magnum fired and the dog's barking cut off in a yelp. A loud voice said, "Get back in the fucking house or I'll blow your head off." As the man with the magnum approached, he blocked the light filtering through the fence. I could hear labored breathing.

I heard scraping at my back where the fence faced the motel. Earl Mitchell materialized at the top of the fence, suspended on his arms, blinking in the glare of the floodlight from the adjacent yard. From inches away, I threw the brick at his face. He dropped from sight so quietly, I wondered if I'd imagined him being there.

Waterfalls were forming in my ears, the thunder creating multicolor explosions in my eyes. I pulled another edging brick out of the ground. When I straightened up, the world tilted. A backlit man appeared at a weird angle and I threw the brick at him. A moment later, something hit my face very hard. Had I been shot?

I smelled dirt. I was face down on the ground. How the hell had that happened? I rolled over, not wanting to die with my face in the dirt. I was in a flower garden, and a snapdragon was a dark column of tiny bells against the low clouds reflecting the city lights. Fragrant flowers colored the air, but I could taste dirt. I wanted to spit it out but I couldn't remember how.

A shaft of light speared the darkness and the snapdragon jerked, bobbing in and out of the light. Other shafts of light appeared, miniature spotlights finding nothing in a darkening world. The explosions from the magnum warbled, as if the gun were under water. Then thunderous vibrations began pelting my body and a blinding white light formed a brilliant tunnel.

CHAPTER SEVENTEEN

Pain stabbed my side. I could see the knife where it stuck out of me, but Toni hadn't noticed. "Damn that hurts," I told her, gritting my teeth against the pain that seemed to be getting worse.

She reached out and stroked my face, letting her warm palm linger on my cheek, then she grabbed my arm. I opened my eyes. A rotund Filipino nurse hung an IV bottle onto a rack beside the bed.

"Am I dying?"

She patted my cheek and said, "No, you're doing very well." She had a kind face. "You just need to sleep."

Day changed to night. The knife protruding from my side hurt, I tried to pull it out. Someone pushed my hand away; a huge man dressed in white was stabbing me. "Don't do that," I told him.

"Got to get it clean, Mr. Charboneau."

"Then put the fucking thing in a dishwasher, don't stab me with it." How fucking stupid could a person be?

My mother had her jacket on; a little purse draped from her right shoulder by a long thin strap. She was leaving. Reluctantly, I guessed, she seemed troubled.

Using a different voice, she said, "We aren't paying you all this money to lie around."

I wasn't sure I'd heard that right. "What?" I opened my eyes.

"Welcome back," Toni said. She was wearing the usual shapeless black suit. Sunlight streamed through the window of a hospital room done in really ugly purple and green, someone's idea of Art Deco. On the wall next to the bed, a machine scratched a line on graph paper. A monitor silently traced my

135

pulse. I expected the green line to stop moving. "Am I going to live?"

Toni sneered. "Come on, Charboneau, it was just a flesh wound."

That sounded good so I made her disappear.

"Okay, Charboneau, time to wake up." Toni stood at the side of the bed. "If you're going to charge us for the hospital stay, I want you out of here. Three days is long enough."

"Three days?" I was stunned.

"At $1,619 a day for expensi—, ah, intensive care."

That made me laugh, which I regretted; it felt like someone stabbed me in the side. I inhaled spit when the pain hit, which made me cough and that really hurt. "Oh, Jesus," I gasped, "you sure I'm not dying?"

"Okay, so the piece of bullet that went through you was a little banged up, and it didn't make a tidy hole. And it did take a tiny nick out of a little bitty artery, and you did lose a quart of blood. But come on, you aren't going to make a federal case out of it, are you?"

Sleep beckoned. I shut my eyes.

"Your mother and brother have been here around the clock for the last three days. I told them I'd stay with you while they went to lunch."

While I considered that, the world evaporated again.

I woke, bathed in sweat, the pain in my side a white hot rod skewering me to the bed. The display on the monitor read 186. Sunlight slanted through the window at a low angle. Late afternoon, I guessed.

Toni woke me up that evening by leaning over the bed and calling my name. When I opened my eyes, my first thought was that her cadaver make-up matched the purple walls.

I asked, "Who shot me?"

"You hit him in the face with a brick and you never saw him? You have some arm. How far away were you?"

"I hit Earl in the face; he isn't the one who shot me."

"You hit both of them in the face, Glen Hubbard right in the chops. He lost three teeth; didn't look at all happy when he was arraigned a couple of days ago. Earl wasn't so lucky. His face was crushed and part of his nose wound up inside his brain. He might not make it."

I could give a fuck about Earl, Glen Hubbard was the dangerous one. "Is Hubbard going to walk?"

"Hubbard? He's charged with three counts of attempted murder. Beside your count, he shot at the helicopter that arrived on the scene as he was shooting holes in a fence. The helicopter sustained a couple of nice fat holes very near the occupants. Those two holes pissed the judge off, so she set the bail at 'No.' Shooting at aircraft is federal, good for several lifetimes in the big house. Now if you'll cooperate and die, they'll put him on death row."

"Okay," I said, looking at the clear fluid dripping in the IV.

She grinned at what she assumed was a joke. She pulled a chair close to the bed, turned it backwards and knelt on the seat. "The shooting put Earl Mitchell and Glen Hubbard together, so now we have a conspiracy to convict Clay."

Big deal, I shrugged. That was very stupid; raising my shoulder pulled on the wound. I groaned at the sudden blaze in my side.

She patted my arm before she continued, "Suppose Sally wanted to see her father in jail for what he'd done to her. Her father scrapes enough together and hires Earl to get something on Sally. Maybe he suspected that she did drugs or hooked. Glen sees Clay playing with hookers, he and Earl get creative and the frame is born. They know everybody has a gun, including Clay, so they break into his house and steal his."

Kneeling on the chair, she towered over the bed, looking like death coming to claim me.

She said, "When Clay takes Sally to the hospital, their plan goes out the window, so they salvage what they can by convincing her father to do a civil suit. Maybe they tell him he's facing a conspiracy rap for Sally's murder; he goes along or else.

"You show up and things go to hell. Maybe they worried that Sally's father would talk if you pressured him. He's their ticket to the money so they can't take him out. That leaves you. Killing you takes care of the problem."

I didn't care. My head spun and I grabbed the side of the bed to keep from falling. "I feel like shit," I said.

"If I can get all that into the trial, it will establish reasonable doubt."

If she said anything else, I lost it in the vortex that sucked me into oblivion.

The soft green glow from the monitor illuminated a bandaged face in the dark room. The ephemeral figure moved in and out of reality. He was next to the tray table, then near the door, then beside the bed, his arm moving in a semi-circle as if he were blind. Metal in his right hand shimmered in the green light.

Afraid, I silently slid out of bed but the IV crashed to the floor. The muffled voice was chilling. "Is that you, Charboneau?" It was Earl. He couldn't see but that wasn't going to make any difference—the automatic in his hand held 17 rounds.

I ripped at the IV needle, pulling at the tape that tethered me to the metal stand. The tape wouldn't break.

Earl ran his hand over the covers and found the IV tube. "You at the end of this, Charboneau?" He was suddenly on the bed, holding the tube, yanking at my hand. His hand slipped along the tube until he touched me. Flat against the floor, I recoiled; the pain in my side paralyzed me. I could only watch as the barrel of the automatic appeared over the side of the bed. In the green light, his head appeared with a hole where his face should have been. Blindly, he pulled the tube taut, and placed the automatic alongside, aiming for my stomach.

The pain in my side intensified. The room was silent; the IV in place but my covers were pulled back. The huge man slid a knife into my side. "Don't do that," I bitched.

"Got to clean the wound, Mr. Charboneau." From the Bronx by his accent.

"With a fucking knife?" That was simply unreasonable.

The short, rotund, Filipino nurse woke me up the next morning. She handed me a hand-printed breakfast menu. I pointed at the IV drip. "No more liquid meals?"

"That's just an antibiotic, we're weaning you off the caviar, baby." She laughed at her joke. "We want you out of here. The place is lousy with reporters and flowers. You famous people are a real pain." That broke her up, and she was still laughing when she walked out of the room, holding the door open for Mom and my brother, Paul.

Paul leaned all six-foot-four over the bed and intoned, "I've seen better looking street people." Mom took a playful swing at him and leaned over and kissed my cheek. "I can see by your eyes that you're finally with the program."

"Can I see the bullet hole?" Paul asked. "I have never seen a bullet hole."

I shook my head in sorrow. "I was just thinking you're getting distinguished looking, then you ask to see the bullet hole. Talk about ruining an image."

"Distinguished," he scoffed. "Why don't you say it. I'm getting fat and bald."

Mom applauded. "This makes me feel so good. My boys bickering, just like the old days."

Their visit was agonizingly short. Mom and Paul had left the bed and breakfast in less than capable hands. Now that I was healing, they needed to get back. Mom pecked my six day growth of beard and said, "Don't try to come home to recuperate. I've told the reporters downstairs that you'll be there for the next few weeks. The publicity should be great for business."

"You're shameless," I said. "Did you really use your son's agony for tawdry publicity?"

She pointed a finger at me, squinted and said, "You betcha." She kissed me again. "Just don't get shot again. You don't get to die before me. You do and I'll kill you." They left after Paul squeezed my shoulder.

I tried walking later that morning. I'd lost the knack. It's really horrifying how fast your body quits. After the tiring 13 foot trip to the bathroom, I went back to bed and fell into a stupor. Intense pain woke me. A nurse gave me two pills that worked, sort of.

Near noon, the bedside phone rang. I watched it until it quit, then a nurse came in, picked it up, and handed me the receiver.

Toni said, "There's a lady in the lobby who tells me that you will torture and kill me if I don't let her see you. It sounds like bullshit to me, but she sounds so positive, I thought I'd better check."

I knew it was Deborah. I asked the nurse to call the lobby and tell them to show her the way. When she appeared in the doorway minutes later, I was too choked up to answer her easy smile and soft, "Hey."

She came over and put her face against mine. As always, her dark brown hair smelled of apricots. I felt her tears on my face. When she straightened, she had a tissue that she dabbed at her eyes. I patted the bed, so she sat beside my legs, one leg folded under the other so she could face me.

The thin white vertical stripes on her dark pantsuit were slimming, or she was thinner, but her face seemed unchanged: heavy eyebrows, eyes set wide apart, a ski-ramp nose, and high cheekbones on an oval face. The large dimple in her right cheek where a wood splinter had penetrated was like a saxophone riff in a guitar solo: out of place yet hauntingly beautiful.

She asked, "How are you?"

"If I'm dying, will you stay?"

In spite of her brimming eyes, she smiled. "That's not gonna work, Fuck-face."

"How are you?"

Her expression said she didn't know.

I asked her to tell me about her life. She was selling machine tools to companies, and the hassles were giving her confidence. "The first couple of times people yelled at me, I really wondered if I could do the job. As I got more knowledgeable, they stopped yelling. Then I learned how to be pushy, and I started making sales."

I asked about the machine tools, where she lived, how she lived, anything to keep her talking. She seemed to be content with her life, and busy. "Busy helps," she said almost sadly. "It makes the time pass and I'm too exhausted at the end of the day to stay awake worrying about the nightmares."

"Still every night?"

"You're in them sometimes."

No doubt telling her things would be fine.

I asked, "If I killed every abuser in the United States, would that make any difference to you?"

"You did what you could, I know that. I've moved on."

"I know, but I can't stop thinking that if I could kill them all, you would come back."

"You'd better get over that, Booger-butt."

I smiled for the joke before I asked, "How's your love life?"

She reacted badly, silently, then her face softened as she remembered that I don't get jealous. "I seldom date," she said in a sad voice. "Men are such slime." She looked surprised when I laughed. "It's true," she insisted. "Every married buyer I work with hits on me sooner or later; every one. Isn't anyone faithful? And why would they think I'm so desperate for a sale that I'd be their whore?"

"There's no one you see? I don't like to think of you alone."

"Alone is comfortable to me." She looked at me as if deciding something, then she said, "There is a guy I see when I'm in Chicago. He's funny and sweet; laid back like you. It won't get serious; he has major commitment problems, just like me."

She smiled and pointed at me. "Your turn."

I told her a blonde joke, trying to convince her it was a story about my latest love. She prodded for more, then wouldn't believe that I wasn't seeing anyone.

She was tired, I could see it in her eyes. I was tired, I kept drifting toward sleep. Finally, she called it a day.

I asked, "Can you come back tomorrow?"

"I have to be in Missoula early tomorrow; I've got a full week scheduled in Montana. I wouldn't have known you got shot if I hadn't been in a restaurant with a TV going. They said you were in very critical condition so I left everything in a rental car and hopped on the first flight out of Missoula last night."

"You could call me if you feel like it."

She leaned over and kissed me on the lips, a light touch that left me breathless. She looked at me with sad eyes as she said, "Ain't gonna happen for a while yet, Barf-breath."

I smiled to let her know that I'd live. She held my hand for a moment and then walked out the door.

As I drifted into sleep, I understood that she was well and almost content with her life, a vast difference from my vision of her cowering in dingy motels. Rather than being afraid of men, she had developed a healthy disrespect. She didn't need to be rescued, and I felt so much better.

Toni's screeching voice yanked me out of a pleasant place. "Hey, Charboneau, how long are you going to baby that scratch? You really expect us to keep paying you for lying around?"

Night, I guessed. No sounds from the corridor. Food was on a metal tray next to the bed, and it looked ghastly in the green glow from the monitor. I was weighing whether I was hungry enough to try eating the green stuff when Toni moved the chair, startling me. I'd forgotten she was there.

I grouched, "Not only is he going to pay me for laying around, I'm going to charge him for pain and suffering."

"Earl owns a mobile home free and clear. You want it? I'll sue him for you."

"No, thanks."

"This Deborah Morgan who came to see you? Is she the abused woman you told me about?"

"Yeah."

"So?" She waited. "Come on, Charboneau, is the love of your life back in the picture?"

"No, and she'll probably never be. She's in love with me, and, to her, that means letting me have control of her life. An abused woman only makes that mistake once."

To change the subject, I said, "You shouldn't wear make-up."

"Really?"

"Sorry. Can I blame that on the drugs?"

141

"I was hoping you meant it."

"I did."

She looked pleased. "You're getting horny, that's a good sign." She laughed, perhaps embarrassed. "Did you see the news last night?"

"I didn't see last night."

"You were featured, looking just like yourself sans the mustache." She seemed happy.

That hurt my feelings. "Shit, how did they do that?"

"The network had footage of you from some local talk show you did during the McBride thing." She grinned malevolently before she added, "They caught me leaving the hospital just after we talked and asked me about the case. I suggested that you might have been getting close to the people who framed Clay. A reporter caught Sylvia by surprise with that same question. Of course she had to say that she would investigate Glen and Earl's involvement."

"How is Earl?"

"On life support. They say he's brain dead."

I had a sudden feeling that I would pay dearly for playing God. Not prepared for the depression that sapped my energy, I opted for sleep.

I woke up early the next morning in pain. I looked at the IV, wondering if they had removed the drugs. I asked a nurse; they had removed the pain killer, so she got me pills. After an hour that lasted for years, the little blue pills finally dulled the knife twisting in my side. Then the huge guy came in and did his thing again, leaving a fire that burned with incredible pain.

Doctor Godfrey came into the room just as the pain was at its worst. Upset, I unloaded on him. The pinched faced, ascetic-looking man listened to me; set his glasses firmly on his nose and said, "The bullet was mangled as it went through the car's door, and it carried all sorts of trash into the wound. We can't let it heal until we're sure we've removed all the foreign matter. Let me put the pain in perspective: you could die if the wound gets infected."

That was a cheap shot if ever I heard one.

About four that afternoon, Toni came in. Her hair fell in loose curls. She'd limited the make-up to subtle eye shadow.

I said, "Very nice, definite movie star potential."

She looked very pleased. "You made the network news again. Did you see it?"

"Fuck! Sorry. Honest-to-God prime-time network?"

She nodded. "It didn't look like you, they used the 60 Minutes footage. They even explained the case against Clay. They showed me speculating that both men were trying to cover up their involvement in the original shooting." She smiled outrageously and added, "If I'd known how well this was going to turn out, I would have shot you myself."

She expected me to smile. When I didn't, she said, "Sylvia was very impressed with the flak the DA on the McBride case took. She has no intention of occupying that same hot seat during the next installment of the Gary Charboneau show. I think she'll drop the charges against Clay."

A nurse brought dinner and Toni made her excuses. I don't think she could stand to look at it. It tasted as bad as it looked, some low-salt, no-fat fanatic had destroyed perfectly good food. I tried to eat, then gave it up.

An hour later, Javier barged in without knocking. "Hey, how they hanging?" he boomed. He winced as he looked at the remains of dinner. "Jesus, is that mashed carrots?"

I nodded. "Something about low residue foods so I don't strain anything shitting bricks."

He looked genuinely sympathetic. "Man, you gonna be ready for tamales when they let you out of here." He surveyed me, critically I thought, before shaking his head. "Some people fall into shit and none of it sticks."

"Toni Conboy thinks I'm dogging it too."

He shook his head and then reset the glasses on his nose. "Not what I meant. Oeland's been telling the truth." He let that sink in before he said, "Last night, Alicia gave us the shooter." He handed me a mug shot of a Willie Elliott.

Willie Elliott's face bore little resemblance to the composite drawing from Oeland's description. Piles of curly hair encroached on three sides of his face. The jutting chin matched a forward swept brow. He had knobby cheekbones over sunken cheeks, as if he were missing molars. A Fu Manchu mustache hardened his face.

Strangely, I felt like crying. I had no idea why. Maybe I was desperate to justify the pain. Whatever the reason, I didn't trust my emotions. To keep from blubbering, I asked, "Alicia came back?"

"Nah, she called. She saw ABC's account about you being shot. She's scared silly that whoever put the hit on you might have a contract out on her, too. She knows Willie didn't set it up. According to her, he's so dumb he would pee in his shoe to hear his foot squish. She wants us to catch him and make him talk."

He pulled a chair from behind a cart and put it beside the bed. Once settled, he said, "We have Willie's warrant on the NCIC. Word on the street has him disappearing at about the time of the shooting."

"Any association with anyone at Microfix?"

He shook his head then settled the rimless glasses back on his nose with his index finger. "We'll check but I don't think so. Willie's a professional bottom-feeder, stands out like shit on white marble. He looks so scummy you'd lock the factory if you saw him in the parking lot. Whoever pulled Willie's strings is the connection to Microfix."

"How much did Alicia know?"

"She knew what Sally knew. Willie was Sally's candyman, but he'd stopped exchanging blow for blow, so she was getting desperate. Willie promised her a kilo if she would take a beating and then accuse Oeland of sexual assault. Alicia was going to back up her story, she was going to testify that Oeland had been to see Sally at the apartment, for a split of any civil settlement. Of course, Willie didn't tell her, or didn't know, that Sally would be dead."

"I wonder why they didn't use that plan. It would have wrecked the merger if that's what the purpose was, and no one would have assigned cops to investigate Oeland's story."

The metal chair scraped the floor as Javier sat back, lacing his fingers behind his head. "I never know how scumbags think. As far as I'm concerned, that's a good thing."

He sighed and sat forward as he said, "You realize that none of this does diddly for your client. Alicia isn't about to return, we don't know where she is, so what she told me is all hearsay. I'm positive it was her, she never could get my name right, she pronounced it 'Haver.'"

Talking to his hands, he continued, "I asked Alicia why Sally thought Willie could score an entire kilo. She said he brought one to the apartment, and let them sample it. That caps it for me, someone with a heavy drug connection was pulling the strings."

"Did Glen or Earl have that kind of connection?"

He leaned forward, scowling. "I don't know, but I do know they didn't set up the frame." He looked at me, then smoothed his mustache. "Glen told me he first met Earl three days after the shooting, and he proved it. Bigger than shit, they met in jail. Earl was in for a DUI; Glen was waiting to be arraigned on a pandering charge." He sat back and the chair made a noise like fingernails on a blackboard. "You see the problem?"

Earl had told the truth. "What are the odds they get arrested for different offenses and wind up sharing the same cell three days after they pull off a nearly perfect crime?"

He sat forward, causing the chair to groan. "It's not impossible but it's damn unlikely. Glen said they were just bullshitting, figuring Oeland was going to get off because he's got money. According to Glen, Earl came up with the idea of trying to get a cut of the civil suit."

"Then why the fuck did the assholes try to kill me?"

"You want to hear Glen's explanation?" Judging by his expression, he evidently thought it absurd. "When you scared Earl into admitting that he and Glen had set up the witnesses and the hookers, they thought you might go to the cops and have them arrested."

The stupidity gave me a headache. I do a B&E; point a gun at him when he catches me, then steal his gun, and he worries that I'll go to the cops? He was brain dead before I hit him with the brick.

Javier puffed out his cheeks as he exhaled, and changed the subject. "Long day. I got volunteered to tell some lady that her cherished offspring had been murdered. No fucking fun at all." He groaned and stood up, preparing to leave.

I said, "If Willie had Oeland's gun, it wouldn't take a rocket scientist to see the possibilities. You sure Willie couldn't have done that on his own?"

Javier was positive. "A couple of months before the killing, a clerk at a 7-11 called. He'd found a dime bag of weed in his parking lot. A plainclothes in an unmarked responds and spots Willie going through the dumpster. He holds up the bag and asks Willie if it's what he's looking for. Willie was ecstatic until the guy busted him." He grinned. "Made Willie famous." He pointed a beefy finger at me. "And don't forget that kilo. No way Willie would have been conscious if it was his."

Something in my side popped. I checked, wondering if the artery had blown out. No blood. Javier leaned forward and put a hand on my arm. "You want me to call the nurse?"

After I assured him, he continued, "Then there's the phone calls." He shook his head slowly. "It's too good a frame for Willie to pull off." He moved to the side of the bed. "At least we know drugs are the connection."

He pointed to the food. "Off the liquid diet?"

"Yeah, I think they want to free up the bed."

"Good," he nodded. "I'll get Ma to whip up another batch of tamales and we'll celebrate being on the same side now. Sound good?"

"Give me a couple of days to get an appetite back."

He nodded. "Just keep repeating, tamales, tamales. It'll come."

Javier visited late the next morning, dressed in a brown business suit, white shirt and brown tie. He blocked most of the sunlight when he stood on the window side of the bed. I touched his suit jacket. "What's the occasion?"

"Been interviewing people at Microfix, trying to find any connection to the players." He sat in the chair and carefully pulled up the knees of his pants. "I'm also supposed to get your statement." He took out a notebook and balanced it on his knee. "Do you remember the shooting?"

I gave him the long version, trying to remember all the important details. When I mentioned that Earl's gun sounded weak, Javier said they had recovered a light, stubby .22 revolver. That explained why he missed. If I hadn't thrown Earl's gun in the dumpster, he probably would have hit me with the Glock. Of course, if I hadn't screwed with Earl, they might not have tried to kill me.

I concluded the story by saying, "As I was passing out, I saw this brilliant light. I thought it was that tunnel you're supposed to see when you're dying."

"Air One thought they were a block away from the scene. They didn't have any speed up when the searchlight spotted Hubbard." Javier laughed in disgust. "Talk about your brain surgeon, Hubbard said he was only trying to shoot the light out. All the judge heard was him admitting to shooting at the helicopter. Now he's eligible for major federal time."

"Couldn't happen to a nicer guy." I hoped the fucking animal rotted in some cage. "Does the DA intend to drop the charges against Oeland?"

A cloud passed over his face. He slid his notebook into an inside jacket pocket. "She's not buying Willie as the shooter. His warrant is for a material witness."

"Does it stay on the NCIC?"

"Yeah, she's run it national; she's covered her ass."

"On another subject?" he began. "Since you're ri—, uh, famous, the regulars from our Tuesday night poker game want to meet you. If you feel up to it, how about we hold the game at your place this Tuesday?"

I nodded. "When I get a place, I'll call you. Will Rita supply some tamales?"

"I'll tell her you're at death's door, and it's your dying request." He

146

laughed, waved good-bye, and left.

As the door closed, I wondered if he was using the poker game to protect me. Was there some danger I didn't see?

That night, Toni came in a few minutes after visiting hours were over. Her hair hung loose. She was wearing a purple dress with matching eye shadow and blush. She had overdone it, but not by much.

"Well?" she asked.

"You look beautiful."

She blushed and muttered, "Asshole. I was asking when you're going to get out of here."

That made me laugh and I hurt myself. When I could talk again, I said, "You don't do compliments well."

"I'm going out on a date. I took your advice and tried for the just-out-of-bed look. Thanks to you, I feel like a slut."

"You look like a gorgeous slut."

She waved that away as if it annoyed her. "By the way, I told the hospital administrator to share the flowers with all the rooms. That okay?"

"That's great. Thank you."

"All kinds of local and national politicians, news anchors, famous lawyers, and a few publications want to talk with you. I've had you under a no-visitors-without-my-okay policy, but you can decide for yourself now."

"I'd be very grateful if you'd stay in charge."

She looked pleased. "Sure." She saw her image in the window. She turned toward me, wincing in agony. "Are you sure this look is what I want?"

I laughed. "You'll hold his attention. Is that what you want?"

"Who knows?" She watched the heart monitor for a few seconds, then asked, "When are they going to release you?"

"Tomorrow if I can find some clothes. According to the nurse, everything I had on was muddy, bloody, and they cut them off. Could you get someone to go by the motel and pick me up something to wear?" I pointed to the night stand. "The key's in the drawer."

She rummaged through the drawer until she found the key. "I'll do it. By the way, the cops released your car. I had it towed to the rental agency; they were thrilled by all the bullet holes. They're thinking of using it in an ad."

"You got all my stuff?"

She patted my arm. "I hired an electrician to remove the computers and radios. He got it all, don't worry." She suddenly seemed awkward. "I have a spare bedroom. Would you like to stay at my place until you're better?"

Her expression changed to relief when I turned her down.

"Suit yourself," she said, "I'll bring you clothes tomorrow morning on my way to work." She made a motion to leave, then she leaned over the bed and kissed my cheek. It surprised both of us.

CHAPTER EIGHTEEN

The white count was high so Doctor Godfrey delayed my release for a day. It was just as well, Toni had to fight her way into my motel room. She was annoyed as she described the scene, finally concluding, "It's those reality shows, the producers want to pay you big bucks to reenact the shooting. You want to be a movie star?"

The publicity was very depressing, I couldn't manage enough humor to kid her about bringing black shoes to go with brown pants. Publicity is great for getting jobs, but I needed anonymity to do the work. The mustache was filling in nicely, and that would be enough if I avoided the cameras.

Toni said, "I paid the manager of the motel to box your stuff after the hordes dissipate. I'll collect it tonight and rent another place."

When the huge guy came in to irrigate the wound, Toni left hurriedly, something in my face, I guessed. As he set up the irrigator and then arranged the towels and a drip pan underneath the wound, he kept up a running banter.

I hated him with every fiber of my being; his attempts at friendly humor pissed me off. Don't fucking try to make me feel better, do what you have to do and get the fuck out of my face. The pain began before he touched me.

Doctor Godfrey came in just after the session. I went ballistic on him. "I can't fucking believe that anything that hurts that badly is doing the wound any good. It feels like the son-of-a-bitch is being ripped open."

The anger was counter-productive. He decided to take the bandages off and look. His technique was shitty, he pulled out half the hair starting to grow back on my belly. He looked into the hole with an ear scope before he said, "Okay, we can stop. Go to the outpatient clinic once a day for five more days. They'll do a wash procedure that won't involve any discomfort." I wanted to use pliers on him, give him a taste of discomfort.

149

At ten the next morning, Toni picked me up at the kitchen entrance to the hospital. The Sunday traffic was very light, and the motel room she'd reserved was only a half-mile away. "I stayed close since you have to go back once a day."

As she pulled up in front of the place, she said, "I put your clothes away. Nice selection of colored underwear."

She couldn't embarrass me; an experienced hospital staff had systematically shredded my dignity. "Just pick out your favorite, I'll wear them when we get something going."

"In your dreams."

I managed to hobble the thirty feet from the car to the ground floor room. I'd let her select my motel any time, the room felt new. The bedroom with a queen size bed was in the back, away from the parking lot. The kitchen had a small refrigerator, stove, oven, dishwasher and utensils. The breakfast bar that hid the kitchen from the living area had three high wooden stools.

Toni left to buy lunch. Feeling suddenly vulnerable, I unpacked the briefcase, put the clip in the 9mm, and put it on the coffee table within easy reach. When she returned with a pizza and a six-pack of beer, her eyes widened and then studiously ignored the gun. We sat on the couch and shared. After two pieces of pizza and one beer, I sat back and groaned, in real pain from the bowling ball inside my stomach.

Sitting beside me, Toni had her feet up on the coffee table while she licked her fingertips. With her hair frizzed and the make-up absent, she looked good enough to eat. The silky pastel blouse would open, the black skirt would slide to the floor, I would take her slowly.

She asked, "Is it safe to play with the gun?" She picked it up by the slide as if it were contaminated. I took it from her, ejected the clip, opened the slide and looked down the barrel. Satisfied that it was empty, I handed it back to her. "The thing under the barrel is a laser." I switched it on so she could see the size of the beam.

"Wherever it shines is where the bullet hits?"

"If you don't yank the trigger and you're within range."

"How far will it shoot?" She put the laser beam on a lamp.

I showed her the top of the reversible clip. "With these, 50 feet." I turned the clip so that the steel-jacketed bullets were facing forward. "With these, about 100 yards."

She took the clip and looked at the aluminum bullets. "These look weird.

150

Are they plastic?"

"No, they're oxidized aluminum, designed to open as they come out of the barrel. Fifteen feet out, they're the size of a quarter and they won't penetrate. At 100 feet, they're going so slow that glass can stop them," I concluded. "I don't want to kill any innocent bystanders if I miss."

"And if you shoot someone only a few feet away?"

"My guess is that they would make very nasty wounds."

She flicked the trigger. "Why does it have this little trigger in the middle of the regular trigger?"

"So it won't go off accidentally. You have to squeeze the trigger before the gun will fire." I pointed to the other safety. "You have to be pressing this in at the same time or it won't fire."

"Really?" She tried to depress the tiny button with the gun held normally. Her thumb just reached. "That's awkward. Why put it there?"

"Most people are shot with their own guns. The idea is to hide the safety so that isn't likely to happen."

"How clever." She smiled. "And you showed me. I'm flattered by your trust." I waved the clip at her so she added, "Okay, so I'm not flattered."

She put the gun down and took another piece of pizza from the box. While she lined it up with her mouth, she asked, "What do you do now?"

"Make a pass at you?" I suggested. She frowned as she bit into the pizza. "Okay, wrong answer. What's the right answer?"

When she finished chewing, she said, "Prove that Sally's father wanted his daughter killed."

It was my turn to frown. "What's his motive? He's dirt poor, so blackmail's out. If she did threaten to tell just to get even, I don't think he would care. At the moment, he's living with an Asian girl who is probably underage."

She dismissed my arguments with a wave of her hand. "You didn't have Willie's picture. Maybe someone has seen them together."

"Fax Willie's picture to the Sheriff in Linda Vista. If Willie was there, he'll know." I laughed at her cranky expression. "All right, wait a day and I'll fax Willie's picture."

She didn't like my laughing. "If you don't want to do the job any longer, I'll understand." There was no trace of understanding in her voice.

The hospital stay had evidently reduced my tolerance to nothing. "You want to tell me how to do the job, you do it."

She grabbed her purse and bolted for the door. The door slamming threatened to take out the front window.

I slept for a while, waking up abruptly as something in my side popped. I went into the bathroom so I could look at the bandage on my back in the mirror. Only a small spot of blood was visible.

I tried booting the laptop, but its battery was dead. As I connected the charger, I wondered if I started bleeding, would I pass out before I could call anyone? I decided I'd go out on the sidewalk in front if I started bleeding, and use the cellular out there. Hopefully someone would notice before I bled to death.

Desperate for a friendly face, I looked up Gina Rawlins' phone number. As she'd said when we met at Microfix, she was in the book. I would tell her that I wanted to talk about her boss and boyfriend, Raul Valazquez. If drugs were the reason for the frame, they were probably coming in through his department. That would be my official excuse. On the fourth ring, she answered with a cheery, "Hi."

"Gina, this is Gary Charboneau. Do you remember me?"

"Oh, Gary, I was so scared. I thought you were...the way they talked on TV...it was very scary. How are you?"

To put her at ease, I asked about her and her work, but she interrupted to ask if I was still in the hospital.

"I'm in a motel about a half mile from the hospital. That's why I called. It's my first time alone in several days and the walls are getting to me. I thought maybe if you were free, you could come over for pizza and beer tonight." When she didn't respond, I added, "I'm not looking for anything heavy, I just need to see a friendly face."

"Do you have a kitchen?"

"Yes, but you wouldn't want me to cook for you."

She laughed. "I like to cook. Don't order anything, I'll bring the food. About 5:30?"

Afraid I'd screw up the successful sales pitch, I gave her directions and tried to hang up. She asked, "Gary, are you all right? Do you need me to come over now?"

Her kindness touched me. "Thank you for offering. I'll be fine."

"Really?" she asked seriously. "Well...okay, I'll see you around 5:30."

While I was thinking about Gina, I thought about Karen Grady, wondering how she was recovering from her broken jaw. To my surprise, the gut-wrenching need to kill her husband was gone. I hated him, but it seemed an abstract notion, as if he were dead. Maybe I had been trying to rescue Deborah.

I still wanted to fix Karen Grady's problem. I had a plan for fucking with

Aaron's head: a fair amount of pain, a lot of waiting to die, and a death sentence commuted at the last moment by sheer accident. I'd used it before, and it worked well, even on experienced scumbags.

Using the cellular, I called Aaron's number. The woman who answered obviously had her jaw wired, she was just barely intelligible. After I suggested that I was from the Santa Clara County District Attorney's office, she told me that Aaron had disappeared, taking all of his clothes and all of their money. She seemed very happy about that.

After I disconnected, I wondered why Aaron disappeared just after I made an appointment to see him. Some government agency asking to inspect his home shouldn't have raised any alarms in a man who had just been released from jail. Maybe my call had only been coincidental, catching him on the way out the door.

At four, moving slowly and trying to keep water away from the bandages, I washed and shaved. When Gina knocked a little after five, I looked presentable.

I opened the door; she walked in carrying two bags of groceries. We were having corn bread and stew she told me as she unloaded the bags. I could reheat it for a nourishing meal for as long as it lasted. "It'll take at least two hours, but the corn bread will be done in twenty minutes. You can eat that if you're hungry." She had bought a cold box of California wine. "For medicinal purposes," she said.

I sat on a stool on the living room side of the breakfast bar and watched her while she worked. Tall and full figured, her face contained a mixture of Italian softness and sharp Nordic features. Two swirls of black hair fell easily on her forehead, contrasting with the pale skin of her oval face. The red of the plain blouse enhanced her skin tone. Red barrettes held her hair behind her ears where red plastic triangles dangled from pearl colored posts. She wore medium heel pumps and black slacks.

When she asked about the shooting, I gave her the long version, trying to be factual. I told her about pantomiming a gun, and the volley Glen let loose from behind the concrete stanchion. She had seen a picture of the car on the news. Glen had hit it eight times, turning it into a total loss. She told me Glen had also destroyed the engine in the helicopter, although they managed to fly it back to the airport. No wonder the judge was pissed, Glen had ruined government equipment.

When the stew was simmering and the corn bread was in the oven, she drew two glasses of wine and handed one to me. Box or no, it was very good.

She leaned on the counter and moved into my space, our faces inches apart. She said, "You're beautiful."

"That's just what I was thinking. Were you reading my mind?"

"I was making a pass at you," she said. Without giving me time to accept, she explained that I needed good food and a sound immune system to heal. Speaking softly, she explained that the immune system could be weakened by stress, and that I needed physical activity to combat stress. I loved her conclusion, delivered with a serious expression. "One of the best ways to reduce stress is sex."

I was grinning like a fool. She saw an insult. "You're laughing at me."

"No, I'm not," I replied seriously. "I'm overwhelmed that you want to make love with me, but why would you think you had to talk me into it?"

She flashed a fleeting smile, and let go of my hand so that she could tug at the collar of her blouse. "I don't know if you feel well enough. Do you?"

"God, yes."

She looked pleased. "Good. When the cornbread is out, we'll do that." She took a sip of wine before she asked, "Are you married?"

"Divorced. I was married for a couple of years. We bored each other silly." That wasn't enough for her. "The divorce was very civil; very polite, no hard feelings." I turned Gina's left hand over. None of the three rings looked like anything a man would buy. "How about you?" I asked.

She nodded and grimaced, explaining with an expression that she wondered how she could have ever been that foolish. The eloquence charmed me. She looked pleased that I'd understood. "Alan. He's a salesman. He did me a big favor when he married me." She mimicked royalty looking contemptuously amused by a commoner. "He's good looking and very polished. Suave, debonair: all those words apply to Alan. He trained me to be a woman he'd be proud to be seen with. I learned to keep my mouth shut and wear plunging necklines."

She'd played it for laughs but the pain was very close to the surface. I leaned over the counter and kissed her cheek, saying, "I'm sorry men are such shits."

She blushed. "It wasn't a total loss. I didn't have a lot of self-confidence when I met him. He gave me that." She almost smiled before she added, "Well, he didn't exactly give me that, I paid for it. He didn't make much, but he spent my money and his to impress people. He drove a Mercedes home to our dark house after PG&E shut off the power."

She turned to peer into the oven. Satisfied with the corn bread's progress, she returned to the counter. She drank some wine and then continued, "He never understood why he couldn't get credit." She sighed. "No one understood him. All those unpaid bills were part of the past, he was trustworthy. As if he was a brand new guy every morning and the rest of the world should have known that." She seemed almost sad when she added, "All the macho posturing didn't convince him that he was brave."

She focused on my face. "Have any kids?"

"No. You?"

"Alan wanted kids." Her face became a montage that included a mischievous grin below innocent, wide-open eyes, and she still somehow managed a sad look. It was an Oscar performance in one expression.

I laughed. "Alan didn't think you could have kids?" When she nodded, I asked, "You didn't want any?"

She rolled her eyes. "Why would anyone? For eight years, you have to deal with someone only slightly more intelligent than a dog. For the next ten years, you have to put up with some smart-ass jerk. Why would anyone choose that?"

She tasted her wine. She put the glass down carefully. "I can still have kids, I didn't get my tubes tied. I just hope Mr. Right doesn't want any. I don't think that I'd be any kind of a mother."

"You seem like a kind and gentle person. I would guess that people with your personality would make lousy parents."

She laughed and still managed to look insulted.

"I'm serious," I said. "Kind people don't like to argue. Kids test their parents constantly. If you aren't willing to fight, you lose, and the kid grows up spoiled."

She seemed pleased. "That explains why my mom had such polite children. She's a real witch."

The timer buzzed. Inside the oven, she poked the cornbread with a knife. Satisfied, she took a dishtowel and put the cornbread pan on top of the stove. She focused on my face, looking almost hungry, then walked around the counter and took my arm, pulling me toward the bedroom.

She was an efficient lover, and it was over far sooner than I wanted even though I'd used every available distraction to hold the moment. Perspiring, she wearily lay by my side as she complained, "It's those damn condoms."

I smoothed her hair away from her face as an excuse to touch her again. "I tried to make it last; you are incredibly beautiful."

She snuggled in and put her head on my shoulder, my arm under her neck. I was absently stroking her back when I felt her fall asleep.

I must have joined her. As she moved to get up, my head came back from a sun-splashed meadow. I held her hand as she stood up, forcing her to turn toward me. "Just wanted a last look." She seemed embarrassed so I let go of her hand, but she dressed without turning away. "Can you stay the night?" I asked.

She looked apologetic. "I don't sleep well with another person." She adopted a motherly look. "Now, come on; get out of bed, dinner's ready."

When we were seated at the bar, eating, I complimented her for the delicious stew, adding, "I don't know how to thank you for this, and the lovemaking."

She looked as if I'd said exactly the right thing. "You can thank Alan for the lovemaking, he taught me well."

"Why did you break up?"

Her expression contained sadness and satisfaction. "I was tired of being his mother, so when his girlfriend called and asked me to divorce him..." Her smile looked wistful.

A silence developed as we ate. Searching for a subject to keep her talking, I settled on Raul Valazquez, her boss and lover. "Do you cook for Raul?"

"I burned the only two meals I've ever served him. He doesn't ask anymore." She pantomimed a helpless look.

I grinned at the duplicity.

She said, "He eats with his mouth open, it's not very appetizing."

"Do you like him?"

She cocked her head to one side as she buttered a square of cornbread. "It's just a thing, it's not like we're long term." She examined the cornbread. "I see him twice a week, but we don't have a lot in common."

Something telegraphed my confusion. She scratched the side of her head with her pinky finger before she continued, "He does things for me. Like he makes sure I have a good job and I get my raises regularly."

When she finished chewing a bite of cornbread, she continued, "He's old fashioned in a lot of ways. He thinks I'm a kept woman." I couldn't think of a thing to say, and she filled in the pause. "It works for both of us. I don't have to do the bar scene. He's married so I don't worry that he might pick up AIDS." Her facial expression implied that it was perfectly logical. "He's paying my tuition to become a x-ray technician." Doubt and confusion battled on her face. "I sound like a whore, don't I?"

"No, you sound like you don't see sex as any big deal."

She looked sideways at me, a potential smile playing with her mouth. "You think that's wrong?"

"I don't make judgments for other people. If it works for you, that's great."

"It does," she said. "Until Mr. Right comes along, Raul keeps me from climbing the walls."

She wanted the feel of fame. Since my recognition was so low, I didn't have much to share. I talked about being an investigator, ending with the discovery of Earl's witnesses. I told her my theory about the blackmail that Clay ruined when he took Sally to the hospital.

She seemed pleased. "Good, I was afraid Raul might have been involved. He has an awful lot of money; I don't think everything he does is legal."

"I asked about his extra money. According to Oeland's secretary, Raul's wife is a successful interior decorator."

She smiled. I couldn't explain how, but her smile communicated that I wasn't much of a detective if I believed that story.

"I took her word for it," I explained. "Do you know it isn't true?"

She puffed up her chest, lowered her chin and in a deep voice, she said, "Effen bitch lays around the house all day watchin' those effen soaps. Place looks like an effen pigsty. She's gettin' fat as a effen pig, I don't even want to eff her anymore." She smiled and added, "Unquote."

"Doesn't sound like a busy decorator," I agreed. If Raul's wife didn't make the money that she reported, the business was being used to launder income.

Gina picked up my bowl, intending to do the dishes. "That's my job," I told her. "Sit here and keep me company." After I filled her wine glass, I took the plates and bowls into the kitchen and rinsed them.

When I turned toward her, I asked, "Why did you think Raul might have been involved? Was it just the money?"

She drank some wine, and then carefully placed the glass on the bar before she said, "No, it wasn't the money at all. Raul was very, very upset after the girl was shot, and that really surprised me."

She responded to my confusion. "Sometimes, Raul calls me 'Snatch' or 'Cunt,' trying to be funny. He doesn't understand why I get upset. He really doesn't understand. I don't think he can see anyone else's viewpoint."

Not following her, I walked over to the bar and put my hand on her arm. "What does that have to do with the girl being shot?"

She emphasized the message by stressing her voice. "If he was upset over the girl being shot, then he must have been involved."

"He said he was upset about the merger falling through."
Again, her smile criticized me for being gullible.
I asked, "He was lying?"
"Through his teeth."

CHAPTER NINETEEN

I vaulted over the railing, and I seemed to be falling forever, watching the stairs approach as if I were in a parachute. When my feet gently touched, I ran toward the parking lot.

On my knees behind the car, I heard the shattered wood on my room door screech as it opened, then a dark figure filled the opening. He searched for me, nervous and unsure, ducking back into the room when a bullet whizzed by my face. Then I heard the hollow pop of a small caliber gun off to my left. I went flat on the ground just before the next bullet dug into the bumper above my head. It ricocheted away with a flutter.

On knees and elbows, I scrambled into the gap between cars. The large man on the second floor walkway aimed his gun, then ducked behind a concrete stanchion without shooting. The gun edged around the corner, and my car's windshield exploded. Glass twinkled like stars as the eruption rose and fell back, sounding like rain on the asphalt. Sparks cascaded from the car door just above my head. The car bounced, the rocker panel gently nudging my arm. I reached underneath the car, wanting to pull the car over me. How silly, I couldn't do that. Then I saw the gun barrel spark, and my ear went numb. I pulled the car over me but it made no difference, blood splashed everywhere as a hot spear penetrated my side. Dust boiled around me and a vice held my head.

Earl Mitchell knelt beside me, a dark hole where his face should have been. He felt for my face, then he held the gun over my eye. I could see his finger tightening on the trigger.

I woke halfway out of bed, my feet tangled in the sheets, my hands on the floor pulling at the carpet, the wound feeling like fire. I hurried to the bathroom mirror, expecting to see blood soaking the bandages, but both were clean. I sat on the bathroom floor, leaning against the tub, the cool metal drawing the heat from my back.

I listened to the swishing of cars on the boulevard, trying not to hear the pulse pounding in my ears. If my heart stopped, I didn't want to know, I would welcome the sudden darkness. I had had enough, fuck it all, I was ready to die.

Despite my resignation, life went on. In the mirror I could see sunlight coloring the drapes with a yellow glow. I hauled my petulant ass off the floor, and washed my hair and face. By the time I shaved and finished dressing, Gina had displaced the nightmare; the interlude seemed more dream than reality.

While I ate breakfast at a nearby coffee shop, I called a cab on the cellular. I finished the meal and I was waiting on the curb when the cab arrived. The tough looking redhead, probably in her late fifties, took me to the nearly empty airport. Inside the terminal, the third agency I tried had a Dodge Neon.

I drove back to the motel, planning to install all the high-tech gear. Gluing the UHF antenna to the windshield exhausted me; installing the radio, antenna, laptop, printer, and the tape machine would have to wait.

Inside the room, I called the Sheriff in Linda Vista. I didn't need his fax number, he had Willie's picture from the NCIC bulletin. He said he'd show Will Krestas the picture.

At eleven, with my heart in my mouth, I went to the outpatient clinic. Despite my fear, the new irrigation was a breeze. The technician was concerned. "The hole will be closed by tomorrow, I'd better call your doctor."

I waited for an hour and a half, certain that the pinched-faced fucker was going to insist on ripping the wound open again. When he did look at it, he wrinkled his lips, slid a piece of tubing into the wound and cut it off just outside the hole. "We may have to remove that in a few days," he warned. After all the pain, he warned me about removing a tube? What the hell did that mean?

Exhausted, I returned to the motel and slept until someone knocked on the door around two. Pat Oeland was dressed in black Levi's and a sleeveless top, a small purse tucked underneath her arm.

Her concerned look felt motherly. "Do I look that bad?" I asked as I stood aside to invite her in.

Her smile fled as fast as it appeared. She moved far enough into the room so that I could shut the door. "You've lost some weight."

"Hell of a diet, I don't recommend it."

She, too, had lost weight since that day in the park. She looked ill, anorexic, her black sleeveless top draped from bony shoulders, her arms skeletal. The black Levi's draped from her waist.

Her body language was uncertain, awkward. "Clay heard you were out of the hospital. He asked me to see if there's anything you need."

While I moved all the electronic gear off the couch so she could sit down, I talked her into trying the wine. She went into the kitchen to serve herself. When she saw the box in the refrigerator, she opted for one of Toni's beers. As she opened the bottle, she said, "You don't have any staples. Let me go grocery shopping for you. Make a list."

I was touched, God bless women. I found a pen and paper and sat across from her in the stuffed chair. While I wrote, I asked her to thank Clay for flying my mother and Paul down from Washington. Pat had hosted them; we talked about the bed and breakfast in La Conner, and about the flower deluge at the hospital. As the conversation lagged, I could sense her sadness. "Is there something I can do for you?" I asked.

She focused on my face. "I'm sorry. Clay and I wanted to thank you for believing in him." She shrugged. "Words aren't adequate to tell you the relief we felt about the outcome of the case."

"I'm not following you; is it settled?"

"You know the charges have been dropped?" When I shook my head, she added, "Oh yes, the District Attorney dropped all the charges against Clay. She issued a murder warrant for this Willie Elliott."

"That's great." Why did she look so sad?

"I feel as if I have my life back." She didn't try to hide the bitterness.

My curiosity erupted. "You don't seem happy."

She crossed one leg over the other, frowning. "Now that Clay's been exonerated, I'm visible again. Clay noticed that I've lost weight. My daughter called, she's coming to visit. Three of my friends, who have been too busy to chat, called this morning to do just that."

She uncrossed her legs and leaned forward, putting her elbows on her knees. She rolled the bottle between her hands and talked to it. "It's a shock when you find yourself alone. After Charlie stopped seeing me, I became invisible. I've heard of that happening to older women who are alone." She looked at me. "It's a shattering experience: being invisible. Nothing my friends or family say will ever erase that feeling, that they once sentenced me to invisibility."

I thought of all the bromides that come so naturally, but this was a smart lady, she needed the truth. I said, "I've been with suddenly rehabilitated people a few times. They try to 'forgive and forget' but it works out to 'forgive and remember.'"

She focused on my eyes. "What did they do?"

"They got divorces and new friends."

She didn't like the answer, and her eyes brimmed. She put the bottle on the table and went into her purse for a tissue.

Needing to change the subject, I asked, "Did you ever use Raul Valazquez' wife for a decorator?"

She shook her head, dabbing at her tears with a tissue.

"Not something you can do, since Raul works for Clay?"

"That wouldn't be an issue," she said. "Clay thinks very highly of him."

"How about you? What do you think of Raul?"

She put the tissue in her purse, folding it carefully first. When she finished that task, she picked up the bottle. After she took a sip, she asked, "So, finished your list?"

I remembered the look that passed between her and Clay in their bedroom. At the time I felt that she suspected who might have stolen the gun. Since she didn't want to talk about Raul, he seemed a logical guess. "You know that Raul took Clay's gun, don't you?"

Again, she looked guilty, as if I had discovered some shameful secret, but she acted nonchalant as she shrugged. "During our Christmas party, he asked if he could use our bedroom to lie down. He said he had a headache. I went to check on him but the bedroom door was locked. When he opened the door, the bed wasn't mussed and my closet door was shut." She held out her right hand, obviously wanting me to look at her fingernails. "The mirrored closet doors are heavy, so I keep mine open a crack. That way, I can use my hand to open it. It isn't a small thing with me, I broke a dozen nails on that door, so I know Raul closed it."

Her momentary smile looked painful, and she waved her hand in a brushing motion. "Ignore that, Clay would be furious if he knew I said it. It's my bitchy side coming out."

I waited, wanting her to keep talking about Raul. She let me wait, watching the bottle she rolled between her hands. Finally, she said, "I detest Raul; he is sleaze. During one party at our house, he made a pass at me that was very physical, so I'm not impartial. But I believe that if one of Clay's managers set this thing up, it was Raul."

Biased or not, two women sharing the same suspicion was a blinking neon arrow.

Pat seemed to have recovered her usual cool demeanor, but her voice trembled when she asked, "Do you think the man who shot you will talk? He must know who stole the gun."

"Glen Hubbard? The police don't think he was involved in the frame." For some strange reason, she looked relieved. I continued, "Sally's missing roommate, Alicia, called and identified the shooter. That's why the police believe Clay is innocent. We still don't know who framed him, or why."

She caught the qualifier. "The police believe Clay is innocent. Does the District Attorney?"

"My experience is that the DA will refile once the media lose interest. She has enough to win the case, truth be damned."

Pat looked shocked; she closed her eyes, perhaps seeing herself as invisible again. Then she smiled, put the half full bottle on the coffee table and said, "Thanks." She got up and I walked with her to the door. She examined my grocery list, asked what brand of peanut butter I liked, and left, promising to return within an hour.

With my hand still holding the doorknob on the closed door, I realized that the case had broken. I counted the reasons on my fingers. "Raul stole the gun; he has a lot of money that his wife's business launders; he is responsible for trucks bringing parts from Mexico as long as he doesn't lose his job in the merger, and from what both Pat and Gina have experienced, the guy is a scumbag."

All I had to do was set him up. Once the police caught him with drugs, they would squeeze him between spending years in jail or giving up the mastermind. When he talked, all the players would be known.

The drugs had to be on those trucks from Mexico; Gina had to have seen something, even if she didn't realize what he was doing. I called her and asked if she'd like to help me finish the stew and cornbread. She said, "I'd like that. Is five all right?"

I tried to keep the slobber out of my voice while we went through the ritual of disconnecting. Afterwards, I knew things were going too well because my Catholic upbringing conjured up an assassin on the sidewalk outside, in the footsteps that paused at my door.

I moved to the window and looked through a part in the drape. Whoever had paused was gone. Maybe the bad guys were feeling the heat. If they were, they wanted me dead.

I took the 9mm out of its case, inserted the clip so that the aluminum bullets would load, and racked the slide to chamber the first round. The gun fit in a kitchen drawer under the pass-through. The bar would provide good cover if the bad guys came crashing through the door.

I had just walked back into the living room when someone knocked. Moving faster than the wound liked, I got the gun and moved to look out the drape. It was Pat Oeland, both arms loaded with groceries. I opened the door, holding the gun in my left hand. She looked startled when she saw it, so I said, "Paranoid."

She accepted that with a head nod. Despite my protests, she put all the groceries away in the kitchen, moving with an easy athleticism that belied her frail appearance. When she finished the job, she asked, "Do you need someone to stay with you? A nurse?"

"I'll be fine," I assured her. "Thanks for shopping."

Despite her doubtful look, she nodded and left.

At five, I was still buttoning a fresh shirt when Gina knocked. She wrapped me in warm arms, and bestowed a kiss that set my rehabilitation back a few days. The full body hug said, "Take me to your bed."

"You want to use my body again, you animal?"

She grinned. "You up for that?"

"Not yet, but give me a second."

She tenderly patted my face. "Good boy." Dumping her purse on the pass-through, she went into the kitchen. She put the casserole dish containing the stew into the oven and turned it on. Then she drew two glasses of wine from the refrigerator. She started toward the bedroom carrying both glasses, pausing to flash a "what are you waiting for" look.

The lovemaking reminded me of why casual sex is such a bummer. She was there, yet she wasn't. I was welcome to her body, but not her. She enjoyed my body, but she didn't need me. Like a warm and caring nurse, her ministrations were all I could wish for, but I missed the passion.

Which is not to say that I didn't enjoy myself, I did. After she drove me over the edge, I was embarrassed by the noise I'd made. I sighed and said, "Damn, I almost came."

She giggled, then broke into laughter. She fell on the bed beside me and laughed helplessly. Her laughter was infectious. I'm sure we looked like fools, lying naked, side by side, laughing.

The pain from the wound got too intense and I had to sit up. She joined me, leaning back against the headboard. She handed me the wine and we were silent for a time before she said, "Thank you for that. You're in pain and you still made me come three times."

I kissed her hand, then I leaned as far as the wound would allow and kissed her cheek. "You give so much of yourself that I can't help admiring you."

She looked as though she might cry, but she said, "Come on, enough playing, we have to feed you." Indeed, the odor of the warming stew had me salivating. I tried to talk her into eating nude, but she told me that could only lead to indigestion. Hers or mine, she didn't say.

In the kitchen, after she nuked the cornbread in the microwave, she filled two bowls with stew. We ate side by side at the bar, the stew better than before. She explained that it needed some time for all the spices to release their full flavor.

She wanted to know how I was sleeping. I related the nightmare play by play, talking about the fear that remained after I woke. Telling the story invoked the same reaction. The fear seemed to prickle my skin in waves. She saw it; she put an arm around my shoulders as if to reassure me that all was well.

She talked about her brother who had died in a car accident the previous year. A gentle and funny man, she felt half her world had died with him. "If there is a Mr. Right, he'll be just like my brother," she concluded.

It seemed like an opening to talk about Raul. "What do you like about Raul?"

She knew exactly what she liked about him. "I'm in control. I haven't been able to control much in my life, especially when it comes to men. With him, I'm in control and I like that." She dunked a square of cornbread in her stew, maybe to keep from looking at me when she said, "I've been thinking about what I said yesterday about Raul being involved in the shooting." She popped the cornbread into her mouth before any of the sauce could escape. After she swallowed, she said, "I don't just think he's involved, I know he's involved."

She had a problem believing that; she shook her head, looking into the kitchen. "He's such a wuss, I can't believe he could have anything to do with a murder." She turned toward me, looking perplexed. "But there isn't any other explanation."

I kept my voice soft, just talking between friends, no big deal. "How did he convince you that he was involved?"

She took the cornbread square that I offered. While she sliced it in half, she said, "When you got shot, Raul was scared. When they released the names of the two men who shot you, he was happy." She put a square of butter on the cornbread as she continued, "When the paper had the picture of the guy who shot the girl, he was scared." She looked frustrated as she concluded, "I know that isn't proof."

I put my hand on her shoulder to let her know I wasn't challenging her. "Yesterday you said he had no empathy; is that what makes it proof for you?"

She shook her head. "More than that, I think he's incapable of empathy."

"Self-centered," I suggested.

"No," she said vehemently. "That's something a person is. Raul has a defect. He can't know what another person is feeling." She ate a piece of the stew-soaked cornbread, giving me time to absorb the idea before she added, "Alan was the same way." Her body language said she wished she had kept her mouth shut. "Maybe it is being self-centered."

"I'm sorry for being so dense, I finally get what you've been saying. If he's emotional about something, it can only be because it affects him."

She looked relieved. "Exactly."

"Do you recall anything unusual on the day of the murder?"

"He was weird the whole week before the girl was shot; afterwards he was panicked for days. He normally visits on Thursday—she was shot on a Thursday—but he worked late that day."

That suggested a question. "Sally was shot around six."

"He worked until nine that night." She shook her head. "That was the first and last time he's ever done that."

I believed her like I believed the sun was coming up tomorrow. She was too generous a person to think badly of anyone. Put together with Pat's observation, Raul had to be the man. I said, "We know the killer had drug connections. How about Raul, does he use?"

She swabbed the lip of her bowl with cornbread while she said, "No, he hates drugs, he's a fanatic about that. Everybody in the department is randomly tested, including me." She stood and walked into the kitchen. Reaching across the bar, she held my arm, preventing me from getting up to help. "You let me do the dishes," she scolded. As she put the dishes in the sink, she continued, "He doesn't do drugs, I'm positive about that."

I said, "People who deal drugs hate to be around users because it's dangerous. If Raul is smuggling drugs, he has to be above suspicion, he's doing it right under the noses of the Border Patrol."

"I don't see how he could smuggle anything on those trucks," she said, rinsing a bowl. "The Border Patrol agent supervises the packing of each box, and puts a seal on each one. He has the trailers searched by a drug-sniffing dog before they're loaded, and he verifies that every box that gets loaded on the truck has his seal. Then he puts his seal on the trailer before it leaves the plant in Mexico."

While she ran more water into the sink, she half-turned to look at me. "When the trucks get here, Raul has another manager with him when he breaks the seal, then he gives me the bill of lading. I check that the Border Patrol seal is intact on each box as it's removed from the truck. Depending on production that week, I decide where the boxes go." She put detergent in the water, picked up the bowl the stew had cooked in, and talked to the stubborn stains. "Besides all that, Quality Control uses random sampling to select units for their testing. I don't know which boxes they'll select, so I know Raul doesn't have any idea."

I could see her face in profile as she worked. Had I just made love to her? She seemed remote, an enigmatic stranger who shared her body but nothing else. Perhaps it was male vanity: how could she not be in love with me?

Still scrubbing the bowl, she said, "Once a box is off the truck, Raul wouldn't know where it went." She turned her head toward me when she asked, "Does that ruin your theory?"

"No, all that means is that the drugs aren't in the boxes." Softening my voice so she wouldn't take offense, I said, "People moving drugs can be very clever. However he does it, he probably picks them up right in front of you."

She straightened as if something hurt, and her face drained of color as she turned toward me. Breathing hard, a wet hand on her chest staining her blouse, she said, "Oh, wow, you're right, I do know how he does it."

She looked sick; a suspicion had become reality and it frightened her. "The truck drivers bring him these black flats, the kind you grow seedlings in? Raul says they're from a cousin in Mexico. Raul supposedly sells them to nurseries, then sends the money to his cousin in Mexico. He said that they sell for ten cents each, he gets about 200 at a time, so that's, umm, $20."

She looked at me as if she expected a comment. I didn't know what she wanted so I tried for a confused expression. Gesturing with dripping hands, she said, "He wouldn't give his mother a ride to the store when she asked. He thinks his relatives in Mexico are," she deepened her voice to imitate Raul, "'a bunch of lazy a-holes.'" She enunciated the words carefully when she added, "Would he haul flats to a nursery to get $20 to send to a cousin? I don't think so."

She turned back to the sink, picked up the sponge, but then she hesitated.

"And another thing. That stack of flats is heavy. He won't lift anything heavier than a pencil and yet he personally hauls those flats to his car." She shook her head. "Just like you said, right in front of me."

"Are you sure they're flats? Could it be a fake pile?"

"No, he stacks them in his office when they arrive, then takes them out to his car at the end of the shift. Once I had to move them to get into the files, so I pulled some of them apart. They're individual flats." Her eyebrows asked if I really thought those flats contained drugs.

"When will he get another shipment?"

"Tomorrow."

CHAPTER TWENTY

The nightmare yanked me from sleep at 2:42 a.m., my heart pounding so hard I was sure it would stop. The nightmare was exactly the same, Glen Hubbard and Earl Mitchell shooting at me, accurately etched in fine detail until the deflating tire trapped my head. Then Earl appeared without a face, blindly groping to find me. As his finger tightened on the trigger, I found myself crawling away from bed on my hands and knees.

With help from two glasses of wine, I got back to sleep at four, only to be propelled from bed at six by a slamming door. I cursed my way through my morning rituals, my legs shaking from the adrenaline overshoot, feeling like murdering the asshole who had slammed the door.

Deluded by the adrenaline, I tried to install all the electronic gear in the rental car. I only managed to fasten the radio to a bracket in the trunk and connect the antenna before exhaustion set in. I needed a tracker on Raul's car to see where he took those flats. For that, I had to have the radio connected to the laptop.

I rested for an hour before I resumed work. I pulled the cables through the back seat opening, rested for a few minutes, then I wrestled the bottom of the rear seat out. I took another break, then ran the cables to the laptop and replaced the seat. I needed to tap into a power wire, but the wound hurt just thinking about twisting my body to work under the dashboard.

Inside the room, I looked in the phone book for a car repair place that specialized in electrical work. After I called, I drove to the shop a couple of miles from the motel. For ten dollars, the guy connected the positive tap and fixed the ground wire under a mounting bracket screw head.

Driving back to the motel, I called Microfix and asked for shipping. A man answered, it might have been Raul, so I adopted a southern accent when I asked for Gina. It was Raul, he sounded surly as he asked, "And who is calling?"

"Mr. Morris from First National Bank."

I was stopped at a red light when Gina came on the line. I asked, "Can Raul hear you?"

Her voice had a smile. "You told him you were from a bank. He's so afraid I'll tell him about my money problems, he'll be gone for an hour."

Too anxious for small talk, I asked, "Is the truck in?"

The light changed to green. I looked for people running the red as Gina said, "Yeah, but the driver didn't have any flats with him."

My life seemed to evaporate, I had expected to wrap up the case by the end of the day. If the police caught Raul red-handed with pounds of dope, he would have no choice except to rat the mastermind into jail.

The identification of Sally's killer, Willie Elliott, must have spooked whoever ran the show. The car behind me honked just as Gina said, "Those flats are important, Raul was very upset. He called someone as soon as the driver told him."

As I moved through the intersection, I asked, "Do you know what time he called?"

"At 10:36. I was writing down the truck's arrival time as he was calling."

There was a thunderous explosion near Gina, I think my heart stopped until she said, "That was rude." I heard a man's laugh before she explained, "Mister dipshit here let a pallet fall."

The gunshot sound had spooked me. I pulled over to the curb, my legs feeling like water. Gina continued as if the incident hadn't happened. "During the call, I could see Raul's face getting red, like someone was chewing him out."

God, I hoped so. If Raul had called the person pulling the strings, Javier could get the phone number. Trying to keep the warbles in my voice under control, I said, "I'm sure that Raul's accomplices are nervous. If they find out you are talking with me, you might be in danger. Don't tell anyone that we know each other; don't come by my place, don't make Raul suspicious." I hated to scare her, but she had to see the danger. "These people killed once, they can do it again."

"Okay." Her voice squeaked; I'd made my point.

"Just in case they're already suspicious, I'll only call you at work, not on your home phone. I'll be Mr. Morris from First National Bank. Make up a story for Raul about how much you owe."

In almost a whisper, she said, "You be careful too," and disconnected.

Just after lunch—a peanut butter and jelly sandwich washed down with orange juice—I drove to the hospital. A nurse yanked off the bandages, extracting more stubble from my belly. The bandages were irritating my skin, and the whole area felt painful. Then Doctor Godfrey came in, gently probed the wound, and then yanked the drain out, pulling something that felt like it was connected to my right foot. As I was sitting there groaning in shock at the pain, he said, "The wound shows no sign of infection, but I do want to see you daily until it's completely healed."

On the way back to the motel, I decided I'd rather die than give the sadistic bastard another shot at me.

I felt better after a nap. While I was waking up, staring at the sparkles embedded in the acoustic ceiling, I tried to put myself inside Raul's head.

Perhaps he had been Mr. Average Citizen when a buddy, maybe from high school, introduced him to a drug dealer. The dealer made an attractive offer: deliver 200 seedling flats to somewhere once a week and collect $10,000 each time.

If Raul had misgivings, the rote mechanics of the task soon erased the concerns, and the money rolling in soothed the jitters. For years, the deliveries went smoothly, the money accumulated, and everyone was happy. Then the merger was announced; Raul would be retired with a very generous severance package.

To the drug dealer, the solution was simple: stop the merger. Perhaps Raul speculated on the only sure way to stop a merger: embroil Clay Oeland in a lawsuit with potentially unlimited liabilities. Soon, Raul was making phone calls with Clay's portable phone to a number he didn't know, in a game that no one explained to him. Too late, he found out that the game included murder. He didn't have to be told, he knew that in the eyes of the law he was as guilty of Sally's murder as the man who pulled the trigger.

Now Willie had been identified; the police no longer believed Oeland had killed Sally. They would come looking for the person with a motive, and there was Raul with all that ineptly laundered money. Raul had to know that the decorating sham wouldn't hold up.

I sat up, excited by how close we were to a solution. If Old Almaden Decor wasn't a thriving business, the money would give the DA enough evidence to put Raul on the grill. Money laundering carried severe penalties. Raul would give up his contacts to avoid a long prison term.

I found the address for Old Almaden Decor in the phone book. According to the map, I was about four miles away. I called and made an appointment with a lady who answered the phone. I put on my shoes, slipped the 9mm into the holster, put on my suit coat, and went to find the truth.

Old Almaden Decor was located in a mobile home in a park on Old Almaden Road. I walked up the stairs into a screened porch area, a wooden sign above the door had the business name carved into the wood. The swarthy Mexican lady who answered the door asked, "You're Mike Smith?"

"Yes, I'm the one who called. You're the decorator?"

"No, the owner creates the plans and I arrange for purchases or fabrication." She invited me in. Furniture overwhelmed the small living room. I sat on an overstuffed couch while she placed four catalogs on a large, marble topped coffee table. She handed me Post-em notes, saying, "Mark the pages that have decorating touches you find attractive. With that information, Ms. Valazquez can come to your house with the appropriate samples."

"She's pretty busy? I need my house done as soon as possible. If there's a chance she might be delayed, I don't want to risk it."

"I'm sure she'll have time."

"Mumm," I murmured as if thinking it over. "You know, I'd really like to see some examples of her work. Do you have a portfolio?"

She smiled apologetically. "She respects her client's privacy so she doesn't take pictures of private homes. But there's no obligation, she'll redo the plans until you're satisfied."

I went through the first book slowly, intending to stay for an hour. A half million dollars of business in a year would require about $10,000 a week, almost $2,000 a day for a five day week. The phone should be ringing, samples and catalogs of tile, furniture, carpets, draperies, and all the other necessities of decorating should be littering her work space. Other than the four books in front of me, there was nothing to suggest any business at all.

Ignoring her directions to the bathroom, I opened the three other doors in the hallway leading to the rear of the home. The business didn't exist in those rooms either.

I left without making an appointment to meet Raul's wife. If she had done a half million dollars worth of business last year, she had suffered a major reversal. Unless that disaster reduced the current deposits, she had some explaining to do.

Back in the car, I called Javier at the police station. He was out; I got his phone mail. Not wanting to transmit what I'd found over the air, and thinking it wasn't smart to mention the poker game, I gave him my motel and room number and asked him to call me if his plans had changed. I could skip the poker game; I'm not a fan, but the thought of the tamales had me salivating. I finished by saying, "If our meeting is still on, I'll see you this evening."

I called Clay, wanting to talk about Raul. He agreed to meet me at four-thirty, which was as soon as I could get to Microfix in the rush hour traffic.

I made it with a minute to spare. Clay met me in the lobby; he wanted to stay out of his office. "This time of day, things get crazy." We took a walk around the parking lot after I assured him I was up to that. As we started walking, he said, "Pat told me you'd lost some weight but I had no idea. You look terrible. You're feeling okay now?"

I assured him I was fine before I asked, "You do know Willie's background was primarily drugs?"

He nodded. "Leads to an obvious conclusion, doesn't it? The merger was going to wreck a drug ring. The only way it could have done that was to interfere with a supply. Since the plant in Mexico delivers once a week, that must be the source." He paused for a moment as the following wind from a passing truck showered us with dirt, then he continued, "Since the trucks would keep running after the merger, the contact here must have been the problem."

I said, "Raul wouldn't have been here to meet them."

That annoyed him. "Nor any of the other managers. Do you know about the procedures Raul set up to make sure there are no drugs secreted on those trucks?"

I nodded. "It was a smart move."

"Don't focus exclusively on Raul. The product from Mexico comes into the plantsite boxed and the boxes are distributed without opening. Anyone in the plant would have the same access."

"Why are you defensive about Raul?"

He looked grim; determined. "Raul's been with me since I started the company 17 years ago. He believed in what we were doing; he stayed when I couldn't pay him for a couple of months. That isn't the only time he's been more than just an employee. I know he's crude and abrasive but I'd trust him with my life."

"You are."

He looked at me, anger or frustration etching his face. "Do you know something?" he demanded.

I nodded, watching his eyes. "Raul is running drugs."

He puffed his cheeks and exhaled explosively. His head slumped. He muttered at the ground. His pace picked up, so I touched his arm to slow him down. He seemed startled. "Oh, sorry," he said, looking at me with concern.

He jammed his hands in his pockets and walked hunched over, looking at the ground. Talking to the pavement, he asked, "You're sure?" He watched me nod before he asked, "Raul's been a really good friend. Why would he do this?"

"For the money. I'm sure he didn't think about anyone getting hurt until his accomplices demonstrated that they had him by the short hairs."

He nodded, looking miserable. "Raul isn't the bravest man I've ever met."

Clay started walking fast again so I slowed him down by touching his arm. He slowed but he didn't look at me. "Pat has become a stranger to me. Raul's involved in framing me. Why don't I know the people closest to me?"

I couldn't help him with any of that, so I said, "Raul may have called his dealer from the plant this morning. Will you let the police look at the phone records?"

"Of course. Come back to my office and I'll write the permission."

When I left Microfix a half-hour later, it was almost 5:30. Eight miles on the freeway took another half-hour, so I had been in the motel room for only a couple of minutes when Javier knocked. He was accompanied by a small, wiry, and obviously nervous kid. Brown scraggly hair that brushed his shoulders and a wispy beard identified him as an undercover cop. "This is Pussy," Javier said.

As I shook his hand, the kid frowned at Javier and said, "Jeff Katz," as if he were repeating it for Javier's benefit.

I held his hand palm down. "Clean fingernails. How do you intend to pass for a scumbag with clean fingernails?"

"Grease off my engine; I use it for shampoo." He looked amazed when I laughed.

"What about your body odor?" Javier asked. "You smell bad out on the street. You gotta earn that."

Jeff said, "I got a bag of cat piss I wear." If he was kidding, he hid it well.

Javier had the tamales in a large cooler that he placed on the pass-through. As soon as he opened the cooler, the apartment filled with the aroma. The tamales were very hot and double wrapped in plastic and towels. "We should wait for the others," he said.

I put five plates and flatware on the table. Javier looked at his watch and said, "That's long enough." He served us three tamales each. They were better than I remembered.

I said, "Would you mind if I asked Rita to marry me?"

Javier said, "Wouldn't work, she only makes these for people she's trying to impress. You think I'm buddy-buddy with you because you do interesting work? Hell, no, it's the only way to get mom to fix tamales."

Ten minutes later, Vic Stauder arrived with two twelve packs of beer. The plump, balding, middle-aged man looked like a banker instead of Javier's partner in Homicide. As he shook my hand, he said, "So you're the fi—, uh, the PI Javier has been telling us about."

"What exactly did he say?"

Vic looked at Javier; shrugged and then said, "That you were dripping money and strung out on pain killers."

"He didn't tell you that I think bluffing is immoral?"

"No need," Vic assured me. "We all feel that way." He turned toward Javier and asked, "Ante a dollar as usual?"

We did our best to get through the tamales before the last player arrived. He was a tall, thin, ramrod-straight, grim faced man with a burr haircut. Les Taylor drew fire from Jeff Katz, the undercover Narc. "Whassa matter, the coven have a meeting?"

"Stake, idiot, Stake," Les said amiably. "No, there was no meeting." He nodded toward Jeff when he told me, "I'm a Mormon; Jeff is scared shitless of us."

He looked into the cooler. His face lit up as he dished up four tamales. "You guys are losing your touch. Any self respecting group of cops should have been able to finish these off." He ate a fork-full and moaned. "Tell Rita that I will crawl the length of Story Road naked at noon to kiss her feet."

"You're late," Javier observed. "It's not nice to keep your buddies waiting, especially when we have a rich fi—, person who wants to play."

"Sorry, takes awhile to tuck the kids in," he explained to me. When I asked, Les explained that he was Jeff's boss in Narcotics.

Jeff said, "Came into Narcotics looking like the man. They couldn't use him on the street so they made him Sergeant."

Les replied, "They needed someone literate to write the reports."

The poker wasn't going to be a serious game, judging by the four nines that Javier dealt me on the first hand. Since I had the first bid, I checked to Jeff who bet a quarter. Up to a dollar when it came around to me, I threw in the hand, saying, "Too rich for me." Jeff and Vic looked at Javier in amazement.

Javier threw down his hand in apparent disgust. "I'm losing my touch. Where did I go wrong?"

"Four nines? That's a little obvious."

Jeff had four kings. He tossed his hand face up into the middle of the table, complaining, "Damn, Javier, how about some help here. That was my best chance to be rich."

Javier said, "We're spitting into the wind. Face it, our friend here is one lucky dude. He developed a new lead while he was unconscious in the hospital." While he dealt the next hand, he told them about Alicia's call naming Willie as the shooter.

The bidding was half-hearted. I folded with nothing. Jeff raised Javier's bet by a quarter and Les dropped out. After Vic saw the raise, Javier flipped a quarter into the pot, which should have been a call, but he said, "See your quarter and raise you fifty."

Jeff had been studying his cards and he abruptly threw them down. "Shit, tightwad raises fifty cents, he's got it and you can take that to the bank."

Javier's partner, Vic, said, "See your fifty cents and raise you fifty cents," while placing just fifty cents in the pot.

As Javier studied his cards, Jeff volunteered, "Finding out Willie was the shooter won't help. Fucker's dead."

Play at the table ceased abruptly. Everyone looked at Jeff expectantly. Jeff looked like they had caught him cheating. Javier broke the silence. "You gonna just dump that or do you have more to tell us?"

Jeff said, "Willie's car has been sitting in front of his girlfriend's house since January. He might leave the chick but never that car, it was his life. He's got to be dead."

"Did you talk to her?" I asked Jeff.

Javier answered. "I did. Willie didn't come home the night of the shooting, and she hasn't seen him since then." He paused before he asked Jeff, "You sure about the car?"

Jeff nodded. "He was my snitch. Asshole could drive me crazy talking about the fuckin' car." Jeff put a hand on my arm. "Willie was slow, maybe borderline retarded. No matter how much trouble he was in, he wouldn't have left the car. He's dead, no question."

"You gonna shit or quit," Vic asked Javier, waving the cards at him.

Javier looked at his hand and then threw them down, saying, "I didn't have anything."

Vic grinned and spread his cards face up. He had a pair of threes. Jeff moaned but didn't say what he'd thrown out. Javier said, "Got to have balls if you want to play with the heavy hitters."

I asked Jeff, "Did Willie pal around with anyone who ran in the same circles as Glen Hubbard?"

"One of his girls used to give Willie free blow jobs," he said, picking at the remnants of the tamale on his plate.

Jeff looked alarmed when Javier reached over and clamped a massive hand around his wrist. "Who?" Javier asked.

"Tiese, the tall one with the white hair."

Javier could look dangerous when he was concentrating. He seemed to glare at Jeff when he asked, "Why would she do that?"

As though trying to mollify the big man, Jeff patted the hand clamped on his wrist. "So he'd fix things at her place. He was handy with tools. To hear her tell it, the guy also had a hair trigger, she could blow him on her way out the door and never break stride."

Javier wasn't angry, perhaps he was preoccupied. His partner, Vic, recognized something because he said, "She'll say she saw them together if she thinks that's what you want her to say."

Javier asked Jeff, "Did Hubbard move drugs?"

"Misdemeanor shit, enough to keep his girls happy."

Javier shook his head when he looked at me. "That's a connection between Glen and Willie that Oeland's lawyer can use, but he isn't our man. We're looking for a major player."

I said, "I've found the contact inside Microfix." The transformation of the group into cops was abrupt, both Les and Jeff pulled out notebooks and pens. I told them about Raul, his money and his wife's sham business. I concluded by saying, "Raul's girlfriend is positive that he's involved, he's had panic attacks every time there's a new break in the case."

"This is the Raul Valazquez that's the shipping manager at Microfix?" Javier asked. After I nodded, he said, "Guy reminds me of the perfect bureaucrat. How reliable is the girlfriend?"

"I trust women's intuition, especially when it comes to lovers."

Javier nodded. "Women can be blind about the men they sleep with, but what they do suspect is usually dead-on."

I handed Javier the note. "That's Clay's permission to look at the phone records from Microfix. I think Raul called his connection around 10:36 this morning."

Les took the paper from Javier and said, "This is a job for us if it's drugs." As he looked at the paper, he said, "Why would Raul call his connection at 10:36 this morning?"

I told them about the weekly shipment of 200 black seedling flats, and Gina's belief that Raul wouldn't stoop over to pick up the $20 the flats earned, much less haul them somewhere. Jeff Katz gave his boss, Les, a weird look when I mentioned the seedling flats. When Les looked at him, Jeff said, "Black seedling flats from Mexico," enunciating each word precisely.

Les flashed him an annoyed look. "You don't have to hit me with a hammer, I got it." He looked at me and explained, "Black tar heroin."

Talking to the table, Jeff said, "Say they weigh six ounces each, take away a couple for whatever binder they use to hold the shape, that's four ounces. Two hundred flats would weigh fifty pounds." His eyes widened. "Twenty-three kilos a week. No fucking wonder this area is lousy with the shit."

Javier needled, "Somebody flooding the market and you don't know who he is?"

Stung, Jeff turned to face Javier. The slumped shoulders were gone as was the street inflection when he said, "We know exactly who he is. You want to hear why we can't nail him?"

"Jeff," Les warned, looking at his cards as if he wanted play to resume.

Jeff whirled to face his boss. "We play poker with these guys, for Christ's sake. If we can't trust them, we can't do the fucking job anymore."

In a soft voice that sounded forced, Les replied, "They aren't the only people here."

Javier reached across the table and lowered the cards Les was holding. "Gary brought you the goods. Vic and I have been busting our asses trying to find out why Oeland was set up. If you know who we're looking for, tell us."

"It isn't that simple," Les said.

Jeff didn't agree. "The name is Deke Horstman."

"Damn it, Jeff," Les yelled, his face reddening. As quickly as it came, the storm passed. Les threw his cards on the table wearily. "Jeff's right, it's not doing any good to sit on it." Les looked at me when he said, "If this gets out, I'll lose my job."

"Gary is good people, Les." Javier pushed his glasses back on his nose. "What's going on with this Deke Horstman?"

Sounding tired, Les said, "We haven't been able to get diddly squat on the guy. It's like he knows when we're interested. We flip some guy, Deke won't do business with him. We set up a tail, Deke is a model citizen. We tap a phone booth, Deke never uses it again." He probed a tooth with his tongue. "You see the problem?"

No one spoke; the idea of a dirty cop required time to digest. Les continued, "It's a lieutenant or above, I know that much."

Javier had to walk around, he uncapped another beer and wandered the apartment. His partner, Vic, said, "If this Raul Valazquez' contact turns out to be Horstman, maybe we can impose on Gary here." Les turned to look at me while Vic added, "He has a knack for knowing what people are saying to each other."

Les asked me, "Can you find out who Horstman talks to?"

"If he's the one Raul called, I'll try." I was surprised that my voice remained steady while my guts turned to jelly.

Les told me, "I'll let you know tomorrow." He smiled when he added, "Do I need to tell you Horstman is one mean son-of-a-bitch?"

He was obviously under the impression that I was brave. To dispel that, I asked, "Can we keep all this between ourselves?"

Les answered. "Until another truckload of flats arrives. When will that be?"

"Next Tuesday, if they ship any."

Les asked, "Do I get my name on TV if we break it?"

Jeff scoffed. "The department won't let you go on TV. The bad guys will be knockin' over places in broad daylight if they get a look at you. They got to figure we can't find our ass with either hand if we put a guy like you in charge."

179

CHAPTER TWENTY-ONE

Post Traumatic Stress Disorder had evidently condemned me to a complete replay of the nightmare each night. It seemed I couldn't wake until Earl, with a hole where his face should be, was aiming the gun at my eye. On the floor when I awoke, I rested there until my heart slowed. With the help of some wine, I was back to sleep by three.

Awake at seven, and I was ready to face the world by eight that morning. I walked to a coffee shop about a mile from the motel. I lingered over breakfast, not at all sure I could do the mile back. Three cups of coffee and two newspapers later, I lost the burning need to call a taxi.

When I got back to the motel, I was ready for a nap. I slept for an hour, then I watched the changing patterns on the ceiling as passing cars reflected sunlight through the drapes. The phone rang just as I nodded off again.

"Good morning," Toni said.

I considered hanging up, but while I debated, she said, "I called Clay this morning and told him I was going to fire you."

That sounded good, I was ready to go home. "And he said?"

"Netting it out, I think he said that I have shit for brains." She waited, giving me a chance to disagree, before she said, "Specifically, he told me to help you instead of trying to run your investigation. So what can I do to help?"

I told her that I believed Old Almaden Decor was a front to launder Raul's unexplained income. I explained Raul's strange behavior with the seedling flats, and that the shipments had stopped, perhaps the conspirators had been spooked by Willie's identification. I relayed the Narcs' contention that the flats were made of black tar heroin, and if that was so, a man named Deke Horstman had to be involved. He was the prime mover of heroin in San Jose. I summed the case by saying, "If all that turns out to be true, we'll know who

181

framed Oeland and why, but proving it won't be easy."

Toni said, "We could inform the IRS that Old Almaden Decor is a money laundering enterprise."

That information would go into someone's in-basket, and maybe, in a year or two, an investigation would begin, not quite the time frame I had in mind. The investigation would be effectively sidetracked if someone blew my brains out. The bad guys knew that, so I needed something to get me off ground zero. I suggested, "If Raul can be charged with money laundering, the DA might force him to talk. Can I file a complaint alleging Raul is laundering money?"

She laughed. "Sure, if you have the results of an audit. Will Raul let you examine his books?"

The laugh pissed me off. When she discovered that she was dealing with a very cranky person, she said she would think about the problem, and hurriedly disconnected. I felt stupid for blowing up at her. Between the nightmares and reality, I was getting a bad case of the shakes.

I rented a pay-per-view movie, and got absorbed in that for the next two hours. Afterwards, I took a nap. At five, I called Javier to see if the phone records from Microfix had turned anything up. When he answered, he said, "See you in an hour, I've got something to show you."

Javier knocked just after six. I tried to ignore the manila envelope he carried while I got him a beer. As I set the beer on the pass through, he took an 8X10 photo out of the envelope and handed it to me. A thin blond guy with a skimpy mustache stared at the camera. Probably in his twenties, he had the vacant look of a man who had done major time. "Deke Horstman," Javier said.

"So the Narcs were right? Raul called him?"

Javier nodded. "It wasn't a stretch." He sat on a stool, overwhelming the small counter with his arms. "If those flats are black tar heroin, he's the only player in town capable of pushing 20 kilos a week. And since Raul called him, we gotta believe those seedling flats are black tar heroin."

Javier tapped the photo. "In the last three years, we've questioned Horstman about two homicides, both former competitors of his. He had an excellent and unusual alibi on both occasions, which means he hired a hit man. Since that's the way he solves his problems, he wouldn't lose sleep over killing Sally to stop the merger."

He drained half the beer with his first drink. He carefully placed the bottle back on the counter. "According to Les, dealers expect interruptions in supply, so most keep a stash to tide them over. Les thinks Horstman won't ship any more for a couple of months."

"Shit." That was all I needed, to be a fucking target for two months.

Javier nodded. "He isn't going to be easy. He's cost the Narcs a thousand man hours, and they still don't know how he moves his product."

Javier began to strip the label off the bottle, working carefully to clean the glass of glue as the paper came off. Talking to the bottle, Javier said, "About a year ago, Les contracted with a PI to take pictures of anyone who talked with Deke. The guy followed Deke for a solid month and all he got was pictures of Deke posing for the camera. Only four people knew about the PI, all lieutenants and above. So when Les found that Raul Valazquez had called Horstman, he didn't tell anyone but me."

I indicated the picture. "You'll give me an address?"

"On the back."

I read the address. "Where is this?"

"South end, a couple of miles from the mobile home park where Earl Mitchell lived. Horstman lives with his folks. No visible means of support for his Corvette." Javier pointed at the photo. "In case I haven't made the point, this guy is a killer. I wish I could give you some help, but if I pass all this on to Sylvia, the brass will hear about Horstman." Javier grinned and then smoothed his mustache with a beefy hand. "This way, you get to earn those big bucks." His grin looked as sick as I felt.

CHAPTER TWENTY-TWO

Earl was aiming the gun at my head when I thrashed my way out of bed at four the next morning. I stood there, angry with the entire world, wondering how many mornings would start this way. From what I knew about PTSD, the replays could last for years.

I went back to bed, slept fitfully for two hours, then got up, still angry. In my jeans, unshaven and probably smelling bad, I went out.

After doing the mile, eating breakfast, and walking the mile back to the motel, my mood had improved to lousy. While I cleaned up, I decided to go see "Mac the Knife," Sally's landlord. If he had seen Raul or Deke Horstman at Sally's apartment, that might be enough for the DA to begin a police investigation.

For early June, it promised to be warm, and the weather lady on the radio sounded grim as she intoned "triple digits." I put on my Puerto Vallarta tee shirt and blue jeans, coaxed the shoulder holster past the wound, then put on an open shirt to cover the gun.

The thermometer must have been bouncing off the triple digits when I drove by Mac's apartment building. San Jose State was doing Finals. I couldn't find a vacant parking spot until I was almost six blocks away, and that was a squeeze—the Neon fit with six inches to spare.

Hot, hurting, and wondering why the hell I'd bothered, I walked into the building's cool interior ten minutes later. After he opened the door, Mac carefully ushered me into his room and solicitously asked if I wanted to sit down. "Heard you got shot, you just out of the hospital?" Mac's hair was rebelling against conformity, heightening his resemblance to Chuck Berry.

I nodded. "I'm supposed to go back every day so they can rip the bandages off my stomach and poke at the wound. My doctor is pissed that I got shot with a dirty bullet, he intends to torture me so I don't make that mistake again."

He gave me a polite laugh. "Wouldn't think he'd screw with you. You tougher than you look, taking out both those guys after they shot you."

"I was lucky." A nervous tremor shook my voice; I didn't want to think about it. "Did you see the picture they had in the paper of the guy who shot Sally?"

"Yes. I told the cop that the guy was Alicia's dealer. Scary dude, big and stupid." Mac grimaced as if something hurt, but his voice was even as he continued, "Strange that the police drawing didn't look anything like him, guy's kind of hard to miss."

"Oeland said that the gun took all his attention, maybe he only thought he looked at the guy."

Mac looked skeptical. "How could he miss those sunken cheeks and the cheekbones sticking out like that?"

I shrugged, pulling on the wound. "How about this guy?" I asked, handing him Raul's picture.

He didn't recognize Raul but when I handed him Deke's picture, Mac looked at me with a perplexed expression. "He's a cop, right? He pestered me a few days after the shooting for Alicia's new address. Told him I didn't have it but he didn't believe me. Must have come back once a week for a month."

Mac had just made the long, hot walk worth every twinge. We now had Horstman looking for Alicia, and Raul had called Horstman. Eager to tell Javier, I made my excuses to Mac, and took the long walk to my car.

When I got to the car, I had to rest a minute before I called Javier. "Bingo," I said when he came on the line. Careful since I was talking on the cellular, I said, "Our man looked for the roommate for a month after the incident."

Javier was quiet for a few seconds before he said, "It's not going to buy a warrant. I think she would say that the roommate was a user and our man is a dealer." I guessed that "she" meant the DA, Sylvia. An overwhelming depression settled into my gut. I didn't want to bug Horstman. Javier continued, "But it sure doesn't hurt the theory, does it?"

"Tantalizing," I agreed. "The roommate is scared to death someone is going to be looking for her, and our man seems to have done just that. I'll do a full court on him and see what I can find out."

Javier was impressed with my bravery, he tossed a "—be careful," into his good-bye. If he only knew how close I was to getting on an airplane and going home.

186

Since I could hardly get in trouble looking at Deke Horstman's house, I let the laptop look up the address and show me the way. Driving leisurely, not in any hurry to get there, I took the city streets to south San Jose. The noon rush was in full swing, hungry high-tech workers smothered restaurants in an avalanche of automobiles.

Deke Horstman's house was one of four two-story designs repeated endlessly in a tract that covered a good portion of south San Jose. Despite the original lack of variety; time, paint, and shrubbery had differentiated the houses. Deke's reminded me of a graveyard; a dozen or more thin cypress shrubs taller than the second story stood guard around the periphery of the tiny lot. A black wrought-iron fence topped with spikes edged the sidewalk and driveway. A padlocked gate denied access to the front door. In case the lock didn't deter a visitor, a large black rottweiler was chained in the front yard. An alarm box hung on the front of the garage. The garage was not used for cars. A late seventies Cadillac occupied the driveway, and a pristine 1967 Corvette was parked on the street in front of his house.

The body language of the house suggested that Horstman expected trouble. The graveyard motif certainly sent me a message, no telling what traps he had set for any intruder. But the large dog was a good sign—dogs set off alarm systems, so the box on the garage was probably a fake. Since Deke lived with his parents, maybe I could get some inside help.

I parked the car on a busy avenue a half-block away, where I could still see the house. I looked up Deke's phone number in the laptop by searching on the address. When I called, a woman answered after two rings, Deke's mother, I hoped. "This is the American Research Institute," I told her. "We're doing a demographic study of your neighborhood. We'll send you two tickets to see the film of your choice at the Century Theaters if you'll answer some questions for us."

"All right, fire away." She sounded excited.

"First, let me get a few facts. We'll send the tickets to 6327 Morning Gate, and the Zip there is 95123, is that right?"

"Yes."

"Can you tell me how many adults and children live in the house?"

"Three adults."

"Any of them married?"

"Yes, me and my husband live with my son. It's his house but we didn't have a place so he took us in."

"You should be proud of having a boy that considerate." I paused to fake sincerity before I asked, "Do you have any pets?"

"A rottweiler."

The dog I'd seen in the front yard. Since she referred to it as a pet, that could mean the dog was allowed in the house, which meant no alarm system. I eased toward that question. "How many bedrooms are in the home?"

"Four."

"Bathrooms?"

"Two. There's a half bath downstairs. Does that make three?"

"I'll put down three bathrooms. How many telephones?"

"Two. No, three. My son has his own line."

That was helpful, I could tap his phone and pick up room conversations with the same bug. "Automobiles?"

"Two cars, my son's Corvette and our Cadillac. There's a motorcycle, too."

"You ride the motorcycle, am I right?"

She laughed. "Not on your life, Sonny. I'm scared to death of the thing."

"Washer and dryer?"

"Yes."

"Dishwasher?"

"Yes."

"Trash compactor?"

"No."

"Alarm systems on your house or cars?"

"No."

"Any major repairs done lately?"

"Yes, my son had a new roof put on this year."

"Was he satisfied with the job?"

"Yes."

"Well, that's the list," I said. "You've been so nice that we'll send you three tickets so you can take your son to the movies with you. The tickets will be for a specific day and time, when would be the most convenient for you?"

"A Sunday matinee is about the only time everyone could go."

Shit, that meant I'd have to bug the house in daylight, while all the neighbors were outside doing whatever. "Very good, we'll send you three tickets to this Sunday's matinee at any one of the seven theaters. Thanks again."

Seconds after I disconnected, the phone trilled. The coincidence startled me, and my heart rate went into orbit as I picked it up. It was Clay Oeland, he wanted to talk about Raul. I didn't want to broadcast our conversation anywhere near Deke's house, remembering the recording setup I'd found in Earl Mitchell's mobile home. I told Oeland that I'd find a pay phone and call him back.

The pay phone outside a drug store was sticky. Judging by the teenagers lounging on the bike rack, ice cream cones were responsible for the goo. I held the handset away from my ear as the phone rang at Microfix.

When Clay came on, he asked if Raul had called a drug dealer. Clay's lawyer had advised him that keeping Raul on the payroll after learning of his involvement with drug trafficking could lead to criminal charges against Clay.

"We have nothing provable on Raul at the moment. Until we get one of those flats, we can't even let Raul know we suspect him."

"Since they didn't deliver last Tuesday, is that a sign they've stopped for good?"

"According to the Narcs, it was probably precautionary, but they might wait as long as two months before they resume shipping."

The teenagers exploded into laughter. I didn't hear Clay's comment. No way in hell did I want to put the handset against my ear. "Sorry, noisy here, what did you say?"

"Nothing. Anyway, I'll hold off on Raul."

After I let the handset ooze back into its cradle, I washed my hands at the nearby McDonald's. After a hamburger, I drove to the Century theaters and bought the Sunday matinee tickets. When I returned, I stopped directly in front of Deke's house. I left the car idling, and the driver's door open with a loud tape playing, hoping to attract attention and perhaps get invited into the house. That didn't happen, so I put the tickets in the slot for mail in the garage door. The lock on the wrought iron gate was for show, it didn't go through the latch.

As I drove away, I wondered if I would break into his house. Sunday at two was only 71 hours away, how much courage could I muster in that short time?

I stopped at a coffee shop for an early dinner. Seated inside, I opted for breakfast. The older waitress who took my order asked if I wanted coffee. I almost refused, but an idea flashed. With the aid of some caffeine, I could put a tracker on Deke's car. If I got lucky, I might help the cops catch him moving some product. With Deke in jail looking at major time, and Raul indicted for money laundering, Sylvia might plea-bargain Raul into talking.

Considering how bad the Narcs wanted Deke, Raul might get a very sweet deal.

After I finished eating, I drove to the motel. Removing one of the square plastic trackers from its shipping box, I set it to transmit its location every five minutes.

At 10:30 that evening, wearing black jeans, and a black windbreaker to hide the gun, I drove to Deke's neighborhood. The Corvette was still parked on the street. Lights were on in the house, so I drove to a nearby shopping center. At a drugstore, I bought a magazine and tennis balls, then I used a corner booth in a doughnut shop to wait.

A little after 11:30, I dumped all the debris of my stay into a trash can, and said goodnight to the garrulous and bored Korean lady at the register. In the car, I inspected the tracker one last time. When its magnet sucked it onto the instrument panel, the infrared meter I held in front of its window pegged. Super snoopy was ready to work.

I drove to Deke's neighborhood. As I idled by, I hit the Corvette with a tennis ball. As his mother had said, no alarm. I parked around the corner at the end of the block and walked back toward Deke's house on the dark and quiet street. A single dog bark rapidly blossomed into a full chorus, ten dogs or more adding tonal variations until the whole neighborhood seemed to be reverberating. No one living on the street needed an alarm system. I'd almost decided to go back to the car, but then the dogs lost interest. A light came on in the upper floor of a house as I was passing. How many others on the street had been awakened?

I took the tracker out of my pocket as I approached the car. The only flat metal facing the ground in the early Corvettes is the differential, more than three feet under the car. Corvettes are close to the ground, and the spare tire housing hides the differential. The wound complained as I slid under the car. As I reached into the dark to place the tracker, it suddenly clamped to the side of a frame cross-member, a useless position. I couldn't get a grip on it, and a long minute passed before it suddenly came loose.

I heard a door shut, then the automatic garage door groaned open, spilling light down the driveway. The tracker went in place with an audible "thunk" as a man approached. I tried to pull my feet up but there was no room under the car. He opened the driver's door and got into the car. The spare tire housing settled into my neck, trapping my head against the muffler. If he moved the car, I was in deep shit.

I heard the warning beep as he inserted the ignition key with the door open. I felt for my gun, yanked on the Velcro, and the gun clattered to the pavement. I had to pass the gun over my belly with my left hand. I put the laser dot on the front tire. If that tire went flat, the rear of the car would rise. I was squeezing the trigger when I noticed that he still had one foot outside the car. I heard music. In a few seconds, a cassette ejected, then more music played. Another cassette ejected. After what seemed like years, the man got out and shut the door, raising the car off my neck. He had two cassettes in his hand as he walked back up the driveway. When the garage door shut, I eased out from under the car and quickly walked away on trembling legs.

CHAPTER TWENTY-THREE

After the nightmare woke me at three in the morning, I watched the ceiling sparkles, trying to find solace in the jewels dotting my sky. The nightly replay of the shooting seemed to be getting more detailed; this time I heard the bullet go through the car door before it hit me. As it came out of my back and hit the ground, asphalt stung the inside of my right arm. Was my brain remembering or creating these details?

At eight that morning, the temperature already in the mid-seventies, I walked to the coffee shop. The mile was a breeze. After breakfast, the mile back hurt. I was too warm in the light jacket I'd worn to cover the gun. The weight of the gun tapping my full stomach vibrated the wound. The sun felt oppressive.

I had plenty of time to recover. Deke's car didn't move until four that afternoon, then the laptop said his car was in east San Jose. As I drove east, the next display showed his car stopped, at a red light for all I knew. Five minutes later, the map on the laptop's screen showed him in the same location.

I turned down that street just as the display changed. He was moving and a mile away. The street I was on had apartment buildings on one side, and a storage complex and two gas stations opposite. The tracker wasn't precise enough to show where he'd been parked on the street. I stopped and waited for the next readout, not wanting to crowd Deke if he was carrying drugs.

The next two displays showed his car stopped two miles away. I drove there, only to find that he had again moved on. At least this time I knew where he'd been, the only structure on the street was a storage rental complex.

The laptop showed him stopped at the next readout, so I drove directly to that location. Deke drove out of a storage rental yard just as I drove by.

A few minutes later, his car stopped again. I found it in a Safeway supermarket's parking lot, and Deke was standing next to a pay phone. Short and slight, with unruly short blond hair, he was wearing buff colored Levi's under a long, tan, slip-on shirt printed with an Aztec calendar design. If he was waiting for a phone call, his body language didn't reflect any tension; he leaned against a wall as he watched the traffic in the busy lot.

I drove to a far corner of the lot and parked. The phone must have rung a couple of minutes later. He picked up the handset and talked. When he hung up, he walked to a coffee shop across the street.

That was too good an opportunity. I walked across the street and went into the restaurant. Sitting at an otherwise empty counter section near the back wall, Deke was facing the door. He watched me, so I nodded at him as I sat down at the counter, five seats away. As I took a napkin, I turned the dispenser so I could watch Deke in the polished aluminum. He was small, five-seven or eight, maybe 120 pounds.

The waitress, a world-weary woman judging by her face, placed water and a menu in front of me, then moved to take Deke's order. Deke's voice had a sharp edge. "I want a hamburger on toasted sourdough with Swiss cheese, tomato, lettuce, and pickles, mayonnaise and mustard." His diction was precise, he sounded educated.

A biker in leathers with chains draped from his belt to various pockets walked in the door. He looked and then walked toward me. In the pincer between Deke Horstman and this huge biker, I entertained some very upsetting thoughts. The biker passed behind me and stopped in front of Deke. The biker said, "Deke."

Deke Horstman looked at the man but he didn't respond to the proffered hand. In a quiet voice that could have been understood in the next county, Deke said, "I'm going to be eating alone here for a half-hour, maybe forty-five minutes. Alone. Is that clear?"

"I thought we could talk some business." The biker sounded belligerent.

Given the disparity in their sizes, I assumed Deke was treading on dangerous ground. Deke knew better. In the same sharp, quiet voice, he said, "If you leave now, you'll save both of us some problems."

The biker mumbled, "Sorry," and left the restaurant.

I ordered soup, something I could appear to finish whenever I needed to leave. True to his word, Deke took his time eating; I was waiting in my car when he left the coffee shop. He got in his car and pulled out into traffic.

I stayed in the lot until the laptop calculated the next fix. He was back at the first storage yard. I waited until he moved to a new location and drove there. He was waiting near a phone in front of an electronics store. When it rang, he picked up the handset, said a few words, and then hung up. As I expected, he went home.

I recognized the modified "body swap" routine from my DEA days. Deke had visited the first location to make sure it was clean, and to replace his lock with the buyer's lock. The next location contained drugs which Deke moved to the third location. This was the only time Deke was vulnerable. Using pagers, he gave the buyer a phone number, and when the buyer called, Deke told him where to leave the money. After waiting a suitable time, Deke returned to the first location and retrieved the money. If that was satisfactory, he then contacted the buyer and gave him the location of the dope.

The DEA called the routine a "body swap" because it usually involved buyers and sellers who had no reason to trust each other. In that case, either the seller or the buyer provided the other party with a hostage, a wife or girlfriend preferably, whose body guaranteed delivery of the dope or the money.

The advantages of the "body swap" are that the money and dope are never in the same place, and neither are the seller and buyer. It eliminates the need to protect the money and the drugs with armed groups, the usual flashpoint in drug transactions. The safety afforded by the "body swap" makes the additional effort worthwhile; that it also complicates law enforcement is icing on the cake.

When I returned to the motel, I called Javier at his apartment. I went through Deke's itinerary, concluding with, "I'll have printouts for the next three days, that should show most of his locations."

"I don't think Les will wait, he'll probably want to take him tomorrow."

"It could be a shell game," I warned. "Does he have the drugs between the first and second stop? The second and third? Or did he add a fourth stop just in case?" I slipped off my jacket while I waited for Javier. When he didn't say anything, I added, "Why don't we wait for the three days? I'll have most of his locations by then. You can get search warrants, find the one with the drugs, and then wait inside until he shows up."

As I pulled the 9mm out of the holster, Javier said, "Once we get search warrants, he's never going to show."

I'd forgotten that the Narcs would need the requests for warrants approved by their bosses. If Horstman had a contact in the police hierarchy, he would be warned to stay home. There would be no proof that he had rented or used the spaces, knowing how cautious drug dealers were about such things. I took off the holster while Javier said, "We should try to take him tomorrow. If he's stopped the shipments to Raul, he might kill him."

Javier was right, killing Raul would be the smart thing to do. Horstman had already assumed that the police were looking for a drug connection inside Microfix, otherwise he wouldn't have stopped shipping those flats. He knew that once the police had the identity of the shooter, Willie, they had to know drugs were involved. Horstman could guess that Raul would be a logical suspect.

I said, "Let me know what you want me to do."

"I'll have Les get in touch with you tomorrow morning. He'll have to set it up." Javier paused, and I thought he was through until he said, "On a lighter note, Earl Mitchell died this morning."

If I had any feeling at all, it was one of relief, as if his death had eliminated a threat. Maybe it was the nightmare, Earl had become a menace by chasing me from my sleep every night. Whatever the reason, the sense of relief seemed peculiar. Was I beginning to see killing as a solution to my problems?

Javier expected a response, so I said, "You think the EPA will charge me with toxic dumping?"

I stayed up late watching a movie on television, and drinking too much wine, hoping Earl's death and the alcohol would let me skip the nightmare. All I did was delay it, Earl's finger tightened on the trigger at 4:11 the next morning.

At eight, someone knocked on the door, yanking me out of a pleasant dream. The furry spider of fear ran up my back and made all the hair on my body stand up. No doubt about it, the mean little guy who could intimidate huge bikers had spooked me. I grabbed the gun from beneath the bed and eased over to the window, using the crack where the drapes didn't quite meet the wall, to look toward the door. A TV crew was set up, taping the door, a nicely dressed young woman with shoulder-length brown hair held a microphone in position, ready to lunge.

I pulled the phone to the floor so that the bed would muffle my voice and called Oeland's number at Microfix. When he picked up his phone, I told him, "I've got a news crew outside. Any idea how they found me?"

"Yes." He sounded discouraged. "Another team just left here. I assume someone was watching Microfix, they probably followed you after we met Monday."

"They won't get a picture of me that they can use on the air. That's all they want, some footage to wrap a rehash of the shooting around. I'll lose them and move to a different place."

Clay didn't say anything, so I told him about Deke Horstman and the plan to take him as soon as he conducted any business. "With Horstman off the street, and Raul looking at major time for laundering money, the DA should be able to extract the story from Raul."

"Thursday, you said you needed one of those flats Raul gets," Clay said. "I thought of a way to push them into sending more flats now. Are you interested?"

"Yes."

"Our inventory of the low-end tables we make in Mexico is too high. I've been talking about that during the morning production meetings, so Raul wouldn't be suspicious if we had the plant in Mexico stop production for two months. If we closed July first, that would give him only three more trucks before the shutdown."

"When would Raul be told?"

"Monday morning at eight. The truck leaves Mexico at seven Tuesday morning."

Thinking out loud, I said, "That would be soon enough to get the flats on the truck."

"So?" Clay asked, "should I plan on shutting it down?"

"Oh, yeah, let's give it a go." Anything to break the case open.

Les Taylor, the Narc sergeant, called a few minutes later. There were street noises in his background, he was using a pay phone. "Javier told me Deke uses storage yards." As he talked, the knocking on the door became insistent. "What's that?" he asked.

"There's a news crew outside that I'm ignoring."

"What do they look like?" He sounded suspicious.

Fear ran over my back. "Two women, one with a camera who looks like she lifts weights. The other is a petite brunette all set to spear me with a microphone."

"That's Rebecca," he said softly. "If I wasn't married, I'd crawl across a freeway in the dark to suck her toes."

Rebecca knocked again, louder, so I said, "The next place she'll be is an emergency room having a microphone extracted."

"You can't do that," he said; paused for a beat and then added, "until I get there."

I laughed for him before I said, "Getting back to Deke, the readout is in the car, and I can't go outside until they leave. I won't know if he's moving until then."

"You won't see anything today, the guy never works two days in a row. When he does go out, it's in the late afternoon, and he's home before sundown. A reverse vampire."

Les sounded irritated as he continued. "He doesn't party, he doesn't socialize, and he doesn't spend money. We don't know how he makes his sales, or who he sells to. When we flipped a couple of guys who had done business with him, somehow he knew, he wouldn't even talk to them."

Les waited for me. I didn't have anything to say so he suggested, "I'd like to wait until we have more information. I know Javier sees a risk to Raul, but we blow it all if we tip Horstman and don't catch him dirty. So can you keep up your tracking thing long enough to get a list of all his locations?"

That meant replacing the tracker on Deke's car every four days, a scary prospect. I said, "Sure, no problem."

When I told Les about the plan to shut down production in Mexico, he sounded happy. "If we get one of those flats, we can put Raul's nuts in the wringer. We'll give him the key to the city, witness protection, anything he wants, if he'll roll over on Horstman. When will Raul be told about the shutdown?"

"Monday morning at eight."

"If Horstman wants to use Raul's delivery service, he'll have to contact his suppliers after that. Any chance you could work your magic by then?"

I couldn't admit that I was a quaking coward. "With some luck, yeah."

After Les disconnected, I called the motel's front desk. I told the lady at the desk that I'd be waiting in the bathroom with a fifty. If she could convince the news crew that I wasn't in, it was hers. In a few minutes, a maid let herself in. Through the slightly open bathroom door, I could see Rebecca standing in the doorway. She watched the maid clean for a few minutes before she left. The maid watched until the crew packed up, then came and claimed her fifty.

I waited another half-hour, packed all my belongings, paid the bill, and put all my stuff in the car. Les was right. According to the laptop, Horstman hadn't moved.

I drove to the hospital and parked in their lot, then walked into the lobby. Hidden by the smoked glass, I watched the parking lot. An older man in a white Toyota Corolla double parked until a spot opened that had a view of my car and the lobby doors. I noted the numbers on his plate, then went to

THE FRAME

find Doctor Godfrey.

Unfortunately, he was in, and he wanted to look at the wound. When I assured him that everything he did hurt, he poked me with a needle and took a syringe full of blood. I had to wait for an hour until he received the results. He looked disappointed when he told me not to come back for a week, as if I'd wasted his time by coming in when there was nothing wrong.

As I left the hospital, the first order of business was to lose the tail. California freeways make that easy. I took 280 north, then took an exit and pulled over halfway down the off-ramp. That move forced the guy in the white Toyota Corolla to drive by me and then make a choice at the signal light. He did the best thing, he turned right and hid in a parking lot. I went straight across the intersection and returned to the freeway. Figuring that it would take him two minutes to make a U-turn and get back on the freeway, I got off at the next exit. Heading back toward San Jose on surface streets, I did some doubling back to make sure I'd lost him.

At six that evening, I finally found a place I liked. The three story motel with the mission motif was built around a central parking lot dotted with trees. One wing of the building included a restaurant. My room on the third floor had a living area, a kitchen off a small dining area complete with two chairs and a table, and a queen bed in the bedroom. The room, the carpet, and the drapes were done in browns and tans. Even the pictures were earth tones. It felt clean.

Pleased with my selection, I unpacked all my stuff. I ate a very forgettable dinner at the restaurant and I was back in my room by seven. I had left my tools on the dining room table, not believing I was actually going to bug Deke Horstman's house, but thinking that I should have the phone bug ready in case I changed my mind.

I selected a bug and programmed it with the laptop's cellular number. When that was done, I took the motel's phone apart and alligator clipped the bug to the proper wires in the phone. I turned the television on and set my timer for thirty minutes. The circuit would store thirty minutes of sound, and then it would dial the cellular number of the receiver connected to the laptop. Once connected, it would send the data to the laptop in about seven seconds. When I wanted to hear what the bug had sent, software in the laptop would reconstruct the original sound.

Just before the thirty minutes elapsed, I put on the holster and gun, donned a light windbreaker to cover the holster, and walked out onto the third floor landing. A brisk breeze was blowing all the smog down from the north bay, I

199

could see it reflecting the lights to the south where the valley necked down. In the evenings, a fifty-mile series of valleys, warm with the day's heat, pulled the cool air above the bay south. In the mornings, ocean breezes came north through the same valleys.

I watched the parking lot for some time. A number of cars circled the lot, most opting for parking spots near the restaurant. The elevator seemed risky. It would stop, the door would open, and the man with a gun would kill me before I had a chance to move. I walked down the stairs, holding the butt of the 9mm under my jacket. I was putting the key in the car door when the night closed in on me. I could feel someone on the upper landing aiming a gun at me. I must have looked like a fool, trying to put the car between the empty landing and me. Regardless, I retreated up the stairs and back into the apartment.

I stood inside the door, feeling foolish. How the hell could I work if I was afraid of the dark? Determined to get past this thing, I took off my jacket and the holster, held the 9mm in my right hand and draped the jacket over the gun. Walking down the stairs with the gun in my hand, I passed a man wearing shorts and a sweatshirt going up. That felt better, I could have nailed him if he reached for a weapon.

Inside the car, I brought up the program to convert the digital data to sound. I was listening to the television program the bug had recorded when a van stopped behind my car. A man got out and walked through the van's headlights. In his right hand, I saw a flash of black steel. I grabbed the 9mm, flicked the laser on and pushed the safety in. As he approached on the driver's side, I could see his hand in the rearview mirror, he carried a large, square gun. As I twisted to aim the 9mm, I saw the drill motor he carried. My screaming nerves barely registered in time to keep from pulling the trigger. He continued by, unaware how close he had come to death.

I switched the laser off, wondering if my hammering heart would hold up. I felt like an armed basket case, I had to get a grip before I hurt someone.

CHAPTER TWENTY-FOUR

I called Javier just after nine the next morning. He sounded so grouchy, I had to ask, "What's the matter, you don't like working on Sunday?"

"Usually I love it, but today, I'm sitting with some slime-sucking mother-fucker who forced his two-year-old niece to drink Drano so she couldn't tell her parents who raped her. If I don't get some cooperation real soon, the suicide rate in holding is going up."

The rhetoric was obviously for the benefit of the accused, but I marveled at Javier's self-control.

He didn't need my interruption so I hurried my request. "There might be a party at our man's house today about two. Can Nora come to the party, or will she be busy?"

"We'll arrange something. Carry when you go, good buddy, no telling how rowdy the party will get."

After I hung up, I propped pillows against the headboard of the bed and sat there with a glass of wine. I shut my eyes and tried to anticipate every problem that might arise during the break-in. I walked down the street, used the lockpick to open his front door, used an ultrasonic to subdue the dog, searched for his office, found his phone, installed the bug, put all my tools away, wiped up any fingerprints, and left the house. Then I went through it all again; this time the dog was in the front yard, the lockpick didn't work, his office was in the kitchen, and anything else that could screw me up. An hour later, I felt ready.

I drove to a pet store. They had an ultrasonic unit capable of 105 decibels. To a dog, the noise would be no worse than the brain rattling blasters kids have in their cars, but, unlike kids, dogs really object to that shit.

When I got back to the motel, I put on my business suit so I'd look like a salesman. In my briefcase, I arranged the tools I'd need. My stomach had a knot in it as I left the room. As I drove toward south San Jose, I sang along with the radio, trying not to think.

I parked on a boulevard where I could see Deke's front yard. Just after one, Deke backed the Cadillac out of the driveway. His parents shared the front seat with him as he made the left turn onto the boulevard. I watched their car until they were out of sight, while I put on my tie and suit coat. I turned on the police scanner, threaded the earpiece wire under my arm and up to my ear, and then put the scanner in my inside coat pocket. Lugging the overweight briefcase with the B&E tools, I walked to Deke's house. I opened the wrought iron gate and walked up to the front door, ready to insert the electronic lockpick. Deke had thought of that, he had a digital keypad lock. If it's not one fucking thing, it's another.

Using the crowbar on the front door was out, there was no point bugging his place if he knew someone had been there. I followed the sidewalk to the side of the house. The eight-foot tall, concrete block wall had a redwood gate that was hidden from the street by several tall cypress shrubs. Using the crowbar, I pried two boards off the gate and slipped into the backyard.

A two-story house to the rear had an unrestricted view of Deke's backyard. From the cover of a shrub, I watched the windows for a minute without seeing any activity.

Resisting the urge to hurry, I examined the rear of Deke's house, finding a sliding glass door into the kitchen. The door was secured by a latch and a bolt lock mounted with self-tapping screws in the aluminum frame. Both screws pulled out easily when I lifted the door with the crowbar, and the latch lost its precarious hold on the frame at the same time. When I slid the door back, the huge rottweiler poked his head into my crotch, looking more interested than angry. Once he got my scent, he changed his mind and started growling. I turned on the ultrasonic, the dog jerked backwards, almost falling on the kitchen linoleum, then he turned and ran out of the room. I stepped into the house and closed the sliding glass door.

Food remnants and dirty dishes crowded the small Formica table and every other flat surface in the kitchen. The house smelled of urine and dog. In the living room, the mess was equally incredible—newspapers and dog toys covered the floor. The whimpering dog was tearing at the couch with his teeth, trying to do something, anything, to stop the assault on his ears. When I shut the ultrasonic off, he barked at me once, then ran up the stairs.

I peeked into the downstairs bedroom. It belonged to Deke's parents, judging by the size of the women's panties lying on the floor. I climbed the stairs slowly, not wanting to surprise the dog. When I got to the landing, he suddenly charged out of the far bedroom, recoiling as if he had hit an invisible wall when I switched the noisemaker on. I stepped into a room filled with exercise equipment to give the dog a clear path. When I switched it off, the dog scurried by, then fell down the stairs, making a horrendous racket but evidently not doing any damage; he was still at top speed when he ran into the kitchen, and something crashed to the floor there.

The next room contained a steel desk with a computer, printer and telephone sharing the surface. Deke's office I guessed. An office chair and two tall steel filing cabinets were the only other furnishings. The filing cabinets were locked with a steel bar and hasp. The computer was on, set up in a phone-answering mode. An Icon labeled "SCRAMBLER" on the screen wasn't active.

In a hurry, I took his phone apart. Bigger than shit, a bug identical to mine was already in place, the fucking DEA probably. Furious that the assholes hadn't bothered to share that with the police, I cut their bug out, leaving the legs in place. Using the magnifying glass and the small soldering iron, I soldered my bug's seven tiny legs to the ones I'd snipped off the DEA bug, then covered it with gray epoxy to fuck up the DEA in case they wanted to replace mine.

As I assembled the phone, the scanner popped to life. "Nora Six, Control."

If I had to run, Deke was going to know I'd been here. As I rushed the screws into the phone, Javier answered the page. There was a man on the floor in McDonald's. Javier told control that both he and Nora Six would respond. As Javier's voice faded, I put the last of my tools in the briefcase.

I came downstairs with the ultrasonic in my hand. I didn't need it, the dog had learned the game. He skirted the periphery of the living room, then scrambled up the stairs.

I screwed the sliding door lock back into the track, and the screws grabbed enough metal to hold the lock for the moment. The door would be unlatched and unbolted, but with any luck, Deke or his parents would blame themselves. Before I opened the door, I watched the windows in the house overlooking the backyard. Seeing nothing, I stepped outside and slid the door closed.

Replacing the two boards in the side gate took forever. I couldn't afford to hammer the nails so I enlarged the holes with a pointed pick until the nails pushed in. With that done, I sauntered back toward my car on watery legs.

As I started the car, I drew my first complete breath in twenty-five minutes. The adrenaline high and the successful B&E brought a feeling of euphoria. I had done it, I had gone into the bear's lair and tweaked the beast, I was tougher than I looked.

I wanted to tell Javier about the DEA bug, since the DEA could be the source of Deke's information about the police. It wouldn't be the first time the DEA protected a dealer so they could identify his boss. Of course, if I told Javier about what I'd found during the break-in, he would have direct knowledge of a felony, not a comfortable solution. Besides, the DEA involvement was supposition; we would still have to assume a dirty cop, just in case.

After I returned to the motel, I checked the laptop every half hour, waiting for the bug to check in. At midnight, it still hadn't sent anything. I didn't know if it wasn't working, or if Deke didn't use his office on Sunday, or if he knew someone had been in the house. I drank a water glass full of wine worrying that the entire exercise had been for nothing.

The wine didn't help. I slept badly until the nightmare drove me out of bed at four. Earl with the hole for a face was standing near the door as I awoke, a solid apparition that slowly faded into the drapes. He seemed so real that I had to touch the drapes. Rummy tired, I got back in bed at six and slept until the ocean sound of tires on the boulevard woke me just before nine.

I was brushing my teeth when the phone rang; all my nerves jumped and I bit the toothbrush. I was picking bristles out of my teeth when I grabbed the handset. It was Clay. "Thought you'd want to know, I announced that we were shutting down production in Mexico at the morning production meeting. After the meeting, Raul left the plantsite."

"To phone Deke from a pay phone, I hope."

"That would be my guess. This thing will have to end soon, I'm to the point I can't stomach being in the same room with him. It's going to show, sooner or later."

"If we get one of those flats, it will all be over."

After we disconnected, I noted the time, 9:24. If Raul had contacted Deke at nine, the bug could check in as early as nine-thirty. My choice for a bug hadn't been the smartest move I'd ever made. Often it took hours for that type of bug to record thirty minutes of conversation; people didn't talk non-stop, they paused between sentences, they were quiet while they looked something up, they waited for the other person to speak, and the bug ignored all that quiet time.

I wouldn't check it until ten. To save my sanity, I decided to go for a two mile run. I put on my grubbies and started off, the gun a welcome presence against my side. The morning low clouds blocking the sun were dissipating. The south wind filled the valley with a faint odor of garlic that made me hungry. Not quite a mile from the motel, I ducked into a restaurant for breakfast.

I didn't get back to the motel until quarter to eleven. With my heart in my mouth, I got into the car and opened the laptop. Bigger than life, the mail icon in the corner of the screen had a question mark. I pushed the record button on the recorder, and clicked the mail button with the mouse.

"Yeah?" Deke's sharp voice filled the car.

"It's me," Raul said. "There's been a development. In three weeks, they shut off deliveries for two months."

"They know?"

"No. Inventories are too high, they're stopping production in Mexico for two months."

"What makes you so sure they don't know?"

"Same ol' shit every day, not one thing different from the last 17 years. That guy hasn't been back, there are no new faces, Clay barely notices me, nobody has been in my office after hours, my girl hasn't heard anything, just nothing."

"So we can do three deliveries, then nothing for two months?"

"If you can still do one tomorrow. Otherwise it's two."

"I'll see." The bug clicked twice before Deke dialed a sequence of digits. A phone rang, then Deke punched in another long sequence. Then, just after another sequence of digits was entered, a female voice answered. Deke's mother said, "Hi," in response.

The woman said, "You're up early."

"Yeah, Dexter got some wild bug up his caboose and went out, so I had to pack him a lunch. He loves tuna fish and cucumber sandwiches, can you imagine? Says he can't get them out. I'm using his phone 'cause it's quiet up here, the old fart watches that shopping thing on TV so loud gives me a headache. Did you ever watch that?"

As she rambled on, I realized that she had saved me weeks of frustration. Given Deke's net way of talking, the bug wouldn't have recorded thirty minutes of conversation in three weeks, if then. Next time, I'd use a bug that I could interrogate remotely.

I replayed the digits Deke had dialed. It took three tries before I caught all the numbers. I called Javier's number and left a message on his voice mail:

"I've got something that might interest both you and Les."

Les Taylor called a few minutes later. After I gave him my new address, he said he'd be by in fifteen minutes. I was watching from the third floor landing when he drove into the lot. Jeff Katz, the undercover Narc, was with his boss. I whistled to get their attention. When they got off the elevator, Les was fanning the air. He had reason, Jeff's odor was physically punishing.

"Let's stay outside," I told Jeff. "No offense, but the room would never air out."

Jeff grinned. "That good? I thought pucker-fucker here was exaggerating." He pulled up his filthy sweatshirt and carefully removed a cloth sack duct-taped to his belly. He leaned over the parapet and let the sack drop to the parking lot. The odor went with it.

Wanting to know that secret, I asked, "What's in there?"

"Rags from a cat litter box. Pure cat piss." He laughed. "Fuckin' awesome, ain't it?"

He was as awesome as the odor. His hair was greasy, dirt and blackheads covered his face, and I didn't want to touch his hands, they seemed to be covered with open sores. When I asked, he told me, "Crepe paper and superglue." He frowned at his hands. "Takes hours to get the shit off."

Les Taylor, resplendent in an iridescent sharkskin suit, beamed at Jeff as he explained, "We're working a scam, trying to get a dealer to show his product. Jeff is going to be walking by while I'm talking with the guy. He's going to recognize me and try to score some dope." He patted Jeff on the back and grinned about the anticipated bust before he asked, "Javier said you had something to show us?"

Inside, I had the tape machine on the coffee table. Les and Jeff sat on the couch. I told them about Clay's plan to push the delivery of more flats. After I assured Les that someone else must have planted a bug in Deke's house, and that I just happened to have a device that would pick it up, I played the tape.

When the tape ended, I gave them a listing of the numbers Deke had used. Jeff knew what they were. "That's the San Diego area-code, Deke called a pager service there. The Microfix plant is in Tijuana, right?" When I nodded, he said, "San Diego pager service covers Tijuana." He pointed to the last seven numbers. "This is their code, it could mean anything, like the quantity and when it's supposed to ship."

I asked Jeff, "How does he know Tijuana got the order?"

"Same way. Someone in Tijuana calls a pager service here and they page

Deke with code numbers." Jeff pointed at Les' watch. "Let's go, that prick ain't going to wait."

Les nodded. As he walked to the door, he said, "I don't want to touch any of this officially until all the ducks are lined up. Whatever help the two of us can give you, we will, but you'll have to carry the load. Can we help get one of those flats?"

"I have that covered."

"How about following Raul to see where he delivers?"

"I have that covered, too."

Les nodded, and opened the door. As he passed me, Jeff said, "You pull this off, we'll give you our poker secrets." High praise from a cop, I was very pleased.

After they left, I called the shipping department at Microfix. When Raul answered, I said, "This is Mr. Morris from First National Bank, may I speak with Gina Rawlins."

When she picked up the phone, she said, "Yes, sir, what can I do for you?"

"I assume Raul can hear you, so I'll do the talking. Flats will be on the truck from Mexico tomorrow. Will you be able to get one?"

"He's gone now, Gary, the bank story has him scared." She giggled before she said, "He puts the flats in his office, then he hand-trucks them to his car when he leaves, usually around six. I don't remember exactly, but I think he usually stays in his office when he has flats. I'd only be able to get one if he leaves the department."

"I'll ask Clay to keep him busy for a half-hour. Will that be enough time?"

"Sure. We keep flattened cardboard boxes stacked in a bin outside his office, I'll slip one in there. I don't know if I can get it out to my car."

"Don't worry about that, I'll pick up the flat from the bin after everyone is gone. What kind of car does Raul drive and where is it now?"

"He drives a brown and tan Lincoln Town Car. You can't miss it, it's the only one parked near the loading dock."

"Can he see it from his office?"

"Yes, sir, I can have the money by then."

Raul was within earshot again. "Thanks again, Gina. Please be careful."

"Yes sir, I'll do that," she said, and disconnected.

I called Clay and left a message. When he called back, I told him I wanted to put a tracker on Raul's car, so would he set up a meeting with Raul somewhere away from shipping? Clay called me back two minutes later;

Raul would be in Clay's office at three.

By three, I was at Microfix. As Gina had said, Raul's car was parked next to the loading dock. I parked some distance away and walked to his car. Hoping no one was looking, I laid on my back behind the car. The wide frame of the Lincoln was flat where the bumper attached, the tracker sucked out of my hand as if eager to do the job. It was programmed to come on the next afternoon at four and to transmit every five minutes.

That done, I walked back to my car, trying to guess what the conspirators would do next. Deke would have to make the arrangements to have those flats processed into usable form. He ordered the flats using his home phone. The only number he contacted was a paging service, but I guessed that he would use pay phones to make the processing arrangements. Since the battery in the tracker on Deke's car would expire before morning, I hoped he would make those contacts while I could still find him.

Taking a guess, I drove to Deke's favorite pay phone near the Safeway grocery store. By double parking and making a nuisance of myself, I got a parking space within spitting distance of the phones.

Just after four, the laptop reported Deke's car on the move. Like the first time, he made three short stops, two in different locations than before. I didn't have to see the locations, they had to be storage units. He wasn't arranging processing, he was selling. After the third stop, I waited for the next readout, hoping he'd be heading toward me.

The best laid plans of mice and men are approximately equal, he was heading away. I made an illegal turn out of the parking lot, ran a red light and made it to the freeway. The accelerator against the stops, the Dodge did six miles in just under five minutes. Getting close, I stopped on the shoulder of the freeway to look at the display. It showed Deke about a mile away, stopped. I took the next off-ramp at some insane speed and made both lights on the boulevard.

I spotted the Corvette in a strip mall but I didn't see Deke. I cruised the lot, looking for pay phones. Finally, I parked and went into a liquor store. The Vietnamese lady at the counter explained where the pay phones were in what I guessed was English. When she noted my blank look, she walked me out and pointed at the gas station on the corner.

Deke was sitting on a low planter next to the phones. The parking lot near the gas station was empty. I drove over and parked there with the passenger side window facing Deke. I poked a hole in a newspaper; settled my back against the driver's door, and watched Deke through the hole. Deke watched me for a moment, then something to his left caught his interest. A man walked past him and used the phone. Judging by his body language, Deke didn't care.

The man finished and walked away. The phone rang. I picked up the directional microphone. Deke was facing away from me as he picked up the phone, so I dropped the paper and aimed the parabola at him and clicked the recorder on. Deke said, "1333 Fremont, number 16. Don't forget to change the locks. Page me with your number when it's done. If I don't get back to you in a half hour, page me again. If we don't connect in an hour, I'll page you with my number and we'll straighten it out."

Deke was listening when a white Japanese compact drove between us. The driver, a man in his fifties, looked at me with a startled expression. The microphone boom extending from the center of the plate sized parabola was a hollow tube, he might have thought it was a gun barrel. He looked at my car's license plate as he drove away.

I didn't want to draw a cop with Deke watching, so I folded up shop and took off for the motel.

CHAPTER TWENTY-FIVE

The next afternoon, Gina called at two to tell me that the flats had arrived, ending hours of nervous anticipation. Clay had called Raul to his office shortly after the truck unloaded, giving Gina the opportunity to hide a flat in the bin containing flattened cardboard. "The flat is between the two tallest pieces of cardboard."

"Thanks, Gina. Did anyone see you?"

"I don't think so." Her voice sounded sad. "Is Raul in danger?"

"The police need Raul alive; they'll protect him."

"It'll seem strange to him if I break our date for tonight."

"Then don't break the date, develop a vaginal infection. Maybe get pissed at him and accuse him of sleeping around. Tell him it could be herpes. Anything like that. Just don't let him wonder why you broke the date."

She said quietly, "Okay, I'll do that. You be careful." The phone disconnecting sounded final.

I believe in Murphy's Law. With the end of the case so close, something had to go wrong. I had worked my checklist: charged the batteries, tested the radios, assembled a collection of easily placed eavesdropping bugs, oiled the gun, wiped dust from each bullet, and, for the first time in months, I bore-sighted the gun to align the aiming laser. I felt ready but the unknown nagged at me.

I called Javier and told him I would have one of Raul's flats that evening. He would be waiting at his apartment. "When do you expect to be here?" he asked.

"I don't know. I'm going to tail Raul until he delivers the rest of the flats, then I'll go by Microfix and pick up the one that's hidden."

"Call me when you know where he's delivered. If you buy the farm, I'll have to tail him next time; I hate that shit."

In my car at quarter to four, I waited for what seemed years for Raul's tracker to check in. Four came and went, and the minutes dragged. I kept reminding myself that the start time was programmed by setting a delay. I'd specified a delay of 26 hours, but from when? Was it exactly 2:00 p.m. yesterday when I set it? Or was it later? I hadn't paid close attention.

At 4:12, the tracker data appeared on the screen. Feeling the adrenaline start, I entered the map coordinates for Microfix into the laptop. I returned to the room, gathered all my gear, rode the elevator to ground level, and then put it in the car. As I waited for a break in the traffic streaming by on the boulevard, I felt the elation beginning to build. That worried me; fate loves a confident man.

I was eating a fast-food cheeseburger in my car at six that evening when the tracker reported that Raul's car had moved. Parked near the intersection he would take, I started the engine, expecting him in minutes. Five minutes later, the next readout showed his car in the same spot. Guessing he had moved his car to load the flats, I stopped the engine.

I watched the readouts for the next half-hour. Two minutes after the last report showed no change, he pulled up on the opposite side of the intersection. When the light changed, he made a left turn. I waited until the cross traffic built up before I started the engine and made the turn to follow him.

At a nearby freeway, instead of turning south toward San Jose, he took the northbound ramp. The short merge lane almost nailed me. I was looking for an opening in the traffic as I accelerated, and some idiot had decided to stop and wait. Luckily, a driver in the slow lane had lagged a car length behind another car, leaving me enough space to swerve by the stopped car.

The concrete interstate snaked over the hills on the east side of the bay. In the evening crush, it was easy to tail Raul, the glut of cars drove north in lockstep. Forty miles north of San Jose, Raul took the off-ramp to an upscale bedroom community named Pleasanton. The ramp ended with me right behind Raul at a stop sign. I turned left when he went right. I took the next right turn and stopped.

The tracker's next readout showed him stopped less than a mile away. I drove slowly by that location. The Lincoln was parked beside a long, single story, corrugated metal industrial building. A man wearing a stained leather apron was loading the flats onto a hand truck. AAA FIBERGLASS SPECIALTIES had fiberglass wheelbarrow bodies and bathtub surrounds stacked beside the building.

A fiberglass business would be the natural distributor for the flats. But would Raul do an eighty mile round-trip to make twenty dollars for a cousin? I could hear Gina's, "I don't think so."

When I returned to the nearly empty freeway going south to San Jose, I called Javier at home and told him where Raul took the flats. After he took down the information, he said, "For a civilian, you do good work."

"How long will it take to analyze the flat?"

"If they find anything, I should be able to get a search warrant by morning. You want to come along?"

"And lose my beauty sleep? No way."

"What's the matter, you don't want to be around all those desperate, crazed people with automatic weapons."

I finished the standard cop joke for him. "No, I don't. And what if the bad guys are armed, too?"

"When do you think you can get here tonight?"

"If I'll be more than an hour, I'll call you."

Minutes later, I took the off-ramp and drove to Microfix. When I told the security guard my name, he directed me to Clay's office.

Clay was on the phone when I arrived at his open office door. He said, "It'll be a minute, I'm on hold." There was a red plunger on the wall near his desk. While he waited on the phone, I wandered over and looked at the sign. It was an emergency circuit breaker for the power in the plant. He nodded toward the switch. "It's my panic button. If anything unusual happens, I get to overreact." He waved the handset at me. "That's the reason for this call, all the emergency lights were removed for battery replacement and... Yes, I'm here," he said into the phone.

Judging by Clay's half of the conversation, the maker of the special battery had gone out of business, and the people servicing the lights couldn't find a replacement battery. Clay was very patient but he finally said, "I do understand your dilemma, but you're giving me all the reasons those lights can't be saved. They can be saved, and they will be, if not by you, by someone else. It's your decision. Return them as-is, or fix them by this weekend."

He stood up as he placed the handset in its niche. "During busy times like this, business people forget the value of long term relationships. He wants to sell me new emergency lighting; he thinks holding my lights hostage will work." Clay suddenly grinned. "He should read the papers, I've been there."

Clay and I walked the silent hall toward shipping. The doors to all the workrooms were shut, the long hall felt like a bowling alley.

As Gina had said, the flat was wedged between the two tallest squares of cardboard. The flat looked as if thick tarpaper had been machine stamped into 24 pockets, and then coated with cloudy resin to both hold the shape and make it waterproof. It was thicker and heavier than the flats I was familiar with.

I borrowed a packaging tape dispenser from a desk, and taped cardboard around the flat. As we walked toward the lobby, I patted Clay on the back. "As soon as the police lab finds dope in this thing, it's all over."

He nodded, looking glum. "What a waste it's all been."

When Javier answered my knock, I handed him the flat. "That's it."

Inside his apartment, I watched Javier bounce the flat. "Katz was right on the money, I'd say it weighs about six ounces." He dug a small pocketknife out of his pants' pocket, scratched the coating with the blade, and then sniffed the blade of his knife. He held the knife out to me. It didn't have an odor but something attacked the lining of my nose. "Jalepeño," Javier said. "Screws up a dog's nose, they don't sniff that twice. Clever." He put on his coat. "I'm going to run this down to the lab now. Hopefully they'll have an answer by morning."

As we parted, I felt a huge weight evaporate. My part was finished, the DA would squeeze Raul until he gave up Deke, and then the bad guys would be locked away.

When I reached the motel, I drove around the parking lot looking for people in the parked cars. I didn't see anyone. I parked close to the stairs. With my hand on the gun, I walked up the stairs, unlocked the door, and went into my room. Leaving the door open, I searched the apartment, the gun in my hand. Convinced my fortress was free of bad guys, I locked the door.

I had poured a large glass of wine when I remembered that I hadn't looked at the laptop's screen since Pleasanton. I didn't know if Deke's phone bug had checked in. I put the holster back on and walked outside.

The night was balmy with a stiff wind that was trying to blow all the airborne trash into Nevada. The lights of the passing cars were bright; jewel-like, their noise muted by the wind. The tropical night suggested romance rather than danger, the tire noise suggested waves breaking on a gentle shore.

Inside the car, I opened the laptop. The mail icon in the corner of the screen had a question mark. I pushed the record button on the tape machine, joysticked the cursor over to the mail button and double clicked.

The playback began when Deke picked up his phone. A male voice asked,

"Can you scramble?" Deke must have engaged the scrambler without saying anything. Since the scrambling unit was attached to the phone line only for the original call, and not the call from the bug, the playback was clear. The caller said, "I tailed Charboneau tonight. He followed our man to our location in Pleasanton."

"Fuck." Horstman echoed my expletive. I hadn't looked for a tail, too busy keeping track of Raul. Horstman asked, "Didn't our man take the required precautions?"

"Yes sir, he followed them to the letter. Charboneau can track a car from a distance. Just like last night, he didn't follow you and your car wasn't transmitting." Fear numbed my body, they knew everything about me. I took the gun out of the holster and put it on the car seat beside me, glancing in the mirrors to check my surroundings. The caller continued in that measured voice. "If I hadn't seen him aiming the microphone at you, I wouldn't have known that he was following you. He's ex-DEA, he might have access to military technology."

Horstman evidently had an electronics expert on his payroll. No wonder the police couldn't get close. Police departments generally have poor radio technology, anyone with a $200 FM interceptor can spot a multi-car tail in a minute. San Jose was no exception.

"Water under the bridge," Horstman said. "I'll have them toss the shipment."

"That isn't the bad news, sir," the caller continued. "On the way back, he called a man named Javier, who must be a cop. Judging by their conversation, the police have a unit under analysis."

I couldn't believe my stupidity, using the cellular to relay that information to Javier. Horstman couldn't believe what he was hearing either. "Are you positive? Oh, shit, of course you're positive."

The caller continued, "And since Charboneau tailed both you and our contact, the police must know everything."

There was a moment of silence before Deke said, "Yes, we have to assume that they know everything." After a lengthy period, he continued, "They can only connect me to the merchandise through the storage yards. They'll watch them for a few weeks. I'll need to know when they stop watching. After that, we'll wait for a couple of months just to be on the safe side."

"So you don't want me to tail you anymore?"

"I won't be working. Just watch the storage lockers."

"What about Charboneau? Do you want me to continue watching him?"

"No, that won't be necessary. Just the lockers."

"Right."

The caller disconnected.

Since the guy was no longer watching me, it was safe to use the cellular. I stopped the playback and dialed Javier's apartment. When his phone machine answered, I disconnected and then called the police department. According to the desk sergeant, Javier, his partner, Vic Stauder, and Les Taylor were all gone for the day. I asked for Jeff Katz. The desk sergeant took my number and name and said he would ask Jeff to call. I must have communicated the urgency, because Jeff called two minutes later. "Hey, Dude, what's up?" he asked. There was street noise in the background, I could picture the scummy looking kid hanging at a phone booth.

I said, "You guys don't have to worry about Deke having a contact in the department, he hired an electronics expert to tail him when he went out on business. He probably spotted your radio traffic when you were near Horstman. He's good, he's been tailing me and I had no clue."

"Fuck me." Jeff sounded depressed. "I been tellin' them we gotta stop using that old crap; get into some digital shit we can encrypt."

"I wasn't any smarter," I told him. "The guy overheard me talking to Javier on my cellular when I told him where Raul delivered those flats. Horstman probably got the word two hours ago; they could have dumped the shipment by now."

Jeff was suddenly all cop. "We'll take a look. Where'd he take them?" I could hear the excitement in his voice.

"To a company named ...do you have a pencil?"

"Hang tight...okay, go."

"He delivered them to AAA FIBERGLASS SPECIALTIES, 10940 River Circle Road in Pleasanton."

"Okay, I'll work on that." Jeff abruptly disconnected.

When I resumed the playback of Deke's bug, he was using a speed dial to call another number. A woman answered, the noise of a television program garbling the playback. "Is Dick in?" Horstman asked her. Her soft voice faded into the noise before Deke said, "Have him call me, it's very important."

Deke used the speed dial to call another number. A sleepy man yelled, "What?"

"Jerry? You awake?"

The man was suddenly very awake. "Yes, sir."

"Come to my house as soon as you can. In minutes, you understand?"

"Yes, sir, on my way."

Deke disconnected, then immediately dialed again. A woman answered and Deke said, "This is Mr. Horstman. He will want to talk with me." The phone played music that seemed to last for a year before a man with a heavy Spanish accent answered. They both activated scramblers. Deke told him of the developments.

His voice calm, the man said, "We must salvage what we can. We can find other ways to deliver the merchandise, but that will be of no value if we lose your contacts. Are you open to a suggestion?"

"Of course."

"Witnesses have seen the product as it's altered for shipment. Units in that form must be disposed of."

"That's being done now," Horstman said.

"Good. Your serious problem is Mr. Charboneau. Only through his testimony can the police make your man give you up. Do you see the solution?"

"I'm working on that."

That rang all the alarm bells. I was the only witness who could tie Raul to AAA FIBERGLASS SPECIALTIES. Deke needed me dead. I had to get inside the room and call for the cavalry, no telling how long ago Horstman had put that plan into effect.

As I opened the car door, I saw a man approaching. Fear turned my guts to jelly. I hurriedly closed and locked the door. The man approached from the rear. I could see in the side mirror that he was carrying something in his hand. I grabbed the 9mm, flicked on the laser, and pushed the safety in, fear drying my mouth. He suddenly raised his hand. I was falling away when the world went white, the blinding flash and the sledge hammer impact on the left side of my face simultaneous.

The sky was bright but the early morning sun hadn't penetrated the valley below; the houses spaced along the country road were still in the shadow of the hills to the east. I pushed off the hill top, the waxed wooden runners making squeaking sounds as the sled accelerated on the short, dew-laden grass that covered the steep incline. The wind screamed past my ears; the barbed wire fence edging the cliff at the bottom of the hill loomed nearer. As the incline leveled, I rolled off the sled, bracing for the impact.

I bounced, waking suddenly, lying sideways on the seat of the car, the laser a brilliant red pinpoint on the dashboard. I could see the lights from the second floor of the motel. The shattered side window dripped glass shards.

What the hell had happened?

Suddenly a gun appeared in the window. The laser's red dot found it and I pulled the trigger. The blast seemed to echo. The car filled with debris as the windshield blew apart in a flash of sparks. It was quiet. I frantically blinked my left eye, trying to clear the fog. I could hear my pulse pounding in my ears; warm liquid trickled down my neck. My left hand came away covered in blood.

Where the hell was he? Crouched down beside the door? Waiting for me to raise my head? I fumbled for the cellular but the handset crumbled in my hand. The laptop was smoking.

I saw a head silhouetted in the window, but the laser didn't show. I blinked and saw Javier there. "Did you call?" he asked.

"What happened?" Instead of answering, he evaporated, the diffused glow becoming a walkway light on the motel's second floor. Had he been there?

A motor roared into life. I sat up quickly. Too quickly. The steering wheel jumped at my face and smashed into my cheek. I lifted my head and turned carefully, in time to see a SUV careen drunkenly out of the parking lot into the busy avenue. A speeding car clipped its rear, the "whump" accompanied by a huge cloud of dust and smoke. The SUV spun out of the cloud, lurching to a stop facing toward me, its rear axle skewed sideways.

I managed to get out of my car, leaning on the side for support. The SUV's driver door opened and a man got out, holding what looked like an assault rifle. He propped it on the hood, aiming at me.

I wanted to fall on the ground, but I couldn't figure out how to do that. Anchored in concrete, I could only watch as he sighted. He seemed to be taking forever to kill me.

The dark colored SUV sitting sideways in the street must have been hard to see, a speeding car never braked before it hit, the sudden impact an explosion that lifted the SUV into a half-roll. Pinned against the opposite side by the force of the collision, the man seemed to sink into the pavement beneath the dark shape.

Sirens were loud and close. People edged out of doorways in the motel, looking at me fearfully. I realized that I was still holding the gun. I turned to put it into the car, which abruptly disappeared. The ground approached at some weird angle and smashed into my left side, bouncing my head, sending bright lights and pain ricocheting through my skull.

I was very tired. I wanted to rest but there was something I should be doing. Oh yeah, I was going to move to another motel. I wanted to get up but

·

someone held me down.

The kneeling cop searched my eyes. "You hear me?" he asked.

I was on the ground. What the hell was I doing on the ground? Had I been in a wreck? My face hurt and I couldn't see out of my left eye. "Do you have any idea how bad I'm hurt?" I asked him.

"No. Lie still, we have an ambulance on the way."

"Do you know what happened?"

He put his hand on my shoulder. "Just lie quietly, Mr. Charboneau."

"Do I know you?" I tried to recognize his face. How much had I forgotten?

"No. I was with you the last time you were shot. You weren't awake."

The last time? "Did someone shoot me?"

He patted my shoulder again. "Take it easy. If they'd hit anything vital, you'd be puking all over my shoes about now."

I wanted to puke but I was afraid my head would split open if I did. The fear came in waves. I might be dying.

A paramedic scared me when he radioed that I had five penetrating wounds to the head. Another strapped an oxygen mask to my face and started an IV. The ambulance driver was in a hurry. I listened to the siren scream as the top-heavy truck lurched around corners.

CHAPTER TWENTY-SIX

At the hospital, the two paramedics from the ambulance used the gurney like a battering ram, hurling me into an emergency room. A trauma team: two doctors and three nurses moved me to a table and began setting up equipment. One of the nurses cut off my clothes. I was cold and shaking, from shock perhaps. A nurse trying to take blood stuck me three times. I lifted the oxygen mask. "If you people will stop moving the table, she'll be able to find a vein."

The words brought all the activity to an abrupt halt. The woman directing the team asked, "How do you feel?"

"I'm cold; I have a bad headache and I'm dizzy."

"Can you tell us what happened to you?" she asked, leaning close to shine a small penlight into my left eye. I could see the light through a red haze. Her breath smelled of coffee.

"The last thing I remember is driving on the freeway."

She told me to open my mouth. She probed my cheeks then deliberately made me gag with a tongue depressor. Satisfied, she told a nurse to get x-rays taken of my head and right thigh.

"What's wrong with my leg?" It felt fine.

"You have six holes in your thigh and five in the side of your face. Whatever hit you didn't penetrate very far, but I don't want to guess."

The x-rays found glass from the car. The pieces in my face popped out with a minimum of pain. The six nodules in my leg took some digging. My left eyelid required thirteen stitches. Altogether, nothing excruciating. I also had a concussion. The lady doctor told me to stay overnight in the hospital for observation.

Javier was waiting near the nurses' station when they wheeled me through. He looked concerned. I asked, "Do you know who shot at me?"

He grinned as if I'd said something funny. He asked the orderly pushing the chair, "Can I talk with him?"

I answered, "I'm okay, it's just a concussion."

We waited in the hall while the orderly made up a bed. Javier squatted beside the chair, leaning his back against the wall. "According to the witnesses, an older couple just returning from visiting the grandkids, the guy walked up to your car and fired through the side window. Since he missed, I'm guessing the side window glass deflected the bullet. "When he stuck the gun into the car to finish you off, the witnesses heard two shots very close together. The perp fell on the ground clutching his hand. I figure that you got yours off just before his, because his blew the windshield out of your car. We found his gun with two of his fingers about twenty feet away from the car."

"Should be easy to get his fingerprints." Talking hurt my head.

Javier chuckled. "Real easy. He's dead."

Had I chased an unarmed man down and killed him? "Do I need a lawyer?"

Javier grinned. "You really don't remember anything. The idiot decided to shoot at you from the middle of Bascom Avenue. A DUI rolled his truck over on him." Javier looked serious when he added, "We're going to charge the drunk with dumping garbage on a city street."

I had a question, then I forgot what it was.

Maybe I had asked. Javier answered, "His wallet listed him as Gerald D. Cornwell, a local boy into assaults and burglary to keep a habit fed, his arrest record is sixteen pages long. Deke might have fed the habit in exchange for his services."

"You think Deke set this up?"

Javier nodded. "He obviously wanted to nail you to keep us from tying Raul to the fiberglass business."

That left Deke only one option. "Since he didn't kill me, that means he has to take Raul out. We don't have diddly if he manages that."

Javier was ahead of me. "We brought Raul in when I heard about your shooting. If the lab findings stand up, we'll have enough to hold him."

The pain settled behind my left eye. "You have a flat?"

Javier looked worried. "How much do you remember?"

"It ends as I'm driving back from Pleasanton."

He hummed. "Yeah, you brought me a flat earlier. I took it to the lab. There's heroin in it, evidently bonded to the tar paper. They won't know how much until they figure out a way to dissolve the resin coating without destroying the heroin."

He put his hand on my arm. "Do you remember talking to Jeff?"

"Jeff Katz, the Narc?"

Javier stood, wincing as he straightened his right leg. "Yeah. You called him, seconds before the shooting."

I shook my head. Pain drove a wedge deep into my brain, and the entire hallway lurched. When my eyes found Javier again, he asked, "You gonna pass out?"

"Just dizzy. What did I tell Jeff?"

"That Horstman had some sort of electronics expert on his payroll who had tailed you and listened when you talked to me. You said Horstman would dump those flats. Jeff got the Pleasanton Police to go to the place. Bigger than life, they nabbed two guys loading the flats into a truck."

"That's good news."

"Jeff's boss, Les Taylor, is a pig in shit," Javier said, wiping at the stubble on his chin. He saw the question on my face. "Les was really worried about dirty cops, he had been afraid to tell the brass anything. You told Jeff that when Horstman was working, he was tailed by an electronics expert. That's how Horstman knew what we were doing. We know that our radio technology needs upgrading, but using an expert to watch us is a new wrinkle. The department is going to go apeshit when that gets around."

The details confused me until I remembered Horstman's bug. I must have heard it all on that.

It came as a relief to know that it was over. Many people could testify that Raul received the flats that had been found at AAA FIBERGLASS SPECIALTIES. With Raul facing thirty years for trafficking, he'd cut a deal and give the cops Deke and the frame. I was out of danger. The relief made me hungry, and I wanted a peanut butter and jelly sandwich.

Javier left when the orderly put me into bed. A candy striper found a peanut butter and jelly sandwich, and I ate that while a nurse hooked me up to several monitors. After some fussing, they shut out the lights, leaving the room darkened except for a night light.

There was a phone on the night stand. I called Toni at home and got a frosty reception for waking her up in the middle of the night. Her attitude softened when I told her I'd been shot again. When I was sure I had a sympathetic audience, I said, "Like last time, they cut all my clothes off. Could you get someone to go by my place tomorrow and pick up some clothes?"

I had to tell her the entire story before she agreed to come get me in the morning. She said, "Every time you get shot, I get closer to winning the case. I'm going to buy a gun." She laughed and disconnected.

Sleep was fleeting. Ghosts materialized and flew in my face. One apparition had glowing eyes. It was so real that I counted the veins in its right eye. Bugs crawled out of the walls and I could hear scratching on the floor. All the illusions were too outrageous to be scary, but they kept me awake.

Toni was leaning over me when I woke the next morning. I thought she might be another apparition until she said, "You look like shit."

I nodded which hurt my head. "Things kept crawling out of the walls during the night. I thought concussions were supposed to be a piece of cake."

"You didn't tell me you'd been cut so badly."

"The doctors had to dig around to get the glass out."

She seemed unable to concentrate. She rambled about the clothes she'd selected until I stopped her. "I'm all right. They only kept me for observation."

"I saw your car. The roof was bent and the doors won't shut."

I managed to stifle a laugh; my fragile head couldn't take that. "No one's going to rent me another car."

She seemed really pissed. "I hate this. I really hate this. It's too dangerous." Her voice was too loud, my head threatened to detonate. She saw me wince. In a soft voice, she said, "The motel doesn't want you there. I packed all your stuff and paid the bill."

"I'm sorry you had to do that again." Did I dare ask? "Did you get all the high-tech stuff out of the car?"

"I hired a man who will do that, but the police haven't released the car yet." She glared at me for a moment before she said, "I've moved you into my spare bedroom, and don't give me any shit about it."

I needed to stay hidden until the police wrapped Deke up, just in case he was a vengeful loser, so her offer was very welcome news. "I appreciate it; thanks."

"With the guard at the gate, you'll at least have some protection from the media." She jerked her thumb toward the corridor. "The pressure on the hospital is intense, all the big shots from the media are screaming at them to hold a press conference. The morning network news gave you forty seconds, and an on-site report. You must be famous, the tax cut only got thirty seconds."

"Crap, that's all I need. Can I sneak out of here?"

"Oh yeah," she sneered. "Like you're inconspicuous. You look like you were put together by a quilting bee."

The doctor pronounced me ambulatory that afternoon. An orderly slipped me into a service elevator. Toni met me outside the kitchen door. As we passed the front entrance, I saw trucks equipped for television remote broadcasting lining the curb for a block.

I decided I would do the talk show circuit after the police arrested Deke. With a fake nose and the mustache, I could hide my features well enough to keep working. The publicity should bring some interesting cases, or, failing that, at least outlandish fees.

I snuggled back into the Jaguar's leather seat, feeling the sun's warmth easing the aches. My work was done, the police would wrap it up while I recuperated. It was over, and I had survived.

CHAPTER TWENTY-SEVEN

Toni was gone when I woke that afternoon. I called Javier at work. He sounded tired. "You made me famous."

"How did I do that?"

"I became an official police spokesman when I walked out of the hospital last night. They showed the interview on 'This Morning.' I am one nasty looking dude." He laughed and then asked, "How's the head?"

"Hung-over."

"Considering he had you cold, that's good news."

"Anything new?"

Javier sighed and said, "It's been a long day. I went along with the Pleasanton detectives when they tossed Triple 'A' Fiberglass this morning. We took Raul with us. He isn't saying anything, he checked with his lawyer before he would tell us his name."

I was sitting in an upstairs bedroom in Toni's townhouse, watching five nearly naked women lounging near the pool. Other than the headache and an itchy eyelid, I felt good. Javier continued, "The lab boys found a strange set of tanks, they're analyzing the chemicals. The company is owned by two brothers. They aren't talking either, everybody has hunkered down." He made some noise before he added, "Despite my warning about the danger, Raul made bail."

"Deke will have him killed." The fucking justice system had its collective head up its ass.

"I told him that," Javier said wearily. "The DA told him that. She offered protection for talking." After a momentary silence, Javier added, "These things take time to work."

A leggy blonde walking around the pool calmed my brain. "So where do we go from here?"

"We're going to baby-sit Raul and wait."

"While we're waiting, I feel naked without my gun. Any chance they'll release it?"

"'They' is me and I just decided we don't need it. You want to come by and get it?"

"I'll ask Toni to pick it up."

"Okay," he warned, "but just make damn sure she's eaten before she gets here."

I was still laughing when Javier disconnected. While I had the phone in my hand, I called Clay to tell him about the developments. Toni already had. "She said you were badly cut up. How's it going?"

"It looks worse than it is, they were all superficial. Did she tell you about the flats?"

"Yes. I've fired Raul." His voice changed. "The DA has said she won't re-file against me. Do you want to go home to recuperate? It will be weeks before the DA needs you."

Sunlight was dancing on the pool. The dry warmth made the District's sticky humidity seem like punishment. "Toni's lent me a spare bedroom. There's a pool surrounded by naked women. I think I'll hang here until she kicks me out."

He laughed. "I don't think she'll do that."

After Clay disconnected, I called Toni and asked her to get the gun on her way home. She grumbled until I told her what Javier said, then she wanted to see him. "I had no idea I scared the big ape." Hearing the lilt in her voice, I felt sorry for Javier.

After I hung up, I thought about going shopping for a new laptop and the software to listen to Deke's bug, but the pool beckoned. I decided to rest my pounding head in several feet of water.

That evening, I held a shot glass with warm, salty water against the side of my face. One of the cuts looked infected. Toni was in the kitchen when the phone rang. She answered and then brought me the portable. "Clay," she explained.

His voice sounded strained. "Mr. Charboneau, can you come out to the plant. I've found something you may find interesting."

I was afraid I'd dump the water if I did much talking, so I said, "Sure. Be there in a half-hour."

Toni looked at her watch. "He's working late. What does he want?"

"Judging by his voice, he's pissed. I think I'm in trouble, he called me Mr. Charboneau." I carefully lowered the glass of water before I asked, "You want to go with me?"

She gave me her "get real" look. "Some of us have to go to work in the morning. Try not to announce your arrival when you get back."

"The point of asking was that I don't have a car." She handed me the keys to the Jaguar without comment. "I'll see you tomorrow then," I said, amazed that she parted with the car so readily. I put the bulky army jacket on over the holster, got the gun and was checking the clip as I walked toward the front door.

"Hey," she said sharply, "what's with the gun?" I didn't understand the question. "Why are you carrying the gun?"

"Because Deke is still loose."

I saw fright in her face but she said, "If they shoot at you, don't use my car for cover."

CHAPTER TWENTY-EIGHT

Unlike the malicious and talented rush hour commuters, the nighttime drivers on the crowded freeway seemed to be idiots. Half were doing 45 in any lane and the others were careening from lane to lane trying to maintain some insane speed. The drivers in the fast lane had reached a consensus around 65, so I plodded along with them.

Microfix's parking lot held three cars and a van. Jumpy and nervous, I drove by each one, getting out to peer into the van. They were all empty. Evidently a few people were sharing Clay's late night.

I walked into the brightly lit, empty lobby. Assuming the security guard was out on rounds, I waited for a while before I walked through the swinging doors toward Clay's office. Just inside the doors, a huge man clamped a massive arm across my face and effortlessly pulled me off the floor.

I grabbed for my gun. My captor ripped it from my hand. I couldn't breathe; my neck threatened to break. I held onto the arm trying to find enough leverage to stay aloft and get some air. He'd opened some of the wounds on my face, I saw my blood join other blood on his coat sleeve. The fucker was incredibly strong, he carried me to Clay's office with unnerving ease.

When I was unceremoniously dumped into Clay's office, Deke was sitting in a chair holding a handgun. Clay was sitting at his desk, sweat pouring from his forehead. His hands splayed on the desk blotter were bleeding; one finger had a bone protruding. A hammer on the desk had blood on the claws, it had taken some effort to get him to phone me. I finally understood why he had called me Mr. Charboneau. Talk about a day late.

The guy who had carried me was barrel-shaped, probably six-five and maybe in his mid-forties. He had done the work on Clay with the hammer, blood spatters covered both sleeves of his brown suit coat. Shapeless pants hung from his waist, the cuffs draping huge shoes. He reminded me of a bear: big, probably stupid, and dangerous. A gray walrus mustache contrasted with his bald head, giving the impression that his hair had fallen off and lodged on his upper lip. Wire rimmed glasses perched on top of a battered, bulbous nose. He grunted with the effort when he leaned over to hand my gun to Deke. "It's his," the bear murmured in a very deep voice.

Raul was standing with his back to us, going through a filing cabinet. He had a Mac 10 submachine gun hanging on a sling from his shoulder. The gun was for show evidently, the bolt was missing.

"Thanks, George," Deke said to the bear. My brain went numb when he used George's name. Everyone had a name; not a shred of disguise, he didn't intend to leave anyone alive who might talk. That's why Raul's weapon was missing the bolt, Raul would be one of the dead. Just looking at the players, the plan was obvious, a murder-suicide with Raul as the perp. Done on the same day that Clay fired Raul, it would be just another berserk employee shooting.

I took a quick survey of the room, looking for possible weapons. George had me wedged between his bulk and a metal chair. Clay had a rock paperweight on his desk; it might do some damage. Deke had an automatic in his left hand, it was a .45 judging by the barrel. He had my gun, although he hadn't yet looked for the second safety. The trigger within the trigger was a normal safety, most autoloaders only had the one.

Deke looked my gun over. "Fucking Star Wars shit." Raul turned around to look. Deke flicked the laser on, put the beam on Clay's forehead, and held the gun out to Raul. "Hold the dot right there and don't yank the trigger."

"Me?" Raul's voice trembled, splitting the word into two syllables. He didn't take the gun.

"We've been over all this, Raul," Deke said patiently. He circled the laser on Clay's face. "He has to go or we all fry. When he popped Sally, you were as guilty of murder as if you'd shot her, we were committing a felony at the time."

"Why the fuck did you have to kill her," Raul screamed at Clay. "None of this would have happened if you hadn't killed her."

"Deke tell you that?" I asked Raul. "If you saw his rap sheet, you'd know that he always kills the witnesses."

Raul whirled toward me, furious. "Willie told me how it happened. The girl was alive when Oeland drove off, but a minute later, as Willie was getting into his car, he heard two shots. He saw Oeland driving like crazy, so he followed him. He saw them wheel her into the emergency room."

I asked Raul, "Why the fuck would you believe him? You can't be that stupid."

I was talking to keep their attention focused on me. Clay was edging his chair toward the corner of his desk for some reason. Did he have a gun?

Raul screamed, "Willie had an empty gun, for Christ's sake. It was empty, on purpose, so there couldn't be any mistake." Raul pointed at Oeland. "And she was shot with his gun. How the hell would Willie get that?"

That shocked me. Either Raul hadn't stolen Oeland's gun, or he was a very hysterical liar.

Deke said quietly, "You can't rewrite history, Raul, what's done is done. Now shoot the fucker." He pointed at Oeland with his automatic while offering my gun to Raul.

"I can't," Raul begged.

Deke reversed the gun and forced the butt into Raul's hand. "No one does your dirty work, Raul, you have to do it. This was your idea, now finish it."

Raul's hand was shaking as he turned the gun toward Clay. I screamed at him, "Don't be a fucking idiot, Raul." Raul was startled, he pointed the gun at me. I continued screaming, "He needs you to shoot the gun because that's the only way this will look like murder-suicide when they find all three of our bodies."

Deke leaned back in his chair as if bored. "Raul and I have been through a lot. He knows who he can trust."

Clay was almost to the edge of the desk. Hoping he had a plan, I yelled at Raul, "He kills all the witnesses, you dumb fuck. Willie's dead, did you know that?"

Surprised, Raul asked Deke, "Is that true?"

Deke nodded. "I gave him money to disappear, but he was scared shitless because he knew he could be charged with murder. He bought himself enough smack to kill four people and took it all." Deke pointed at Clay. "Now, come on, shoot him, we can't hang around here forever."

"Raul," I said, "he has to kill you, you're the only one who can tie him to the drugs." Pointing at Deke, I told Raul, "Use the gun on him while you have a chance."

Deke told George, "Shut him up."

George whirled and swung a massive fist at my head that just missed. Clay dove for the wall, hitting the red button with his elbow, plunging the factory into inky blackness.

I grabbed the empty chair on my left and swung it toward where George had been. It hit him and hung there; he must have grabbed it, so I shoved with my whole body, feeling the big fucker go over backwards. I scrambled out the door, coming to an abrupt halt when I ran into the secretary's chair.

Deke sounded annoyed. "Raul, get the fuckin' lights on."

I felt someone run by. Hoping that it was Clay, I pushed the secretary's chair into the doorway of Clay's office. George's eerily deep voice rumbled and I heard him fall over the chair. I turned and ran down the corridor, sprinting headlong in the darkness.

I was using my right hand to keep track of the wall. When I felt a doorway, I stopped, found the knob and opened the door. As soon as I'd closed it, the lights came back on. Rows of steel work benches had open gridwork legs. Steel shelving lined the walls. There was nowhere to hide.

Two people ran by. Then slower footsteps approached, the stalker opening and closing doors. I flattened against the shelving on the hinge side of the door. When George walked into the room, he had me cold. He had shed his coat and he was pissed, his forehead was bleeding profusely, staining a plaid shirt that contained enough material to drape a moderate sized house.

He could have easily strangled me with one of his hands. Instead he tried to shoot me with my own gun. He fumbled with the safety. With the laser playing around my eyes, I grabbed the gun by the barrel and kicked him. The toe of my shoe caught his privates, something there absorbed the blow, it felt like I'd kicked a pillow. He went down immediately, releasing the gun, his wire rimmed glasses shattering with the impact. While he moaned and writhed on the floor, both hands holding his crotch, I put the muzzle against his knee and pulled the trigger. The slug exploded his knee; bone and blood spattered me. He grabbed his calf, almost hitting himself in the face with his own foot as the leg bent backwards. His wounded animal screams seemed to rattle the walls.

I ran back down the hall toward Clay's office, looking for a defensible hiding place. A space between an I-Beam and a steel locker offered shelter, and I wedged myself into the narrow slot and tried not to breathe.

George's screams eased into long moans. I couldn't hear anything else, were Deke and Raul gone? I dared a peek. Raul was flattened on one side of the door to the room, Deke on the other, both easy shots. I switched on the laser but Deke slammed through the doorway before I could target him. I put the laser on Raul's stomach and fired.

The expanded slug probably didn't penetrate, but the impact bounced him off the wall, a long loop of bloody vomit exploding from his mouth when he landed on his back. He was gagging and coughing, moving around as if trying to escape the devil that had landed in his belly.

Time ceased, Raul gurgling and George's moans were the only sounds I could hear. I put the laser on the door frame, hoping Deke would look out.

Two minutes or two years passed. My eyes were tearing from staring. I strained to hear some sound, hoping Deke would make a mistake. Boxes blocked my view of the bottom foot or so of the doorway; had Deke crawled out of the room? I should have moved to a better vantage spot, now I was trapped if he knew where I was. But time was on my side, I could afford to wait, Deke couldn't.

Suddenly, he was beside me, his gun in my ear. "Move, motherfucker, and you are dead." He slid his hand up my arm and took my gun, then backed away. That he hadn't killed me was so shocking, it felt surreal.

He motioned me down the corridor toward the front of the building. I tried not to walk in the pools of vomit. Raul watched me without expression, making some gurgling sound with each breath, as if he had liquid in his lungs. Deke paused and patted Raul's shoulder. "Hang in there, buddy, I'll be back in a minute."

We continued toward the front of the building and into the area behind the lobby. The room was empty. "Aw, fuck," Deke said quietly. Keeping me in the center of the room, he checked the adjacent rooms. He motioned me out through the lobby into the parking lot, keeping the litany of "Aw, fuck," going like a mantra. He made me circle the van and the other four cars while he searched them, bending down to look under the vehicles. He was groaning as if he were in pain.

Back inside, he pushed me down the hall toward Raul, stopping in each doorway to look into the rooms. Finally, he grimaced and shrugged, saying, "Well, that's that."

He would kill me at any moment. I strained to hear sirens, hoping Clay had called the police. He had to have gotten away, but had he found a phone?

As I passed the door to the room where I'd shot George, Deke said, "Stop." Then he shoved me into the opening.

George was face down and not moving, his wounded leg bent backwards so that his foot pointed toward his head. The floor underneath him was a pool of blood. Deke held his automatic on me with his left hand while he aimed my gun at George. When he couldn't pull the trigger, he searched for the safety and found it. Then he placed the laser dot on the top of George's head and fired. The slug blew George's head into three large pieces, spraying the room with bits of brain and blood.

Deke motioned me back into the hall. He told me to stand against the wall, my feet almost touching Raul's belt. Raul's breathing was ragged, each breath a long agonized gasp for air. He was still conscious. Deke looked at him when he said, "Oeland got away, amigo. It's all over."

Aiming his automatic at me, he moved some distance away. He put the laser on Raul's head. Raul tried to talk. Deke fired. I caught a face full of gore as the slug exploded Raul's head. Deke continued to fire into Raul, splattering me with blood as hydrostatic shock tore Raul's body apart.

When the automatic's slide remained open, Deke winced at the mess that used to be Raul. "For a citizen, you use nasty slugs."

Deke looked into the slide to make sure the gun was empty; he could only see the top of the clip being used, enough to convince himself that it was empty. He wiped the smooth parts of the gun against his pants, and then tossed it to me. I caught it by the grip. Holding the gun against my leg to keep the magazine from ejecting all the way, I pushed the magazine release. If his attention lagged, I'd have the magazine reversed and the gun loaded in a second.

He waved his automatic at me. "You get a ride because I don't want my picture on the networks." He looked at the mess that used to be Raul, and he sighed. "None of this would have been necessary if Oeland hadn't killed Sally." As he walked away, he pointed the automatic at me and said, "You peek out the door before I'm gone, and you're fuckin' dead."

I waited until the corridor doors slammed shut, then I reversed the clip, racked the first steel jacket into the chamber, and edged my way into the lobby.

Deke had started the blue van parked just a few feet away from the entrance. I raced out through the doors, put the laser on the driver's door, and fired six rounds, spacing them evenly across the door. The van lurched into motion and idled a straight path across the lot. It came to a stop in the perimeter shrubbery. A moment later, the horn began a lonesome dirge.

I called 911 from the lobby desk. Mine was the first call. Clay hadn't gotten to a phone. I searched the factory but there was no sign of him. I walked outside intending to circle the building. As I passed, I heard a whistle from behind a large juniper. Clay and a security guard were wrapped around a chair, Clay handcuffed to the back and the guard taped to the chair.

"I carried Ernie out here, but once I fell down, I couldn't get both of us up," Clay explained.

By the time the police arrived, the adrenaline shakes had taken control of my body. Clay was whisked away by an ambulance. When Javier and his partner, Vic Stauder, arrived, Ernie told his story. Luckily, the cadaverous little guy in his seventies weighed just 105 pounds, so even with smashed hands, Clay had managed to carry him out of harm's way. Ernie hadn't seen anyone but Raul. Raul had entered the lobby alone. While Raul talked with him, someone grabbed Ernie from behind, taped his eyes, and then taped him to the chair.

While I was telling my story, my nerves collapsed, I started shaking as if I had palsy. While an evidence technician took swabs of my hands, Javier assigned another cop to follow me back to Toni's, explaining, "We'll need to confiscate your clothes." He watched me for a moment, then asked, "Can you drive?"

I wanted to, needing to lose myself in a mundane task, anything to forget the sight of those bodies being ripped apart, but the drive was uneventful and quick. Inside Toni's apartment, I saw myself in the bathroom mirror; blood and bits of gore covered my clothes and face.

After the police left with my clothes, Toni brought me a water glass full of wine. I kept seeing the laser playing around my eyes as George searched for the safety. He'd touched it once but he tried to push it down rather than in. That instant kept replaying, over and over. I felt like the gun might go off, and then I'd be dead.

The wine didn't relax me, so I finally went to bed to rest. I fell asleep almost immediately, waking up in a sweat a half-hour later. That pattern repeated until I heard Toni leave for work in the morning.

CHAPTER TWENTY-NINE

Javier knocked the next morning. I heard the banging as I stepped out of the shower. After checking, I let him in. He pointed at the towel around my hips. In a passable John Wayne impression, he said, "Put some clothes on, Pilgrim, 'cause ya gotta go meet the bad guys."

I shook my head. "I did that yesterday and I didn't like it."

He stayed in character as he closed the door. "Shoot, Pilgrim, those guys only had guns. I'm talkin' lawyers." He slipped into his own voice to add, "Sylvia wants a sample of the bullets that hit Raul and the big guy."

When I was dressed, I came downstairs to find Javier tasting Toni's coffee. He looked at the cup in amazement, asking, "Was this coffee or was she cleaning out the pot?"

"I'm never sure, so I wait until she's gone and then I brew some decent stuff. You got time?"

He shook his head. While he seated his glasses, he said, "Your friendly prosecutor awaits."

I gave him a box containing 25 bullets. I explained how the slugs expanded, and then said, "I had no idea how much damage they would do up close."

"Sylvia is convinced you were using explosive bullets." Javier read my face and nodded. "She thinks you may have used excessive force." He laughed abruptly. "She upchucked when she saw Raul's remains; she's really pissed that I saw her do that."

Javier drove me to Microfix. The news media had the parking lot there under siege, trucks with satellite dishes mounted on their roofs pressed against the police tape. I sat on the car's floor, my jacket covering my head, as Javier negotiated the crowd.

Inside Microfix, Javier introduced me to three cops who would videotape our reenactment. In the hallway behind the lobby, Clay saw me. He walked over and abruptly hugged me, holding his bandaged hands away. The video crew thought that was worth recording.

He seemed upset; near tears. "I can't thank you enough for what you did last night. I'm ashamed that I called you. I was in so much pain, I couldn't face having another finger broken."

I nodded at his bandages. "I wouldn't have lasted as long as you did."

He held up his left hand and wiggled three fingers. "I caved as soon as he hit the first finger on this hand."

We walked through the events for the tape. After Clay hit the Emergency Power Off switch, he crawled around the desk, brushing by George as the big man untangled himself from Deke and Raul. Once through the door, familiar with the factory, he ran to the lobby.

Assuming that I was out of the factory, guessing that I would call the police on my cellular phone, Clay decided to release Ernie. With his broken fingers, he was still working on the tape when Raul and Deke arrived. While they locked him to the chair with Ernie's handcuffs, they heard the gunshot and George's screams, and they ran off. Pulling on the back of the chair with the handcuffs, Clay managed to balance Ernie and the chair against the front of his legs, and waddle out the door.

When it was my turn, I pantomimed disabling George, running to my hiding spot, and shooting Raul. A cop crawled out of the room while the cameraman taped the scene from where I'd been standing. I'd made it easy for Deke. A gap between boxes revealed my position. He should have shot me; he risked his life to capture me alive.

I traced the path Deke followed in his search for Clay, and where I'd stood while he executed George and Raul. I demonstrated how Deke had wiped my gun on his pants and how he'd thrown it to me. My gun was in the police lab; using an officer's nicely balanced S&W 9mm wasn't the same, the gun rotated too fast. With the weight of those 16 bullets inside the handgrip, my gun had made a lazy half circle, arriving butt first.

After the video session broke up, I called Toni and told her about Sylvia's planned interrogation. "I'll be there," she said tersely.

Three men and a woman walked into Clay's office a few minutes later. Sylvia Vance, the DA I'd heard so much about, was a petite brunette in her mid-twenties with pale green eyes. A cute lady, she had a deferential demeanor; she would be shy in a crowd, I thought.

Then she looked at me like I was some kind of bug, perhaps reacting to the wounds.

At her direction, we went into the large conference room that adjoined Clay's office. Sylvia had each person state their name and address for the stenographer. That done, she told Clay and me to wait outside while she questioned Ernie.

As Ernie exited the conference room, Toni walked in. She and Sylvia traded frosty greetings at the door. Sylvia motioned Clay inside, and the door closed. Ernie leaned against the credenza next to me. Whispering, he said, "That ball-breaker thinks you murdered all those people."

My emotions were still screwed up; I thought that was the funniest thing I'd heard in years. I was just barely managing to stay in my chair when Sylvia opened the door and glared me into silence.

When it was my turn, I gave Sylvia my version of the events. I expected her to be interested in Raul's outburst accusing Clay of killing Sally, but she made no comment. I almost suggested that Raul hadn't taken Oeland's gun, but since that was speculation on my part, I stuck to the facts. Other than occasionally writing in her notebook, she might not have been listening. When I was through, she asked, "Why did Deke Horstman use your gun and not his own."

Toni objected. "The question is speculative and not relevant to establishing the facts of the shooting."

"Your objection has been recorded," Sylvia answered.

Toni nodded at me and said, "You can answer the question."

"You want speculation?" I asked, astonished.

Sylvia nodded, then noticed the stenographer frowning and said, "Yes."

"I thought that he intended to kill Clay, Raul and me with my gun, make it look like a double murder and a suicide. Since he asked Raul to shoot Clay with my gun, I guessed Raul was going to be the suicide."

Sylvia sneered. "That's ludicrous, why would Raul agree to that obvious a plan?"

Toni raised the objection in a singsong recitation. "The question is speculative and not relevant to establishing the facts of the shooting."

"Your objection has been recorded," Sylvia said wearily.

I finally understood the form when Toni said, "You can answer the question."

"Deke said that they were all guilty of murder for Sally Krestas' death, he must have convinced Raul that killing Clay and me would fix his problem. Raul had a machine gun, maybe he felt safe with that, assuming he didn't know it wouldn't work."

Sylvia tried out a poker face; it didn't fit. "You knew that the gun was inoperable?"

"Yes, I could see that the bolt was missing."

Instead of regarding that as new information, she asked, "What was Raul carrying when you shot him?"

"The machine gun."

"Why did you shoot him then." Sylvia liked her little trap, she couldn't hide a brief smile.

"At that range, the bullet should have been non-lethal. I needed to take him out of action."

Sylvia hammered in another nail. "The man we presently know only as George was also unarmed when you shot him. Is that correct?"

Anger was starting to build. I didn't want Sylvia to see that, so I put on my bored face and shrugged. "I don't know if he had a weapon."

She decided not to tell me. "And after Clay Oeland escaped, Deke Horstman allegedly used your gun to kill Raul and George. Why?"

Toni broke in. "The question is speculative and not relevant to establishing the facts of the shooting."

"Your objection has been recorded."

"You can answer the question."

I leaned back in the chair, adopted my least interested face, and then said, "I haven't the vaguest idea what Deke was thinking. I do know George was too big to carry away, and Deke needed Raul dead. He probably used my gun so you would think that I executed both men."

Sylvia took the bait. "Is that why he allegedly gave the murder weapon back to you?" She saw her error in time to tell the stenographer, "Erase that." Fixing me with those pale green eyes, she asked, "Why didn't you try to stop the van without shooting into it?"

I asked politely, "How? Like walking in front of it and holding up my hand?"

Javier laughed. Sylvia didn't see the humor, she looked a warning glance at Javier, then said, "Yelling? Holding the gun against the driver's window?"

"He thought the gun was empty."

"Why didn't you let him drive away?" I could see the gleam in Sylvia's eyes, she had sprung her trap. "You knew who he was and where to find him, so why did you kill him?"

Putting my need to kill him in specifics required some time, and Sylvia was impatient. "He might tell a different story?" she suggested.

I ignored that, remaining silent until I had my story complete. Then I said, "For all I knew, Clay and Ernie were running down the same road he would take. He might have killed them both and then come back for me. I needed to stop him, but I was in a bad spot. I was backlit by the lobby lights and I couldn't see into the van. He had a gun; he said he would shoot me if I opened the doors."

Sylvia watched me as she said, "That would have been difficult, his gun was empty."

"You've got to be kidding." I thought maybe she was, but she held up a police report. Without meaning to, I asked, "None of them had loaded guns?"

Sylvia said, "You had the only bullets."

Remembering Raul's near hysterical defense of Willie, I could believe that Horstman had given Willie an unloaded gun. Maybe that was the way he worked, unloaded guns meant no mistakes. If he wanted to set up a murder-suicide vignette, he had to use a gun that belonged to one of the three intended victims. If Raul didn't own a gun, that left only mine. He must have known that I wouldn't go out without a gun, considering the attempt on my life the night before.

When all three of us were dead, George and Deke could sneak out, leaving Ernie alive to testify he hadn't seen anyone but Raul come in. Raul had been fired that day, he came back and smashed Clay's fingers, one-by-one, until Clay called me. When I arrived, he got my gun, shot Clay and me, and then killed himself. Just another disgruntled worker.

Sylvia wrote something in her notebook as she asked, "It's your contention that you didn't know his gun was empty?"

"I didn't know his gun was empty."

"Even though he didn't shoot during the alleged gunfight?"

"Even though."

Sylvia clearly didn't believe my story, she summarized everything to show me how it looked. "By your own admission, you shot all three unarmed men. By your own admission, you intended to execute Deke Horstman. We have only your word that you didn't execute the others as well. Judging by the blood spatters on your clothes, and the lack of any such spatters on Mr. Horstman's clothes, you were standing very close when both men were executed inside the plant. Your story of the incident begs credibility, and I intend to prove that you executed all three men."

I kept my mouth shut, not wanting to add resolve to her anger; prosecutors have incredible power. Sylvia waited for me to put my foot in it, then warned me not to leave town. In frosty silence, she gathered her notes and slipped them into her briefcase.

After Sylvia and her entourage left, Javier joined me as I walked out of Clay's office. He wrapped his huge right arm around my shoulders and confided, "You mad dog killers are all alike: do your dirty work and then try to pin the blame on the innocent guy running for his life."

"And I thought she'd be grateful I saved the city all that money."

"That's why she's pissed, she loves trials."

When we got to the lobby, I could see the crush of reporters straining at the yellow police tape. With only my skimpy mustache for protection, my face was about to get singed into the collective American memory.

Javier came to the rescue. He draped a coat over one of the uniformed cops and they both rushed out and got into his car. Most of the reporters mounted up, and followed him when he drove out of the lot. While the attention was focused on him, I walked out to Toni's Jaguar and got into the back seat. With me laying on the floor, Toni drove to her home.

I was exhausted. My nerves jumped at each sound. Toni dropped a spoon in the kitchen and I leapt to my feet. Something snapped in my side and I groaned. She thought I was having a heart attack.

When we'd determined that I wasn't bleeding to death, she fixed me a gallon or so of Brandy Alexander. In an hour, I was totally wrecked.

CHAPTER THIRTY

I woke up the next morning on Toni's couch. She'd taken off my shoes and covered me with a blanket. Her VCR showed 9:48. I felt great, no nightmares at all. Perhaps Brandy Alexanders were a cure for nightmares.

Toni had left me coffee that I didn't try. I brewed another pot, then took it upstairs where I could sit in the sun on her small balcony. Saturday at the pool was busy, and watching the barely clad residents soak up sun gave me perspective. I felt wonderful, no one had any reason to kill me.

That afternoon, wanting to stay at Toni's until Sylvia decided to drop the foolishness, I rummaged through Toni's kitchen to see if I could do some cooking for her. She had a cupboard full of cake mixes, so I made a chocolate marble cake and put it on the pass-through to cool. At six, I fixed meatloaf with hamburger I found in her freezer; washed off two very old potatoes and put both in the oven with the meatloaf. I made the chocolate frosting recipe that's engraved on my brain, and iced the cake. I found a half full package of frozen corn, I put that in a pan without turning it on. I'd wait until she came home.

When she came in the door, she asked, "Meatloaf? Am I right?" I nodded. She put a hand on my arm and asked, "Is there an aroma of chocolate?"

I trotted out the cake. She laughed. "The entire world is going nuts trying to find you, and you're cooking for me. Who would believe it?"

Toni was hooked on the evening news. The local station was going with the footage of Sylvia and her loose cannon theory. I'd already seen the headlines in the San Francisco paper: "PI BLAMED FOR DEATHS." Under the headlines, an article was labeled, "Six Dead in Shootings." Earl, Deke, Raul and George made four, the shooter nailed by the drunk driver accounted for another, and Sally's death had started the whole thing. The actual total was seven counting Willie, but his body hadn't been found.

Toni was trying to spare my feelings, I guess, because she watched the news with her finger poised over the mute button. Her hair-trigger nerves nailed the network anchor twice in mid-sentence.

I was trying to read a paperback, just something to get lost in, but Toni's tension had me on edge. "I guess I'll turn in," I said. She nodded, as if going to bed at seven was normal. I didn't want to go up to my bedroom, it had no place to sit and the lighting there was too dim to read.

"Unless you want to talk," I suggested.

She mashed the mute button and looked at me, registering surprise. "About what?"

"Why you don't want me to hear that I'm a loose cannon and a killer? Are you afraid that I'll go berserk and start shooting?"

"It's so unfair," she said.

"Life's a bitch and then you die," I said, grinning. "Sylvia is frustrated and she's running her mouth. As long as I'm not sent to prison, I'm happy about the publicity. Being known as a mad dog killer will help my business."

The next morning, I rented a car and drove around collecting my stuff. I didn't see any reporters or cameras as I drove by the electrical shop Toni had chosen to remove my gear. Forgetting that my face looked like I'd lost a cat fight, the surreptitious glances I received from the employees worried me. Had they called the media? I asked the man who waited on me to hurry. "You gonna shoot me?" he asked, smiling uncertainly. Sylvia had made her point.

While I waited for the asshole to collect my stuff, I called Javier on the cellular. Vic answered, and he gave me Javier's pager number. Javier called right back, they were dusting Deke Horstman's house for fingerprints, and looking for bugs. "Sylvia's sure you pulled some illegal stuff; she's out to prove it."

"You might call the DEA, on the off-chance they had a bug in Deke's phone."

"Boy, that would really piss her off." He sounded delighted by the prospect.

I told him why I was calling, I hoped to recover the trackers that I'd put on Raul's Lincoln and Deke's Corvette. Both cars had been impounded by the police. I described the trackers for him, he said he'd remove them.

"One more thing?" Javier asked. "In the calls from your cell phone, there was one to an Aaron Grady's house. You know him?"

Ever so grateful that I hadn't found Aaron, I said, "No, but I wanted to. I like to fuck with wife beaters, try to make them appreciate what their wives are going through. I never found Aaron; he seems to have vanished."

"Did you ever talk with him on the phone?"

"Yeah, once. I made an appointment to see him, but he wasn't home when I got there."

"Well, that explains it."

"Explains what? Do you know what happened to the guy?"

"Probably." He didn't say anything more, so I waited. Finally he said, "We'd like to keep it quiet."

"If you've got some way of scaring these scumbags, I sure would like to hear it. I get around, I could share it with other police departments."

He liked that idea, so he told me that a San Jose cop had made up a scrapbook of mostly fake newspaper articles describing the torture deaths of several dozen wife beaters in cities throughout the United States. "Whenever we get a wife beating that makes the newspaper, whoever handles the case shows the guy the scrapbook, gives him all the time he needs to read the articles, then tells him to be sure and call us if he ever gets any calls where a stranger tries to set up a meeting. We let that news age awhile, then somebody gives him a suspicious call. If he calls us, we handle it like we would any chance to catch a serial killer. While we have the stakeout inside his house— we insist that he stays with us to identify any legitimate caller—the cops talk about how this guy disembowels his victims so that they die slowly, and any other gruesome lie we can think of. Of course, nobody shows, but the guy does get another call the next day. This time, the caller tells him all he did was delay their meeting. If the guy calls us again, we tell him we can't give him full time protection, his best chance is to go into hiding."

"Does it work?"

"Fourteen last year. Some, like Aaron, disappear right away. You must have spooked him when you tried to set up a meeting with him."

"Do they take their wives with them when they run?"

"Never. The first two articles in the scrapbook mention how the guy evidently tracked the abuser through his wife."

The irony of having the abusers living like fugitives was beautiful. In a way, Deborah was still running from the man who abused her. Considering the crime, I liked the cops' solution, killing the assholes was no punishment at all for the torture they inflicted.

I asked if I could pay to have the scrapbook duplicated. With the right leaks, the story of a serial killer targeting abusers could become an urban legend, a legend that might make abuse a thing of the past.

Javier liked that idea, he said he'd get me a copy of the scrapbook. While we'd been talking, the service manager had stacked all my stuff on the counter, so I said my good-byes to Javier and disconnected.

After I returned to Toni's, I called Gina. Her voice sounded husky, as if she might have been crying. "Oh, Gary, I feel like Judas. I didn't want him to get hurt."

"It really turned out badly." Gina didn't respond, so I added, "You couldn't let them convict Clay of Sally's murder, you had no choice." The line was silent. Finally, I said, "I haven't told anyone how much you helped. With your permission, I'd at least like to tell Clay. He should know."

"I could use some help; the new manager will fire me as soon as he can." She sounded lost and alone when she asked, "Does anyone else have to know?"

"I'll get a promise from Clay before I tell him." I waited but she didn't say anything. "Can I do anything else for you, Gina? If you'd like some company, I can come over."

"No thanks, Gary. Take care of yourself." She abruptly disconnected.

While I waited for Clay to come on the line, I watched a lone swimmer doing laps in the pool. He might have been in his eighties judging by the papery skin, yet his stroke was true and beautiful. He acted as if he could go on forever.

When Clay picked up his extension, he talked as if he'd left me a message. "Gary, thanks for calling. I have the check ready."

"Give it to Toni, she has a deposit form, she'll see that I get it. I'm going to stay out of sight until Sylvia decides whether she's going to indict me."

"For what?"

"Javier says she's looking for illegal bugs that she can tie to me."

His phone crashed, sounding like it had fallen. When he picked it up, he was chuckling. "I forget my hands. I tried to write a note and dropped the phone."

"How are they?" I asked.

"Hurting. How are your injuries?"

"Getting better, but I still look like shit."

He said, "I thought, if you'd allow me, I'd hold a party to thank you. Nothing too big, just a few people from the plant. I want to do something to show how much I appreciate what you've done."

"Thanks, but I don't want to be out in public until the media loses the scent. There is something you can do for me."

"Sure. Name it."

"A person who works at your plant really broke the story for me. Contingent on you not revealing the name to anyone else, that person has given me permission to give you a name."

"Gina Rawlins?" he asked.

"You have to agree not to reveal the name."

"Sure, I'll agree to that. It is Gina, isn't it?"

"Yes."

"She's a smart lady," Clay said. "I guessed that she was the one who hid the flat."

"The new manager in Raul's job doesn't like her. I'd hate to see her lose her job when she did so much to help."

"Don't worry about her, Gary, I owe her more than a job."

"One more thing?" I asked. "She wouldn't hurt a soul if her own life depended on it, and now she has Raul's death on her conscience. I'm worried about her, she's very depressed. If you call her, that might make all the difference."

"I'll do that," he said.

Just because it was on my mind, I said, "Judging by his hysterics in your office, Raul didn't steal your gun. Do you have any idea how Willie got it?"

Clay pushed all my buttons when he said, "Let it go, Gary."

I made all the right parting noises and disconnected. Then I called Javier.

Pat Oeland answered the door wearing ragged blue sweats spattered with white paint. My appearance shocked her, she put a hand over her mouth before she recovered enough to say, "Clay doesn't live here anymore, he's got an apartment."

"I came to see you."

"Me?" Her thin face paled.

"You."

She nervously patted an errant strand of dark hair back into place. "Come in."

The paint odor was strong, but it faded as we descended toward the ground floor. Walking ahead of me, she seemed to be in a hurry, taking two steps at a time with those long legs. On the ground floor, she crossed the living room to the wet bar; put one glass on the counter and filled it with scotch. As she held up the bottle, she asked, "The wounds look painful, are you sure you won't have some?"

Quietly, I asked, "You want to tell me why you killed Sally?" She shook her head and downed half the drink. "You heard him arrange to pick Sally up. You followed them and waited somewhere, maybe on the highway, because you didn't see what happened, did you? When they did come out, you shot her. Miss Rich Bitch sees her meal ticket slipping away, so she kills the whore to teach hubby a lesson?"

She finished her drink, and placed the glass carefully on the bar. "You get the police to arrest me, and then I'm calling my lawyer."

"You don't understand," I said softly. I undid my belt and pulled it from the loops of my pants. I held an end in both hands.

"You're going to strangle me?" She thought the idea was ludicrous.

"I was shot twice; seven people are dead, and you stand there grinning like a fool. Big fucking joke, lady?"

I moved into the center of the room, cutting off any escape; she was trapped behind the bar. As I moved toward her, she put both hands out, saying, "It wasn't like that."

The bar formed a protective barrier across the corner of the room. Wedged into the corner, her hands were almost on my chest when the bar halted my advance. I grabbed the front of her sweats with my left hand, pulled her halfway across the bar, and raised the belt as if I intended to hit her in the face. She begged, "Please, I didn't mean to shoot her."

I wrapped the belt around her neck, twisting it to choke her. "You didn't know it was loaded?"

Her skin had turned ashen, she was feeling the horror, she grabbed the belt, trying to find air. I loosened it so that she could talk.

In a hurry, she clawed at the belt while she explained, "You don't understand, it wasn't like that. As Clay drove toward me, the sun was glaring off the windshield. All I could see was that she was in her bra and Clay didn't have a shirt on, like they had just had sex. When Clay stopped the car, I saw the fingernail scratches on his face and chest."

"Didn't that give you a fucking clue?" I yelled.

Wincing, trying to loosen the noose around her neck, she said, "I thought the sex had gotten wild. The scratches infuriated me, didn't he care that she'd marked him?"

"You shot her because she scratched your husband?"

Her mouth almost refused to work. "Try to understand, I had the gun pointed at him but he wasn't scared, he looked like he pitied me. Then he said, 'You don't want to be here,' as if I was a naughty child. I screamed obscenities at him; I almost shot him."

Pat's eyes lost focus, she seemed to be back at the side of Clay's car, the gun in her hand. "Then she laughed." She was still hearing Sally's laugh, she seemed to sag, I had to hold her against the bar to keep from choking her with the belt. In a voice so soft, I worried that the wire wouldn't be able to pick it up, she asked, "Why did she laugh?" She looked at me as if I had the answer. "I was feeling foolish and betrayed and worthless, and the woman responsible for that laughed at me. I was so furious, I swung the gun at Clay, but he ducked. Then I could see her belly, it was shaking as she laughed."

She shuddered, her knees gave way and I had to hold her up by hugging her. Her mouth was near the microphone when she whispered, "I don't remember how it happened, but I was inside the car and the gun kept going off." Her voice weakened as she said, "I saw her stomach explode; parts of it hit my face and I dropped the gun. Clay drove off while I was vomiting."

CHAPTER THIRTY-ONE

The tape of Pat Oeland's confession was inadmissible. I had clearly threatened her, but she couldn't stop confessing, even after Javier read her her rights. Her arrest dropped me off the front pages.

I called Javier two days later. He had the trackers but he also had a shadow who belonged to NBC. "Wait awhile, until the lady gets tired of bothering me." He waited a beat and then said, "Or until I get her into the sack, whichever comes first. She's a cutie."

He abruptly switched subjects. "Oh, hey, I didn't tell you. The flats were black tar heroin pressed into a paper binder. They found two chemicals at the fiberglass shop. One dissolves the resin coating, the other dissolves the paper. Skim the residue off and presto, heroin. The lab people are pumped, they get to enter the process into the NCIC computer with their names attached."

"And how's Sylvia coming with my indictment?" I asked, feeling my heart speed up.

"Well, she's having some trouble. Deke had traces of blood on his pants that belonged to both Raul and the big fucker, who has been identified as George Biolley, muscle out of San Diego. Your bullets used a slow-burning powder which matched the residue on his hands. It seems inescapable, even to Sylvia, that he fired your gun. Since every round from your gun hit someone, she was forced to conclude that Deke must have fired the gun at either Raul or the big fucker. She ignored my suggestion that maybe you and Deke took turns." Javier laughed before he continued. "Since the only prints on Deke's gun were his, how would you know that his gun was unloaded? Her theory that you forced him to run and then gunned him down is somewhat shaky."

"She didn't find any illegal eavesdropping devices?" My poker voice failed me, I sounded like an adolescent.

"Yes, the investigation turned up three bugs in Deke's house. The DEA was a little upset that she made a public statement referring to their bugs, so they talked to her boss. I think she may also be in a little trouble with her boss for some of the statements she made to the media. The 'loose cannon' comment has the City worried that you might sue." He adopted a southern accent when he said, "Yep, looks like Sylvia's case jest plum fell apart. She might have to give you a public apology."

Javier was on the mark. That night, I watched Sylvia on the network explaining that the evidence she'd developed supported my original story. The apology she read from a note was brief but it contained all the right words.

Toni watched with undisguised glee. "Suck it up, bitch. Look us in the eye when you eat crow."

I surprised Toni the next morning, telling her that I was leaving. "Going to drive across country and see some of the sights. Yosemite, Tahoe; maybe I'll drive home through Yellowstone, I don't know." Deborah was in Montana, maybe I'd go there to see what it was like.

When I was ready to leave, Toni shook my hand and then hugged me. "Take care of yourself." She didn't want me to see the tears. Life is full of twists, I had expected to see relief.